What She Told Him

What She Told Him

Carolyn Doty

Viking

VIKING
Viking Penguin Inc., 40 West 23rd Street,
New York, New York 10010, U.S.A.
Penguin Books Ltd, Harmondsworth,
Middlesex, England
Penguin Books Australia Ltd, Ringwood,
Victoria, Australia
Penguin Books Canada Limited, 2801 John Street,
Markham, Ontario, Canada L3R 1B4
Penguin Books (N.Z.) Ltd, 182–190 Wairau Road,
Auckland 10, New Zealand

First published in 1985 by Viking Penguin Inc.
Published simultaneously in Canada

LIBRARY OF CONGRESS CATALOGING IN PUBLICATION DATA
Doty, Carolyn.
What she told him.
I. Title.
PS3554.O79W4   1985   813'.54   83-40670
ISBN 0-670-71087-3

Printed in the United States of America
Set in Caledonia

For
GARDNER H. MEIN

Part One

The football field and the two small sections of white-washed bleachers that flanked the track of Yellow Fork High School were deserted except for two young men who were casually jogging around the oval. It was late afternoon, early October, and the two ran easily, keeping a steady rhythm.

Callant Newkirk had much to think about—his mother's trouble, the beginning of his senior year, the never-ending pursuit of small-town dreams, the growing problem in a place called Viet Nam. He ran comfortably next to his best friend, Dave Langley, hearing only the crunch of tennis shoes in the ash, the steady labored breathing of two runners, so in tune their hearts must have been beating together. It dulled the worry for him, that steady relentless sound of breath, the concentration on the stride.

His mother, typically shy about the situation, had tried to reassure him. "It's nothing," she said. "It happens to lots of women." He had been terrified during the surgery, too numb with it all to even consider the reality.

Cal resumed counting, concentrating on the vibrations that shook his body as each foot hit the track. But she was better now. "Coming along nicely," the doctor said.

They were nearing the end of the workout. Cal would jog peacefully home, grab something to eat, shower, and be at the hospital for the visiting hour. She'll be coming home soon, he thought. Coming home, coming home, each step repeating, keeping the steadiness, com-ing-home.

Dave momentarily broke the pace, and Cal waited to resume the rhythm. Dave was off today. Probably too much worry about Susan McGregor. He smiled.

"One more," he panted to his partner. "Hit it at the twenty."

"Right," Dave said.

"Winner gets Susie's pink lace panties," Cal said, turning to look at his friend, still keeping the easy pace. Dave's face reddened, and Cal decided it wasn't a good day for teasing.

They ended each workout the same way. A fifty-yard dash.

"Now," Cal shouted, and digging in, took off with all that was left of his running energy. He concentrated on the line, feeling himself pulled toward it, his chest out, legs kicking, grinding in the ash, the pounding dissolving everything but the finish. Everything except the feeling that Dave had fallen back, and it made him go for the line even harder. It didn't seem fair, he thought, as he crossed the thirty, for Dave to be so easy.

"Hey," he said to his friend as they walked to the empty bleachers, "don't take it so hard. Just an off day."

They sprawled back against the bleachers. Both wore gray sweatsuits, stained with perspiration. Both lounged, waiting for their breathing to return to normal. Cal looked at the nearly cloudless sky and thought there was just the touch of winter on the way. Something about the blue of the sky turning slightly white. The taste of a chill.

"Hey," he said, "only kidding about Susie. You know that." He took a deep breath. "Good news," he said. "My mother's getting better."

Dave leaned forward, dangling his hands between his knees.

"She should get to go home next week sometime."

"I've got to tell you something," Dave said. His breathing was still slightly irregular, but it sounded serious all the same. Like the sky, a touch of winter, Cal thought, and he turned to his friend, only to have Dave look away.

What was this?

"It's about your mother," Dave said.

"I told you, she's almost better," Cal repeated. "They say the operation went fine. It'll just take some time for her to get her strength back." He laughed a little, and imagined he could see the two of them, himself and Dave, running the track. He saw them from above. A bird's-eye view.

"I wouldn't tell you except someone else might."

Cal felt a quickening in the pit of his stomach. He'd known Dave all his life. What could he possibly say now about his mother? That he liked her? Maybe even loved her? It made Cal jealous sometimes, to see how Dave looked at her as the three of them played board games on the porch. Parcheesi, Monopoly, Sorry. When Dave had his arms around her, a little stiffly to be sure, as she gave them dancing lessons, one at a time. Surely the doctor wouldn't have told Dave something he hadn't told Cal.

"So what is it?" Cal forced a smile.

Dave took a breath. "My mother's got some second or third cousin visiting from Four Corners," he said. "And she saw that picture I took of you and your mother last year. Junior Prom night."

"So?" Cal could remember the photograph perfectly. Dave had given them a print. It sat in a small gold frame on the round table in the living room right next to the picture of his father in his uniform.

"She recognized your mother."

"From Four Corners?" He was puzzled. "She never mentioned being there."

"She used to live there," Dave said. "She grew up there. This cousin even remembered her name was Carlotta."

"She's from Cambrick," Cal said. "She would have told me if she'd lived in this Four Corners."

Dave chewed on his bottom lip, still avoiding Cal's stare. "Shit," he said, folding his hands together, and Cal could feel his friend's fear. "Christ, I..."

"Just say it," Cal said, an anger to which he was not accustomed rising in his throat. What was this about?

"When your mother lived in Four Corners," Dave went on, and his slowness of speech made Cal want to shout at him, "when she was about twenty—this woman says—she was sort of attacked." He squirmed.

"Attacked? Attacked by who?" He couldn't get any image at all.

Dave shifted again. "Assaulted, I mean," he whispered. "You know, raped."

Now there was more than a touch of winter in the air. Now there was a sharp chill that began in his bones. "I don't believe that," Cal said. "Your relative must be wrong. Don't you think my mother would have told me?"

Dave sighed. "Maybe not. She moved away, I guess, or this woman said, or something…moved here when she turned out to be pregnant."

Cal clenched his hands together to stop the shaking. "Wait a minute," he said, and Dave finally turned to look at him. He could see the pain in his friend's eyes, and he wanted to hit him anyway.

"She'd gone to some carnival, or something. Hell, Cal, the woman even remembered when—the July before you were born."

Cal tried to figure. July to March. Without wanting to, he counted silently on his fingers. March. Nine months.

"You've seen that picture of my father," Cal said carefully, unwilling to release Dave with his eyes.

Dave shrugged. "I'm only telling you what this woman said. Maybe your mom didn't want to hurt you."

"Hurt me?" Cal was stunned. Raped. Pregnant. No. His mother couldn't simply have made up all those stories. *Wouldn't have.* No. One, two, three, four. He trembled with each number. A square-jawed man in a uniform. His father, the war hero. Six, seven, eight, nine. A sick feeling in his stomach. No. It couldn't be true.

"Look," Dave said. "I'm sorry. I thought you should know. That's all."

"You're lying," Cal said, struggling to his feet. He stood looking down at the bowed head of his friend. "You are fucking lying to me."

Dave shook his head slowly, and then it was over. Cal jumped down from the bleachers, looked back once at the boy who had been his best friend, and then he was gone. He took off running, running to the sound of his beating heart, running as fast as his labored breathing would allow, and he cut diagonally across the fading green of the football field, his steps soundless on the grass. He ran, leaving Dave with his head bowed and his hands folded.

He ran past the high school, his feet hitting concrete now, sending sharp slivers of pain up his legs into his lungs. He ran past Dave's house, thinking about hurling a rock through the damned front window, hearing the glass shatter, a scream from some lying bitch whose face was covered with blood. He passed two girls who waved to him from a porch, and he shouted "Shut up" to a chained barking dog frenzied at the sight of the runner.

He felt the pounding of his heart, and the cold omen of a new season in his lungs.

He turned the corner and there it was. The house where he lived with his mother. The yard surrounded with dying chrysanthemums, the tree whose last leaves hung tentatively, waiting for the final wind.

He leaped onto the porch, and threw open the front door as if he were in time to catch an intruder.

The house was warm with day-old sun, and it was absolutely quiet. He leaned against the door jamb, gasping for breath, thinking there was no air in this place, none at all. No voices, no teakettle whistling on the stove, no relentlessly ticking clock. Nothing. He was burning alive in the silence.

He looked around the living room. He searched the corners with his eyes, and remembered countless games of hide and seek, the wonderful element of surprise when he jumped out at her and her hands would fly to her face in mock terror. She, when it was her turn, always hid in the closet or behind the chair in the corner. He pretended he didn't know, although he had been dismayed at her lack of imagination then.

There weren't any secrets in this room. The man in the photograph gazed steadily at him. There he was, right where he had always been. No secrets.

He went down the hall to the door of her room. It was exactly as she'd left it. He'd had no reason—not until now—to enter it when she wasn't there. Her bed, a nightstand with a crystal lamp on it. A library book, a small heart-shaped box. He walked over to the stand, picked up the box, and removed the lid. It was empty. Not even a trace of powder, a button, or a needle. He had given it to her one Valentine's Day when he was in the sixth or seventh grade. He placed the box back on the stand.

He could hear his breathing again. He still could not get his heart to quiet.

It had to be here, here in this room. A clue, a memento, something that would explain the story. The heart box, empty. Her bureau. People hid things in the deep corners of drawers, money, tickets, letters. He pulled open the top drawer. Her undergarments, folded neatly in pastel-colored rows. A quilted satin box, a tiny compartment for each pair of stockings. In each corner, a small satin square, or oval, soft little pillows— scented. The perfume attacked him. He was breathing too deeply. Two silk scarves. He pulled the drawer out and dumped the contents onto the bed. No letters, no envelopes. He went back to the second drawer. Her nightgowns, slips. A black gown he'd never seen, didn't know she had. He was tempted to crush the fabric with his hand and walk into her hospital room waving it in an accusing fist. *Who did you wear this for?*

God, what a question. He had not meant to even think it. There had never been a man in this bedroom. Never.

He mixed the black nightgown in with the blue one, the pale pink, and a camisole, a beige satin slip. A crazy erratic black line through a pastel sea, still visible like a pulsing vein in someone's temple. More flowered sachets, a white satin heart. He went on. Drawers full of soft and furry sweaters, fine cotton blouses. Nothing.

He opened every drawer of the vanity, upending them onto the floor. Bright tubes of lipstick, a powder puff, more scarves, gloves. A white leather jewelry case on the top. He spilled the necklaces, earrings, pins out onto the mirror surface. A mother-of-pearl button, a ring with the stone missing. He tore everything from the closet, looking in the pockets of coats, jackets, skirts. He tossed them all behind him. A penny, a quarter, a crumpled dollar bill. He shook every shoe.

On the top shelf she kept shoe boxes full of small scraps of fabric, labeled according to color. He dumped the contents of *red* onto the bed, and raked his fingers through squares of vermilion satin, scarlet silk, coral ribbon, burgundy chiffon, rose voile, flag-red cotton, Christmas flannel. Nothing. Box by box, the blue, the green, the yellow, the white. Lavender. The bed like a rainbow, frozen, then shattered, its pieces blown here and there across white sand. Unrecognizable.

He looked in every purse, in every compartment. He opened a large dress box on the floor of the closet and found every drawing he'd ever given her from school, carefully marked with the year and the teacher's name. A horse, a dog, a house, a thunderstorm. And a scrapbook of pressed leaves, blossoms, and carefully printed names. A man, a boy, a woman, holding hands. He ran his fingers over the picture, the childhood crayon sketches.

What had he done? Why? He looked at the clothes he had ripped from the hangers, a robe thrown over a chair, shoes scattered, boxes, scarves. Her jewelry glittering in a wanton heap on the vanity—tangled.

Whatever had happened, it hadn't been her fault. He sat down on the bed. It was getting dark. What was sunset-orange light in the bedroom window one moment, was blue smoke the next as the sun fell behind a mountain. Everywhere he put his hand, he touched softness. All those dresses she had made for others, the dresses gone away, gone to weddings, dances, parties. The scraps left, in labeled boxes telling *nothing*. The occasional glitter of a gold or silver thread running through, catching, then losing the light.

How would he ever explain to her?

How could he ask such a question?

He picked up a flowered sachet on the bed next to him and threw it at the gaping chest of drawers. As if he had thrown it against the wind, it fell soundlessly short of the mark. Even now she waited for him. She would be wondering where he was. Thank God she could not see him, sitting in his gray sweat clothes in the midst of the colorful destruction of her room in the company of an invisible vandal.

He had to get ready. Shower, shave, look normal so she wouldn't worry. Normal. Could she have kept that secret from him, from herself? He got up from the bed. He could do one thing. He would find Dave before school and say just one thing to him: He was never to mention the story again. To anyone. Cal would deal with it his own way.

And as he walked through the darkness to the hospital, he rubbed the ends of his fingers. Something there. A light dusting of talc, powder, perfume. He raised them to his face. A sweet forbidden scent the water had not erased.

He could still feel the powder as he sat next to her bed, as he listened to her ask about the plants, the Wandering Jew in the kitchen, the African violets in the living room. Her usual questions about his day, the brightness in her eyes and in her cheeks as she assured him she was almost well. A few more days, maybe a week. And when she grew short of breath and lay back on the pillow and closed her eyes, he looked for any trace of a lie, and found none. The slight shadow of blue lines beneath her illness-paled skin could hardly be construed as a sin.

"Give me a kiss, now," she whispered. "I'm sleepy. You be on your way."

He did as she asked.

As he walked home, it occurred to him that he had never seen his mother naked. He heard Dave's words, Dave in a fit of temper at his own mother over something Cal could not remember. "That bitch. You should see her without her clothes. Her tits hang almost to her knees." Cal had been unable to look at Mrs. Langley for months after that, that sagging image making him both guilty and embarrassed.

Cal had never seen his own mother in her underwear, let alone naked. A satin strap here and there, a frill of white lace at her hem. "It's snowing down south," he would say, laughing, and she would go to the mirror in her room to look. A robe pulled not quite tightly enough. Now he wondered. Had she been hiding some mark, some eternal bruise or silvery scar?

The next day he stayed home from school and restored her room to order. And for the next five visits he sat calmly by her bed watching. Only once, thinking of trickery, he asked if she wanted him to bring his father's picture to the hospital. Did his eyes narrow as he asked, did a corner of his mouth turn up in mockery?

"Don't be silly," she said laughing, a laugh that quickly turned to a dangerous cough. "I'll be home soon. You're the one needs company." She patted his hand and looked at him. She was as lovely as ever. "I have nurses, doctors, and dear Mrs. Marlowe." She smiled in the direction of the ancient woman in the bed next to hers.

Cal would have to wait until she was well, until she came home, and they were alone again.

The following Tuesday, the high school principal appeared at the door of Cal's English class. He summoned him into the hall.

"The hospital called," he said, simply. "They want you there right away."

A trembling began at Cal's ankles, and he wondered how

he would run, without falling, the necessary blocks.

His mother was dying. He sat by her bedside holding her hand, thinking only that he needed more time, there had to be more time. She had to open her eyes, those eyes that could tell him something, anything to save them both. The doctor and the nurses moved in and about, and he could hear the rubber-soled whispers, the hospital innuendo. "She developed pneumonia," the doctor said. "It happens sometimes, but this came on so fast, and the drugs aren't working." He shook his head.

He tried counting her eyelashes, too black now against the paleness of her cheeks. The sheets were too white, the blanket that covered her a dull dying blue. All he could see was the maze of color he had created in her room and the ugly gray question that lay in the middle of it all. Dave's words, whispered now, fading away, then coming back at him in pieces. The look in the eye of the girl at school who had whispered to him about a secret meeting, and a place where he could touch her and no one would know, no one would see. And then the girl moved away, making the same promise to every young man who lounged against the lockers in the hall. Down the line, the whispers, then the laughter. The girl in a driven daze of undetermined despair, peddling her whispers in the corridor. He hated her then for coming at him, and he hated himself for remembering it all now.

Callant. He thought he heard his mother call his name and he leaned forward only to see that she had not moved at all. Callant. The children who had discovered the rhyme, "Callant, the gallant," his anger, the accusation. "I hate my name. Why don't I have a regular one like everyone else?" A flash of anger from her then, a fire in her eyes. "There's nothing wrong with being a gentleman, nothing wrong with being 'gallant,' nothing wrong with being different."

She'd created that name for him. How could he be so ungrateful? He needed time to make that and everything else all right.

"There's nothing left to do but pray," the white-coated doctor said.

All the color in the world was locked away, hidden in the boxes in her bedroom at home. If only he could bring it to her now, the red for her cheeks, the green of spring, the blue of a faultless sky. He wanted her to have music. He wanted to bring the records, the old ones that would shatter on the sidewalk if they were dropped, and he wanted to play them for her now. He wanted to close his eyes and see her dance to "Moonlight in Vermont" wearing the dress she had made for someone else. He wanted to hear the sound of the chiffon as she moved, a sound as soft as the breeze by the lake in summer.

All she had to do was open her eyes, and they would both hear the music again.

"Mother?" he whispered. Nothing. He closed his eyes and held the pale white hand. He had to know. "Please," he sighed.

Suddenly her fingers curled around his, and he opened his eyes. The grip was not the solid, protective one he remembered; it was a plea. He was amazed at the strength of the grasp, as if all her being centered there. His eyes flickered, a slight uncontrollable tremor.

He waited, still. Her eyes did not open for the longest time. And when they did, and Cal had to restrain the desire to scream for the white-cloaked people who roamed the halls, she only sighed.

"Callant," she whispered, and her eyes fluttered and sought the ceiling. "Cal?"

"I'm here," he said, leaning over her face so she could see. "I'm here."

"Your father..." she whispered, trying to moisten her lips with her tongue, trying to remember something.

He saw it then. A drawing from the collection on the closet floor. A man, a woman, a little boy. Holding hands in front of the house in which they lived. A family of three. He took a deep breath.

"Was a wonderful man," he said. He knew the rest of the lyrics, could hear the melody.

"Yes, but..."

Her eyes seemed blurred by still waters, too bright for an instant, then clouded.

"My father," he said, and the words caught in his throat for just the smallest time, "was a wonderful man. He loved you more than anything, and then he loved me."

"We danced," she said, and the waves of an ocean far distant muffled the words, and the question he had put away.

"You danced, and he held you close and you were happier than anyone had ever been."

"Danced…"

Cal pushed the buzzer that called the running feet. Already he could hear the whispers and the cries.

"Danced until the moonlight vanished," he said in a voice he could no longer call his own.

"Moonlight," she said, then opened her eyes as wide as seemed possible, as if searching for the source. Then her eyes closed again so tightly that Cal gripped her small hand hard enough to break the fingers.

"It didn't matter," the doctor would say to him later when he tried to explain. "You didn't hurt her."

"It was too late," the nurse would say.

Her eyes drifted open and fixed at the ceiling as if to say, this is where we leave it. This is the way it will be.

He imagined that she went to sleep, frozen in the moonlight in the blue silk chiffon dress fluttering in the late summer night breeze with the arm of her love tight around her waist, her head against his shoulder.

He dropped his tears on her hand as the doctor and the nurse shuffled around him murmuring apologies.

They begged him, in the most sympathetic terms, to let go.

He held her hand until everything closed in white, until he was certain the orchestra was gone, the music over. He did not want her to miss one single infinitesimal moment of the dream.

It was midnight in his mother's house. He sat in the darkness on the edge of her bed. He remembered her laugh, the slight dancing steps, the sound of her sewing machine, the evening call to dinner. She clapped her hands at some amazing trick of his; she placed his track trophy on the coffee table.

He lay back against the pillows of her bed, and closed his eyes. He thought he heard music from somewhere, but knew he must be mistaken. He could feel the tears warm on the sides of his face, and he wondered if he would ever be able to sleep again, although the darkness was warm and soothing in her room. He rolled onto his side, and slipped one hand under a pillow. Tomorrow. He just didn't know. He was certain of only one thing. His mother and father, one way or another, were gone. He was alone.

Your father was killed in the war—a hero, my love—but oh, he would have been proud of you had he lived. He would have loved you just as much as I do now, she whispered.

"I know," he said, "World War Two." He was sleepy now, too tired to move. "Proud."

He would have been very proud.

"Yes," Cal murmured. "I know. I know."

Two and a half years later, Cal was a groom, tall and dark. The bride was small, blond, and dressed in white.

"Here comes the bride," a girl child sang softly in the corner of the room. "Big, fat, and wide."

"There stands the groom," her friend giggled behind her hands. "Skinny as a broom."

A mother's hand clapped over the child's mouth.

Cal would have smiled at the singsong if he hadn't been so nervous. He seemed to be responding to everything about twenty seconds too late. He had not understood that there would be so many people. So many watchers.

"Congratulations, buddy," Dave said, and Cal gripped his hand, holding it for too long. Dave's mother kissed him, not completely missing his lips, and there was something about the sound of things that rattled rather than soothed.

He glanced at Mary Beth. It had been a shock to his senses when he kissed her at the altar. Her lips were soft, but the lace of her dress was almost sharp under his hands. That was the trouble with it all. He had somehow expected a filmy, moonlit wedding. "No one gets married at night, silly," Mary Beth had said, and that ended that.

He had to relax, so he put his arm around Mary Beth's shoulders and hugged her to him, in spite of the lace. They stood together in the receiving line in the armory, and they smiled at her relatives, and his friends. A happy, Technicolor couple.

Her brothers came at him, one by one, and pounded him on the shoulder. They winked and said, "Hey, Cal," and they shook his hand and said, "You take care of baby sister." He tried to laugh too, and he ended up looking over the shoulder of each of the brothers in turn, slightly to the left. Dave stood by him, occasionally, as if able to read Cal's mind, nudging him, saying, "Everything's going just fine."

Mary Beth's mother kissed him on the cheek, and he could smell something powdery, and he could feel her lips tremble. Mary Beth's father shook his hand, an unfeeling handshake from a rough-edged man. Mary Beth's three best friends and bridesmaids giggled in pink net, jiggling bouquets of carnations, and moved off in search of the brothers.

Cal stood in his new blue suit, a handsome young man of twenty, and felt thin. He rubbed his hands together as if to erase the feel of the lace, and Mrs. Langley, as if she too could read his thoughts, came up to him again and said, "It's a pity your mother did not live to see this day." He avoided her eyes.

His mother would have had a lovely dress for the occasion, one she made herself. His mother, her dark hair streaming down her back, her foot on the pedal of the sewing machine, satin and lace skimming by under her fingers, the fingers with the red-painted nails. Scraps of fabric on the floor, stubborn threads caught in the carpet. The smell of his mother's perfume, and the dinner in the oven. His mother, standing before a mirror in a blue chiffon dress she had made for someone else. Turning around for Cal to see, the dress flaring at the hem as he watched, as he checked for evenness, and he could see her knees as she turned. A dress for someone else's party, dance, wedding.

"I don't think," Mary Beth said softly into his ear, "that it was very nice of Mrs. Langley to bring your mother's death up on a day like today."

Cal looked at Mary Beth, puzzled for a moment as to what she meant. "It was all right," he said, pulling her closer to him, arm around her waist, the veil stiff under his chin. "It *is* too bad my mother isn't here."

"But death..." Mary Beth shook her head. "It seems like bad luck."

Mary Beth's oldest brother handed Cal a beer, and Farley, the brother he knew the best, took a picture of him, and the flash put little flecks of light in his eyes. Mary Beth clung to his arm, and he could feel the lace even through the fabric of his suit. He reached for her hand, for the flesh of it, and caused her to drop her bouquet.

"Silly," she said, resting her face against his arm. Cal was ten inches taller than Mary Beth, and he was suddenly aware that he was holding her hand much too tightly. Tina, with red hair and freckles and crooked teeth, quickly rescued the bouquet from the floor, and ran away in her pink net dress. "I caught it," she giggled. "I caught the bouquet."

"Not yet, silly," Mary Beth said, releasing Cal and pursuing her friend, while Cal marveled at the childishness of the chase, then remembered that was one of the things he liked best about Mary Beth—that she was young and sweet.

"It's not time yet," Mary Beth said as Tina held the bouquet behind her back.

"Tonight's the time," Farley whispered to Cal. "That's the time."

Mary Beth's mother, passing by, seemed to pretend not to hear.

Mary Beth's oldest brother lined them up for more pictures. Farley put his fingers behind Cal's head, and everyone laughed and Mary Beth's brother took just one picture that way. Then he insisted on seriousness. All of the bouquets were back in place.

Cal could smell the carnations, and he turned to look down the wedding party row. He smiled and surrendered to his place in the portrait. And he tried to remember, while he and Mary Beth were arranged and rearranged with various members of the wedding party, when his mother had first told him the story. In the cradle, probably, he thought. Whispered in the night to an infant while her hand rocked the cradle.

But usually when she told him things—those stories about his father—they sat at the kitchen table. It might have been a bouquet of bachelor's buttons from the garden that triggered the story, or a dress she was making for someone, sitting at the table where the light was good, taking tiny hand stitches, biting the thread with her teeth, a bad habit she admitted but did not break.

Maybe it was something bright and deep blue, like the glass bowl on the table. He'd heard the story so many times, it ran before him like a favored scene from a movie. A man and a woman danced in the moonlight on a terrace that extended over the water. The music is soft, the trembling tones of a clarinet, perhaps a violin. Something reminiscent of wartime. The woman wears a dress of blue silk, and her skirt moves softly as they dance. It moves the way the slight waves lap against the pier. She holds a bouquet of tiny yellow roses. "Tea roses, Callant." And she holds it tightly against the man's back. They dance slowly, gracefully, the man in the uniform, the lovely woman in the blue silk dress. On her finger is a new gold ring. In his lapel, next to the decorations, is a single yellow rose that matches the ones in her bouquet. There is night-blooming verbena and the scent fills the air. There are stars in the sky, strings of white lights, and spots of moonlight falling indiscriminately on the water. The band, still out of sight, plays "Embraceable You."

Cal shook his head in slight irritation at the memory, and Dave handed him a glass of champagne. Someone made a toast. Mary Beth giggled and said the bubbles tickled her nose. There was orange sherbet with soda in glass cups for the people who did not want beer. Three girls in flowered aprons served glass plates of cake, mints, and coconut macaroons. The reception guests sat around the hall on metal folding chairs and compared stories of other weddings, other times.

It was a good thing, they commented for example, that Cal would not have to go to Viet Nam. They were proud of their armory and their boys in the National Guard.

There were three long tables set up along the walls of the room. Two of them displayed the gifts. The third had the beer and potato chips. In each of the four corners of the room was an American flag. Mary Beth took Cal's arm and led him to the first table.

"A toaster," she said. "Isn't it pretty?" Towels in shiny cellophane, a set of dishes, an iron. White sheets tied with a purple ribbon. A cut-glass candy dish. A set of dishtowels for every day of the week embroidered with cats.

"Sue did those," Mary Beth's mother said. "Look at the fine stitches."

Sue was not one of the pink ruffled bridesmaids. Sue was in a wheelchair across the room, legs withered from a childhood accident.

"They're really cute," Mary Beth called to her. "Look at the kitties."

One cat was hanging the washing on the line. The word *Monday* was embroidered in red.

It seemed amazing to Cal that people were giving all of these things to them, and he felt warm with the affection of it all.

"Maybe we can get a kitty," Mary Beth said, squeezing Cal's arm. "I'd like a little yellow one."

"We can get two, if you want," he said. He put his arm proudly around his wife's shoulders as they walked alongside the gift table.

"Oh, look. From Mr. and Mrs. Barnard. Red and blue flowered sheets. They must have cost a fortune."

Farley, behind them, hit Cal right in the middle of the back and laughed. "Lots of sheets," Farley said over Cal's shoulder. "And lots of fun between them."

"You hush up, Farley," Mary Beth's mother warned.

With the champagne, the beer, and Mary Beth's arm, Cal was feeling warmer all the time, and yet as they walked, as Mary Beth called, "Cally, look at that casserole," Cally this and Cally that, he felt as if he were walking through waist-high water. The sounds of the slight waves against the shore, the slowness of it all. And the scene returned, blurring for a minute the set of steak knives and the lettuce keeper.

The men in the orchestra wear white jackets and have slick dark hair and small mustaches. The light catches in the silver circles on a saxophone or burns gold in the cone of the trumpet. "We danced to 'Stardust' because it was as slow and as close as we were, and we called it our wedding song, and I held onto my bouquet as tightly as one would to a priceless heirloom. I was convinced the moment could be caught, like the silver rings of light, or the soft glorious notes of the clarinet, and held in my heart like the bouquet in my hand."

He could hear his mother whispering the words through time, even while he walked and listened, nodded and smiled. It was a comfort to him. He could feel the loosening in his wrists as he shook Mr. Harper's hand.

Dave appeared beside him. "You're holding up just swell, buddy," he laughed. "You're going to make it yet."

"I don't know why," Cal whispered to his friend, "it didn't

occur to me that there would be all these people watching us all the time. I mean, I've been to weddings before." He pulled at his collar to indicate his discomfort.

It was time to cut the wedding cake, and the cameras were ready. Cal could feel his face begin to burn again under the flash, and the many eyes that were upon them.

A silver cake server with a white satin ribbon.

"Now you put your hand over mine," Mary Beth said.

Callant felt like a child until he looked into her eyes. She was beautiful. A beautiful little girl, and she looked at him with bright flecks of love in her eyes.

"Smile, Callant," Mary Beth's mother called, and to his own surprise, he did, and he meant it. He and Mary Beth were going to live both parts of his mother's dream.

He lost sight of everything but his hand over hers. The pink ruffled bridesmaids and Mary Beth's brothers faded. His hand over hers holding the silver knife with the white trailing satin ribbon. His hand over hers, hers still guiding his from underneath, moving him at will. He thought perhaps his eyes filled with tears. With the precision of a surgeon, his hand over hers, together they sliced right through the middle of the prettiest white rose on the wedding cake, and the knife hit the plate with a vibration that no one other than Cal would have felt.

And then Mary Beth was laughing and pushing a piece of the cake into his mouth, and he tried, for then his hands were shaking, again to cut a small perfect piece for her, and trying, trying to be steady, moving the cake to her mouth, Mary Beth turning, smiling, laughing, people moving closer, and he put the piece of cake on her tongue because she opened her mouth wide, wider than he would have expected and looked up at him with an expression that would have seemed like a dare had he not been so puzzled by it, and so bent on getting that piece of cake just so.

With the tip of her tongue, Mary Beth licked the white frosting from her upper lip, and she reached up to put her arms around Cal's neck. She pulled him down to her, and kissed him until he could taste the sugar from the cake, and smell her perfume all at once.

The applause, like crackling wings of giant birds, took him away.

"Whooee," called Farley. "Come up for air."

And someone handed them plates, a square of ice cream puddling around the edges, and a spoon awkward in his hand, Cal smiling, wanting it to be all cold in his mouth, hoping to cool down his brow. With the first bite of the ice cream, all smooth, smelling of time gone by, he was lost again. Rock salt and hard-time turning of the crank. Water seeping out the wooden bucket, puddling on the basement floor of the house he had grown up in. They sat on child-sized chairs, his mother and himself. Pour on the salt, the quartzlike crystals. He wanted the beaters, and had the patience for it. An hour and a half of turning. Custard. The old wooden handle, rough in the hand, still at last. The ice cream dripping white to be smoothed into blue dishes and eaten with silver spoons.

He shook his head, moving back to the present, took another bite of ice cream. That old freezer was in the basement somewhere, and he'd teach Mary Beth how to make ice cream.

Then the music began. The bridesmaids all kissed him again, and someone gave him another beer. Drink it as fast as you can, they suggested. Chugalug. Chugalug. People began to dance to the orchestra, comprised of middle-aged men from the community who played at every major occasion. An old man swept a woman in a red flowered dress around the floor in a waltz. A man in a short-sleeved shirt and blue pants danced with his hand in the middle of Mary Beth's aunt's bare back.

There wasn't any more champagne, but there was plenty of beer. The edges of things were beginning to dissolve for Cal, and Mary Beth said "Kiss me again, kiss me again."

And he did, without blushing.

"Finally made it legal," Kirk Sutter from the track team said, shaking Cal's hand.

Legal, legal, Cal thought. Legal, legitimate. There was that small painful dark spot again. He shook it away.

"Promise me a kitty," Mary Beth said.

"I promise you a kitty."

He had made it legal. Every single step of it.

"You are my pretty little wife," he said into her ear.

"And you are my handsome husband."

With those words, he noticed the rise of her breast, and he looked closely at the wedding gown for the first time. It promised white things, like the ice cream and the cake, and he longed for her. Longed to have all this pink and musical confusion over. He had felt her breasts against his chest when he kissed her, but everything else was still to come.

"The bride and groom haven't danced yet," someone shouted.

"Now, now, now," the chant began. The militant clapping of hands, and Cal thought, this I know, this I can do. The floor cleared, and he took Mary Beth's hand and led her to the center of the dance floor.

He wished, in honor of his mother, that he had remembered to request "Stardust." And in fact, when the music began and he took the first gliding step, he could not remember the name of the song. Mary Beth, soft in his arms, following him in the waltz.

Everyone loves a man who can dance. His mother and Dave in the living room. The old seventy-eights. The rug rolled and pulled to the side, and he remembered feeling jealous as he watched his mother dance with his best friend. She with her head held high, her back straight, her slim legs forming the steps perfectly, and Dave, his shoulders dropped, his eyes cast down upon his hesitant feet. Dave still couldn't dance as well as Cal could, but then had not had nearly the practice.

They were young then. The dancing lesson took time. It was a secret from everyone else. Dave had not even told his mother. The waltz, the foxtrot, the samba.

Mary Beth pulled back from him slightly as they danced, and looked up at him. "One of the reasons I love you," she said, "is that you can dance like this. So close."

And he held her again, ignoring the people who ringed the room, making the carefully measured steps, still unable to remember the song. And he had to have it, had to be able to sit with his own children someday and tell them a story that was true. "Your mother and I danced to—something—on our wedding day."

"I feel like a fool," he whispered to his bride. "I can't remember the name of this song."

"'True Love,' silly," she said. "Everybody knows this song."

And suddenly it was time to go, time for Cal to take his wife by the hand, the bride trailing her wedding skirts, her bouquet, her ribbons, the whiteness of her hand waving, and her red mouth laughing and her eyes flickering with that new strange something.

So Mary Beth tossed her bouquet of white roses high into the air, and in the skirmish among the pink-ruffled bridesmaids and the girl who had been in charge of the guest book, the bouquet bounced above their heads, pushed higher by the desire, until it flew up and over, and to the discomfort of everyone, ended in front of Sue's wheelchair. Sue picked it up and waved it like a torch before anyone was foolish enough to protest.

"Oh, thank you," Sue called to the newlyweds, who were out of her vision. "Oh, thank you, Mary Beth."

"Can you believe it?" Mary Beth asked Cal as they ran through the hail of rice. "Of all people..."

He looked at her, surprised. He'd never noticed that little cruel whisper before. But then she kissed him, long and hard, in the car, the car that was decorated with clever phrases— SHE GOT HERS TODAY, HE'LL GET HIS TONIGHT—cans and streamers, and he thought everything would be all right after all.

"I love you," he said when she released him.

"Of course you do, silly," she said, looping her arm through his. "We're married."

As soon as they were outside of town, Cal pulled the car off to the side of the road and removed the cans and the rough-sketched words from the car, while Mary Beth, who did not agree with the act, waited impatiently in the front seat.

"You'll like this place," Cal said as he drove. He had rented a cabin in the mountains. "And the food in the cafe is just fine."

"I've been to Parker's Camp before," Mary Beth said as if he had accused her of stupidity. "I mean, I've never stayed in the cabins, but I've been there. You think I'm just a little girl who's never been anywhere, or seen anything, don't you?"

She tickled his ear, and he shuddered.

"Of course I don't think that," he said.

"I'm a woman," she continued. "You'll see."

He smiled. There had been other girls he had been with who were willing to give it a good go on the back seat, in the dark, on the edge of the gravel pit, but Mary Beth had not been one of them. *Married. Not until I'm married.* He supposed that was one of the reasons he loved her.

They drove from the high valley floor, away from the lights of the smelter, the sprinkling street lights, and the low frame houses. They drove up a narrow asphalt winding road into the foothills of the mountains. Cedar, pine, and oak. A creek alongside the road swept through willows. There were occasional picnic tables, flat spots by the roadside, and cars and coolers, and children stirring up fires with sticks.

They listened to the radio, singing along with the Beatles, changing the station when the news came around with its disturbing accounts of protest against the war. Mary Beth reached over and plucked the carnation from his lapel and held it to her nose.

"It doesn't seem fair to have to throw the bouquet away," she said.

There was that slight doubt again. His mother had told him about taking the flowers out of her bouquet, one by one. In the morning the flowers were on the pillows, and she'd laughed with her soldier husband. *No one gets married at night, silly.* Things must have been different in wartime, Cal thought. That was it.

It was just past eight in the evening and still very light when he turned the key in the door of Cabin 14.

"Aren't you going to carry me over the threshold?" she asked. "Like in the movies?"

She was teasing him, but he didn't mind. He put the bags inside the door.

"I can pick you up in a minute, sister," he said, sweeping her up into his arms. "You're just as light as a feather."

She kissed him on the mouth as they entered the cabin, and he had the strange sensation again of being close to tears. Happiness, he decided.

The cabin, while small, was comfortably furnished with a double bed, a dresser, and a table and chairs. They would be able to sit at the table later, look out over the lake, play gin rummy, plan their life together. Gin was the only game Mary Beth knew so far, but he intended to teach her others. Chess, the game he played most often with Dave, but that might take some time.

"Pretty nice, huh?" he asked her.

"You want to unzip this dress for me?" she asked, turning her back to him. "It's too hot."

His hands shook only slightly as he lowered the zipper. She stepped out of the dress immediately, and turned toward him. In the white underslip, she looked like one of the roses from her bouquet. He put his arm around her, tipped her head back, and kissed her.

"Hungry?" he asked, hoping she would say "no," not wanting to stop now and sit anxiously in the cafe.

"You bet," she replied, and her breath was soft against his cheek. "I'll get ready."

She opened her suitcase, took something from it, and went into the bathroom. He'd seen her in a bathing suit before, but the slip was different. Later, with the lights out, in the dark, he would run his hands all over her body. Explore it all. Slowly. Gently.

He took off his suit coat and hung it in the closet. Carefully he removed the rest of his clothes, and as he did so, the light in the room took a different turn, as if in one instant, the sun had dropped behind the mountain. It seemed ridiculous to sit in the cafe. Everyone would know right away they were honeymooners, and he didn't want the sidelong smiles, the whispers. He sat down on the edge of the bed in his shorts. Maybe he could just get them a couple of hamburgers to eat in the room. He could ask.

"Aren't you going to look and see what's special?" Mary Beth asked.

He turned immediately.

He could not believe his eyes. Mary Beth stood in the doorway, the bright light from the bathroom casting her sharply, as if she were on a small stage. She was not wearing the white or pale pink negligee he had imagined those nights he had spent alone in his bed waiting for this day. She no longer looked like a rose from her bouquet. She was wearing something black, something utterly transparent, and she was walking toward him. He could see the nipples of her breasts, the dark patch of hair. The thing she was wearing had a little red ruffle on the bottom, and that didn't even quite reach far enough to cover the hair. And she just kept walking to him, slowly, deliberately.

"Takes your breath away, doesn't it?" she asked him as she slid onto the bed next to him. "I had to hide it from my mother."

To his embarrassment, he wanted to run and turn off the bathroom light, the light that destroyed the darkness that was falling, but not falling fast enough. He had the awful feeling someone was watching.

"Mary Beth," he said, and he could barely hear his own words. He stared at the thing she wore, the thing that was secured in front by one tiny red bow. He'd seen pictures of clothes like that. He'd seen them in magazines that were filled with photographs of women with their legs spread wide open. Blaine Wells had kept a collection in his locker at school until the principal found out, and Blaine was expelled. Those magazines, tattered from eager hands. "Look," Blaine had said to him. "You can buy a doll, a doll that you can fuck if you can't get a real girl. A girl like this one." Blaine had licked his finger and put it right in the center of the photograph of a woman who had a ring of black hair around what looked to Cal like a wound. "And if you'd rather diddle a guy..."

And here was Mary Beth, right there with him on their wedding night, fiddling with the little red bow with one hand and stroking his bare thigh with the other. "I knew you'd love it," she said, putting her arms around him and pulling him back onto the bed. "I showed it to Tina."

He couldn't think of what to say, and she leaned over and kissed him. Tina, watching, waiting, knowing. The nightgown parted, and he could feel her breasts against his chest, and something made it hard for him to breathe.

"Let me help you," she said, her voice the voice of a woman he had never met, a woman he had never intended to touch legally. He closed his eyes against the remaining light, felt her hand on his groin, and he lay there as she reached inside and touched him, and he wanted to shout, Wait, wait. No. *Wait until dark.*

He was barely aware of her moving away from him, only slightly conscious of her removing his undershorts. He moved just enough to help her because he had to; he couldn't just do nothing.

"Move up to the pillow," she whispered, and he obeyed, keeping his eyes shut against what he feared would be a blinding flash. He groaned, and she said, "That's wonderful, darling," her voice growing older.

He tried to reach for her and she said, "No, you're supposed to lie still," and he wondered why he didn't know that. He felt her settle down next to him, could feel her bare legs and arms. Why shouldn't he bury his head in her arms? Why should he feel it was too light? She could see him too well. That was it. He was afraid of what she might see. He touched her hair in spite of what she'd said, and although he knew it was golden against his stomach, it felt black. And what happened next was so unexpected, it sent a convulsion through his body, and he moaned.

She took hold of him, her hand moving up and down. Then

the coolness of her lips, the tip of her tongue, circling, then taking him in her mouth. His mind was lost to his body and the stiffness grew. She moved faster now, and her hand was unaccountably strong. And he wanted to scream for release.

And then she was on top of him, those strong fingers putting him in the place, that ring of red surrounded by black, and he had to move with her. Her hands were on his chest, and she moved back and forth, around, and up and down. He had to regain his position.

He turned her onto her back. "Oh," she sighed, and he was in the darkness now, in the back seat of a car with a girl from another town whose name he did not know, and he heard the words "I love you," and he drew away from her, raised his hand, and slapped her across the face.

But no, he didn't do that. He opened his eyes and saw Mary Beth, he heard her whisper again, "I love you," and as he tried to keep going, he thought of blood, and how they should have a towel.

He did not know he had stopped. That he had frozen above her, his eyes wide open. He thought he pushed her, pushed so hard it hurt her, violated her, raped her. The pictures flashed by, and then everything was liquid and he was floating somewhere in space. Something warm, sticky, salty. Blood, he thought, running everywhere.

He collapsed onto her breasts, felt them flat against him, and when she reached with her arms, he rolled off, closing his eyes, gasping for breath.

"You didn't need to do that," she whispered to him. "I'm on the pill."

He did not have the slightest idea what she was talking about. He wanted to beg forgiveness for hurting her, and all he could manage was a faint, "I'm sorry."

"It doesn't matter," she said. "You didn't know, that's all."

She was talking in riddles. But he *didn't* know. He had only suspected. That small dark circle of doubt he had tried to ignore had surfaced again. Had he slapped Mary Beth or not? No, only that memory, that girl who had whispered love when only darkness was there. He had been afraid then to consider his act. He was afraid now.

But he loved Mary Beth. He shouldn't want to hurt someone he loved.

The room was dark now, and Mary Beth quiet, her breathing soft in sleep. He could see the white heap of wedding dress flung over one of the chairs. It looked like a huddled, mourning ghost.

There would be blood everywhere, he thought. He tried moving a little at a time so he would not wake her. She sighed only slightly as he got up from the bed.

In the bright white glare of the bathroom, he could not find so much as a trace of a stain.

He stepped into the shower. He could only hope that the water would wash away the confusion, for at that moment, that exact instant in time, he did not know what had happened. He had no evidence to help him distinguish between the unwelcome dreams of the past and the reality of the day.

Cal leaned against the blue pickup truck and listened to Kenny Larkin tell one of his endless stupid shaggy dog stories. He had to smile and shake his head. The only beauty of the whole thing was that Kenny laughed like a maniac at the end of his own stories, and the rest of the men couldn't help but laugh with him. Unfortunately, it had created the illusion for Kenny that he was a truly funny man.

It was cooler than usual for the middle of a summer day. A slight breeze blew down from the barren hills that surrounded the concentrator. Cal and his friends all wore safety boots and some had goggles dangling around their necks. The noise from the rod-and-ball mill was muted by the distance.

Kenny finished his story and howled with laughter, and tried to swallow a bite of sandwich at the same time and choked. The rest of the men doubled over at his red face, and Dave reached over and pounded him on the back.

Cal and Mary Beth had been married for nearly three months, and he had to admit he preferred the good-natured company of the men he worked with to the sulky girl his wife had become. He'd begun to wonder what had made him want to get married, what had happened to his dreams of going over to Justin for a couple of years at the junior college.

That was something—the college—that had just seemed to get away from him. None of his friends were planning to go, and it had seemed so natural just to settle in at the smelter where the money was good enough, and to simply keep in the back of his head somewhere that when he got some money together, he'd go to night school. Or something.

And he had been very careful making love since that honeymoon night, to keep his mind from leading him into that mysterious brutal space he did not understand. He would never raise his hand against his own wife. Funny. Every time he thought that, the words seemed to be the very ones his mother might have said had his father lived long enough to prove the fact. He had forced from his mind any questions about Mary Beth's virginity. After all, he'd had his share before they were married. And he listened to the way his married friends talked and thought, we're not so different, not so different at all. He'd taken all the kidding about being a newlywed, all the remarks.

"Mary Beth makes a great lunch," Kenny Larkin said, back on the laugh track, snatching the uneaten half of Cal's sandwich.

"Not to mention midnight snacks, I'll bet," Luther Mergin chimed in. "She's some girl, that Mary Beth."

"Don't act like you know something," Dave said quickly, "you big mouth, because you don't."

"'Course I don't," Luther said. "Hell, Cal knows I kid."

"La de da," Kenny Larkin said, wadding up his lunch sack.

"Christ, don't get her pregnant," Luther said. "My wife sits around the house like a big balloon and don't do nothing but watch people wail and moan on TV. Her back hurts, her legs hurt, her head aches. She still throws up. I haven't had a decent meal in months."

Pregnant. Mary Beth wasn't entertaining any notion of that. The vial of pills clicked and turned with absolute regularity. When Cal had suggested they have a baby, Mary Beth had run into the bedroom and cried for two hours as loud as he had ever heard anyone cry. She had slammed the door to the room that had been his mother's and kept him out, the door that had never been closed to him before. It was all he could do to resist putting his fist through that door, or going through the house, room by room, and taking down the ridiculous treasures Mary Beth had placed on every available surface. A collection of plush animals he had never known existed. A green dinosaur on the couch. A huge blue bear in the corner by the dusty sewing machine.

But then he would soften, and stop by Mrs. Hughes' porch where she sold summer flowers from her own garden. He would pick up a six-pack of beer, and a couple of hamburgers. He and Mary Beth would turn the lights down when it got dark and dance. When they went to bed, he kept things gentle and slow, and for a time, it would seem all right.

But Mary Beth had taken recently to getting up in the middle of the night and pacing in the living room. Sometimes he could hear music turned down low, but when he asked her what she was thinking, she just looked at him as if she herself did not know. Eventually she would sleep, but she was always too tired to get up in the morning.

The whistle blew, and Cal closed his lunch pail. Once again, lost in his own thoughts, he'd missed most of the conversation and the last joke that had everyone else yelping with laughter. It didn't matter anyway. The talk was always the same. The married men complained about the lack of sex, and the single bragged about the excess. He would be glad to get back inside the crusher where the noise prevented any more words.

Mary Beth had been so cheerful before they were married. Now, often when he came home from work, Mary Beth and Tina would be in the living room drinking beer. He thought Tina looked at him suspiciously, and he wondered what she knew. She always left quickly once he arrived home.

In the meantime, dust collected on the tables and in the corners, and he found himself cleaning up secretly when Mary Beth was away.

That afternoon, he tried, as the railroad cars dumped ton after ton of ore into the crusher, to think of how he might talk to Mary Beth about her responsibilities. He didn't want to make her cry.

He arrived home at ten minutes after five. The first thing he noticed was that the living room was uncommonly dark. The drapes were still drawn as they had been in the morning when he left. The radio was on, but not as loud as usual, and Mary Beth was asleep on the couch. She was stretched out on her back, one knee bent slightly, and she was naked. Cal quietly turned off the radio. He looked at his sleeping wife. He loved her, didn't she understand that? He wanted to take care of her, to dress her in silk, to bring her flowers and dance with her under the stars. Maybe if he just came right out and said that, she would understand.

He went into the kitchen and placed his empty lunch box on the counter. He felt strangely uneasy as he went into the bedroom and took Mary Beth's bathrobe from the chair and walked back into the living room. Maybe she was sick or something, and this wasn't the right time.

"Mary Beth," he whispered, and her hand moved across her face as if she were trying to block the words that might wake her.

"Mary Beth," he said again. "Please wake up."

She moaned slightly but opened her eyes. "What time is it?" she asked, raising up on one elbow to look at him.

"Little after five."

"It's too hot to cook," she said. "I want to go get a hamburger or something."

"I know it's hot," he said, and pushing away his sense of arousal, he handed her the robe. "I want to talk to you."

"About what?" she asked, sitting up. She pulled the robe around her. "Could you open a window or something?" she asked.

He opened both side windows as far as they would go. He'd never seen the living room in such a light of despair. He heard her yawn behind him.

"Want a beer?" she asked. "I'm going to have one."

"Sure." The blue bear in the corner looked monstrous in the duskiness, and it seemed to him that the glass eyes caught a light somewhere that did not exist. It added to his discomfort; the eyes made him feel like a stranger.

When she returned from the kitchen, she sat down on the couch next to Cal and handed him a cold can of Coors.

"I know the place is a mess," she said, giving him the opener. "I didn't feel so good today."

He opened both cans.

"You don't seem very happy," he said, and he took a long swallow of the cold beer. "I'd like to know what's wrong."

"I wish I had a cigarette," Mary Beth said.

He laughed a little in spite of his fear. "That's all? You just need a cigarette?"

Mary Beth gave him a cold look, and took a sip of her beer.

"Sorry," he said. "I want to know why you're not happy."

She took a deep breath, and the robe parted again, revealing most of her breasts. "All right," she said, brushing the hair away from her face. "I'll tell you. You're not what I expected at all." She paused and withdrew her glance. "Still waters run deep. That's what everyone used to say about you. What a laugh. They don't run at all."

Deep. Run deep. What was she talking about?

"You know, *Callant,* I've got six brothers and I know something about men, and there's something wrong with you."

He could feel the damned shaking begin inside. Wrong. Had he been wrong all along? Those horrible dreams of hurting her. He'd been positive they were just that—nightmares. He'd been so careful to stop before they took him over. He had never been able to find so much as a mark on her body. Didn't she understand how much will that took? Her brothers? Those crude baboons. The shaking turned to anger.

"Your brothers?" he said. "Those assholes taught you about men?"

Mary Beth slapped him, and he grabbed her wrist. "Don't," he warned, and he saw that her eyes were filled with tears. "Don't you swing at me, little girl."

"Don't you call me little girl." She struggled, and he freed her wrist at the moment he realized what he had said about her brothers. God, he hadn't meant to imply that she'd done anything with them, but he suddenly saw Farley spreading her legs, plunging inside her. A bright red stain spreading beneath her. Stop it. Stop, he pleaded with his mind.

"I just listened to them talk. You know, when I was a kid. I couldn't help but hear," she said. "And I used to sneak into their rooms and look at their magazines. The ones where men write in and say what they like." Her eyes were wide and afraid now, as if the confession were being made to her mother.

"Magazines?" He saw her in the doorway on their honeymoon night. He saw her posing for a picture, stretched back on a bed, her legs apart, a stranger holding the camera. "Those magazines are filled with crap. Crap and lies."

"You looked at them," she said softly. "Why shouldn't I?"

He didn't even know where to begin. None of this made sense. For a moment there he had thought perhaps she wanted the kind of gentle, tender lovemaking he wanted to give her, and now she was talking about *magazines*.

"Tina has sex and she says it's fun," Mary Beth went on. "It makes her feel good, and Tina's not even married."

Tina. So that was what they talked about. No different than the lunch-hour locker-room talk at the smelter.

He turned to her slowly. She looked pale and frightened, and it quickened the anger he felt.

"Well then, little..." He stopped. "Why don't we go in the bedroom right now, and you can show me what's *fun*."

"I don't feel like it right now."

He stood up, reached down, and grabbed her by the arm, pulling her to her feet. She dropped the beer she held in her other hand and it landed dully on the table, then rolled to the floor. She struggled against him, and her robe fell down off her shoulder.

"Come on," he said. "You show me now."

"All right, damn you," she said, pulling her arm away from him. "I will."

He was left to follow her down the hall, to keep up with her determined pace, and he was that stranger again, that interloper in his own home.

She began slowly enough, offering him first one breast then the other, pushing her soft flesh into his mouth, moving his hand where she wanted it to be, caressing him with her own hands, moving her body under him. At first, he thought, this is no different, this is fine, this is what we always do, she must be wrong, and then he stopped thinking anything and gave in to it all, and he moved with her, not against her, and her words gave way to moans and he could feel her warm breath as they continued. All the while he could feel that heat rising in his body, and his mouth was eager, and everything loomed larger than before.

"Not yet," she whispered, and the shadows of the room moved from the corners where they hid, moved in ever-expanding intensity toward the struggle. Then they had him and something came loose in his soul, and all he could see and feel was red and black. He imagined ropes around her wrists and ankles, a dirty blanket, and the smell of hay. He had to tie her up. She would scratch him with those long red nails. He had to cover her mouth with his hand so she would not scream. Her face was already covered with bruises, and there was a trickle of blood on her throat, and all the time, he just kept at her, kept that pounding steady determined rhythm that would break her, and set him free. He saw the glistening blade of a knife by her side, felt her teeth against his palm, and he tasted blood. The ropes had made ugly red circles on her wrists and ankles, and it only made him stronger. The shadows exploded into a series of bright lights, and he thought he had been caught, that there were men with lights, and weapons, and that he was surrounded, but they wouldn't get him before he was through. A loud crackling noise that was either a gunshot or the sound of bones breaking all at once mortally wounded him, and, gasping for his last breath, he moved away from her, rolled onto his back, and died.

In the midst of the darkness and the silence came the gradual intrusion of a quiet crying. He did not understand. To his amazement, he was able to open his eyes.

The shadows had receded, and next to him, Mary Beth was crying, her face buried in her pillow. There were no ropes, no marks, no men with flashlights and rifles, nothing except the small pale body, huddled, hiding from him, shaking in the bed.

He touched her shoulder, and she pulled away.

"I'm sorry," he whispered, although he didn't understand the nature of the crime. "I don't…"

She turned quickly and faced him. The tears made her eyes dark and yet brilliant at the same time. "You did it again," she said. "Like you just become someone else, or go someplace else in your mind."

His fear, as if he had been shot, drained the blood from his body, and he could feel it filling her eyes as she stared at him.

"You go along," she said, "just as if everything is fine, and then you just stop. You look at me like you hate me." She shook her head. "Why does that happen?" she asked. "What goes wrong?"

He covered his eyes with the back of his hand. He was cold all over now, and in his darkness, the musty smell of hay returned. He shook it away. "Sometimes you push," he whispered, desperate to explain. Was it true? Had he simply stopped? Frozen? It didn't make sense. He felt the release of tension in the bed springs as she got up. He heard her close the door to the bathroom, heard the sound of running water.

The nightmare had never been that bad before. Asleep or awake, it had never been so real. Exhausted, he rolled onto his side, his back to the bedroom door. Gary Martin was an epileptic, and he had "little" seizures. Was that what he was like when he just stopped, when his mind kept going on alone? He began to count backward from one hundred, slowly, methodically, the sound of running water blurring the numbers, erasing them completely at seventy-three.

He woke with a scream lodged in his throat, the shadows coming at him once again. He sat up in bed, perspiration running down his sides. The house was dark and silent.

"Mary Beth?" he called.

Nothing.

He struggled up from the bed, pulled on his shirt, and checked each room of the house.

On the kitchen table, beside an empty beer can, he found a note. "I've gone over to Tina's," it read. "Don't come after me. I'll come home later."

He opened the refrigerator door. There was a can of beer on the shelf, chili uncovered in a bowl, leftovers from a week ago. A wilted head of lettuce, and three jars of pickles with one or two left in each. He reached for a carton of milk, only to find it empty. He could never understand why she put empty cartons back on the shelf.

He opened the last can of beer. He put his hand on his stomach when it growled, and thought, I have to eat, have to get something down to calm me.

He sat in the darkness at the kitchen table and finished the beer. What, he thought, in hell am I going to do?

He closed his eyes, and thought he could smell chicken roasting in the oven. He thought he could hear his mother running water over the fresh vegetables from the garden, the sound of the opening and closing of cupboard doors. *Callant, be a love and set the table for me, will you, honey? This will be ready in just a few minutes. Use the red flowered table cloth and the blue napkins. Thank you, sweetheart, you're such a good little man. That's right. Fork on the left. Salad's in the refrigerator in the blue bowl.*

He opened his eyes, knowing she would not be there.

"Why can't you help me?" he asked anyway. "Why in hell didn't you tell me the truth?"

No answer came. Although he waited with quiet respect, no one spoke.

He showered and dressed, anxious to escape the over-powering sense of density in the house. Outside, the night had cooled the air, and there was just the slightest breeze as he walked. He tried counting his steps. The lines in the side-walk, the number of actual maple trees on Maple Street. He thought about telling Mary Beth the truth, and it made him laugh. He didn't even know what the truth was. He walked around a chalk hopscotch on the sidewalk as if he would ruin it by stepping on it.

He thought about going by Dave's. If Mary Beth could run to Tina, why not? He thought about going to Hawley's for a hot dog and beer, and the thought of smoke and noise made his stomach turn.

Dave. Dave and his mother's cousin's damned story. Why was he letting that bother him now? He had promised himself it was not true. He'd made Dave promise. Worst of all, he had sat at his mother's bedside and denied everything. He had promised her, although even his mind had not formed the words.

He stepped on a crack in the sidewalk and thought about broken promises. Broken backs. Mr. O'Leary on Cedar Street was hosing down his front walk as if it were a secret task to be done only at night. Cal crossed the street to avoid the water, and any kind of greeting.

That was it. His life needed cleaning. His house was filthy, his job covered him with dust from the moment he entered the crusher every day, and his mind was giving in to a damned dirty story some whispering gossip had chosen to tell. His garden was overgrown, and one of the clotheslines was broken. A loose wire that angled to the ground, and made scratching noises against the pole on windy nights. He would fix that, and take every damned piece of dirty linen in his home, and wash it. He laughed. He didn't know how to use the old washing machine. Mary Beth did the wash at her mother's house once a week in an automatic washer. She spun their clothes dry in a white box with a door that rattled. His mother had never asked him to do anything except fold the sheets. She had performed her own miracle in the basement, the smell of water and soap, the winding of the wringer. Then she'd taken a basket into the backyard, and strung up the clothes and secured them with wooden pins from a bag that slid along the line. The skirt of her cotton dress caught up from the hem by a breeze, the snap of white sheets as the wind took a turn around the garage. She'd never asked him to do anything other than believe.

He turned the corner and saw the giant neon ice cream cone that identified McNee's parlor. A milkshake would taste good.

At the counter, Mrs. McNee herself asked Cal how Mary Beth was, and how married life was treating him.

"It's fine," he stammered, and looked past her to the list of flavors on the wall. "How about a boysenberry shake?"

"Those little seeds get caught in your teeth." She laughed. "Or at least they catch in my dentures."

A kind person, he decided. One who knew nothing about what could happen behind the doors of his soul.

"Well, they'll get caught in my teeth just as easily," he said. He squinted at the list. Mrs. McNee didn't seem in any hurry.

"Hot, isn't it?" she said while he read.

"Sure is."

The sound of giggling girls turned Cal's attention to the back of the parlor. There, in one of the red leather booths, were three girls in sundresses.

"I figure they stop that around fifteen," Mrs. McNee said, shaking her head.

Or when they get married, Cal thought. He discovered he could watch the girls in the mirror once Mrs. McNee moved.

"I think I'll have a hamburger, too," he said, watching the

girl with curly brown hair. "And a plain old chocolate milk-shake."

"Sure thing," Mrs. McNee said.

Now he could see that the girl in the pink sundress was Kenny Larkin's little sister. What a contrast. He couldn't remember her name. She was three or four years younger than Mary Beth. They were all pretty, he thought. Sitting in their summer dresses in a pink-and-white-striped ice cream parlor. Giggling, he supposed, about boys. One of the girls wore a white bracelet, and she kept sliding it up and down on her arm. Her smooth young suntanned arm. He thought of how Kenny talked about his wife, and he bet he didn't talk that way around his sister.

Mrs. McNee put a glass of water in front of Cal. "Little low on ice, if you don't mind," she said, and moved back to the grill to watch his hamburger.

Mary Beth and the magazines. Mary Beth, a sweet little girl listening to the talk of her brothers. He didn't believe it. Why wouldn't she have put her hands over her ears and run to her mother for help? He could hear the words, the low laughter, the cheers and jeers and hip-swiveling gestures, the rough hands clutching imaginary breasts. No.

He looked to the mirror. The girl with the darkest hair had particularly long eyelashes. They shaded her eyes. He smiled. He could sit and watch them, and they had no idea. Like an old man with dentures who was afraid of seeds.

They toyed with the straws in their glasses of lemonade or Coke. They leaned into the middle of the table and told secrets, then laughed, their hair with curls of different colors bouncing in the light of the ice cream parlor, and Cal couldn't take his eyes off them.

"Want the mustard, too?" Mrs. McNee asked, placing the hamburger in front of Cal. Open face, a pickle round, a piece of lettuce, a slice of pale red tomato. The bottle of catsup right in front of him.

"Yes, please," he answered, still watching the girls in the mirror, and a yellow bottle came sailing down the counter at him, and Mrs. McNee laughed at herself and her accuracy, and called to him, "I should have been a bartender," and Cal took the first bite of his hamburger, just as Kenny Larkin's sister's shoulder strap slipped off, and she let it stay there a minute, then with two fingers pulled it back up. On the fourth bite, the strap fell down again, and this time she just left it.

The chocolate milkshake was cold and thick, and Cal thought maybe he would order another hamburger, but the girls were getting ready to go. They searched in little straw summer purses for the coins to pay for their drinks. The girl with the white bracelet dumped everything out of her purse, looking for a lost quarter, found it, held it up with fingers with pearl-painted nails, laughed, and tried to make it stand on its side.

Cal wondered where they were going now. He wished there were a carnival in town. He would take them all for a ride on the Ferris wheel. The three of them could sit in the seat in front of him, and they would go up and down and around, and there would be music.

"Now you girls be good." Mrs. McNee laughed as they gave her the money. The tiny ring of the cash register, the slipped strap, the bracelet dangling down around the slender wrist.

They stopped by the door, and Cal hurriedly finished his milkshake and examined the check. They were giggling again, over something in one of the magazines on the rack. He moved to the end of the counter, money in hand.

"You tell Mary Beth hello for me, and that she shouldn't be such a stranger," Mrs. McNee said. The tiny cling ring of the register again. The louder sound of the bell as the door to the parlor opened and closed behind the girls, and all Cal could think was that it would be nice to see the summer whiteness of them against the moonlight. He would just stroll along behind them for a few minutes, just to watch.

He was in luck. They turned off the main street onto one filled with houses and fences and porch lights that helped him see. Light streaming from windows where the residents had not bothered to pull the drapes because they had nothing to hide. And it was on his way home so no one would suspect him of following them.

They huddled together midway down the block, and then the one with the bracelet, he could see it even from that distance, pulled away from the group, twirled around and sent her skirt flying up so that Cal could see her legs and the trace of a slip, and then she danced back to her friends. Cal passed a house with red climbing roses blooming all along the low fence, and although he felt like a thief, he picked one quickly just to feel it in his hands, to smell it when he wanted, and the trio of girls danced and dipped along the walk, and he thought crazily, crazily, that someone should be in front of them strewing rose petals, and what a pretty picture. A summer night vision.

The girls stopped in the middle of the sidewalk. Cal didn't know what to do. If he stopped, too, they would know he was following them. He had no choice but to keep walking, and then he would pass them, and it would be all over. He would have to go home to Mary Beth and the drawn drapes and the smell of what he had done.

And so while he tried to walk slowly, each step put him nearer, and the girls began to loom large in front of him. Still they did not move, and he considered crossing the street, but that would look odd, and what if one of them called out to him, what if one of them were to say something. And he was almost to them, and then he saw the light, the striking of the match that for a minute illuminated the face of Kenny Larkin's sister, and she looked older, more like Mary Beth, and there were three little girls in summer dresses standing in a circle on a street filled with blooming rose bushes, lighting cigarettes, inhaling, blowing the smoke up into the sky.

Cal stepped off into the street to pass them, and it was as if they did not know he existed. The one with the white bracelet said loudly, "Fuck, I lit the filter, give me another," and Kenny Larkin's sister shook a cylinder out of a pack and Cal kept walking. He dropped the rose in front of him and stepped on it. He ground it into the pavement, and imagined that it left a red stain.

Mary Beth was still not there when he got home.

He began in the kitchen. He turned all the lights on, and opened the doors and windows. He cleared dirty dishes from the table and counter, and ran hot sudsy water into the sink. He washed away the most prominent fingerprints from the cupboards, and mopped the floor. From there he moved to the living room, again opening the door and the rest of the windows. He straightened and he vacuumed, arranging Mary Beth's animals in one corner next to the flowered chair.

By the time Mary Beth came home a little after midnight, every room in the house was ablaze with light, every room filled with cool night air, every surface free of dust.

He faced her in the living room. He could see from the wavering look in her eyes that she had been drinking. Before she could speak, he walked over and put his arms around her gently.

"Everything will be all right," he said. "You'll see. Everything will be just fine."

He thought she looked at him trustingly, as he moved away to turn out the lights.

By the time he went through every room, closing windows partially, locking the doors, and returned to the bedroom, she was asleep.

That's all I need, he thought as he climbed into bed next to her, is a little trust. A little faith. Time to clear out the debris.

The last thing he remembered before he slept was the perfect red rose he had held in his hand earlier. Everything else was gone.

Cal and Mary Beth lapsed into an uneasy truce. Even when Cal heard Mary Beth giggling over the telephone to Tina about his new compulsion to clean up the house every Saturday morning, he thought he detected a slightly embarrassed note of guilt. In fact, Mary Beth did begin to make at least an attempt to keep things in order. At Christmas time, she made Santa cookies that were burned around the edges and whose hats tended to break off. She'd laughed and made Cal eat three, one right after the other.

In turn, Cal concentrated on being a better lover. He devised a thought pattern to keep his mind away from the danger area. He kept his eyes open, forcing himself to see Mary Beth and no one else. But some nights, after it was over and Mary Beth had gone to sleep, Cal found himself wide awake for hours, and when he finally slept, a dark, heavy-set man would loom on the edge of his dreams. A little girl with dark curly hair would try to explain the man's presence, but she spoke only Spanish, a language he did not understand. He would wake in the morning, baffled by the presence of these strangers, and it would take two or three hours for the irritation to subside.

Cal and Mary Beth spent New Year's Eve at a party at Junie and Billy McKenna's, drinking beer and dancing, only Mary Beth was tired of Cal's slow dancing. She wanted something a little more *modern,* and she seemed to be getting it from Sammy Petroni.

For Valentine's, Cal bought her a box of Whitman's chocolates, and she finished the box in a day and a half. "You'll get fat," he said, giving her a playful pinch.

"So what," Mary Beth said to him, but she had gone on a diet the next day, and soon was even slimmer than when they were married.

At Easter time, Mary Beth decided she was tired of hanging around the house and took a job at the Mercantile in children's clothes. "You do the housework," she said, accusing him. "I mean, there's nothing for me to do here." And although he felt some embarrassment at having his wife work, Cal had to admit she was happier. Even though she had to work late a couple of nights a week—inventory, she said—he thought the job was good for her. She spent most of the money she made in the very store in which she worked, charging new clothes against her pay. "I get a good discount," was her explanation, as if he had complained.

Because she was tired—she said—she was less interested in making love. And although he was ashamed to admit it, Cal was relieved to be spared that mind-bursting concentration the act required.

Dave's younger brother, Joe, was killed in Viet Nam a week before the Fourth of July, making the parade in Yellow Fork a rather somber affair. Cal and Dave marched with their guard unit, but Cal, for one, wondered how many people along the route whispered that they, too, should be in the jungles fighting rather than safe in weekly meetings and weekend drills in the armory.

He remembered, as they marched in cadence, the photograph of the man in the uniform—his father—which was now in his bottom dresser drawer. He'd placed it there along with the pictures of his mother because he was afraid their presence would depress Mary Beth, he told himself. But he thought about it now, as he marched.

The next week, at work, he tried to talk to Dave about it. They were sitting around eating lunch, and Cal leaned back against a company truck and looked down at Dave, who sat on the wide running board. "Do you ever think," he began slowly, "especially after what happened to Joe, that we should be there?" He screwed the lid back on his thermos. "I mean, sometimes when I think about it...when I remember how everyone had to go in World War Two, it seems funny to be so far away from it."

There was a burst of laughter from the other men who were standing around Georgie Tillman's truck, and Cal was irritated. George had another damned magazine he was waving around.

"That's stupid," Dave said. "We might have to go anyway, so we might as well wait for the invitation. The Langleys would like to keep one of their sons alive."

"I know," Cal said. He stared out at the dusty trails of tailings, the white wisps of fine dust that tiny whirlwinds caught and made into spirals that dissipated in the sky. It was a jungle in Viet Nam, hot and overgrown green. Swampy. He'd seen pictures. Men crawling through the tropical marsh, camouflage, uniforms, branches on the helmets. He could see it so clearly, he didn't realize what he was hearing at first. Georgie Tillman's singsong voice. At Dave's "Let's go back inside," the jungle vanished and Georgie's words came back, "Guess whose wifey was hanging out at Hawley's again last night, and I do mean hanging out."

Cal looked at the four men who stood with Georgie. All he could see was five smiles, and Georgie's mouth moving, singing that song about Mary Beth. He blinked. He started toward the group, and Dave grabbed his arm.

"Five to one? Shit, dummy," Dave growled. "Forget it."

Cal shook his arm free. Georgie was laughing now, backing away from Cal. "Hey, buddy, no offense, no siree. Just a little joke. You didn't think I was talking about M.B., did you?"

Cal stopped. "You're an asshole, Georgie, anybody ever tell you that?" He turned away. How had he known they were talking about Mary Beth? Christ, he knew because he knew. He'd tried to believe she worked late, that she only went over to talk to Tina. He looked at Dave, who stood looking down at the ground. "Did you know about this?" he asked him.

"I don't go to Hawley's much," Dave said. "But I'd tell Tina where to go if I was you," he added. He crumpled up his lunch bag and walked away.

Another guffaw from Georgie and his boys, and Cal turned, his fists clenched at his sides, only to see that they had gone back to the magazine.

Shit, everyone knew. He was the only one who refused to

face it. There she had been last night. Standing over him. From half sleep, he felt the presence, and he had opened his eyes, almost expecting to see the silent man from the disturbing dream. She just stood there, staring down at him, and even in the darkness he could see the cold look in her eyes. "I'm home," she said, unsteady on her feet. The look was still in her eyes this morning when he left for work. She had lain there with her eyes open, not moving or speaking, just watching him dress. He'd avoided a fight by saying nothing, too.

Now Georgie's song. "Hanging out at Hawley's." Whose wife? His wife.

The whistle blew, calling them back to work, and Cal started back to the crusher. Dave was waiting for him at the entrance.

"I like Mary Beth," he said to Cal. "Just rein her in a little."

"You watch," Cal said. Christ, he'd like a minute's peace.

He was glad to be back inside the crusher. His job was simple enough, although there always seemed, perhaps because the noise was so overpowering, an impending sense of danger. Perhaps it was the notion that if one were to fall, to slide down across those rails into the center of the cone where the pestle reduced huge boulders to pieces of ore less than six inches in diameter, they would never be able to stop the mechanism in time. It would be an instant, though perhaps not instant enough, death.

In a sense, all Cal had to do was make certain that he did not fall, and that the railroad cars were properly coupled once they were on the drums that turned them so they could spill the entire load of ore in four or five tips.

He wore ear plugs and a mask against the dust. Then a light flashed indicating that they should hold the next dump. A large boulder was lodged on top of the pestle. They weren't supposed to send pieces of ore that big from the mine, but some got by. Costello, the man behind the green glass in the booth, would have to maneuver the boulder with a crane into a different position. It would take some time.

As Cal waited for the all-clear signal, he remembered that strange look in Mary Beth's eyes. Where had he seen it before? The face of the man in his dream was still indistinguishable.

A dark-eyed woman. It came to him with such a flash of light, for a moment he thought it was the signal to begin rotating the railroad cars again.

He might have been ten years old. The middle of the night. He'd heard his mother moan. Then a short cry. The darkness. The sound woke him. A moan, a cry. He'd been too terrified to move for a minute. Then he had remembered that he was the man, he was the one who took care of his mother, who protected her from harm, from evil, and he'd gotten out of bed. The feel of linoleum under his bare feet. The silence. He crept down the hall to the open door of his mother's room, prepared to banish the intruder, his knees trembling under the weight of his fear. There she was in the moonlight, her hair dark on the white pillow, and while she moved her head, the tresses swirled in arcs.

There wasn't anyone there. She was alone, tossing and moaning in her sleep. He had only to wake her, to tell her she was dreaming, and he crept to the bedside, the feel of the soft rug by the bed replacing the linoleum. That was the way his mother was, all softness in a world that was too often hard and cold, and he put out his small hand and touched the side of her face and thought she felt too warm. She moaned again as if she simply could not escape, and so he had to take her shoulder and shake her, shake her hard until she stopped rolling her head from side to side, until she stopped tangling the black curls in the fingers of her right hand. She opened her eyes.

That was the only time. The look of something so dangerous, *he would never be able to describe it.* A frightened boy. A whispered "Mother?" The look. He started to cry. The next thing he knew, his mother's arms went around him, and her hair was soft against his face, and she was rocking him, soothing him. "It was just my nightmare, just a nightmare," and all he could think to say was "I heard you, I heard you."

She took him back to his bed. He lay awake the rest of the night trying to understand what had happened. He could hear her soft breathing. He was afraid to move.

Bad dreams. Hereditary defect.

The all-clear signal came, and Cal turned the railroad cars and the ore went crashing down the slated steel that screened out the pieces that were already less than six inches, slipping down the steel, the gray rock shooting sparks of blue-white, sparks that looked a little like stars.

Waggling it around for everyone to see.

Turn. Another rumbling crashing turn of ore, the grinding gyrating motion of the pestle in the bottom.

A little girl speaking Spanish. How could someone in his dream speak a language he did not know? At least not in this lifetime.

The rest of the afternoon passed as he contemplated that question. Finally Costello signaled the end of the day.

Outside, he removed his goggles and watched Dave strip off his.

"Let's go to Hawley's and have a beer," Dave said, brushing the white dust from his mustache and hair. "It's early."

"Christ, we're damned dirty," Cal said.

"This isn't dirt," Dave laughed. "It's pure white dust."

By the time Dave and Cal arrived at Hawley's the place was already crowded. They took two stools at the bar near the door.

"I bet Costello will chew some ass about those boulders," Dave said. "We had to stop every other dump, it seemed to me."

"Blasting must be sloppy or something," Cal said, and had one of those quick flashes of wishing he'd gone to college. Taken engineering. Something that would put him in a cleaner place. Maybe he could take some courses by mail. He needed more order, more plans for the future. Words and numbers on a printed page that would make him forget the damned past.

Hawley himself brought them each a beer.

"Costello seems real calm, you know," Dave went on, "sitting up there behind the glass, but I've heard him bring it down like nobody else."

"You think Costello went to college? He seems to know a lot."

"I think he's just been working there all his life." Dave drank his beer in almost one gulp. "Listen," he said, "why don't we try that new place? The Roughrider."

"No. This is okay," Cal said, sipping his beer and looking into the mirror. The white dust at his temples made him look middle-aged. A little distinguished. He was feeling better.

"It's too crowded in here," Dave said. "It's getting to me."

Cal turned to face his friend. What was this all about? Dave's face was flushed, and he did not look at Cal directly, but shuffled his feet and looked toward the door.

Cal started to search the bar, using the mirror to bypass the crowd that blocked entrance to the booths and the other end of the bar. Men in plaid shirts and Levis and hard hats, and safety glasses, goggles still slung around necks. Men with burly arms and short hair.

"Where is she?" Cal asked. "That's it, isn't it? You think Mary Beth's here."

"Nah," Dave said, but Cal did not believe him.

He grabbed Dave's arm. "Where is she?" he growled under his breath.

"I just thought I caught a glimpse of her in a booth down by the end, then a guy stepped in front. Probably wasn't her. Not this early. Not this crowd."

God, Cal thought, it never ended. Intruding everywhere. Maybe he should just walk out, ignore it. If she was there, he would have to do something about it, and he looked past the shoulders of the men who worked in the mill, the men who walked the catwalks of the concentrator. All men. No women.

He caught just a portion of a bare shoulder, a white halter, and a shock of hair the color of Mary Beth's, and he was off his stool, pushing through the crowd, Dave following, muttering something at him, touching his arm but not holding him, and when he pushed someone who spilled some beer, the man just shrugged and moved out of the way. The laugh. Now he could hear the laugh, and then the last wave parted, and with Dave in back of him he looked down into the surprised face of his wife, his Mary Beth who was laughing at something, at a joke, and Tina said, "Oh no." And Mary Beth said, "Well, hello, honey. I took the afternoon off."

And the man sitting next to her, Kenny Larkin, the man with the little sister who smoked cigarettes, who had a wife God knows where, said, "Hey Cal, why don't you pull up a chair? And hey, Dave, how's it goin'?"

"Why don't we go on home," Cal said slowly to Mary Beth, never taking his eyes away from her pretty little face.

Her cheeks reddened. "Listen, honey," she cooed, but she did not look at him. "We're all going to have a little party tonight. At Tina's. We're going to get a pizza at the corner and drink a little beer. I was going to call you soon as I figured you were home. We've got to have some fun."

His wife sitting in a goddamned bar with the likes of Kenny Larkin, sitting there in red short shorts and a white halter, and one would have thought she would be freezing what with the fans and all, even if it was a hot September, sitting there cool as a cucumber as if he wasn't anybody who mattered to her, as if he were just some goddamned casual friend she could invite over for pizza.

"Come on, Cal," Kenny Larkin said. "Sit yourself down."

"Why don't you just come with me a minute, Mary Beth," Cal said to her, "and we'll discuss this party."

Mary Beth toyed with the paper napkin she held in her hand. "What's to discuss? You run home and change if you want, and we'll meet you at Tina's."

"You come with me."

"Hey," Dave whispered behind him.

"But I'm all ready," she said sweetly, finally looking up at him. "Silly."

He started to say, listen, I'm your husband, you come with me now, when I say, but his mind got caught on the word *husband*. He wasn't her husband; he didn't know what he was and he wondered, looking down at her, her fine blond hair, the low-cut halter that revealed too much of her breasts, why he had decided to love her, and with a noise as loud in his heart as the ore slamming down the slats into the crusher, with as many tiny sparks of light that blazed tinsel for a fraction of a second then vanished, he knew he didn't care.

"You," he said, leaning down close to her, and Kenny Larkin said, "Hey wait, Cal, you got the wrong idea," and Dave pulled on his arm. "You," he said, taking Mary Beth's chin in his hand and turning her frightened face to his, "can go to hell."

He released her with a snap, and saluted Tina, who looked scared to death. As he walked away, he heard his wife say, "He's sick. I mean, really."

"Tramp," he said to Dave on the porch of Hawley's. "Slut."

"Calm down," Dave said. "Probably isn't as bad as you think." He shook his head.

"I know it's as bad as I think."

"Want a lift home?" Dave asked. "I think I'll move along."

"I think I'll walk," Cal said. "Thanks."

"Don't do anything…"

"I won't."

Cal walked down the street and around the corner to the liquor store, the words Mary Beth had said to his back singing in his mind. Sick. He wasn't sick. He had wanted decency, and he had gotten deceit.

He stood in front of the counter and scanned the bottles while the clerk waited. He didn't, he thought, even do enough hard drinking to have a preference. He settled on a bottle of Jim Beam. When he put the change for the tax on the counter, he thought it sounded louder than it should. Like the cracking of a bone.

He clutched the bottle, the brown paper bag rough in his palm, the bottle weighty and conspicuous. He could not bear to go home, and the thought, the very idea of going to one of the local bars and running into someone, anyone who might have witnessed the scene, or even just heard about it, made him tremble. It wouldn't be dark for another hour or so. He walked along the street, wondering. Mary Beth in July clothes in September. He imagined her naked, climbing on a table. He shook his head and closed his eyes for a moment, then kept on walking with the same relentless pace, going nowhere. He turned up an alley, anxious to escape any contact with another person. He walked along the irrigation ditch, and listened ever so vaguely to the sound of running water. He would simply have to get used to being alone. He passed a fenced-in horse and the horse tossed his head, rattling his mane, turning his gaze away from Cal, and Cal paused, as if to taunt the horse, and opened the bottle.

The bourbon burned his mouth and throat, and it still was not enough to destroy the taste of blood that he felt lingering too near the surface. The horse flicked his tail, whether at an insect or in irritation, Cal didn't know. He shuddered. He longed for the noise of the crusher and got instead the quiet early evening sounds of water in the ditch, the buzz of a wasp, the gentle snorting of the horse, the slam of a screen door in the distance. He could smell meat cooking somewhere, and an old woman in the lot next to the horse was picking tomatoes and putting them into a coffee can.

He passed her by without so much as a nod, although he knew it was Petroni's grandmother, and without turning around to see if she noticed, took another drink from the bottle.

A pickup truck, with a light toot of the horn, passed by him, kicking up the dust, layering yet another coat on the white that still clung to his clothes and to his eyebrows. He coughed.

He would ask her to leave. Send her home to her mother. Maybe she would move in with Tina and they could have pizza parties every night, and she would get old and fat and ugly quickly. He would pretend he had never known her, never had anything to do with her. He would clean the house and sacrifice everything that had ever belonged to her. He would put his mother's blue table and chairs back on the porch.

He did not understand justice.

Maybe he should move away. His mother had told him stories—how many were true—one about her best friend. A pretty blond girl who had gone off to Hollywood to become a movie star. They were silly then, his mother had explained. It all seemed so simple. And she'd been in some movies, although he had never seen her, but then she'd died a simple tragic early death in a plane crash. He would move away; he just wouldn't fly. The bourbon was making the thinking easier.

His mother had known a movie star, but it had to be kept a secret. Small towns had a way of misunderstanding such ties. He laughed.

He traversed the town by way of the alleys, following the water. He thought it was amazing how different the town looked from the inside of the blocks, from the back side. Facing the streets were clean, painted houses with dark red or green porches. Neatly trimmed lawns and picket fences. Lampposts with house numbers attached. But the backyards. A different story. The blocks were big, square, and the lots stretched back perhaps 150 feet. The lawns and patios and picnic tables were set off from the part that ended at the alley by trellises covered with honeysuckle or columbine. Then came the underside. A horse tethered, chickens with dull gray feathers flying in low rusty cages. Hollow shells of old automobiles. Rolls of unused barbed wire. Hunting dogs kept behind chain-link fences. Sometimes an ill-kept orchard of old apricot or peach trees. Sour apples. In short, overgrown, fallow victory gardens. Where once the people had grown fruit and vegetables in a spirit of patriotism, now the land collected the junk of a more affluent time.

Like a person, Cal thought, like Mary Beth. Looks one way from the outside. Behind the fence, the facade, the little girl innocent, another thing altogether.

He stopped to look at a hutch of rabbits, the big brown and gray hares lying low in small cages, their eyes closed and their ears twitching, and a little boy that Cal had not noticed came by with a pail of cast-off lettuce leaves and carrots.

"Big, ain't they?" the boy asked, and looked at Cal. "I bet we'll have to eat one of them soon." He stared with clear blue eyes, and Cal felt compelled to deny it.

"Don't look ready to me," he said, smiling at the boy. He would never make any son of his eat a rabbit he had hand-fed.

It would have been nice if Mary Beth had had a baby, and he would have kept it for himself. A son or daughter, it didn't matter which. He wanted to reach across the low fence and pat the boy on the back and comfort him, but he did not. The boy was tearing the lettuce into small pieces and placing it in the cages.

Cal had to be on his way. What was it they used to sing in school? Something about a happy wanderer? "Meat nor drink..." He laughed, holding the bottle high. "Nor money have I none." That was a different song. "Still, I will be ha-a-app-ee—Hi, ho..." He stopped. "Fee-fi-fo-fum. I want the blood of an Englishmun." He was mixing everything up.

The sun dipped behind a mountain, and the air was immediately cooler, and the greens were softer, and he could see some lights begin to flicker on in the back rooms of the houses he passed.

"Jerry?" a woman called. "Dinner."

He took another drink. Families were gathering. Men and women and children were sitting down to the evening meal.

Sure you can have Dave stay for dinner, his mother says, wiping her hands on the towel that hangs on the cupboard door. Pull some carrots for me, will you? That's a good boy. Dave, you can pick out three of the best tomatoes you can find. Call your mama on the phone first so she won't worry.

The best tomatoes are closest to the ground. You have to look under the vines. Carrots sliced in small perfect circles and hamburger patties with melted cheese on top. Slices of red garden-ripe tomatoes, and the three of them sitting around the blue table, the table that was always covered with a bright colored cloth, and Cal notices how Dave looks at his mother, and he smiles because he, too, knows she is beautiful. She doesn't look like a mother; she looks like a girl.

After dinner, they put up the Monopoly game, and she manages to get Park Place because she always does; it is a tradition. If Dave or Cal lands on it first, they say it is too expensive, and she claps her hands and says, you'll be sorry. Cal settles for St. Charles and St. James, and Dave collects the railroads and utilities. His mother counts out her money, her red shiny fingernails the object of attention for both the boys.

Cal paused at the end of the alley, and tried to decide where to go. He decided on the park. It was nearly dark, and if he picked a bench that was mostly hidden from the street, he could sit in peace and think of words to say to Mary Beth. "You were a lousy Monopoly player," he says as he walks. "Lousy."

From where he sat, he could watch the people walk along the main street of town. Not many that night. An occasional woman with a bandanna on her head running into the corner market for some last-minute thing. A quart of milk, a loaf of bread. No one could see him as he sipped from the bottle and watched the people pass underneath the street light. Into the spotlight, and out. His mother's dead Hollywood friend. Jeannette was her name.

Three teenage boys who reminded him of his friends in the days gone by, the simple times when a job was a paper route, or delivering groceries, or mowing summer lawns for widows and the town wealthy. They spent their summer salaries on hamburgers and the pinball machines, and an occasional clandestine six-pack of beer. There were girls with cut-off jeans and hair tied up in ponytails that swung in the night light as they walked. A young woman in a white dress and a flash of gold in her ear that caught the light and caused him to sigh as she walked alone.

The neon ice cream cone of McNee's began to multiply before his eyes.

Where were the pretty girls in their summer dresses? Where were the blushes and the eyelashes that hid lowered eyes, resting on the porcelain faces of the innocents? A man and a little boy stood on the porch of McNee's while the father wiped the child's chin, and then they were off, down the street toward a home with white curtains at the windows and soft music on the radio. The sound of a mother rinsing dishes in the sink.

Cal got unsteadily to his feet. He was hungry, that was it. He would amble across the street as if nothing were wrong, and slide up onto one of the stools and order his usual, and Mrs. McNee would serve it up with a smile, and the girls would come in and whisper "Hello, Cal," and slip into the booth in the corner, and he could watch them again while he ate, and he would remember that Mary Beth was not one of them, nor had she ever been. Was Mary Beth the one who had gone to Hollywood and come home an actress? Was that how she fooled him? No. Dead Jeannette.

He had difficulty locating the door handle, ended up pushing on the glass. He could barely make out the form of Mrs. McNee as she came forward to take his order.

"Evening, Cal," she said. "What will it be tonight?"

"Hamburger," he muttered.

"You want two to go?" she asked. "One for you? One for Mary Beth?"

He shook his head and the salt shaker wavered before his eyes.

"Me," he said. "One for me. Here."

He put his hand in front of her to show her exactly where.

Mrs. McNee shuffled down to the grill, and he heard the sound of the hamburger, the spit and sizzle, as it hit the grill. A wave of nausea, a rough swallow, and he focused on his own reflection in the soda fountain mirror. His hair, something wrong. One side all ruffled up like the backside of a bird, and he moved his hand to smooth it, to concentrate, and he thought his head was too big for his body, and he had trouble finding the exact place to reorder it.

A man and a woman came in and sat at the far end of the counter, and he thought he recognized them, but could not make his eyes focus enough. He blinked. He leaned forward over the counter. Mrs. McNee, coming at him with a plate in her hand. A slice of tomato, a ring of onion, a piece of lettuce, and a round of meat on a toasted bun.

"Where are the girls?" he asked her as she put the plate in front of him.

"Girls?" Mrs. McNee leaned into him. "My girls?"

He shook his head. "No, no, no," he said, reaching for the paper-napkin holder. He knocked over the pepper, and Mrs. McNee quickly righted the shaker. "The little girls, the pretty girls."

"You're drunk, Callant Newkirk," Mrs. McNee whispered, and the couple at the end of the counter turned to look. "You eat that hamburger, and I'll get you some coffee."

"The little girls in pink dresses," Cal said, determined.

"You want me to call Mary Beth to come and get you?" she asked, putting a mug of coffee in front of him. "Oh dear, Cal. You look terrible."

"Mary Beth," he said, pulling himself up, straightening his back, "is not a little girl. Believe me, she is not."

"You lose your job?" Mrs. McNee asked with narrowed eyes.

"Little girls," Cal said, still amazed that she did not understand. "One's about this high." He watched his hand waver in the air. He couldn't lift it as high as he had hoped.

The man at the end of the counter cleared his throat, and Mrs. McNee moved away from Cal. "This high," he whispered, trying to manage the hand. He looked for the mustard, could not find it, and gave up. He picked up his fork to spear the tomato slice, and it slipped around the plate. Dropping the fork, he picked up the slice with his fingers, mashed the lettuce on top of it, and put the bun in place. It was not easy to remember how to chew, and he thought he must look silly, but something was wrong with his jaw. No little girls to see, anyhow. No mother to say, Callant, wipe your chin. No mother to pick up a napkin and dab away the crumbs. A father and a little boy. A dribble of chocolate ice cream.

The coffee looked deadly, but he drank it anyway. He could not tell how long it took him to eat, or how long he sat there after he had finished. It was like being asleep, he thought, and he stared into the white circles of the onion slice until it became a pale yellow moon in a winter-white sky.

A man touched his arm. "We'll drive you home, Cal," he said, and Cal turned to see Dave Langley's mother and father standing beside him.

"You go with them," Mrs. McNee said.

"I'm waiting for the girls," Cal murmured, and he felt the tears come to his eyes.

He rode in the back seat. Dave's mother and father whispered in the front seat, and he could not understand a word they said.

"Mary Beth," he murmured, and Mrs. Langley turned around to look at him.

"Don't worry, Callant, we're almost there."

Where, he wondered. Where was almost there?

When they stopped in front of the house, Cal could see the moon shining through the tree leaves, and could just make out the sidewalk that led to the door.

"Is Mary Beth there?" Mrs. Langley asked. "Do you need help?"

"Mary Beth," Cal said as he struggled out of the car, "doesn't like me anymore. Ha."

Mrs. Langley looked embarrassed. "You go to bed, Cal. Everything will be all right."

He slammed the door and nearly fell against the car doing so. "Thanks," he muttered. "Thanks for the lift."

Determined, he turned toward the walk. He didn't think there were any lights on. Nobody home. He wanted to giggle. Hi ho, anybody home. "Meat nor drink nor money have I none." None. Boy scouts. Good scouts. Funny songs.

He turned at the corner of the house and waved to the Langleys, and their car moved off down the street. He felt his way along the side of the house. The moon wasn't as much help as he thought it should be, and he tried to locate it in the sky to tell it so. Damned dark.

Girl Scouts. Mary Beth should have been a Girl Scout. Then she'd know how to make cookies at least. Ha. Leave me and join the Girl Scouts, he would shout at her. Little girl. Mean little girl. Curl right in the middle of her forehead. War head. Whorehead.

He fell against the side of the house. What was the day? Work, work. He held his head against the sound of the crusher.

Saturday tomorrow. He'd help Mary Beth pack up her things. Going camping with the Girl Scouts. When she was good, very, very good. Bad, horrid. Hit her in the forehead.

He turned the corner of the house, and reached for the back door. He had trouble with the small step up, and at first he thought he had grabbed the wrong handle. The screen door wouldn't open. He pulled again. Hooked, hooked from the inside. How could that be? He rattled the door again.

Ah, she was home and had locked the damned door against him. The door to his home. The place he had lived all his life. His home. Never a door locked against him. Never darkness waiting for him.

"Open this door," he shouted, and began to pound with both fists.

A light went on in the hall.

"You get away from here," he heard Mary Beth shout. "Get away or I'll call the cops."

Was it Mary Beth? Was it the right house? He pulled the door again.

"I mean it," she called again, and he was certain now. His house, his door. Locked.

"I'll break a goddamned window," he yelled. "Let me in right now." He could feel the door loosening.

"You are drunk. You sober up first," Mary Beth screamed.

He kicked and pulled at the door. He could hear her sobbing, and all he wanted to do was to get in there and make her quiet. "Hush," he shouted. "Be quiet."

A light went on in the house next door, casting a square of light into the yard. He turned. Mrs. Perkins in a pink hairnet and tiny glasses squinted at him. "Don't look," he shouted to the old woman, who moved quickly out of his sight, but he knew she was there, watching it all. Seeing him locked out of his own house.

"Get away from me," his wife cried. Cal heard another door slam, the back door next to his, and before he knew it, Mr. Warner was standing by him, pulling on his shoulder, pulling him away from his own door.

"Listen boy, you calm down, you waking everybody for miles, and you don't want the police to come, now you just calm down here. You go stay with some friend till she simmers down."

Mrs. Perkins was back at the window, leaning forward for a better look. Mary Beth was crying, "Go away." A flash of light in Mrs. Perkins's spectacles. Mr. Warner's hand on his shoulder. A strong hand. A father's hand.

With one quick move, he pulled away, gave the door a final kick, and turned to run. He ran back through the yard, through the open place in the fence, through the vacant land where they should have had a good garden. He ran into the alley before he paused to look around. The back of the house was obscured by the bushes, and there was nothing like the sound of footsteps following him. It was absolutely quiet, and it was as if nothing had happened, as if he had imagined it all. Like a woman who runs from the man who does not exist. He shook his head.

Where to go? He had been evicted. Park Place and St. Charles. Then the dizziness. He leaned over the ditch, held his stomach, and vomited. He choked and cried with the sickness of it all. Tears burned his eyes and the inside of his throat.

He did not know how long or how far he walked. Through the alleys, looking for a place to sleep, looking for a barn or a cool green grave. Finally, in exhaustion, he crept inside a wooden fence and curled up in the long grass of someone's back lot. The house was far away and dark. The only light was from the moon. And then the grass was cool and lovely against his face, and moved in the slight breeze like a lover's hair on the pillow. The sound of the water, running clear from the canyons, drowned him in sleep.

Something tickled his nose, brushed by his face, vanished. A floating web perhaps, a long-legged spider. Something burned at his forehead, then slipped into a pounding as he contemplated opening his eyes. He knew he was lying on his back in the grass, knew without risking the look. But where?

Get away. Get away from here. Locked, his house locked against him.

The heat on his forehead must come from the sun. Stretched out in the center of the park? Grass too long. In a mountain meadow in another state? Something brushed him again, and before he could open his eyes, he felt a soft weight on his chest, and then he had to look.

He stared into the pale blue eyes of a gray kitten. A tiny creature perched on his chest, four legs straight, intent on the conquest of the giant. He reached up to stroke the cat's fur, and the kitten stiffened, arching its back, and he could feel the slightness of tiny claws. Soft, the kitten was soft like the grass around him and the sunny day. There was no smell of autumn in the air.

Get away. Can I have a kitten? A little tiny kitten? One, two?

He could feel the low rumble of the kitten's purring under his hand as he stroked it. He closed his eyes against the bright light and the heat of the sun. What time could it be? Where was he? What in hell was he going to do? The feel of the kitten's fur under his fingers. The cat sat down on his chest,

curling its paws under, prepared to stay, and Cal thought he
might cry with the affection of it all, and the brilliance of his
grief.

"Pretty kitty," he whispered instead.

It was almost too quiet. The occasional bark of a dog in a
fenced yard somewhere. The sound of a bird in the tree above
him. Not singing, just the rattle of wings at flight. The kitten's
gravelly purr. The persistent ache in his head, the dry throat
that felt like the kitten sounded. What in God's name was he
going to do about this mess.

"That's my cat," a little girl said, and Cal's eyes opened
abruptly.

"That one you're holding," the girl said, pointing to the
kitten.

Cal blinked. With the sun hitting him almost directly in the
face, he could not see much more than a silhouette against
the sky. She seemed impossibly tall and dark in the day. He
squinted at her. He took his hands off the cat, but the cat did
not move.

"Sorry," he said, and he poked gently at the cat.

"Her name is Dusty," the little girl said.

"Cute cat," Cal muttered. He should try to sit up, to get
himself together to move.

"This is my yard," the child said, and her white anklet
stockings and black shoes came into focus. He followed the
line of the legs up to the ruffled hem of a light green dress.
Above the knees. Following up until he saw that she looked
down on him, and her long straight hair fell over her shoulders,
and she stood with her hands on her hips staring down. He
squinted again to make out her face and could not. Alice, he
thought. Alice in Wonderland. A Cheshire cat.

"I was just resting," he said, moving closer to a sitting position, and the kitten extended its claws in objection, and Cal
lifted the cat with his hands, held it around its small furry
belly, lifting it up to the girl whose face he could not make
out. The kitten struggled out of his grasp, and bounded away
through the grass.

"Come back," the child called, and turned after the kitten,
and Cal remembered the irrigation ditch, and heard the sound
of the water. He got to his knees to look after them both. He

imagined the kitten in the ditch, fur plastered against the body. Drowning. Drowning.

"Dusty," the little girl called, down on her knees, peering through the tangle of brambles near the edge of the small stream. "She's caught in there," the child said, turning to Callant.

Down on her knees, peering into the maze, her ruffled skirt up enough so he could see the white lace of her underpants. Little girls in ruffled things with kittens, soft voices, skin as smooth as dreams of satin. No screams, no threats. No locked screen doors with rusty panels and splintered wood. Satin. Just a touch of that, he thought, then shuddered, actually trembled at the notion of it all. The kitten. Trapped in the brambles. He needed to free it and be on his way. A small act of chivalry to atone.

He moved over to where the child kneeled and got down beside her to look into the tangle of vines.

"Feel these little stickers," the child said, and Cal put his finger to a needle of the fruitless raspberry vines. "She'll get all scratched."

He could see the kitten peering at them from the center of the knot. The sunlight filtered in dusty streaks onto the top of the kitten's head, and flecked the dry bed of leaves on which the kitten sat.

"I don't think she's caught," Cal said to the little girl. "I think she's teasing."

"She's caught," the child said determinedly. "Can you reach in and pull her out?"

Tiny thorns, razorlike edges. A brave act. Daring. He felt the hair on his arms rise in anticipation. His arm, snaking through the veins and arteries of the brambles to rescue the soft ball of fur with the unblinking eyes.

He looked into the face of the little girl. Ten years old, maybe. He couldn't tell. He was wrong about so many things these days.

Her eyes seemed to be filling with tears.

"Now don't cry," he said, and touched her shoulder. She turned her face away.

And it was true. She was as soft as he had imagined. Her bones were tiny and fragile underneath his grasp, the grasp of the hands made rough by work with rock, and he knew the thorns could not hurt him enough. He could use his arm and his hand to sneak into the thicket and somehow, he knew the kitten would wait for him like a promise. Wait to be enveloped in his palms, to be comforted and saved by his strong fingers and his courage. He would stand, bow to the little girl as a prince would to a princess, hand her the cat, and say, "Two damsels in distress, rescued."

Bracing himself against the attack, he stretched out full length on the ground and began to slide his arm into the brambles, carefully, slowly, flinching only slightly at the pin-pricks of pain, a pain that excited him as he guided his arm toward the kitten in the center. "Come on," he crooned to the kitten, "Come on to me, come on." He moved his fingers slowly, beckoning without frightening. "Come on, Dusty, " so low in his throat, he could feel the words vibrate in his chest. "Come on."

Almost there. Tiny lines of red appearing on his arm. Slight slivers of painful pleasure. The kitten stood, and still the blue eyes stared at Cal, daring, expecting, promising.

"Oh no," the little girl said, and the kitten backed out of Cal's reach. "Oh, I've scratched my leg. It's bleeding on my dress."

He turned to see a scratch on the girl's knee, a trickle of blood, and he thought she must have knelt on a stone, something sharper than the grass and soil. A jagged unexpected wound. He watched in fascination, forgetting everything, as the child licked her fingers and rubbed at the blood, as she lifted the hem of her dress where bright red stained the ruffle, and put the material in her mouth. Small tears streaked her face, but she made no crying sound. All she wanted to do, Cal could see, was remove all trace of red. As if it were his own blood, he could taste the salt of it, and it made his head pound, and his stomach tighten.

Then the kitten inside licked his hand, splitting him in two. A child, injured, crying. A kitten within reach. One hand in, one hand out. Up to the shoulder blade, stretched along the ground. A child bleeding. A kitten washing his hand.

"Hush," he whispered to the little girl. "I've almost got her."

"Hurry," the child cried. "Oh, my mama will be so mad."

"It's all right," he sang to her, touching her with his free hand. "All right." He turned back to the kitten. "Come on, now, you come on out," calming the kitten, coaxing it along. Trust. Everything depended upon trust.

"This is a new dress," the little girl said, and yet she stretched out on the ground alongside Cal, trying to keep the scratch out of the dirt, her knee up, and still see her kitten.

Cal had the tunnel of vision.

Then, as the kitten sniffed at the suspense, Cal grabbed it. He felt the sharp stabs of the briars, but the kitten, struggling yet, was locked in his hand. He had only to remove them both. Close your eyes, he wanted to cry to the kitten. Don't let the thorns puncture the pale blue water of the eyes, and now the child was on her stomach next to him, venturing into the brambles herself, reaching for the kitten, and her leg was against Cal's and the cat was struggling. Cal thought he felt her tears falling on his lips, but that could not be, and he almost had the cat free.

Exquisite. The whispering pain in his arm, the rocks of the earth beneath him, he could feel the centuries of them, blooming up through soft black soil, penetrating his own soft flesh, and that of the squirming child next to him. The warmth of the sun on his back, the feel of her leg next to his. She was so close under him, reaching for the kitten, that a strand of her hair caught in his lips, and then it was so close, so close to the edge. The kitten, wiggling in his hand, the girl moving in closer to see, to help, her own arm springing with small red lines.

Cal put his other hand into the brambles to calm the frightened cat, and with the cocoon his two hands made around it, pulled the kitten through the final web, rolled onto his back, and pushed the kitten down against his chest. "You tease," he said, and the girl moved in beside him and began to stroke her pet as Cal held it prisoner, and her hand would trail off the cat's back onto his chest, and still tears wet her cheeks.

"Listen," he said to her, whispering in her ear, "everything's okay." He turned onto his side. The kitten was warm and soft between them now, and to comfort the girl, only to comfort her, he drew his hand down the side of her body the way he had stroked the cat. "It's all right now. It's all over." She moaned into his shoulder.

"My dress," she whimpered. "My mother."

He told her it didn't matter and moved to hold her closer, to make her feel the wonder of the softness of the earth, and the kitten struggled free again, and ran away from the brambles so quietly no one noticed because the girl continued to cry, and Cal held her against him. "It's all over," he repeated, and he moved to touch the scratch, to test the power of healing.

"Lord God," a man said. "I'll kill you."

Cal moved quickly away from the girl. "Wait," he said, rising on one elbow.

The little girl started to wail. "Look at my dress, Daddy."

"You son of a bitch, if you move I'll tear your head off." The man's voice broke, and Cal looked up at him. Even against the sun, he could see the man's face, distorted with a terrifying rage. The man, all in blue against the sky, looked like a giant and he held a hoe as if it were a lethal weapon in both hands.

"Wait," Cal began, "I was just..."

"Shut your mouth. Lila, baby girl, you run to the house and tell your momma to call the police."

"But," the little girl said, getting to her feet, brushing her dress down as if she were ashamed, and Cal knew she was terrified, too, senseless in the face of her father. "My kitten..."

"Do as I say," the man said. His voice was dusky, insistent, boiled down to an instinct strong enough to strangle him on his own words.

"Her kitten," Cal muttered, trying to get up, "got caught." It suddenly occurred to him that in a town where he knew almost everyone, he had never seen this man before. That, and the touch of a southern speech. "I was just..."

The man stepped toward him, and Cal could hear the girl crying as she ran toward the house. He heard the screen door slam, and the word *police* kept ringing, and the scratches on his arm stung him. His head pounded, and he looked up at the man, and tried again to form the sentence, and it was, "I helped her get the kitten," but he did not finish the thought. The man's boot came crashing at the side of his head, and he heard the thunderheads of curses and darkness and rage, and he turned over into the soft black soil, and melted into the mound of earth on which he lay. A sharp pain moved like a freight train up his spine. A noise like metal wheels on iron tracks, then nothing.

He awoke alone in a cell at the city jail. He opened his eyes to a solid wall of gray, with the scratches of a hundred desperate men recorded in a space of a concrete block. He stared at the white chalky lines, and they meant nothing to him. He licked his finger and tried to wipe out the word that was right in front of his eyes.

Christ, it was all true. Every word of Dave's evil story. A little girl. What would he have done to her given the time? The blood on her dress. The goddamned cursed blood in his veins. It made him sick.

Cal did not move from the bunk until they came for him.

He knew both policemen, had known them all his life.

"Goddammit, boy," Buck Nelson said. "This is some mess."

Neither one of the men would look him in the eye as they read the charge.

When it came time to raise bail, Cal refused. He had nowhere to go, and no one to see. He would wait it out alone.

Cal was moved twenty miles to the county jail. He was moved on the day that the leaves turned bright red and yellow. He felt the chill in the air even in his cell. The frost that was white on the ground had changed everything. The long green grass of summer was gone, and the lawns turned blue-green, the precursor of yellow. Later, everything would be disguised in white.

The jail was in the basement of the courthouse, a large adobe-block building, gray and imposing in the center of town, a three-story cube with ivy curling toward the red roof. The lights in the basement burned against yellow walls, emphasizing the bars on the windows.

The court-appointed lawyer, to whom Cal had tried to explain, had nodded with narrowed eyes, and said, yes, they could try that story, but he was not optimistic. The man, Cal noticed, had large farmboy hands, although he professed to come from the city. Yes, the man understood Cal had never been in any kind of trouble before, but that was not uncommon in cases like these. It was not, after all, petty theft leading to burglary.

"Get out," Cal said. "I need somebody who can help me."

The new lawyer blinked at Cal, said he was having trouble with his eyes, apologized, and said he would try to get him as light a sentence as possible. Perhaps Cal did not understand the general reaction to a situation like this. People got funny, crazy, when they thought a child had been threatened in any way. A kind of blindness prevailed. A willingness to think the worst. It didn't help any, he added, that Cal had no family in the area, although, fortunately, Mary Beth could not testify against him.

The man rubbed his pained eyes, and Cal wanted to laugh at the irony of it all.

"We're better off to just go before the judge," the lawyer explained. "You open this up to a jury, and they'll hang you just for being in the neighborhood."

"I did not," Cal said to the lawyer, "do what they are accusing me of. Remember that. I did not *do* it."

"It's more a matter of what it seemed you intended to do," the man said, taking his handkerchief from his pocket. "We can only hope that the judge will believe you." He dabbed at his irritated eyes. "They seem," he went on, "to have come up with a bunch of witnesses..."

"There weren't any witnesses."

"I mean, as to your state of mind at the time."

A flicker of fear. Was that possible? Could someone have read his thoughts? Impossible.

Witnesses. The yellow walls of the jail, the neon lights, the small polished light oak table where they sat while Cal told his story again and again. The oak chairs with curved backs and slats. There was nothing on the walls except for light and an occasional shadow.

Mary Beth was in possession of his house and everything in it. Glasses his mother had used, the blue fruit bowl. Well, that was the least of his problems now. When it was over, he would deal with her.

Dave came to see him.

"This is big trouble," he said to Cal. "I don't know what to tell you. The guy's new in town, and every time someone tries to defend you, he suggests they are unfriendly to newcomers." Dave shook his head. "Costello will come and testify for you. He's a tough bird; that should be good. He'll sit there and look that judge straight in the face and tell him about your work record."

"What about Mr. Leone?" Cal asked. He knew his lawyer was going to contact the school counselor to speak on his behalf, to point out his good grades, his remarkably clean record.

"I think they can call him, but I don't know what he'll say. He didn't want to do it. Says it jeopardizes his position at the school. He was never exactly a hero," Dave added.

"They can't convict me of something I didn't do," Cal said.

Cal mistook the hopelessness in Dave's eyes for sympathy at his plight. He could not imagine the whispers, the shouts that Dave must have heard. Conviction seemed out of the question. There was this matter of the truth.

He had not actually *done* it.

And while Dave went on to try to console him, Cal knew that now, finally, after all the time that had passed between them, he had to ask that question. While Dave talked to him about current gossip, Cal needed the rumors of another time, another war.

"Dave," he said, his tone stopping Dave in mid-sentence.

"You want me to bring you a file in a cake?" Dave giggled nervously as if he knew what was about to come.

"I want you to tell me exactly what that cousin or aunt or whatever of your mother's told you."

"Hey, buddy, I don't think now's the time…"

"Tell me."

"It was a long time ago."

Cal stared at his friend. "Tell me what you remember."

Dave shook his head. "All I can recall is that this woman said she'd been…I told you that part. Apparently some guy followed her home from a carnival, or maybe he didn't follow her home. Maybe he took her outside of town. That seems right. Like held her prisoner and someone finally found her."

"A man from a carnival," Cal repeated.

"I guess. Or at least, he was at the carnival." Dave looked confused. "Hell, I can't remember. I was pretty shocked."

Cal nodded.

"Look, I don't think you should be thinking about this now," Dave went on. "It shouldn't really come up."

Cal laughed. "Don't you think," he said, "that it's pretty damned funny? I mean, if what you say is true, that man doesn't seem to have been caught. Is he in jail? No. I'm the one in jail. Sins of the fathers…don't you think that's funny?"

"No," Dave said. "Forget about it."

Cal saw a look of sadness in Dave's eyes, and it was that look he remembered when he tried to sleep. He imagined

Dave trying to defend him against the tongues of the skeptics of Yellow Fork. What if they brought all this up at the trial? Dave's mother knew the story. Had he imagined it, or had she looked at Cal suspiciously ever since the incident, the visit from the story-telling cousin? Did she think all of this was in his blood? Somewhere, deep inside, did Dave believe that, too?

Was it? Was that tainted streak the origin of all of his violent thoughts, his trouble now? And his mother whispering her gentle lie. But a lie, nonetheless.

And so, as he tried to sleep, he found himself wrapped in the conviction of others, and he was visited by an unwelcome dream. A dream in which he lay in the soft grass with a girl, the girl whose face he could no longer remember, but who now shone before him with the radiance of an angel, a round-cheeked, blue-eyed, golden-haired child, and she wrapped her arms and legs around him. He felt the tiny ruffles around her thighs, and the delicate give of the elastic as he first reached inside. Her arms, covered with golden down, circled him, and she whispered in his ear in a language he did not understand, but the sense of it all came through to him. The fine white cloth slid down over the legs, the faultless flesh previously unmarked. It slid down over the white anklets and the patent leather shoes, and the child turned on her face in the grass, the breeze blew strands of something across his face, and someone breathed *please* into his ear. The legs spread apart, and the blades of grass sprang up between them. Then he buried his face in those strands, and the smell of damp earth made him thirst. But he moved up and over her and covered her, hiding her from the sparrow that perched in the tree overhead. He protected her from the other bird, too, the one with the flashing black eye and the razor-sharp beak that punctuated the silence with his rat-a-tat-tat against gray bark oak. A red head and stripes. The rat-a-tat-tat of the woodpecker. Cal covered the white legs, and the child's arms, and the blue eyes that the birds lusted after, and the two of them sank together into the soil, impossibly entwined, and then the earth closed in over them, and Cal knew it was a grave with the soft shovels of the diggers tossing and clanking the spades together in the curious toast of farewell.

He was all alone.

But when he woke in his cell, it would take a litany of the actual event to convince him of his own innocence. Intent. His only sin was dreaming, and he wished he could stop. He was afraid that he had a guilty look about him because of what went on uncontrolled in his sleep. Someone might see the image of the child made naked without the consent of anyone. He looked at his hands, and thought he could see them soften with each passing day. He missed the sound of the crusher.

Dave brought him books. Detective novels. The guilty were always brought to justice, the innocent set free. Yes, he could count on that. But who was guilty here?

"This is coming up too quickly," the lawyer said. Now he wore lightly tinted glasses to protect his eyes from the neon glare. "I'd hoped for a delay, till folks could calm down, but they're pushing it. I've tried everything I can think of."

Cal nodded. He didn't think it really mattered. People weren't ever going to calm down about it if they believed he was guilty. He would not accept the possibility of that kind of error.

"Another setback," the lawyer said, "though they shouldn't be able to use it."

"What?" Cal asked.

"The man—the girl's father—just lost his only son in Viet Nam."

"I think we might as well get it over with," Cal said.

It was snowing, and it was that peculiar snow that seems to catch a light of its own, making the day bright without sun. A white light without warmth. From the table where Cal sat with his lawyer, he could pick one of two windows to look out of, and he decided on the one that made it appear as if he were looking slightly to the right of the judge. If things went badly, he would merely stare at the falling snow until it hypnotized him. He liked snow, he reminded himself. It covered any number of imperfections.

To his relief, Mary Beth was not going to be at the trial. "My mother won't let me go," she had informed Cal's lawyer. "She doesn't want me to be embarrassed." Embarrassed. The irony made Cal want to laugh. The world was filled with "embarrassed" little girls.

The courtroom was on the third floor of the courthouse.

Yellow neon lights washed the color from the faces of the witnesses and made the falling white snow even brighter. In the corner, one bulb flickered, and Cal thought he could hear it. His lawyer shuffled papers, arranging, rearranging. A door opened, and Cal turned, hoping to see Dave. Instead, he stared right into the face of Mrs. McNee, who quickly looked away, and he thought, oh no. He decided not to look again.

"Dave's testimony should help," the lawyer whispered. "It's just a little odd to have his parents called by the prosecution."

"I don't know what they can say except that I was drunk the night before. That's not a crime."

"We'll make a point of that."

He could hear others entering the room, and finally the familiar hand on his shoulder, and the encouraging words from Dave.

"Good luck, buddy."

And suddenly the judge was there, a man with too black hair, and a small mustache, and he reminded Cal of someone, but he could not think of who it might be, and he had the uneasy feeling that whoever it was that the man resembled was someone he had created in his own mind. The judge looked slightly Latin, that too black hair, the slight olive cast to his skin.

His mother's dark hair. His mother with a handsome man who looked slightly Latin. He shook his head, and looked out at the snow, not wanting to risk catching the man's eye directly. He'd never seen his mother with any such man.

"Un-predictable," his lawyer had told him about the judge, making it into two words. Then he added, "He dyes his hair." Disguised, like everyone else, Cal thought.

And so it began.

The prosecutor stood. A tall thin man with a slight stoop to his shoulders. Crisp gray suit. Cal looked at the cut of the man's clothes, then toyed with a button at his own wrist. He was wearing the suit he had been married in, and he hoped this was going to go better than that had.

And then horror of the words struck him, words that were being said about him.

"This man, Callant Newkirk, was caught right in the middle of this fiendish act by the poor child's father. Imagine if you will, the effects of this outrage on this entire family. And we will show, not only that he committed this assault against the morals of decent people everywhere, but that it was premeditated. Imagine that. This man went looking..."

Cal could not believe his mind was translating this correctly. His own lawyer looked baffled, and Cal whispered even though everything else said, scream, shout, *I am innocent.* "I can't believe this. I can't believe it."

His lawyer, making notes, brow wrinkled.

"Not a singular act of passion, but a planned conquest."

There were murmurs behind Cal. How many people lurked back there, sighing, murmuring, rumoring, believing. His own lawyer making frantic notes. The judge, face turned to the tall, thin man who walked up and down in front of him, occasionally turning to face him, pleading for justice.

He wanted Callant Newkirk's soul.

"How many others might there be or might there have been? Little girls out there. Prey for the beast in this demented man's skin. Victims of this monster's perverse passion."

How many.

And it was then that Cal turned to the snow, to the bright white falling outside where things were free and buried. This was craziness. His world, this world, was evil, insane. The lights flickered, the radiator hissed. The judge adjusted his spectacles, and the snow kept falling.

Then his lawyer stood before the bench. He stood there, and Cal hoped he was looking the judge straight in the eye, and he said, "This is preposterous. This is all a misunderstanding created by a man so blinded by rage at what he *thought* he saw that an innocent man is being tormented in this way." Yes, he could understand how it happened. He, too, was a father. Little girl about the same age. No malice intended, he would agree to that, but to accuse a man, a man like Callant Newkirk who had never been in any trouble with the law, never any history that would suggest he was capable of such an act, never, never, never...

The words, running together. Never, never. The snow falling, the words still coming, and Cal thought he heard someone snicker.

Where are you, you damned rapist bastard, he wondered.

And then it was time for the witnesses. Mrs. McNee, dabbing at her eyes with a handkerchief. "He wanted to know where the little girls were. If only I'd known what he meant, I could have called the police, something."

"And was that exactly what he said?"

"Exactly. Where are the little girls. The ones about this high."

Another murmur.

"I just thought it was because he was drunk. But then after this terrible thing happened, then I remembered one night when I think he might have followed some girls..."

"Objection."

Cal closed his eyes. Twisted. Everything was being twisted. The judge would have to see that.

The Langleys. One by one. He said he was having trouble with his wife. That she didn't like him anymore. That she was not a little girl. He was definitely drunk.

And to the defense? Yes, he was a longtime friend of their son's. When it came right down to it, they had always felt that Callant was a little unusual. An odd situation with his mother.

He was not going to let them, let her, Mrs. Langley, bring that up. He began to pound the table with his fist. "No, no, no." His lawyer first touched, then grabbed the hand.

"Quiet," said the judge, rapping the gavel.

"That won't help," the lawyer whispered.

And Cal thought he could keep pounding his fist in his head, and it would keep perfect time with the judge's gavel, and no one would be able to tell them apart.

"But this is just normal conversation," his lawyer protested. "It's being used out of context."

"He was dead drunk," Mr. Warner said. "Like to have waked up the whole neighborhood if I hadn't run him off." He took a deep brave breath. "Wife had locked him out. He must have done something."

"Objection."

"He woke me up," Mrs. Perkins said. "He was like a mad man."

"Objection."

"He was clearly drunk and shouting profanities. His wife was screaming. Scared to death."

"Objection."

And then there was the man. The big rawboned farmer of a man with his rural shock of hair and his homegrown dignity, a man who testified, crying the rough angry sobs of a man whose foundation has been shaken, and whose soul has been wounded by the transgression against his child, against that fruit of his seed, that flower to his passion and his blood, and his lines of immortality, already clipped—his son, his poor dead son—and now his flower of a daughter, that flower he was entitled to hold in his hand and watch blossom in the purity of it all, white petals spreading from the center that he, the father had created.

His flower was stained now, and he ached in his loins with the horror of the assault against his line.

"That's him," he said, pointing a shaking finger at Cal. "That is the man I found in my garden with my little girl."

And under cross-examination he stared first at Cal's lawyer, and then at the judge, and said, "I'm not the criminal here, and you aren't going to make me sound like a liar, either."

Back at the table, the lawyer whispered to Cal, "If I attack him any harder we're going to lose whatever sympathy I might be able to get for you. He *believes* his own story. He believes he saw the situation accurately."

"She'll tell them the truth," Cal said, speaking of the child. "She'll tell them about the kitten."

But that was not to be. The child had only one line to say, and she did so with the expression of a singer who knows the notes and how the words of the opera sound in Italian, but has no notion of the meaning. She came into the courtroom, the courtroom with the highly polished wooden pews that made it resemble an exceedingly pious church with a no-nonsense congregation, and she looked at Cal, who caught her eye and frightened it away. She sat there and said her sentence in her little-girl voice, wearing her little-girl anklets and a wool plaid jumper because now, after all, it was winter, and the chill was everywhere. The snow was falling, and she had on a yellow sweater under the jumper, and a note in her pocket that said, "Please excuse Lila for being late to school," signed in the rough script of the father who sat with his large hands folded in his lap.

His daughter had not had to listen to his words. She merely came into the courtroom in her little-girl clothes, and she said, "That—is—the—man."

She was then whisked away, having suffered already the

trauma of a hundred lifetimes, the judge said.

"I demand the right to cross-examine," Cal's lawyer shouted. "We have that right."

"Leave the child alone," someone behind him hissed.

"May I approach the bench, your honor?"

"No, you may not."

And while they argued, all Cal could think was that the little girl believed the lie. And the judge was unrelenting. Over the continued protests of Cal's lawyer, he insisted that identification was all that was necessary. The child had been quite enough of a victim already.

And, Cal thought, secrets come out. Someone would tell her sometime. A friend or an enemy. Her classmates would hear it discussed in the whispers at home, and those whispers would come into the corners of her life the way they had into his.

The jeers of children, the children who played in circles ringed in chalk, or who swung from the same jungle gym that he had climbed as a boy, and sat on the same seesaw on which he had balanced with Dave, carefully avoiding the certain death, one foot in front of the other, arms extended. It was like walking on a pirate's plank. But she would be a little girl in the middle of the ring, and the children would dance around her singing. He could hear the music, but he could not make out the words. But he knew, in this case, they would not sing the truth. They would lure her onto the rocks, and kill her innocence. Children, whispering evil in secret codes. Guessing.

It was not the same, he decided, as what had happened to him. The story that was a lie would be vicious, sordid, in this case. The truth, innocent and unspoken.

No. Not like the stories he was told, where the lie was the beauty, and the truth, the beast.

Child whispers. He, that man, tried to put his you-know-what inside her. He saw her you-know-what. He touched her you know where. The circle widened and the child spun in the center.

And the snow kept falling, and the words in the courtroom kept falling, and Cal thought about the truth in the midst of very little of it.

There they were, he and the child. Lovers by misconception. Centers of separate but ever widening circles. They should have been banished to an island where they could have learned to love each other alone. He would have made her his daughter. As it was now, they were merely victims of an uncommitted crime. A day had dawned and ruined them both.

His mother, the prophetess.

Mary Beth, the temptress.

He could not think about her, couldn't remember how she looked, the sound of her voice. Her name, a fleeting shadow of her, brought him a quaking sickness, the memory of the symptoms of an illness. The word *wife* held no meaning for him any longer.

And while Mr. Costello, with cold-eyed surety and very few words, explained Callant's work record to the judge who looked only bored by it, while Cal's lawyer pleaded, Cal himself decided that there was no truth. There was only belief. The father *believed* and made it reality. One could believe bad or one could believe good.

The time did not matter. The moment. He no longer heard the words, the words that had no meaning anyway. He no longer cared that his lawyer leaned over to him and said, "This is a travesty, insane. If he decides against us, we'll appeal so fast it will make everyone's head spin, and we'll get this whole goddamned mess out of this county."

It was as clear to Cal as if a shaft of summer light had suddenly pierced the courtroom in spite of the now gray falling snow.

There was only one believable story here. His, or that of the man who had come along just at the right moment to convict him. There was Mrs. McNee and the boysenberry seeds in her dentures, and Mrs. Langley who had never trusted him since... since what? Since the story. And Mary Beth. That would have been something had she been able to testify against her husband. *Sick.* Would she have told them about their honeymoon? Modeled the outrageous black thing she had worn? Yes, she had her own illustrated version. His mother's story. Dave's.

What a collection of stories. An anthology of mysteries. In the middle of a winter day in a courtroom filled with artificial light, there were any number of fascinating tales being written, and they were all being put down as history by the woman with the nimble fingers, the court recorder. And since she needed no inspiration, Cal found her face expressionless. There was no light in her eyes.

By the time the judge spoke, Cal was filled with a complete and immovable anger. He pushed his will into every portion of his body in order to avoid screaming his own creations at the circle around him.

That—is—the—man.

Three years.

Part Two

It was true. Prison was gray. A movie filmed in black and white. Cal was taken there in a gray car, led into a gray building, issued a suit of gray clothes, marched down a gray corridor into a gray cell.

After the trial, before he had been moved to the prison, Mary Beth had come to visit him. He had refused to see her, and took some pride in doing so. Dave had come to apologize about not being able to raise bail money. He couldn't even begin.

"Don't worry," Cal had told him. "I don't have anyplace to go anyway."

The lawyer, increasingly outraged, assured Cal that he would file an appeal immediately. It would actually help them that the judge had set such unreasonable bail, if he would just wait it out. "Senile old bastard," the lawyer said. "Cross-examination is a damned right."

He dyes his hair, Cal thought, wondering if that fact would help.

But in spite of all that, he was in prison and he was going to be there for some time. He intended to use that time to figure out exactly what had happened. He was going to review every step of the case, every damned incident in his life. A prison. A place that had never even been a possibility.

He took the folded sheets and blanket on his bed and made it up while his cellmate watched silently. He stretched the sheets and the blankets as tightly as he could and thought he should have been in the army. He heard a slight clicking behind him, and turned to face the man as if it were some sort of order to stand at attention.

"Don't fit right," the man said, staring at him with uncertain pale eyes. "Dentist here ain't up to much." He pointed to his teeth. "Been back to him three times."

Cal opened his bag and put the last four books Dave had given him on the table beside his bed.

"What'd you do?" the man asked, and the slight click was still there.

"Nothing."

The man laughed, and Cal avoided looking at his mouth.

"What I mean is, what'd they say you did?"

"Assaulted someone," Cal said, sitting down on the bed.

The man shifted his jaw. "Was she a looker?" he asked, his hands dangling between his knees.

A little girl in Sunday best, skipping down the sidewalk to church. A handful of petunias.

"I can't remember," he said.

"Lots of us here," the man said. "Women, they ruin you every time."

"Right," Cal said. "What did they *say* you did?"

"They *said* I robbed a market." A pause, more clicking, then a raspy, bronchial laugh. "Took them eight months and sixteen days to find me. Not a penny left."

"Eight months, huh," Cal said, smiling again at the man's pride of tone.

"And sixteen days."

"Did you assault a woman, too?" Cal asked, trying to make the connection.

"No," the man said, putting his feet up on his bed and leaning back against the wall. "Spent all the money on one."

"I know how that goes," Cal said.

"Last guy they put in with me was a fag," the man said. "Glad to hear you aren't one of those."

"No," Cal said, opening a drawer in the desk to put in paper and pen. "Not one of those."

"You gotta let them know that right away," the man said, "then hope they leave you alone."

"I will."

"Name's Howard," the man said.

"Cal."

They were marched down the gray corridor for the evening meal. Everything, Cal thought, is a straight line. Gray trays sliding along chrome bars. Gray tables and benches that pretend to be green without much effect.

"Follow me," Howard said, and the two of them slid to the end of a table next to the wall.

Cal stared down at his tray of food. He poked at the meat with his fork, trying to identify it. As if Howard knew the question, he said, "They call it Swiss steak. We think it's dog." He laughed, his mouth partially filled with food, and his bottom plate protruded and Cal could see the glistening pink gums. "Goddammit to hell," Howard said, pushing the plate back into place.

A large man joined them, sliding in next to Howard, facing Cal.

"Irv," Howard said without pausing to swallow. "Cal."

The man looked at Cal with suspicion, and nodded.

"Nearly three hundred of us here," Howard went on, "if you count the niggers."

Cal looked around the hall. The tables filled unevenly. Some groups of ten, some of three. Occasionally a man sitting alone. It was almost like a high school cafeteria, except there was no music, and the people that heaped the food on plates were other convicts, not the plump women dressed in white that Cal recalled. Of course, there were no women. *They ruin you every time.* He and Dave, and usually Kenny Larkin. A couple of Mary Beth's brothers. Laughing, shuffling around. The constant pranks. The salt shaker turned upside down so that when Dave picked it up, a river of salt flew across the table. A hidden spoonful of pepper in someone's rice pudding.

It was difficult to believe, Cal thought as he looked around, that this group of men had ever lived such a simple life. No pranks now. Felonies. No high-pitched girl giggles. Laughter that sounded hard. No elbowing and pushing and straw papers flying back and forth. Menace.

He had to swallow his own terror along with the food on his tray. He had to do that.

"There's groups here," Howard went on. Irv sat silently and ate his meal in perfectly rhythmical fashion.

He leaned over the table in confidence. "That big table

over there," he said, gesturing with his head toward a group of a dozen or so men who sat nearly in the center of the room. "The guy at the head, the fat one with the glasses. He can get you anything if he likes you. Don't like many."

"Likes killers," Irv said, not looking up from his place. "Ones that did it on purpose and got something for it."

"And crooked cops," Howard added.

"Those ones over there," Irv said, moving a shoulder indicating the table closest to them. "Embezzlers and forgers. The white-collar group. Short-timers."

Cal wondered where the child molesters were. Did they sit with the rapists and compare notes? The sex offenders in general. Let me tell you about my Daddy, he would say to them, and how I came to be here. He was getting dizzy with the din of it all, the matter-of-fact passing of information. He wondered why Irv was there. Was this the armed robber table? It was better, he could tell, not to ask too many questions here.

He pushed his tray aside. He would try to get used to the food tomorrow.

That night, he lay on his back, his hands behind his head, and tried to think. Howard slept, snoring lightly, clicking occasionally. He wondered what kind of woman Howard had spent his money on. He wondered how he had lost his teeth. He wondered where the man was that Irv had stabbed in a barroom fight, the man who now only had one eye, but according to Howard, the bastard didn't even deserve that, that one right to see. If someone tried to take your woman away, even if that woman was a bitch, a man had to fight.

Another thing his mother had not explained.

The prison was not as quiet as he had expected it to be. He could still hear voices, although he could not make out the words. He swore he could hear the opening and closing of cell doors, but thought he must be mistaken.

It wasn't as bad as he had thought it was going to be. He wasn't so afraid anymore, just restless. Sleep, he thought, like the food, was going to take some getting used to.

He remembered his own room, searching for the ordinary to soothe him. The three swimming trophies on the bureau. His mother clapping her hands in pride and delight at his victory. The letter sweater for track. His mother in the stands, a light blue sweater around her shoulders, cheering him. Had

he run every race, done everything simply for her applause?
Three certificates for academic achievement, framed, under
glass. The brown clock radio that woke him every morning,
and the dresser with one drawer pull missing. The poster of
North American birds. The woodpecker and the sparrow. The
cedar waxwings and chickadees. He'd never actually seen a
bluebird or a cardinal. Maybe he could really study birds
while he was in prison. That would add a nice ironic touch.
Flightless birds.

He thought he heard murmuring, a slight moaning. His
mother's head upon her pillow. Tossing.

And then she came to get him. His sleeping bag was on the
bed, and his suitcase was packed. Ah, she said, putting her
arms around him, how I've missed you. A whole week. It
seemed like forever. Her hair brushed across his face, and she
kissed him on the cheek. Ah, but such fun you must have had.
He handed her a small cabin made of Popsicle sticks. As she
took it, he noticed she wore a ring on every finger. And it had
only been one week. She led him out of the Popsicle-stick
cabin into sunlight so bright he was nearly blinded, and then
they were walking down a corridor. A corridor inside and she
had her arm around his shoulders and his sleeping bag kept
bumping against his leg as he walked. They passed doors with
numbers on them, and he thought they must be in a school
and he wondered how they got there. He could hear the click
of her heels on the tile. They stopped before a door with a
frosted-glass panel, and she said, Now you wait here for me,
I'll be just a minute, and she put her hand to his face, and he
felt something sharp like a thorn tear his flesh.

Oh, she said, looking at a sharp white stone on her hand,
I've scratched you. Oh, she said, drawing a finger over the
scratch, and he knew the pain disappeared. Then she reached
up to the glass with the ring, and drew a perfectly straight
line down the middle. Just a minute.

He sat on his suitcase in the corridor, his sleeping bag at
his feet. Perhaps he went to sleep. He woke and it was cold
and dark and still she had not returned. He rubbed his eyes
and reached for the door handle. He could still see the line
she had made with the ring. He put his fingers to the scar on
his face. He could feel the welt. He turned the handle and
opened the door.

Outside it was snowing, and the flakes blew in and caught on his lashes and his lips. He didn't have a coat, and the field in front of him was white in the moonlight. He opened his mouth to call to her.

The sound of a bell. A profusion of yellow light. The noise of men in steel gray halls.

"Turn to," someone said, and he sat up in bed.

"I forgot to take my damned teeth out," Howard said, rubbing his jaw. "Got to remember to do that."

It began at breakfast. Cal and Howard went to the same table as the night before. Howard chattered away, explaining the rules, repeating the gossip.

"Stay away from the niggers altogether," he said. "They got their own groups and they think different than we do."

Perhaps twenty-five percent of the men there were black, and they even, it seemed to Cal, kept their space to about one square quarter of the cafeteria. There might as well have been a wall. "And you don't want to accidentally sit down with one of those guys that sits by themselves. They do so for some reason. Either they like it that way, or we do." He said this last with the distinct air of the man on the inside.

The eggs looked less than authentic, and Cal decided it was like the army. Like summer camp in the Guard.

Howard worked his way methodically around the tray as if prison eating were a learned skill. A march around the yard for a purpose. The eggs, the toast, the oatmeal. Something that tasted like Spam. Dentures clicking, fork on metal tray, the murmur of voices, indistinguishable words.

Cal thought for a moment that it seemed as if everyone was telling some odd secret in a voice just low enough to be misunderstood. Perhaps confessions.

"Hey," Howard said, "what the hell?"

Cal looked at him. The man was staring down the cafeteria to a far table against the wall.

"What the hell is he doing over there?"

"Who?" Cal asked, straining to find the place Howard watched.

"Irv. We been eating breakfast together every day for the last three years. Now he's over there."

He pointed with his fork, jabbing the air angrily at a table three rows down and against the opposite wall.

A slight quivering of uneasiness began in Cal's stomach. Maybe it was simple. Just a matter of dislike. Maybe it was something else.

"Maybe he just doesn't like me," Cal said. "That happens sometimes. For no real reason. Two people just don't like each other."

"You didn't like Irv?" Howard asked, turning to face Cal, his eyes opening slightly wider.

"No. I didn't mean that." Cal looked down at his tray and poked the piece of Spam with his fork. "Maybe he just took a dislike to me. Maybe he'd rather just have breakfast with you."

"Irv's a nice guy. I know the stabbing business and all, but he's just a regular guy."

High school. A girl with a bad reputation, an easy girl sliding up beside you in the hall. That uneasiness. The tough boy. The one who all of a sudden when it had been just fun and games and horsing around had you by the shirt collar with a look of madness in his eyes. The small boy in grade school. No one would sit by him because he smelled like pee. Cal was one of those who avoided him.

"Maybe he's just doing some business," Howard said. "Lots of that goes on here. If you want something from the outside, there's those that can get it for you."

Like what? Cal wondered. Howard was obviously disturbed about his friend's absence from the table. Why did he feel so certain it was because of him? Strange being around all these men. It wasn't the same as working at the smelter with the same bunch you grew up with. The smell was even different.

Men.

The little girl, alone in the center of the circle. The children ringing around her, whispering, singing, spinning a cocoon of barbed wire.

He took a deep breath. Swallow it, he thought.

"I guess you ought to just ask him," Cal said, and he could

feel the coldness he forced in his voice. "And if it's me, I can just sit somewhere else."

Howard did not disagree.

He was assigned to the laundry and things got worse there quickly. The trustee who was to explain the procedure to him moved about the room, and Cal was certain that every time they approached someone else that man stopped and turned away. Did the large black man who oversaw the ironers mutter something under his breath? Stop it, Cal thought. This is no good. They passed the line of large stainless steel industrial washers. Already the men were loading them from bins of gray uniforms and dull white linens. Already the air was filled with steam.

"What you're going to do is take these bins with wet clothes over to the dry area and load them." The trustee grabbed one of the empty wheeled bins. "Like this," he said. "Follow me."

How hard could it be, Cal wondered, to wheel a bin of wet clothes over to the dryer? The man talked to him as if he were a dim-witted two-year-old.

"Like this," the man said, above the noise of the washers and the clatter of the wheels as he rolled the empty metal bin.

He pushed the bin up in front of a large empty dryer. He opened the door and began to scoop the imaginary clothes into the dryer. Cal wanted to laugh.

"The grays take forty minutes. The towels take fifty. The linens, thirty-five. Don't waste no dryer time."

Cal smiled. Thirty-five, forty, fifty. Memorize the formula. The binomial theorem of the laundry room.

He heard another bin rolling up behind him and before he could turn, it hit him in the back of the knees, nearly knocking him to the floor.

"Hey," he said, and the trustee turned back to look at him as he whirled around to face the clumsy operator of the bin.

Above a batch of steaming gray clothes, Irv looked at him. His eyes, cold and steady. His mouth turned slightly in a barely hidden sneer. Cal waited for a gruff sorry, and got nothing.

"Move along," said the trustee, and Cal felt his hands tighten at his sides. Relax, he told himself. Maybe this is their own brand of welcome to the laundry.

"Now you take this bin back around this corner, and you see you find yourself right back to the washers, and there should be another load about three machines down from the last one you picked up." The man scratched his head. "You just got to look and see what's done, but we work right to left, you see."

He seemed to have difficulty with the complexity of it all, or at least with the description. Cal could still feel the cut of the edge of the metal bin against his thigh, although it wasn't that painful. What the hell had Irv meant?

"I sit right up there," the trustee said, pointing to a table and a chair. "You can ask me if you have any trouble. Don't try sandbaggin', though."

"I won't," Cal said.

"You don't need to talk, neither," the trustee said.

"Fine."

It was a little like the crusher, Cal told himself. Lots of noise. The constant churning of the washing machines, the rolling drums of the dryers, the clatter of the rolling bins. A little like a joke. He imagined the grimy men from the concentrator immediately placed at work in a laundry. What an ironic juxtaposition. One place they essentially made finer and finer dirt, and the other they tried to get rid of it. Dust. Ashes to ashes. Dust to dust. Dust to nothing. The other washer unloader was a young man who looked about Cal's age who wore thick glasses that covered over with steam every time he opened one of the washers. It made him seem strangely blind. He did not speak to Cal. He reminded him of someone, glasses, dark hair. Short, stocky.

Angelo Calese.

A tall thin man came toward him, looked as if he were going to pass him, and Cal moved in closer to the washer that was nearly complete in cycle, averting his eyes from the oncoming man, and the man leaned into him as he passed and said, "You little prick," hissed it under his breath, bumped him into the vibrating washer, and went on.

"What?" Cal moved out into the aisle, stared at the man's back, and perhaps his words were drowned by the final throws of the spin. The end clunk of the motor as it shut down. What?

This was not right. He opened the washer door and began scooping the warm wet grays into the bin. Prick. Angelo Calese.

Dead now. A car in the canyon when he was sixteen.

A voice startled him, a hand on his shoulder. He turned up from the bin to see Irv standing there.

"You have a pecker for little girls? A tiny little thing?"

Cal clenched his fist and stared at the evil face.

"You better not move," Irv said, "you slimy pervert."

"Newkirk," the trustee shouted from the table. "Back to work."

"Get off my back," Cal said to Irv, and the huge man smiled at him.

"Don't turn it, baby boy," Irv said. "Your *back*."

Cal pulled the rest of the laundry from the washer and slammed the door. Watch it, watch it, watch it. When he looked up, two men were motionless, staring at him.

Angelo Calese. He and Dave had gone to mass with him. That's what Cal remembered at that moment. The litany. Like the litany of looks that seemed to fill the steam of the laundry. The rhythm of the spinning machines. Angelo, a nervous young man, devout. Holy Mary, mother of God, holy Mary mother of God. Cal wished he had paid more attention. A chant to get him through this. Angelo Calese, crossing himself before a basketball game, before an at-bat in baseball, before a ninth-grade history test.

He rolled the bin toward the dryer. Holy Mary, mother of God. Holy Mary, mother of God. There had to be more. He could feel the tremor in his legs. In the corridor of dryers, he would be out of sight of the trustee. Keep your head down, roll that bin. His mother had not believed in churches. God in the heart, or not at all, she said. Buildings filled with hypocrites. His mother who was never bitter, uncharacteristically harsh about the matter. They did not need a church. Sneaking off to Catholic mass with Angelo, watching with curious eyes, listening with superstitious ears. Holy Mary, mother of God, if you'd let me go to church, holy mother, I might know the rest of this song. Holy Mary, holy holy, blessed. Around the corner, down to the far end of the line of dryers, the bin vibrating as he rolled it, the morning not even begun and already this, this trouble.

He was here, he reminded himself, because he was stupid. Because someone had neglected to tell him the truth about life.

Holy Mary, mother of God.

Two men waiting by the empty dryer, waiting, lounging as if they had nothing to do, thugs on a street corner, no way to cross around them, leaning there looking at their hands, and Cal refused to slow the bin, to hesitate, and he thought, move them out of the way, use the bin, move them with the power of a steam shovel with a lowered blade, push them away. Holy Mary, mother of God, please let them move, move them around the corner, blow them away.

They did not move, and Cal stopped the bin just short of contact.

They stared at him.

"Get out of the way," he said.

They did not move.

It had to be now, he decided. Now. He rammed the bin with all the force he could muster into the side of the first man. It was like hitting a wall.

"Move," he shouted, hoping the trustee would hear, hoping someone else would round that corner and put a stop to all of this.

One man grabbed the side of the bin and the other came around to him.

"Thought you should deal with someone your own size," the man said.

"We don't like men that pick on kids," the other muttered, leaning over the bin.

Cal released the bin and stood up straight.

"Two against one? That's fair." The words sounded strange to him. As if they could not possibly have risen from his throat. "Real courage." He couldn't stop. Not now. It would never end if he did. He clenched his fists.

The man holding the bin laughed and stepped back, and Cal could see the other man knot his own fist and prepare, and it was as if his own body was ten seconds ahead of his brain, and he whirled before the man could get his fist up and caught him full on the jaw, sending the man staggering backward against the dryer across the aisle, causing his eyes to open in surprise and pain, and then it was the beginning of the end. The man pushed the bin at Cal, catching him at the knees, knocking him backward, and the bin tipped onto its side, spilling the wet clothes onto the floor and the man was on top of him, and his face was down in the warm mass of material, and he felt an arm twisted impossibly behind his back. His own weapon became his foot, and he kicked, catching the man behind a knee, knocking him to the floor, the arm releasing his. He kept thinking, this is instinct, not training, instinct. He was tangled in the clothes, and he had the man's head now, his hands around his throat, and the man punched at his side, and he could hear the shouts, the cheers, the accolade of the group that had gathered, and for one strange incredible moment, he thought they were cheering for him.

But then he was pulled to his feet, and his arms were pinned behind his back, and a succession of men, two, three, maybe four, Angelo Calese with his steamy glasses and his Hail Mary, full of grace, Holy Mary, mother of God, and he thought he heard his own jaw crack, and he would not yell. He would not. No uncle, no uncle, no mother of God. No mercy, no Mary, no Monday morning mass.

And he thought he heard running, and knew it wasn't him. He thought he heard wheels, a squadron of metal bins rolling across the floor to mangle the enemy. Shouts, curses, another blow to the face, and he could not see anything, could not feel anything except that he was released, released, freed, sent flying down, down down somewhere through space, landing in a cold damp swamp. Dying on a battlefield just before the end of the war. Wrapped in the clothing of his birth, Holy Mary, mother of God. Away.

When he opened the one eye that he could, he saw a perfectly white ceiling that he mistook at first for the back of a sheet. Then the light came into focus, and he turned on the bed to see a guard at the door. He knew enough not to speak. He wondered if he could feign sleep, or death, until his lawyer could get him out.

He awoke in the middle of the night, furious. It took him a minute to remember where he was, but when he did, he had to restrain himself from sitting bolt upright in his bed and shouting. Had a dream led him here? He gripped the sides of the bed in the darkness. It wasn't just the fight, the beating. It was something else that lingered around the edge of wakefulness.

Betrayal. He had been betrayed.

Many had lied to him. He closed his eyes thinking maybe he was just overcome by panic, by fear of the future, but that didn't feel right either. Where was he going to find his refuge? Where he had always found it in the past, in the lap of his mother? Mary Beth had betrayed him. Was it as simple as that? He was just like the other men there. A woman had done him in. A wife, a little girl. Mrs. McNee. Dave's mother.

Just like them, and they had attacked him anyway.

God, he had to go to sleep. He had to forget about what had happened.

Goddammit, he couldn't. He had to figure out how to survive.

His mother, sitting as placidly as ever at the kitchen table, his mother with her soothing words, her stories about his father. He was a wonderful man, kind, considerate, honorable. She brushed her hair back from her face and looked at him with love and conviction. The face without lines of aging, without the marks of fear or stress. Her smooth cheeks with just the trace of color, the eyes that promised grace. The soft red lips that formed the words of love and hope and great expectations. The breathless gentle song that defined the world for him, the arms that created a universe that encircled him.

And she, she of all people knew it wasn't true, and she had chosen not to warn him.

He felt the tears come to his eyes. That world, he thought, clenching his fists. That *woman's* world. No words of love or lamentation were going to bring it back.

Now he could not hear what she said; he could only see her face as she formed words, could only remember the look in her eyes.

You should not, he thought, as he watched her speak, as he studied her as if she were a portion of moving picture film without the sound, you should not have *lied* to me. You. You with your dreams and your stories, your goddamned fairy tales.

You come back to me. You come back and tell me the truth, dammit.

I told you all I knew, she whispered, and then she was gone as if that last lie had destroyed her even in spirit.

She could not come back, and he felt betrayed. He had no where else to go, nowhere to hide from those faceless men in gray who attacked him.

His head began to throb, and the men began to march. He closed his eyes, placed his fingers to his temples, and tried to coordinate his vision. A blinding flash of light, an almost religious burst of passion made him catch his breath and stop it. Now the marching men had faces, and one by one they marched into the spotlight, paused, and turned around. With each man, the face became more and more familiar, as if the sculptor had not succeeded in the likeness the first time, but was willing to try again and again and again.

There was only one person who could possibly answer his questions, Cal thought, as the men marched closer, and the light became brighter. A gray needle in a gray stack.

That bastard had to be somewhere.

He stood before the warden's desk the next day, one eye swollen shut. He stood at attention, and tried to remember the National Guard. The warden was bent over a file, and a guard was by the door. Cal could see that the warden's hair was thinning on top. He had combed long strands from the side up and over. Cal wondered if his own father was bald.

The warden closed the file, took off his glasses, and placed them on the desk. He sniffed, cleared his throat, and looked at Callant.

"Do you know," he asked, and Cal thought the man looked at him but did not see him, "what we have to do with troublemakers here?"

"No, sir," Cal said.

"Solitary."

"That's fine with me."

"You think that's fine until you've been there." He folded his hands. "You ones that think you're so tough crumble and end up crying on the floor like little babies."

"Maybe," said Cal.

"Christ, I wish they had a separate goddamned place for you mo-lesters." The warden's voice was cold and contemptuous.

"I'm not a molester."

"Right," the warden said, nodding. "You're just another innocent man. Shit."

"Right," Cal said, fixing his stare above the warden's head.

An old map of the United States was tacked to the wall. Like a schoolroom, Cal thought, and he wondered if the man would get up soon with a pointer and tap out places like Albuquerque, New Mexico, or Charleston, South Carolina.

"There isn't a real man inside or out who doesn't detest a molester," the warden said.

Where exactly was the Natchez Trace? Cleveland, Ohio? Cal squinted at the map and said nothing.

"You hear me? You're going to have nothing but trouble the whole time you're here, but by God, you're not going to cause trouble for me."

Dallas, Cincinnati, Salt Lake City.

"And I don't give a damn how long or how short a stretch you're here—your lawyer talks like you're just here for the weekend—you will stay out of trouble. You got anything to say, boy?"

"I didn't start the fight. I only tried to defend myself." The Mississippi, the Missouri, the Columbia, the Snake. The sound of water in an irrigation ditch. A cat with liquid blue eyes.

"Well, now, that's an unusual story," the warden said, picking up a pencil. "It seems no one ever starts these things."

"You know I didn't start it." Nashville, Little Rock, Cheyenne, Wyoming.

At the sound of the pencil cracking against the desk, Cal looked at the warden.

"Pay attention, boy. It'll serve you to do that."

"Yes, sir."

"I've got some questions," the warden went on. "I want simple answers."

"Yes, sir."

"I've read over the transcript of your trial. Like to do that to see exactly what kind of SOB I've got here."

Cal stood at attention, his hands at his sides.

The warden leaned back in his chair, the open file before him.

"Why didn't your lawyer question the little girl?"

"The judge wouldn't let him."

"Sure he didn't decide it wasn't in your interest to let her talk?"

"I'm positive. He kept yelling about it. Said it was illegal." That term again. Illegal. Cal looked at the warden, who was twirling a pencil between his fingers.

"And you got no record, no trouble before, and they threw the book at you?"

My father was a rapist. Cal blinked, the thought amazing and terrifying at once. He caught his breath. "No trouble, sir. No record." Was his voice trembling? Did he look guilty?

The warden stood up from his desk. "You stand right there, boy."

He left Cal alone with the guard, left him standing at attention in front of an empty desk and a map.

Rapist. Father. *My father was killed in the war.*

The grave away from the main part of the cemetery. He was a man apart, his mother had said. I didn't want him there with everyone else. No marker, just a slight rise in the earth. They had prayed over that grass-covered spot. Placed delicate-stemmed spring flowers where his heart would have been, and watched the wind blow the flowers away. Holly at Christmas. A birthday visit. September 20. It's a secret ritual, just the three of us, she had whispered to Cal. We don't talk about it to anyone or it will spoil it. Her soft breath tickling his child's ear.

He had not even dared look at the oddness of it all before. Now it seemed like an act of madness.

Finally the warden returned.

"Watkins is going to take you down to 114. He'll move your stuff from the outer cell. You'll be alone." The warden scratched his chin while Cal wondered what it all meant.

"The way I see it," the warden went on, "is that I got two kinds of real trouble here. The damned child molesters, and those hippie draft dodgers. You, unfortunately, look like you might be both."

"I'm in the National Guard," Cal said.

The warden frowned. "Well, you can't wear that uniform here, boy." He shook his head. "Take him to 114," he said to the guard, and Watkins stepped forward and grabbed Cal's arm. Cal turned quickly, almost struggling, and looked into the passionless eyes of the guard.

"And get me Melvin Ruggles on your way back," the warden added, and he turned his back on them both. As they left the room, Cal imagined the warden listing the cities he had been

to, the places he would rather be. New Orleans, Nashville—
Boston, Massachusetts.

He walked with the guard to a new empty cell. Gates opened
and closed, and there was only the sound of footsteps in the
corridor, and the customary clanking of iron. He had another
set of folded sheets and blankets on his bed. It gave him
something to do.

My father was a rapist.

He felt he should apologize to someone.

At dinnertime, they brought him a tray. He sat with his back to the cell door as the other prisoners filed past. "Prick," a man hissed. "Little girls, shit," another said, and Cal was sick to his stomach as he looked at his food and tried to ignore the words. His eyes hurt, and he was still stung by his own admission. Rapist.

Where had she gotten the damned picture? Who was the man in the living room picture, the man he had looked upon with love and trust for all those years? Had she paid good honest money for the photograph, framed already by someone who actually knew the man? Who would sell a picture of a war hero? Did she buy it at the ancient junk store on the corner of Third, the one run by a man who sold only guns that wouldn't shoot? Cal had tried to buy a .22 there when he was sixteen years old, and the man had yelled at him. He had Civil War guns, ones used for something meaningful. Not toys.

Cal covered his tray with a napkin to avoid looking at the uneaten food. How had she managed? Not just the stories, but just sitting around the kitchen table. Sometimes she would pretend to be her actress friend, the one who had died tragically, and she would quote lines from a play while peeling apples. She made quarts of applesauce every year. Upside-down mason jars bubbled in water on the stove, sterilizing. Maybe he was using the old apple corer. His favorite job. Undoubtedly, they were sitting at the table in joint effort while she waved one hand in the air, bringing it to her forehead,

"Oh, darling, I can't go through with it, don't you see?"

"With what?" he would ask in his deepest voice, not knowing the lines.

"With the murder, of course. You'll have to do it for me."

Apples. It would have been apples lining up on the table. She peeled them with a paring knife, and the red skins came off in spirals. She was quick and only occasionally nicked a fingernail, stopping to lament it when she did. The spirals of red and white danced in the water of the pan in front of her, and Cal had thought at the time they would make great toys except that they wouldn't keep.

Sometimes there were worms, and Cal, the man of the house, or the lover, partner in crime, disposed of them with malicious glee.

"Here he comes, Reginald, that awful man. Kill him for me, dearest." She would hand Cal the apple.

"Squish," said Callant, murdering the worm.

"My hero," his mother would say, the familiar make-believe expression in her face and in the way she held her hand.

Cal always blushed, but he liked it. Then he thought he was a hero, a hero like his father.

It was odd to think she had played out all her stories to an audience of one.

"Let me tell you again," she would say, turning the bright apple in her hands, "about how I met your father."

And then she would be into it. The weaving of lights and color and smells. It was as if Cal were there, peeking around the corner of the ring-toss booth with his small boy's eyes, looking right at the past.

A carnival. A carnival like the ones she had taken him to in the summer, the ones that traveled from small town to small town and set up the lights and the noise in the town's vacant dusty lot. She would take Cal and together they would ride the Ferris wheel, and she would watch as he rode the merry-go-round, and she would applaud every time he came by. She wore light summer dresses, and sometimes she put a flower in her hair. Sometimes a man would approach her, ask her name, say "What a cute little boy," and she would take Callant's hand and say "Thank you, but no thank you," and the man would slide away through the yellow dust of a summer night.

The evening she met Callant's father she was wearing a
dress with pink flowers embroidered around the hem and the
neck. She had done the work herself.

A young woman with long dark curly hair in a pink dress.
Her friend, Elizabeth by name, the girl who was destined for
a new name and short-lived stardom. A girl with a light in her
eyes. Two girls at the carnival. Two young women, he corrected the vision. They walked slowly, shyly from booth to
booth. They rode together on the Ferris wheel, gently rocking
baskets, swaying at the top over the trees. They pretended it
was dangerous.

And then Elizabeth met her aunt, a harried-looking woman
carrying a child. "I can't do nothing with him," the mother
said. "Too tired to have any fun, but if I take him home, all
the other kids got to go too, and then I'll have an uprising on
my hands."

"I always thought it was funny," his mother said. "*Uprising*.
Like Indians, I suppose. And that's a little how they looked.
A small band of Indians."

And then she would stop and explain to Callant that when
she told him how other people talked, it did not mean it was
all right for him to speak in that way. "'I can't do nothing' is
not good English."

And then she would be back into the story, taking the parts
of the people.

"I'll hold him for a while," Elizabeth said, taking the child
from her aunt's arms.

There wasn't anyplace to sit. The two young women walked
around the games, listened to the barkers, stepped back as the
team of dwarfs came through the crowd and called to takers
for the show.

"He's feverish," Elizabeth said with her hand on the baby's
forehead. "I ought to take him home."

"I'll go with you," Carlotta said.

"But maybe I can come right back. Why don't you just wait
for me here?"

The baby screamed and struggled in Elizabeth's arms.

Carlotta looked at her watch. "I could do that. If you're not
back by ten, I'll just walk on home."

Together they found the aunt, who was loading the three
other children onto the merry-go-round.

There was something pleasant about wandering through the dust and noise and music and color alone. She saw people whom she knew, nodded, smiled, stopped to say hello. There were children with snow cones and cotton candy. There were people lined up to buy feathered dolls and American flags.

Carlotta stopped to watch the people who were flipping pennies into orange and green and yellow glass bowls and plates and she thought, what a pretty sight. All that glass glittering under the lights of a summer night. She watched a tall handsome young man in a uniform flip penny after penny at a deep blue dish. It was as if that were the only thing he wanted, and he would stay there until he won it. She looked at his hands as he held the pennies. Nice strong hands, she thought. Clean fingernails. He had dark hair and blue eyes, and he was all alone.

She was almost hypnotized. Penny after penny tossed at the bowl. Other players came and went, but the young man stayed. Carlotta moved up to stand closer to him, to be able to see more precisely the click of the fingers and wrist.

"Move away," the man who ran the concession finally said to her. He had Indian black hair and a long drooping mustache. "You're taking up space. Come on, pitch a penny and win a dish," he called to the crowd. "Plenty of room for winners." He looked again at Carlotta.

Callant could see the evil in his eyes. He could see that he meant to do her harm. He could feel his mother's fear.

"You play or you move," the man hissed at her. She took a step back from the booth. The man had a stick. She thought he might hit her with it. Strike her right in front of everyone. Too frightened to move. The man had eyes like a snake.

The lights and the noise of the carnival ceased to exist for her. It was as if time stopped.

"Hey," the young man yelled, and the evil one turned his eyes away from her. "Hey, get me that bowl."

It was the young man with the blue eyes and the blue bowl. In the center of the bowl was a copper penny. The vendor moved to him, picked up the bowl, held it high, and shouted to the crowd. "You can be a winner, too, just like this young man here. Pitch your pennies, step right up and trust to skill and lady luck."

Carlotta was still frightened. She wanted to run home and

hide, but she was unable to see anything but a dark path. Suddenly the young man was at her side. He had the cobalt blue glass bowl in his hands. It made the color of his eyes seem deeper. He held the bowl out to her.

"This," he said, "is for you."

And there they stood, in the center of the dust and yellow light, the kickup of color and the sighing of the merry-go-round. They stood there as the town siren rang ten o'clock, rang over the town, rising and wailing and dying so that everyone heard. The carnival began to ring down, as people stopped and listened, and began to turn away home. The single wail of the siren in the time of war. Ten o'clock. All is well.

They turned, she holding the bowl, freed from the man with the stick. The winner put his arm lightly about her waist.

"May I walk you home?" he asked as the siren faded into memory.

And that was how it all began.

Or so she had told him.

Cal put his head into his hands. It was peculiarly silent in his cell, as if he had a wing to himself. Or like a movie theater after the last show. That's what his mother's story was like. A movie.

Perhaps it really did begin that way. Carlotta and her friend, a sexy blonde on her way to Hollywood. Perhaps Elizabeth had met some handsome boy and gone off with him, leaving Carlotta alone. Someone who had promised her something. A ticket to stardom.

There was no blue-eyed man who threw a copper penny into the middle of a cobalt glass bowl and offered to walk her home.

Someone followed her. Perhaps the man with the evil eye and the stick.

Perhaps Carlotta heard his footsteps behind her as she turned down the dark street where she lived. She began to run, looking fearfully behind her. Her long dark hair would have obstructed her view. Her dainty shoes would have been difficult to run in. She would have thought, even though her heart was beating faster and faster, that someone was playing a cruel joke on her. Any minute, some of the young boys on the block would jump out and yell "Boo hoo, we scared you," then run off down the street and around the corner laughing at their mischief.

Nothing ever happens around here, she would have thought. My imagination. But she would have run along the sidewalk anyway, wishing she were younger and faster and less out of breath. Maybe she slipped off her shoes and carried them. And then there would not be any footsteps at all. Not hers, none behind her, and she would slow down, concerned now with listening, looking back over her shoulder, back down the tree-lined street and the moonlight shadows of leaves that barely moved, perhaps didn't move at all in the summer night, and perhaps a block away she would hear someone laughing, then another, then another, and she would think, I am not alone. Not alone on this dark street. There is no danger, and it is only silliness that makes my heart pound, and she would be walking, looking behind her, her long hair falling into her face. She would not hear anything, nothing at all. No shadows behind her. No footsteps. The sound of a car a block over. The barking of a dog in the distance. The white streak of a cat crossing from the field across the way, low to the ground, slinking home under the light with a field mouse in his mouth.

And then he would be there, in front of her, and he would grab her before she saw him, and she would wonder, but only for a moment because then it would no longer be important, how he got in front of her, where he had passed her by without so much as a breath, and he would hold his hand over her mouth.

She would think of tobacco, and the fact that he was crushing one of her breasts. She would try her teeth against the palm of his hand. He would cover her nose, and her mouth until the world turned blue then black, and then buzzed like the swarm of summer bees that circled the honeysuckle in the garden. His eyes would stay fixed, eyes that carried the flicker of light, a porch light three doors up, and it was too far, and too late.

Who knows how long it might have been or what happened to her before she woke.

He guessed he had decided it was a barn where his mother was held. Those musty visions of straw, of damp isolation. The nightmares with Mary Beth. That was the end of the story Dave had inspired.

Carlotta would have felt the sharp straw against her leg, against her back. Certainly she would have felt cold even though it was summer warm, because she was naked. Her wrists would be raw from the rope that held her, and there would be indescribable pain between her legs, and blood smeared down her thighs. She would turn over in the straw, burning her wrists more, and she would hide her face.

Perhaps then he came at her from behind. Perhaps he lifted her up and rutted like a pig making that same noise, the horrible grunting noise, and she was only ears and no mouth, her mouth bound so screams burst in her own head. Perhaps a moan-smothered cry. A knife held to the tips of her breasts, a demand that she open her eyes. The breasts no man had ever seen—the place between her legs now a gaping wound.

The man was the devil, cruel and pointed, sharp and searing. The man was a man.

She thought she was going to die. She wished it would come quickly now that it was inevitable. The slats of light that came in through the half-collapsed roof of the abandoned barn burned across both the man and the woman, making him pierce her even more deeply, and she thought she was on fire.

Someone found them there, and the man escaped.

Had the man raped other women? Did he always get away?

Where was that man, Cal wondered. Did he have a side to his story? What possible excuse?

He was exhausted, and the thoughts of his mother made him queasy. He could feel himself changing, something growing like a stone within him. God, he thought, I'd better hope it grows quickly. Something to make him invulnerable. He was going to have to concentrate on survival here. He didn't have time to misunderstand.

Watkins came for Cal the next morning, after Cal had managed to choke down the breakfast he was served in his cell. As they walked to the warden's office, Cal could only keep time with the step, and hope that the warden was not going to send him back into the laundry. His dreams the night before had been a strange combination of running track, and rolling in a dryer, the heat and smoke smothering him, the dirty water making him sweat, turning him gray and limp.

The warden was signing a stack of papers, and to Cal's dismay, a large man stood in the corner glaring at him. It was the very man Howard had pointed out. The large man with glasses who supposedly ran things.

The warden finished, and looked up at Cal. "I'm turning you over to Ruggles," he said, and Cal thought, I'm a dead man, dead. Turning over in an empty grave. He could feel his eyes flicker and he tried to find Kansas on the map on the wall.

"He's your new cellmate, and you'll be working under him in the library."

Library. Ruggles worked in the library. Cal turned to look at the man, and his gaze was returned with contempt.

"He'll explain how things work," the warden added.

Cal continued to stare at Ruggles as if his life depended on this initial scene.

"And you'll listen good," Ruggles said, leaving no room for doubt.

Cal turned back to the warden. "Yes, sir," he whispered.
What was happening here? Yesterday he'd thought the warden
was on his side. Now this. Ruggles was twice his size; he'd
never make it against him.

"That's it," the warden said, nodding to the guard.

Cal walked between Ruggles and the guard through a cell
block, to a large gate, through that, up to a smaller gate, with
a cardboard sign that read LIBRARY in black ink letters. It might
as well, he thought, have said GAS CHAMBER. Then, as another
guard appeared to open the smaller gate, he felt a surge of
relief. He wouldn't be there alone, at least, but when he looked
at the face of the tall lanky man who held the key, there was
nothing there to comfort him. Inside the room, he saw the
shelves of books with an element of surprise that made him
feel weak again. *There are books,* he wanted to shout, then
realized he would sound insane.

Watkins left with a few muttered words to the other guard,
and the gate clanked shut, leaving Cal facing Ruggles with
nowhere else to turn.

Ruggles took a package of cigarettes and a book of matches
from his pocket, his eyes never moving from Cal's face.

"I don't like being a babysitter," Ruggles said. "You get that
straight right now."

He blew a cloud of smoke directly at Cal. Babysitter?

Ruggles moved around to the back of a large wooden desk
and sat down. Cal stood facing him. He had nothing to do but
wait. "Yes, sir," Cal stammered, finally.

"That's a good idea," Ruggles said, inhaling again. "You call
me 'sir.'"

Cal nodded.

"You ever been in a library, boy?"

"Yes, sir."

"Well, now, that's a distinct advantage." He grinned, and
Cal noticed for the first time how thick the steel-rimmed eyeglasses were. They made Ruggles' eyes larger, but no more
sympathetic. "That means you are probably also familiar with
the alphabet."

"Yes, sir."

"Well, a genius."

Cal swallowed. Ruggles ground his cigarette out in an ashtray. "These taste like shit," he growled. "There's three boxes

of new books on the floor over there."

Cal looked to the cartons stacked in the corner.

"You're going to catalog them and get them on the shelves. I don't look kindly on mistakes."

Cal nodded. Catalog. Cards. Files. Where was the kindly gray-haired old lady of library dreams? Mrs. Herman who'd helped him find material for his paper on the assassination of William McKinley? He shook away the clouds. Before he could catch his breath, he was seated at a table in front of Ruggles, the cartons at his side, a stack of cards, a pen, and a copy of the numbering system. He had filled out ten cards before his hands stopped shaking. He had red ink from the stamp that read PRISON LIBRARY on his hands.

Fortunately, he did not have to ask Melvin Ruggles any questions.

And he listened with fascination as other inmates came into the library.

"Read this one, Lister," Ruggles said. "It has words of more than four letters and you might learn something."

"Take this book on Spain, Gonzalez. Tell you something about your ancestors, if you had any."

No one disagreed with Ruggles' choice. It was something to remember.

A guard brought sack lunches at the noon siren, and Cal and Ruggles ate in silence at their respective tables.

In the afternoon, Howard came to the gate, but left quickly when he saw Cal.

"You ain't much good for business," Ruggles said. "Shit."

Irv wasn't so reticent. "You know who you got there?" he muttered to Ruggles, clearly loud enough for Cal to hear.

"I know everything, fat ass," Ruggles said. "You're the one who's got to watch being stupid."

Irv left the book he'd selected on the desk, and went out. Cal felt only relief when Ruggles didn't mention that.

And as the afternoon passed, Cal gained more courage and began to watch Ruggles when he could do so without being detected. The huge man sat engrossed in a large reference book of some kind, making occasional notes in a loose-leaf binder. It seemed odd to think of him studying, but Cal did not think it wise to ask quite yet. He began to wonder what crime or crimes Ruggles had committed, where he was from.

How he commanded such respect from the position behind a desk in the library. He looked about forty, maybe forty-five. Had he ever worked the carnival? Was he from up north, say around Four Corners? Cal shook his head.

"You got a book about some kids that grew up in a boxcar?" a timid middle-aged inmate asked Ruggles. He'd come in without Cal's noticing.

"That's a kid's book," Ruggles said.

"My mother used to read it to us," the man said nervously.

"Lucky you," Ruggles said in little less than a snarl as he went to pull the book from the shelf.

After the man left, clutching the book from his childhood in his hand, Ruggles spoke. "We got more kids' books here than any other goddamned place I've ever seen," he said, sitting down at his desk. "People are right generous with their kids' things."

"I guess everybody likes to remember when they were a kid," Cal ventured.

"Most these so-called rough little buggers are still kids," Ruggles said. "They don't have far to think. The warden's do-goody wife ought to scare up some law books, something useful."

"You read a lot when you were a kid?" Cal asked.

"Don't recall," Ruggles said, closing the book on the desk with a snap. "If you're done cataloging, busy yourself with something else, boy. Read a book."

"Yes, sir."

"Shit," Ruggles said. "Damn slow day."

It took some time for Cal to get the courage to start going over the shelves for something to read. He could feel a tension filling the room like a yellow fog smelling of sulfur. It reminded him of the smelter, and he wished he was back in the crusher where at least the overpowering noise dissolved everything else. He was about to take down a copy of Dickens' *A Tale of Two Cities* when Ruggles spoke again.

"Come over here, boy," he said.

Cal guessed he would get used to being called that soon enough. Boy. Yes, massa, he thought. Shit.

He stood in front of the desk again.

"Since I'm going to be stuck with you twenty-four hours a day, I want some things straight right from the start." He lit another cigarette, and blew the smoke straight forward. "I have my own way of doing things, and I don't like a lot of talk. I transact a certain amount of business. You keep your eyes closed and your mouth shut, understand?"

Cal nodded. What kind of business?

"You ever see those three monkeys? Hear no evil, see no evil, speak no evil? You just practice being all three."

Monkeys. Cal couldn't place it for a minute.

"You're going to be hounded some, and I don't want you to do or say one damned thing about it, hear?"

"They beat me up in the laundry," Cal said. "I didn't do anything then."

"Christ, you dummy. I know that. Why the hell do you think the warden put you with me?" He ground the cigarette out again. "That bastard is going to have to get me better smokes than this, I tell you. The point is, I can throw you back in that water faster than you can pee your pants if you cause me any trouble. My deal with the warden only goes so far."

"Yes, sir," Cal said. A deal, just for cigarettes? There had to be more than that.

"You remember that at the table tonight," Ruggles said. "You aren't no cat with nine lives."

"Shut it down," the guard at the door said. "Hour's over."

"Stuff it up your ass," Ruggles muttered, and gave Cal one last menacing look.

Dinner at Ruggles' table came off with less difficulty than Cal had imagined it would. Except for one painful jab in the back as he stood in the line, and a series of threatening whispers, he might as well have been invisible. Ruggles explained nothing to the others, and Cal sat staring at the food on his tray, and kept his mouth shut.

And as he listened, it was almost possible to imagine that he was back at the concentrator, listening to Kenny Larkin and his friends tell the stories, the endless tales of sexual gratification, or the lack of it.

There was one addition, however. One that made Cal's face feel hot at first because he thought perhaps the men at the table were talking to him, about him. But as he listened, he realized that the jokes about homosexuality at Melvin Ruggles' table served as a notice, a kind of position taken. They said—not me. Not us. We're big boys, the all-men. Then they moved on to women, to ladies of the evening they had all known. A woman from Denton, Texas, with an extra little tit in the middle of her chest. A circus acrobat who could wrap her legs around her own neck. A woman who weighed four hundred pounds and always took on two at a time, and longed for three. Henry Whitehorse had run into a woman who liked to be chained in a doorway and whipped with black leather. Unfortunately, he had been unable to convince the judge and jury that it had been her idea, and she had, for some unknown reason, turned on him. He laughed as if the whole business were one monumental joke. The man next to him suggested that perhaps Henry had run into too many women of that ilk for the common man to understand.

"Bees to the honey," Henry had sneered. "Old Indian tale."

In the cell later, as he sat quietly on his new bunk with his book open, Cal thought about Mary Beth. The flimsy black nightgown. What a fool he'd sound if he told that story here.

He heard Ruggles turn a page in the book he was reading. Christ, Cal thought, he'd been such a sucker. All his nice little notions, all his mother's pretty little stories. It made him shiver. A woman with three tits, an acrobat and a fat lady. Carnival characters all. An evil-eyed man with a stick. Henry White-horse and the captive woman.

It was time to go to sleep. He wondered whether to say good night to Ruggles, but decided he'd let Ruggles make that move. He closed his eyes.

An exotic dancer with seven veils coming off one by one. A woman with long dark hair, gold loops in her ears, and red paint on her nails.

A man at a long gray table somewhere telling a story about a woman he had followed once, a particularly beautiful woman who had struggled at first, but then...

"You did a right good job of keeping your mouth shut," Ruggles said. "You're a right smart boy."

Cal nodded, still with his eyes closed. "Yes, *sir*."

Ruggles laughed.

It was the twelfth note since Christmas. It fell out of Cal's book when he picked it up to read in the quiet part of the afternoon. He stared at the awkward letters and felt the same combination of fear and annoyance he experienced each time another threat appeared. As if the holidays had not been bad enough with the feeble attempts at festivity inside. An oddly misshapen tree in the mess hall, a few red and green crepe paper streamers, and a box of cookies Cal received from Dave, most of the cookies broken into crumbs in transit.

The first note had been under his dinner tray, and he'd been lucky enough to pick it up before anyone noticed. The others had come in new uniforms from the laundry, and now, too close to home, in the library.

They all said the same thing. He wasn't safe. He would turn a corner someday and someone would be waiting. Someone his own size. Not a little girl. This one said simply, WE GET RID OF SCUM. YOUR NEXT.

Cal stared at the misspelled "your." He hoped that eliminated Ruggles as a suspect. He didn't know who to trust, though weeks had passed. Could it be a guard? Did they have their own vendetta against people like him?

"What the fuck is that?" Ruggles said. Cal had not heard him come up behind him.

Cal wadded the paper in his fist. "Nothing."

"Give it to me, you little fuck," Ruggles snarled, grabbing Cal's hand.

"All right," Cal shouted. "Look at it." He opened his hand and the paper fell onto the table. Ruggles picked it up and unfolded it. He was still right beside Cal, and Cal could hear the man breathing.

"Christ," Ruggles said, throwing the note down on the desk. "I thought..." He stopped. "How many of these you gotten?"

I thought you knew everything, Cal wanted to yell, you and your damned power. "Six," he said instead.

"Forget it. They'll stop. Bastards don't even have the guts to sign their numbers."

That was easy enough for Ruggles to say, Cal thought. He didn't have to look around all the time, have to wonder what was going to happen next. It was bad enough to be locked away in this place, without some damned conspiracy from people he didn't know, could not explain anything to. Keep your mouth shut, Ruggles said. He'd done that. No explanations to anybody. No fucking apologies.

Ruggles went back to his desk. "I hate a goddamned man who won't stand up," he said.

Then it struck Cal. "What did you think it was, anyway?" he asked Ruggles, his voice still shaking in anger. "A damned love note?" The words were out before he could consider.

Ruggles glanced toward the guard at the door. "Dummy up, kid." The guard appeared not to have heard. "Later." Ruggles mouthed the word.

Later. Later he might get out of this damned place. Later someone might get him. Later he might learn something. Shit. He sat in stony rage for the rest of the day in the library. Ruggles hummed a little tune under his breath, and Cal wanted to hit him. He seemed almost pleased at the whole thing. That damned unidentifiable tune. It made Cal's head ache.

He tried to look around the table at the evening meal to see if anyone watched him. Nothing was different. He might as well have been an empty chair. Ruggles was his usual gruff imposing self, as if nothing had happened. Cal wondered if they all knew, if they all waited for him to stand up at the table and say, "Who the hell is leaving these threats," so they could all have a good laugh. He saw Howard and Irv, heads together at a table across the room, and he wondered if he had any rights at all. A six-handed monkey. Shit.

Later. Later he would hear from his attorney. Right.

By the time Cal and Ruggles were returned to their cell for the night, Cal was burned-out calm. He sat down on the edge of his bed, and as soon as the line of prisoners had passed by, he looked over to Ruggles and said, "Well?"

Ruggles narrowed his eyes. "Well, what?"

"You said, 'later.'"

"Oh, that," Ruggles said, the slightly mean smile twisting his mouth. "I thought you might be making deals with some other bastard."

"Deals?" Cal asked. "What kind of deals? I don't know anything, I don't have anything. The monkey, remember. Your deaf, dumb, and blind monkey?"

"I forgot," Ruggles said sweetly. "I forgot what a good boy you are."

"Shit," Cal said, and rolled back on his bed. He stared up at the ceiling. He couldn't get anywhere with anyone.

"Listen, you little bastard," Ruggles said in a low growl, "I got the sweet deal going here, and you aren't going to fuck it up for me."

"Yes, *sir*," Cal said, putting his hands behind his head.

To Cal's surprise, Ruggles laughed and it made him even more furious.

"You little know-nothing," Ruggles went on, "I've got that warden right where I want him. I could be out there breaking rock or breaking heads or pushing some stinking load of laundry around. I could have been one of those stupid bastards that tried to break your scrawny little neck, but I get to sit in a nice clean library reading books because I know how that warden works. You understand me?"

"Right."

"I've been in more jails and prisons than you been in ladies' beds, boy, and I'm looking at the long time. I got this nice little *reciprocal* deal with the man. You don't get hurt, and I get to do what I please."

You can't get out, Cal thought. *I am going to get out.*

"You forget about those sissy notes. Save them up if you want. Send them to one of them 'poetry-in-the-prison' magazines run by some long-haired draft-dodging hippie. I don't care what the hell you do as long as it is *nothing*."

Something in the sound of Ruggles' voice. A distinct change in tone. Was it fear? No. Something else. A masked longing.

Cal turned on his bunk and faced the large man.

"Nothing, do nothing."

"It's my business to make sure they don't get to you. Don't you think I can handle my business?" That sweet sarcastic tone again, the sly creeping smile.

In spite of himself, Cal felt a welcome trust in the man across the cell from him. There was a light in the eyes, magnified by the thick lenses, unmistakable.

"I expect," Cal said carefully, "that you can handle anything."

"Well, you're finally right about something," Ruggles said. He shook his head. "I ever tell you how I snaked that warden?"

Cal leaned forward on his bed. "I don't believe you did." He paused. "Sir."

Ruggles leaned back against the wall and folded his arms on his chest. "It's a damned funny story," he said. "A real barrel of ya-hoo laughs."

For the next half hour, Cal sat fascinated as the toughest man in town told his tale.

According to Ruggles, it hadn't taken him all that long when the warden was appointed to see a pattern. Oh, he was a tough talker, but nothing compared to the former warden the inmates had called Big Hitler. One of the first words out was that the warden had a book-loving do-gooder wife. While the other convicts looked for the weakness this might indicate in a man, a man that let his wife into the stone walls at all, Ruggles was smarter than that. No warden was going to be any pushover. He wasn't going to snicker in any damned corner about a sissy book reader. He was going to use it, and use it he did.

"I got the word out," Ruggles said, "that I was one of those closet scholars. You find them in here sometimes. A real misfit who uses books to pretend he's better than someone else."

The warden, according to Ruggles, had fallen for it, "hook, line, and sinker."

And there was some truth in it, Cal could see. Ruggles had been reading. The Bible, of all things. "Trying to figure out," Ruggles said, "why so damned many people put so much stock in that little black book."

It wasn't long before Ruggles was called to the warden's office, and the proposition made. Ruggles, the perpetual troublemaker, was to be given one last chance.

Ruggles laughed. "You see, kid? See how that works? You want something, and you get someone to think it's their idea. Make them think they're saving your soul, and all that horseshit."

Cal nodded at the concept, trying to see if he could use it, too. Hell, he didn't even know who was sending the threats, so he couldn't exactly work on that.

"So you see, boy," Ruggles concluded, "I got what I wanted, and the old man thinks he won."

He did, Cal thought. He could suddenly hear the warden giving his side of the story. Two sides. How the warden reformed Ruggles. Another two-sided tale. Which was true? He'd have to think on that.

First of all, he would have to decide what he wanted and who could get it for him. His lawyer was at work on the appeal. That he would have to trust to him.

He knew what it was; it had just taken him a couple of weeks to admit it, and another week to come up with the plan.

On the day he planned to approach Ruggles, word came from his attorney. He was meeting with some others to discuss the appeal. He'd been able to get it set for the next week since the judge in Cal's case was gaining an increasing reputation for creeping senility.

That dyed hair wasn't fooling everyone, Cal thought as he read the letter.

And at the same time, the threats stopped.

"Bigger fish to fry," Ruggles said. "We got two new peaceniks in here amongst this band of patriots."

"I guess they might as well start their own table," Cal said, trying to be clever.

Ruggles glared at him. "Don't get any ideas," he said. "You just stay right where you are."

"I intend to get out," Cal said stubbornly.

"Chickens counted too soon can end up to be dead chickens," Ruggles said.

Cal had to admit he never heard it put that way.

Cal waited a couple of days. He had to worry about the appeal, and at the same time concentrate on the right opening to Ruggles.

It came in the late afternoon after a slower than usual day.

"Fascinating," Ruggles said, closing *The Maltese Falcon* for the last time. "What a mind."

Perfect. A man who loved a mystery. Cal was going to give him the opportunity to solve a big one. He had gone over the opening to his story so many times, he almost believed it himself.

"Hey," Ruggles interrupted his thought. "You with us today, kid?"

"Sorry," Cal said, getting to his feet. "What did you say?"

"I said we got to check with Leroy about that book he's got. It's been too long, and he's a sneaky little bastard."

"Sure," Cal said, sitting back down in his chair and making a note, "Look for Leroy."

"You act like you're in a goddamned daze," Ruggles said, leaning over his desk.

"I was just thinking about mysteries. Real ones, you know. Not those in books."

"The meaning of life, or some other crap, I suppose," Ruggles said. "You stick to the simple ones like Perry Mason, who always gets his man and all the answers."

Cal winced. This wasn't going to be as easy as he had hoped.

"My mother used to tell me about a rape case that was never

solved. Twenty years ago or so. Just curious."

"Curiosity killed the cat."

Ruggles had one of those damned sayings for everything, Cal thought, and he took a breath.

"I thought it would be interesting to see if anybody in here knew about it. I thought maybe I could ask a couple of questions at dinner, or when men come into the library..."

"Shit," Ruggles said. "You're not thinking of writing a book, are you? An unsolved rape case. That's about as unusual as tits on a cow."

"But I think this might have been a *famous* rape case. Hell," Cal said, trying to be daring, "the bastard might even have ended up right in this prison. It would be a good story. I could just put out some feelers."

Ruggles glanced toward the guard as he always did when Cal was saying something that might be trouble. Then he turned back to Cal, and there was ice in his magnified eyes.

"Listen, you little punk, don't you pull this shit on me. You don't have the sense God gave a horsefly. I don't know what you're up to, but I can move you out where you'll have plenty to do if you're bored."

Cal could feel his heart pick up the pace. Ruggles was furious and he didn't know why.

"I didn't mean..." He couldn't finish the sentence.

"Hour's over," the guard said in his daily monotone.

Ruggles was gruffer than ever at the table. He ignored Cal, and even told Henry Whitehorse that he was damned sick and tired of hearing about Henry's women and his fucking Indian proverbs. Cal dreaded returning to the cell. He tried to figure out what had gone wrong and came up empty. He concentrated on the appeal and his lawyer's optimism. Maybe that was it. Ruggles hated him because he might get out. At any rate, it was going to be a damned long night.

But as it turned out, it didn't take long at all. The minute Cal and Ruggles were alone in the cell, and only muttered speech could be heard from the other inmates, Ruggles stood in front of Cal.

"I don't know," he said staring down at Cal who sat on the edge of his bed, "what the hell you were up to and I don't care. Whatever it is I want it stopped."

"It wasn't anything really," Cal said, "I just..."

"You listen to me. You know who the most hated bastards are in this place next to you mo-lesters and the fucking hippies? I'll tell you, boy, because you're stupid. The informers that's who, and you're starting to look just like one. Curiosity. Shit. Everybody in this goddamned place knows you're likely to be short time, and you don't want them speculating on why."

Cal could feel the blood pounding in his face. He could only continue to stare at the button on Ruggles' shirt. He didn't dare look up.

"And don't you think you're walking out of here, boy, and leaving your shit on my shoes. Got that?"

Cal felt faint with the foolishness of it all. Why hadn't he thought of that himself? Always having to have someone yell the facts into his face. *She was raped. That is the man. You're a goddamned fool.*

"I didn't think," Cal said. "Sorry."

"You stick to reading books and keeping clean, boy," Ruggles said, and turned away. Then he added in the sickeningly sweet tone Cal hated, "I most sincerely expect you to do that."

"Yes, sir."

Ruggles snatched a new book off the desk, and leaned back in his bunk. "Christ," he muttered as he opened it.

Cal lay back on his bed and closed his eyes. He thought of nothing except getting out until the guards signaled the end of the day.

What had ever made him think he could trick the old dog in the bed next to him.

The next few days passed unbearably slowly, impeded by Cal's anxiety about the appeal and the general hostile mood of Ruggles. Cal's skin crawled, the soles of his feet itched, and he felt slightly sick to his stomach most of the time. Why hadn't he left well enough alone with Ruggles?

Then the anger would return and he would repeat again and again, I have a right to know. It is my fucking *right*.

The problem was, nobody had to tell him anything.

The day of the meeting came at last, and Ruggles acknowledged it with a single comment.

"I hope to hell it goes your way, boy. I'm sick of the sight of your face."

So Cal sat in the library, watching the door, watching Ruggles. And as he waited, he had to wonder at Ruggles' continued anger. There had to be more to it than he understood.

Finally, Watkins appeared at the door.

"Call for you, Newkirk," he said. "In the warden's office." Watkins' face revealed nothing.

Cal's knees shook as the guard escorted him to the office. What if there was another delay? This might all mean nothing at all.

The warden nodded to Cal as he entered the room, pushed a button on the telephone, and handed the receiver to Cal.

"Yes?" Cal whispered.

"We got the date," the lawyer said, and Cal felt his knees momentarily go, and he pulled himself up.

"When?" he asked.

"Seven weeks from tomorrow," the lawyer said. "Not as soon as I'd hoped, but the court's bogged down with new draft trials. We'll just have to live with it."

I'll have to live with it, Cal thought.

"But that's not the best news," the lawyer went on. "I've got more. New evidence. I could get a new trial on that even if the judge wasn't a crackpot."

What new evidence? "I don't understand," Cal said.

"The little girl," the lawyer said. "She told her teacher all about it. That father of hers has made such a perpetual pest of himself, he's made everyone a little crazy. The girl ended up in tears, so scared she had to tell someone that her daddy was wrong about what happened."

"Why don't they just let me out then?" Cal asked.

"I wish it were that simple, but it's not," the lawyer said. "But what it does mean is that we can probably count on a change of venue and lowered bail. The teacher will testify at the trial."

"Bail?" Cal asked.

"Bail. I'm working on that," the lawyer said. "And I'll be up to see you soon and we can go over everything." He paused. "There's one more thing, Cal," the lawyer went on. "Your wife is divorcing you. I don't know what you want to do about that. I can stall if you want to try to reconcile."

Reconcile. Mary Beth. Wife.

"No," Cal said. "Let her go ahead. I don't want to see her."

"You're certain?"

"Yes," Cal said, a strange feeling of ending coming over him. "I'm positive."

"Well, I have to say, it's better in the long run—for the case. Her behavior has been less than exemplary since the trial, and that's got people talking."

Mary Beth at Hawley's in her honeymoon black. Cal closed his eyes.

"If the appeal goes through, how long before the trial?" Cal asked.

"Hard to say. Might be months, but as I said, I'm confident about the bail. If we get the trial date, you'll be out." The lawyer laughed. "We've got them on the blocks, Cal. Just hang in there."

"I don't have any money," Cal said.

"That's what I'm working on," the lawyer said, and then it was over. Cal handed the receiver to the warden, who replaced it.

"Well, boy?" the warden asked.

"Appeal date is seven weeks from tomorrow."

"Well, that's step one."

Cal nodded. He had nothing else to say.

Ruggles didn't even bother to acknowledge Cal's return to the library. Cal stood in front of his desk, waiting, and finally Ruggles looked up.

The bastard would not ask.

"Seven weeks to the appeal," he said. "My lawyer thinks he can get me out on bail right away if they give me a new trial."

"Try and live that long," was Ruggles' only advice.

Cal passed the next week in a daze, immersed in uncontrolled dreams of freedom. With his eyes closed, he could see wide green pastures, fields of grain. The flag in front of the post office, a playground filled with children. But when he opened his eyes, the walls of the prison seemed even closer than before. At times, he thought he had difficulty breathing the air, and it began to feel as if his lungs could not stand the pressure. He noticed a peculiar steady odor he could not recall from before. He repeated *I'm going to get out* so many times that the very litany of the phrase seemed to be driving him mad. So many things could go wrong.

Ruggles was as angry as ever, and Cal had no one to talk to about anything.

Finally his lawyer arrived, and they spent the morning going over what was likely to happen at the appeal. Cal watched the man speak, and thought it was strange, all that enthusiasm and energy. Out of place inside the prison.

"I want you," the lawyer told Cal, "to spend the time you've got left here doing some preparation. You just pretend the appeal will go through, and think about getting ready for the trial."

"Like what?" Cal asked.

"I want you," he said, "to be prepared this time to testify on your own behalf. Go over and write down everything that happened. Get it absolutely clear in your mind."

Cal nodded in agreement, although he could feel that stone

of terror forming in his stomach. He would have to answer questions from the prosecution.

When it was over, he was taken back to the library only to have the fear grow in the silence imposed by Ruggles.

What if they asked about his father?

And as if that wasn't enough to make him shake through the day and the dinner, he returned to his cell to find a letter from Mary Beth. The sight of the pink envelope and her childish scrawl made him want to tear it up without regard to the contents.

Ruggles made that impossible.

"Getting threats from the outside now, are you boy?"

Cal ripped open the envelope. A money order fell onto the bed and he picked it up. $265.00, made out to him. What the hell? He opened the folded pink note.

The letter was brief.

> Dear Callant,
>
> I couldn't afford to pay the rent on the house myself, so I moved out. I sold the furniture and stuff, so here is your half which your lawyer said I had to give you even though I did all the work. The furniture was all pretty old, so I couldn't get much money. Your lawyer said I should have asked you, but that's too late now, since it's all gone. I live at Tina's now and I stored some of your junk in daddy's garage but the water got to it, and since it was all rotten my mother threw it out. I'm sorry about that.
>
> I hope you have a good life some day.
>
> Mary Beth
>
> P.S. The divorce takes six months to be final so it will be the end of the summer, I think.

The words danced before Cal's eyes. Divorce. Final. Six months. Gone, everything gone. The pictures, the scrapbooks, the drawings. The dishes. His clothes. The evidence. Gone.

He stood in the middle of his cell, the letter in his hand, the money order on the bed. $265.00.

His words from his soul came half strangled from his throat. "Goddamn her," he muttered. "Goddamn her to hell."

He looked at the door of the cell. No one. No one anywhere, nothing left. He turned to face Ruggles, who stared at him through those damned thick glasses, and Cal thought the man smiled even though he wasn't sure, and he moved toward the man with the open book, the letter in his hand.

"She sold everything," he shouted, and Ruggles straightened as if he were ready and able to defend himself. "She sold every damned thing I ever had, my life, for two hundred and sixty-five fucking dollars."

Ruggles put up a hand, and Cal thought he was going to hit him.

"Shut up," Ruggles hissed. "Shut up and show me the letter."

Cal could not move. He was melting, his face falling, sagging, and he could not move.

Ruggles snatched the letter out of Cal's hand, and read it quickly. "What was so damned important?" he asked Cal. "So the bitch sold it?"

"You bastard," Cal said, and reached for the letter, only to have his arm grabbed by Ruggles.

"You best settle down, boy," the man said, and once again, his massive body overwhelmed Cal. He could not stand there and face that sickening shade of gray.

"Leave me alone," Cal said, freeing his arm with a quick yank.

"You want me to call a guard?" Ruggles asked, his own voice low in his throat.

"I don't give a damn," Cal said, and he moved to his bed. There was, he knew, no damned place to go. No way to get out of this box he lived in. He sat down and put his head in his hands. He rocked back and forth, feeling the veins in his temples. Gone. The color, the pictures, the last remnants of anything gentle. He was only dimly aware of Ruggles in the cell. The silence was killing him.

Finally Ruggles spoke. "Why don't you just tell me what the hell this is all about?"

"It's a long story," Cal said. A long story indeed.

He heard Ruggles light a cigarette. "Is it an interesting one?"

"It's fucking fascinating," Cal said.

"Good," Ruggles said, and the smell of smoke filled the cell. "You got my undivided attention."

As he spoke, Cal marveled at Ruggles' grasp. It was a difficult story to tell although he had been through it in his mind many times. Back and forth in time, dancing between two tales. Dave's. His mother's. His own speculation.

"So," Cal said, "I figure this all happened in July 1944."

"You should've asked her, boy," Ruggles said.

Cal took a breath. "Well, I decided not to. And it's too damned late now, isn't it?"

Ruggles shook his head, but Cal wasn't discouraged. There was something in the set of Ruggles' shoulders.

Cal glanced at his watch. "Anyway," he said, "she told me this story about the carnival, so I figure the first part is close to true. The guy likely worked for the carnival. That makes sense, doesn't it?"

"I used to know a guy from Four Corners," Ruggles said, rubbing his chin. "He's dead."

Cal didn't see what that had to do with it, and the panic started to surface again. Who was the man? What would happen if he had to sit up there and be asked about him by some stranger who wanted to send him back to prison?

"Christ," Cal said, and he could feel his voice shaking. "What kind of a kid doesn't know who his father is?"

Ruggles straightened immediately, and Cal saw the flicker of anger again.

"I don't know, kid. What kind?"

Cal just stared at him. The conversation, he could tell, was over.

When Cal woke in the morning, he knew only one thing. His dreams had been filled with questions he could not answer, all the way from those asked by a dark-eyed man with a stick, to those put forth on paper by a long-forgotten history teacher. He was empty, and tired.

Ruggles acted as if nothing at all had happened, and the day passed slowly. Cal was irritated by everything, as if some parasite had taken up residence under his skin. He waited for Ruggles to make some crude joke about his story, to ridicule him for his stupidity. It was only a matter of time, he was certain. Cal would just have to wait until he was released, and then he would go about the search on his own.

That night, in the cell, Cal tried to concentrate on the book he was reading, but the words kept drifting before his eyes, and he would turn one page after another without understanding.

Then he heard Ruggles close his book with a dull thud.

"I've been pondering your situation here," Ruggles said.

Cal closed his own book. Here it came.

"Nobody's going to tell you anything, you know that, don't you?"

"So you say," Cal said.

"So you *know*," Ruggles said. "Who do you think could get this dope for you?"

"You," Cal said.

"Right."

Cal swung his feet off his bed and faced Ruggles. It was going to work after all, and he hadn't even seen it coming.

"How would you explain why you were asking?" Cal ventured. He didn't want the whole prison talking about the dumb boy who couldn't find his daddy.

Ruggles lit a cigarette. "Shit," he said. "Just when I think you've smartened up some. Since when do I need to explain what I do to any goddamned fool?"

Cal had to admit that was true. "Why would you do that?" Cal asked. "For me?"

Ruggles laughed, but Cal could see a strange distant look in the man's eyes. As if he remembered something a long way back. "Because I'm bored, kid. You just remember now, to keep your eyes and ears open, and as usual, your mouth shut."

When the lights were out, Cal lay with his eyes open. He couldn't wait to see how Ruggles handled this. He smiled in the dark.

"You know," Ruggles spoke from his bed, something Cal could never remember his doing before. "When I was a kid, my mother ditched out on my old man and me. Or he ditched her. Never knew for sure."

"You never heard from her?"

"Don't think so. My old man wasn't a talkative sort. Shit, she was probably living in some cheap-assed hotel turning tricks. But I used to wonder..."

"That must have been tough," Cal said. "You..."

Ruggles interrupted. "That's enough jaw, boy. Get some sleep."

Cal took a good deal of comfort in Ruggles' admission; it was the first thing he remembered when he woke. He wondered then if Ruggles had told him the truth, or merely wanted to give him a reason for agreeing to help. And although he waited for Ruggles to say more in the library when they were alone, no new revelations were forthcoming.

Ruggles didn't, however, waste any time. It was almost as if he called the dinner table to order the way board presidents in old movies did. And he was nothing if not to the point.

"I'm looking for someone," he said, "and I thought with all you boys' traveling experiences, you might have run across him. I got a *personal* reason for needing to find him."

Cal was filled with admiration. Ruggles said the word *personal* in a way that absolutely precluded any questions as to what it was.

"Christ knows what name he might be using." He shook his head as if overcome by memories. "Toughest buzzard I ever came across." Ruggles paused. "Except for me."

Cal had the silly vision of Ruggles accepting an academy award, and he shook away the giddiness lest it show.

"Probably worked a circus, or a rodeo. Maybe a carnival. Slick-tongued boy. Eye for the ladies."

A beautiful girl with long dark hair and gold loops in her ears. Running along a street in terror.

Cal looked around the table. He wondered if his hand shook. Most of the men were staring at their trays. Ancient Horace

Millward, a small-town petty thief whom Ruggles had already described as the biggest charity case at the table next to Cal, cleared his throat. Cal thought he detected a tremor in the man's voice as he began to speak, something he had not done since Cal joined the table.

"Knew a guy like that once. Worked the carny, yes he did. Mean bastard. Heard tell he cut the midget's throat one time over a game of penny-ante poker. Thing is, I think he was an Indian. Crow or Blackfoot. Carried a knife in his boot and wore a feather in his hat. Fearsome bugger."

"Indians don't cut throats," Henry Whitehorse said, his big brown face solemn. "Take-em scalp." The men at the table erupted into huge guffaws, and Ruggles squinted at Horace as if to warn them all.

"What I want you boys to do," Ruggles said, "and you know how nice I can be when you men do what I want, is to ask around a little. I need this information now."

Cal thought several of the men looked suspicious and the itch began on the soles of his feet. Careful, he thought.

"You just point out anybody you come across you think might know something," he said. "And keep in mind I ain't looking for an Indian or a nigger."

Stifled laughter. Cal scratched the side of his face.

Ruggles then lapsed into what seemed to be a no-nonsense silence. The effect was impressive. It was as if every man at the table was searching his mind for the currency Ruggles demanded. Amazing, was all Cal could think.

In the library, Ruggles took on the look of the fat satisfied cat.

"Think you might be part Indian?" he asked Cal.

"No," Cal said.

"No Crow, no Blackfoot? Ever feel like scalping a man or burning a town?" He slapped his knee at his own joke. "Firewater make you crazy?"

Banging on the doors and windows of his own home. Shouting to Mary Beth. Running, fleet-footed across the fields. Cal's hands went involuntarily to his face, as if to feel for a new formation of bone.

"Shit, you aren't part Indian," Ruggles said, seemingly annoyed at being taken seriously, even for a minute. "Any fool can see that."

"Maybe Italian," Cal ventured, trying to recover. "Dark hair and all." The fact that he didn't know began to bother him. Hell, his mother had never even told him where she got her dark hair.

"Mongrel," Ruggles said, "like me."

"I guess," Cal said.

"You know," Ruggles said, suddenly thoughtful. He tapped the eraser of a pencil on his desk. "We're going to hear more damned stories from this." He smiled. "Maybe I'll write one of those best-selling books and make a fortune."

"What would you call it?" Cal asked.

"*Bullshit Behind Bars*," Ruggles said. "Keep a shovel handy."

It didn't take long. That very night, at dinner, a man came up and whispered something to Ruggles. Cal could see Ruggles look over the heads of the other inmates to another corner of the room. "Bring him over," Ruggles said to the man. "You clear out," he said to Horace and another man who was still nameless to Cal. Two other men left, leaving Ruggles and Cal alone at one end of the table.

"Louis Malveso." Ruggles leaned to Cal. "Bad-check passer."

The nervous little man sat down on Ruggles' right and looked suspiciously at Cal.

"He's my secretary," Ruggles said. "What you got?"

Cal could see the man had a glass eye, and it struck him, as the man began to speak in quick quiet statements, that the glass eye looked at Ruggles, the good one at him.

"Back in the forties," the man began, and Cal heard Ruggles sigh, "when things was going better for me, I married this woman from up north. Ugly woman, but she had something, you know. Can't think for the life of me what it was, but there was something. Come from one of those big families spread over five counties. Goddamned if I can remember why I married that woman."

"Get to the point," said Ruggles.

"Am getting there," the man said. "Funny family. Married each other, if you know what I mean, and they got so's they had a little twisted look to them. Funny-shaped faces, if you know what I mean."

Malveso took his own face in his hands and pushed one side up and one side down. "She wasn't so bad. Hadn't gone that far yet, I guess."

Ruggles cleared his throat. "Don't sound like my man's type," he said. "He liked them young and pretty."

The man went on. "They was the ones that talked me into starting that damned turkey business. Turkeys are the stupidest animals that ever lived, did you know that?"

Ruggles looked at the man as if he might be giving them some competition.

"Drown in the rain, the dumb buggers do. That's no joke."

"What's this got to do with the man I'm hunting?"

"Well," the man said, leaning over to whisper, the blue glass eye glittering more than the real one, "that's when I hired me this man to help out. Big guy, like you described. Even looked a little like you. Smart bastard, too."

"He have a mustache?"

"Think so. Haven't thought much on him. Long time ago. Forty-six or forty-seven."

"Stay with you long?"

"Too long. Crazy devil. Said he was a wanderer, liked to roam around. Seems to me said he'd worked the carnival circuit. Seems to me he said that."

"Dark hair?"

"Those goddamned gobbling birds. Never knew how to shut up. All they thought about was eat, eat, eat. Turkeys stink, did you know that?"

Ruggles nodded again.

"Anyways, this big guy, he commenced to knock up one of my wife's sisters. Can't say I could see what he saw in Lorene. Funny gal. Didn't have the twisted face, but she always had the strange look in the eyes, if you know what I mean."

Cal stared at the man's glass eye.

"Right," Ruggles said.

"That family was a bunch of odd birds, let me tell you. One kid who had three toes on each foot. Poor bugger couldn't walk."

Ruggles shot the man a fierce look, and Cal began to feel nervous.

"Anyway, the old man—Lorene's father—my wife's father too, of course—he was hot. Seemed to me he just wanted someone outside his own family for a change, and he was threatening all sorts of mischief if the big man didn't do right by his little girl." Malveso laughed in a short croaking way. "Little girl. Hell, she was six feet if she was an inch. Funny family. Little men, big women. My wife, may her soul rest in hell wherever she is, was three inches taller than me."

"Where's this guy now?" Ruggles pressed him.

"So's anyway, this here big guy, he's supposed to drive these turkeys to a slaughterhouse. Had no taste for that myself. Dumb birds." He sniffed as if he could smell blood and feathers right then and there. "Can't eat a piece of turkey to this day. Still remember the smell."

"Get on with it."

"So's he gets in my truck. I must have still owed a thousand dollars on the mother. Maybe not. Maybe four hundred. Can't remember exactly. Gets in my truck and takes off with them gobbling birds. Have to tell you, I wasn't sorry to see them go."

"The bastard drove 'bout ten miles down the road, stopped the truck, and let every one of them prime-fed turkeys loose, that's what he did. Hell, they was run over by cars and eaten by dogs. Stupid bird, the turkey. There was feathers in the air for days."

Cal had to smile inside at the picture of fleeing turkeys even though Louie looked remorseful.

"So what happened to the man?"

"Don't know," Malveso said. "Never saw hide nor hair of him again."

"That's it?" Ruggles asked, irritated.

"That sound like your man?" Malveso asked, and Cal thought the man was blind in more ways than one.

"Messing with turkeys?"

"I just thought maybe..."

"Turkeys. Shit."

"He looked like you, I remember now. Funny man. Big and strong."

"What'd his kid look like?" Ruggles asked, and Cal knew he would have winked at him had he had the chance.

"Lorene's girl?" The man paused. "Looked just like her. Big girl." He paused again and smiled. "But she got the black mustache."

Ruggles chuckled. "Yeh," he said, "maybe that was him. Letting a bunch of fucking birds loose."

"I guess it was funny," Malveso said tentatively.

"A million laughs," Ruggles agreed. "Don't ring right though," he said, staring at the man. "Not mean enough."

With that, Louie Malveso swallowed hard, shook his head, looked up at the ceiling, and waited to be dismissed.

Instead, Ruggles got up from the table, and Cal rose with him.

"I'd stay out of the turkey business if I was you," he said to the nervous man.

As they walked to the guard by the door, Ruggles whispered to Cal, "Maybe you got a long lost sister, too, six foot tall with a mustache."

Cal had to admit it was funny, but the nagging notion of other relatives gained credence. Maybe he didn't want to know as much as he thought.

Not all the stories they heard were as amusing. They listened patiently while other convicts spilled the stories of their own downfalls with men who might have passed for Ruggles' man playing secondary roles. A man with a black mustache who had taken the rent money in a game of five-card stud, and forced the loser to rob a local bank. A man whose wife had been seduced by a dark-haired drifter. He had subsequently beaten his wife into oblivion. Tears ran down that man's face as he told his story, a fact that raised no sympathy from Ruggles. "It didn't go well with me," the man sobbed, "because I already had the record, you know. Other things that weren't my fault."

"I hate that kind of whining," Ruggles told Cal later. "Gets me in the gut every time."

Cal wondered if he had been sitting in the prison for years the way some men had if he would come to the conclusion that everything was Mary Beth's fault. Or his mother's.

If he located his father, would he blame him? He would try to remember how pathetic the other men seemed when they told their stories of misunderstanding.

And any fears that Cal had that Ruggles would get discouraged at listening, would give up the search, were soon put to rest. If anything, he became more determined. Cal thought it became a real test of him in some way. First of all, he managed to locate a map of the area and began marking times and places and possible sightings. A list of vile acts. A network of petty larceny. He decided to "sweeten the pot" with a few fancy tales of the man, and Cal sat at the dinner table with a certain amount of discomfort as he listened to Ruggles. The man had taken on the given name of Gene, although God knew how many aliases he had used. He was so convincing sometimes that even Cal momentarily forgot he was talking about a man who did not actually exist.

"Good-lookin' guy," he said with real admiration. "Had to beat the women off with a club." He shook his head. "Got so's he couldn't stand it, them after him all the time. Wanted to tie him down, keep him for themselves." His face took on a peculiar twist. "Nothing worse than a pawing woman, a grasping one."

Cal wondered if Ruggles was remembering someone in particular from his own life.

"They'll ruin you," another man said mournfully. "Bleed your last drop."

"So you can see why he was the way he was," Ruggles said with authority. "Why he turned on them the way he did."

"You think he kills women?" Henry Whitehorse asked.

"Maybe. Can't say for sure." He looked thoughtful. "Mean sucker."

"A real lady killer," a young man with twelve service station holdups to his credit said.

The laughter was cut short by Ruggles' hand hitting the table. "I want," he said, catching the frightened look on the young man's face, "some real information, and I want it now. I figure it's about time you all start repaying some of the favors I show you. I'm starting to feel you all aren't taking this serious enough."

There was silence then until the guards signaled the end of the mealtime and the prisoners were ushered back to their cells.

For the next day, Ruggles employed a new tack. Glowering looks. Not a word. The nervous itching began to plague Cal again, and he began to fear that Ruggles was taking it too seriously himself. What if he was out of control? What if he started to take even more extreme steps? It was as if, in fact, the search for Cal's father had been replaced by Ruggles' quest for someone he actually knew. A man who had run off with his own long-lost mother. Did Ruggles remember what was true?

Just as Cal was about to suggest they forget the whole thing, a man came into the library.

"Maybe got something for you," he whispered to Ruggles, and Cal strained to hear.

"Pennington. The strange guy who keeps to himself. Been in and out. Assaults. Bad temper. Here and other places. Says he knows about a guy, but wants something in return."

"Tell him he can keep his teeth," Ruggles said.

The man squirmed.

"And breathing," Ruggles added.

"Listen." The man bent closer to Ruggles and Cal could barely make out what he was saying. "This guy's a little nuts. Quiet, but mean."

"Meaner than me?"

"I mean, something's eating at this bastard."

"Tell him I'll talk to him tonight."

When the man left, Ruggles turned to Cal. "Shit," he said, "I hope this bugger's got something interesting. These boys're starting to bore me."

"So do I," Cal agreed. The appeal date was getting closer all the time.

The redheaded man wouldn't come to Ruggles. Ruggles was going to have to go to him, and Cal could see that annoyed him. "I hope you appreciate this, kid," he hissed at Cal as they walked across to where the man sat. They sat down, and the man, whose face was covered with freckles, continued to eat his dinner. He ate slowly, patiently, as if they were not there at all. He said nothing.

Ruggles shook his head, and for a minute, Cal was afraid he was going to get up and leave.

"Hear you might have something for me," Ruggles finally said.

"Who's that?" the man asked, nodding his head in the direction of Cal.

"My fucking research assistant. Got something or not?"

"Depends on what you got for me," the man said. He had just the slightest trace of a Southern drawl, unusual in the prison. It made him seem even more like a big ranch hand. And the contact had been right, Cal thought. Something simmering there, just beneath the surface. Beneath the innocence of freckles and the eyes that were pale blue, was a festering of some sort.

Ruggles drew back. It was almost like watching a dance. Cal could see him calculating how to proceed. Sizing the red-haired man up in his own way.

In a surprisingly soft voice, he said, "Why don't you tell me what it is you want, *Red.*"

"Don't try to rile me," the man said, putting his napkin over his tray. "Red's what I go by."

"Lucky guess," said Ruggles.

Red folded the largest hands Cal had ever seen over his tray.

"Hear you got kin around Four Corners," Red said.

Cal wondered when Ruggles had added that part of the story.

"Maybe," Ruggles said.

"I want someone there watched," Red said. "I'm from there. Sort of."

Ruggles narrowed his eyes. "Born there?"

"No. Wife's there. From Texas first off."

Four Corners. Where his mother was from. Maybe this was going to be it after all. Cal wished Ruggles would let him ask just a few questions.

"Something's going on with her," Red said. "And I want to know exactly what."

"Might handle that."

"I got two more years," Red said. "And I want that woman waiting on the front porch for me when I get out."

"Some women aren't the kind to wait," Ruggles said.

"This one fucking better be," Red said, rubbing one of his gigantic knuckles. "She's just got to stay out of temptation's way."

And Red's, Cal thought. If she valued her life.

"I got an idea," Ruggles said.

"She's real young," Red went on. "And don't always know what's good for her." Her name was Lucy, he said, and he had a child, a red-haired boy of four. "Waiting for his daddy to come home."

"You tell me what you've got for me," Ruggles said, "and I'll take care of it."

"Don't want her hurt," Red said. "Just so's she understands things."

"Right."

"Lucy's mother, she was born right there in Four Corners, too. So was her dad. Lots of family up there, but they didn't really take too kindly to me. Can't depend on them, if you understand. Always treated me like the outsider. They're funny up in that part of the woods. Funny about that."

"What about my man?" Ruggles asked.

It was odd, to hear a man talk about people who would have known his mother. Small town. Knew everyone.

"This ain't a short story, mister."

Cal and Ruggles both leaned in toward the man. So intent was Cal on the man and his story, that he didn't notice the guard approaching.

"Warden wants you, Ruggles. Right now."

"Christ," Ruggles said. "I'm busy."

"Not too busy. Now."

"This man's telling me a joke," Ruggles protested. "Wouldn't want me to miss the punch line."

What was Ruggles doing? He was going to have to go with the guard. Was Cal supposed to stay and hear Red's story?

The guard answered that question for him.

"You, too, Newkirk."

Cal could see Red physically and mentally withdrawing from them both.

"Later," Ruggles said as he and Cal stood to go with the guard, and the look in Red's eyes said, never.

"You'd think," Ruggles said as they walked, "the warden could do without my advice for one damned day."

The guard snickered. "You're full of shit, Ruggles."

"Leave us alone," the warden said to the guard once Cal and Ruggles had been delivered. He did not offer them each a chair.

"Now," the warden said when the door closed behind the guard, "what the Christ is going on?"

Ruggles said nothing. He stood with his hands clasped behind his back and stared over the warden's head at his map. Cal tried to do the same, but he felt shaky.

"Who you looking for with all these questions, Ruggles?" the warden asked. "It can't be your long-lost brother because as far as *you* know, you *ain't* got one."

Oh God, Cal thought. Why was the warden determined to make Ruggles mad? It wasn't going to make him tell him anything. He looked sideways and saw Ruggles' clenched fist.

"Don't know what you're talking about," Ruggles said through his teeth.

"Want me to leak it out that you're snooping on commission from me?" the warden asked. "That ought to liven things up some."

Ruggles didn't say anything. He just stood and stared.

The warden turned to Cal. "You tell me what's up."

Cal took a breath. "I haven't really been paying much attention, what with my appeal, and all, and..."

"Don't give me that crap," the warden said.

"I'm looking to locate a guy," Ruggles said. "Owes me some money."

"Right," the warden snarled. "The world is just filled with your debtors. Christ, don't you buggers ever learn?" He sighed. "Maybe you're tired of that nice cushy job in the library," the warden added. "Maybe you'd rather be out breaking rock."

"I don't mind breaking things," Ruggles said.

God, he was stubborn, Cal thought. Maybe he should just tell the warden what they were really doing.

"This isn't going to help you, boy," the warden said to Cal.

"He's got nothing to do with it," Ruggles said. "He just stays with me. Like to remind you, at your request."

The warden leaned back in his chair. Cal watched as a slow smile spread across his face. The warden looked first to Ruggles, then to Cal, and he buzzed for the guard.

"You boys got till tomorrow this time to tell me the truth," he said sweetly.

Cal scanned the Canadian border on the warden's map. Ruggles was going to be furious, what with the remark about the brother and all. He hoped Ruggles understood that Cal hadn't said one word to anybody.

And when the door closed behind them, Cal could have sworn he heard the warden laugh.

Ruggles sat on the edge of his bed, thinking. Cal didn't know what to say or do about the expression on Ruggles' face. It could only be described as profound annoyance, but Cal supposed he ought to be grateful it wasn't blind rage. *A brother you know about.*

And it seemed to Cal as if word of the difficulty had somehow spread down the corridors of cells, along the walls, into the whispers of the other convicts. Something sinister afoot. Some strange overtone. How many other men had the warden already asked about Ruggles' questions? Maybe Red was a setup, another story going nowhere.

And why had the warden laughed? If he was contemplating the joy of making a fool of Ruggles, Cal was dead. The memory of the beating came back, the Hail Mary full of grace, mercy, mercy, only this time Ruggles was in the pack.

And just when it looked as if they were getting someplace. Hell, everything was just another trick, another damned made-up story. How many lies had they listened to already, how many more were about to be told? He was even afraid to tell Ruggles just to forget it. It would be like asking him to admit defeat.

Well, dammit, he wasn't going to be caught again. If he had to make it alone, he would damned well do it. He would become just like Red Pennington, keep to himself, look so ferocious no one would dare come near him.

"Why don't you read or something," Ruggles finally said. "You're making me nervous as hell just sitting there while I'm trying to think."

Cal picked up his book dutifully, then felt his face redden at his own obedience on the heels of an oath. There was an odd flickering of the lights, and when it stopped, they were dimmer than before. The damned air was attacking him, too, he thought. Something as impersonal as electricity. He clapped the book shut and closed his eyes. He heard, or thought he did, the sound of running feet. Maybe there would be a riot or a jail break, and he would just slip out with the rest.

The warden had laughed.

Ruggles was tapping one finger on his knee, a tapping that might as well have been some kind of code. Cal thought he heard shouting in the distance. Running. What was happening?

"What the hell is going on?" Ruggles said, his back straightening as if it would improve his hearing. "You hear that?"

All Cal could do was sigh with relief that Ruggles had heard it, too.

"You don't think it's a break-out, do you?" Cal asked.

Ruggles looked at him as if he were a moron. "If it was a fucking break-out, I'd know about it," he said.

Two guards walked by with Red Pennington between them, and he looked furious. It was time for lights out, but they did not go. They were dim, but still lit.

"Something's up," Ruggles said, standing by the door of the cell. He leaned casually there, waiting for some word. A tide of whisper like a low single wave in an otherwise still sea rolled toward them. But before it reached them, two more guards appeared at the door.

They wanted Ruggles.

"Jesus Christ Almighty," Ruggles said. "Office hours are over."

"Stuff it," the tallest guard said.

Cal was left alone, and the wave rolled away and was quiet again, stopped by the presence of three guards stationed at equal intervals down the corridor.

All Cal could do was wait.

The warden had been angry about Ruggles' questions, Cal understood that. But nothing to cause this kind of shakedown. It was like an aroma of death, the kind of atmosphere he assumed prevailed every time some new speculation about using the firing squad came up. They couldn't be taking prisoners from their cells and putting them to death without notice. Without notice. He was thinking like the outside again. Where things were fair once in a while. He had too much going on in his head, causing him to understand nothing.

God, he was tired of never having an answer. And here he was, once again, without anyone to ask.

It was over an hour before Ruggles was returned to the cell.

"Somebody hit that kid," he said simply, as if it were enough of an explanation.

"What kid?" Cal asked.

Ruggles shook his head as if Cal were an idiot, this time. "The draft dodger, the skinny blond kid who came in a couple a days ago. Don't you listen?" He sat down on his bunk. "Going to be a fucking long night, but it's going to get the warden off our backs, at least for a while."

"Hit him?"

"Somebody took him in the shower."

"You mean he's dead?" Cal could not place the kid.

"You're a genius," Ruggles said. He shook his head.

"Why did they send for you?"

"Because they're so stupid they think I might mess with something like this."

"Do you know who did it?"

"Boy, I don't care about the fuckers and I don't care about any war in some gook country."

"What did they want with Pennington?"

"They don't exactly confide in me about the other prisoners," Ruggles said in his phony-baloney snob voice. Then he frowned. "Now let's get back to business. There's something funny about the warden's interest in my questions. I want to know exactly how much he *knows* about you."

Cal could not get rid of the picture of some pale thin boy dead on the shower-room floor. Blood growing out from under him.

"You listening, boy?"

The question. Cal thought. "He's read the trial transcript, but there's nothing there about this. He's talked to my lawyer, but I don't think he knows anything. Except about my wife. *Ex*-wife." Cal could not remember telling him anything else.

"That bastard knows something. You tell him about some bugger raping your mother?"

Cal burned at the words. Spoken words. "Maybe he thinks you're after some man that got away with your woman?" Cal said without thinking.

"Don't go guessing, boy. It doesn't suit you."

"I don't know why you think it's me he wonders about."

"Because he knows I'm not dumb."

That didn't make any sense to Cal, but he wasn't about to

argue now. A bloody naked kid crumpled up on the floor of a shower. A man with mean black eyes and a mustache, unflinching before the questions.

"The way I see it," Ruggles said, "I've done all the goddamned work so far. Now it's your turn."

What if whoever killed the boy decided Cal was to be next? He couldn't shake the thought.

Ruggles took out a package of cigarettes and shook one loose. "Now this is the way I figure it," he said, lighting one. "We're going to turn the tables completely and tell the truth."

Cal wondered immediately exactly which truth that was. The story about the turkeys, the one about Ruggles' mother, or perhaps a completely new one that he was supposed to make up?

"This Pennington thing might not pan out at all. Another dead end. The *man* who can find the man is the warden. He's got all the sticks."

"I don't know why he'd do that for us. For me, I mean."

"Let's assume he *might*. We'll get the story out of Pennington while the warden's occupied with this latest crap, then when he calls us in again, you can spill your guts." He took a long drag from the cigarette. "Spill your guts," he repeated with a laugh. "We're going to operate on the truth here, boy, and we don't want the patient to die on the table." He laughed again, and Cal wished he could find the situation that amusing, too.

"What if he doesn't believe it?"

"'Course he'll believe it," Ruggles said. "It's the damned truth, isn't it?"

Ruggles leaned back against the wall, and blew a stream of smoke at the ceiling. He smiled, obviously pleased with his idea.

Cal rubbed his eyes. He wondered when these confessions would ever end. "It's the truth," he whispered.

They waited in the library the next day. They watched the clock and they watched each other. No one came in. Activity had been suspended while the investigation into the killing proceeded. There had not been enough time at breakfast to try to get to Red. They would have to hope for lunch or dinner. Cal sat at his own desk, a book open in front of him, but spent most of the time staring into space thinking. He finally took out a pencil and a pad of paper and began, in a slow careful script, to organize his story.

"You don't think Red killed that kid, do you?" he finally asked Ruggles.

"That would be a stroke of bad luck," Ruggles said. "But I don't think so. He strikes me as the type who worries about himself. Can't see him killing anyone who hasn't messed with him directly."

Cal thought he detected a slight note of warning in that statement. Pennington with the soft drawl and the boyish manner and unmistakable violence beneath it all. If prison had taught Cal anything, it was to see that. He thought of Red's wife and son, and was fearful for them both. If he had to get the information, should he tell the truth then, too? Regardless?

The clock turned closer to noon. "What do you think?" Cal asked Ruggles.

"I think no news is good news."

"I'll be ready," Cal said, looking at the notepad.

"You better be."

The cafeteria was filled with the hushed conversation of conspiracy. Who had been questioned, who knew what? Cal watched anxiously for Red to appear, and listened with half of his mind to the talk at the table.

"I think it was more than one," Henry Whitehorse said. "These things," he said solemnly, "they aren't one man's gripe."

"Makes sense," Candy Rumford said, the liquor-store robber with the both likely and unlikely name. "They won't get nothin' out of anybody on this one."

Ruggles rubbed his chin. "You always got one weak link in a chain," he said. "That's why I never use one."

Cal wondered why Ruggles seemed to deliberately cast suspicion on himself. Another facet he did not understand.

Red was almost the last man to appear, and Cal tried to contain his impatience as the man slowly moved through the line, as he walked to his own lonely place. Had they been questioning him again? Was this killing going to make him clam up tighter than ever?

"Bastard got what he deserved," Ruggles said, looking at Cal. "Got to remember that." Cal saw him look over at Red.

"Come on, kid," he said to Cal as he stood from the table. Together they dumped their trays and walked over to where Red sat. Cal was certain that every eye in the place was on them.

Ruggles sat down and leaned over the table. Cal sat nervously, his back turned partially away from Pennington.

"Ready to make the deal?" Ruggles said.

Red looked across the table. "They're trying to nail this killing on me."

"They're trying to nail it on everyone," Ruggles said.

"They pulled me in twice already."

"Listen, we haven't got that much time," Ruggles said. "I can do your little favor, got it all lined up," he said. "Now, let's hear this little story before the lid clamps on real tight."

"When can you get me the information?" Red asked.

"Maybe a month, maybe a week. I said I'd get it and I will."

Red looked around as if to make certain no one could hear, and Ruggles tapped a finger on the table. Cal began to manufacture a kind story about Red's wife. Faithful, true, weeps every night for her beloved husband. Shit, he could be as good as his mother if it came right down to fairy tales. He wanted Red's story now.

"I wouldn't miss this chance if I were you, buddy," Ruggles added.

Red leaned even closer across the table.

"'Bout five years ago," Red said, "when I was on the circuit, I ended up in the Wade County jail overnight with a guy that sounds like your man. Black hair, mustache. 'Bout the right age. I'd had a little skirmish with some suit-wearing dude who thought we was abusing the animals. They don't give one damn in hell if some bull tromps all over a man, but let them think you've shocked up an animal and they're all fancy mad."

Wade County. About the middle of the state.

"Get on with it," Ruggles said, looking around. Cal looked too. The hall was thinning out if you didn't count the extra guards.

"Guy was hauled in for assaulting some woman, and had a big mouth. Liked to brag."

"Old Gene can get real funny about women," Ruggles said, and Cal marveled at the naturalness of the lie.

"Seemed more than a little crazy to me," Red said. "Something weird about him. Said he'd been arrested before, and he was right proud that they'd never been able to make it stick. Got to tell you, I had the feeling he was making a goodly portion up... Hated women, though."

"They make it stick that time?"

Red shook his head. "Woman went to pieces and wouldn't identify him. He just laughed. Seems they brought her in with her husband. Seems she had been punched around by him, too. Seems like maybe she asked for it. I tell you, the guy just laughed and they had to let him go."

"That isn't much," Ruggles said. "Ever run into him again?"

"No."

"Tell you anything else?"

"There was the carnival business. He talked about what a great scam that was, and about how women would just do anything he wanted for one of his prizes. Some cheap piece of glass or a statue of a cat."

A dark-haired women with gold earrings eyeing the blue glass bowl. "Oh, I want it so badly," she said, leaning closer over the counter to pitch her coin. "You're such an old meanie for not giving it to me."

Cal shook his head. The voice belonged to Mary Beth. The buzzer signaling the end of lunch sent a tremor up Cal's back.

"See that was the thing. We was both in town for the Fourth of July. He was with another carnival then. Me with the local rodeo. We talked about being in the same places, what with the circuit and all, at the same time."

"Exactly five years ago?" Ruggles asked.

Red scratched his head. "About. No. That's wrong. Six years ago."

Wade County. Six years ago. July Fourth. Flags waving. A dead draft dodger in the shower. Everything connected, Cal thought. This was more preposterous than his mother's story.

"You come with me," a guard said, and for a moment, Cal thought the man was talking to him.

Red sighed and stood. "Again?" he asked, his eyes hardening into bright angry specks of the present.

"That's not bad," Ruggles said to Cal as they got up from the table. "If I didn't know better, I'd think you blabbed your story to him, too."

Cal couldn't shake the image of the young woman leaning over the penny-toss counter, and he thought he had heard everything before. It was just another recitation.

All carnivals had barkers. All of them had penny-toss booths. The prizes were pretty much the same. One man who worked the circuit was much like any other who did. A small circle. Like the world of Dickens.

A man who hated women. Mary Beth would argue that he had inherited that tendency directly. That was an interesting idea. In his own stupidity, had he married her to punish her along with women in general? The little girl? It sounded like something a psychiatrist would come up with, but it didn't feel right to him. Maybe the man had a good side. Women did seem to take to him. A braggart and a liar. Hard to know. For sure a rapist and a woman beater. Nice blood.

It made him feel right at home. One of the boys, finally.

So Ruggles and Cal had to wait for the warden to solve his crime and get back to them. Cal, having gone over his story many times, was starting to have the same feeling about it as he had about most things these days. A fairy tale of sorts where all the characters were evil. Now, whenever he wrote something down, it became a fiction. After all, nothing happened in prison.

"You ready to spit this out?" Ruggles said, as if the warden had an unfailing nose for the truth. Cal had to admit, though, the man did seem gifted in that area. He hoped to hell the ability came with age. He watched Ruggles wait right along with him. The remark the warden had made about Ruggles' *brother*, the insinuation about Ruggles' mother. It amazed Cal that Ruggles had never mentioned it since. As if no reference had been made at all. Perhaps he had gotten used to it long ago.

The guard brought a letter from Cal's lawyer. Everything was going well, very well indeed. In his consultations with others, the lawyer was more confident than ever. Cal should start making plans. He didn't advise starting up in Yellow Fork again. The people there had softened some, but why not get a new start somewhere else?

Cal put the letter on his desk. The lawyer sounded so certain, it seemed unlucky.

Ruggles looked at him expectantly. "The lawyer thinks we've got it knocked. Even thinks I'll get out on bail if the appeal goes through," Cal said.

"Hmm," Ruggles said, puffing on a cigarette. "You better be ready for the warden then. Time's running low."

"I will be ready," Cal said.

"When you get out," Ruggles said, "*if* you get out, I got some things I want you to get for me." He paused. "Some books. I'll make a list. Some chocolate. Some cigars. And Jane Russell."

"Jane Russell?"

"Right. Ever see *The Outlaw?* She's my type of woman."

"Well, I'll go right to Hollywood and get her," Cal said. He had a dim memory of Jane Russell sprawled against a bale of hay. Blouse off the shoulder. A lot of leg. Ruggles and Jane Russell. Cal smiled. Hell, the gate might as well be open right now.

Start planning, his lawyer advised.

Don't go back to Yellow Fork.

The big-boned stupid farmer might harm him. How did his lawyer know but what he might, he just might have a surprise for that liar himself?

It didn't matter. The minute he was released, he was going straight to Four Corners and find out all he could.

"Goddammit," he said, laughing, pounding his fist on his desk. "I just can't fucking believe it."

"I might want some magazines, too," Ruggles said, still dreaming of Jane Russell. "Under the counter."

Ruggles and Cal were summoned to the warden's office just before lunchtime the next day. Ruggles grumbled. "Right, get us when we're hungry. Make us miss a meal, shit."

"I didn't know you were so crazy about the food," Cal said as they walked. He could not stop smiling, no matter how hard he tried, and Henry Whitehorse, at dinner the night before, had accused him of grinning like a dying coyote, whatever that meant. Henry often said things that didn't make sense to Cal.

Plus, he'd been over his reasons, and he thought they sounded pretty good. Something that would appeal to the warden. He hoped to hell Ruggles wouldn't laugh.

The warden looked tired and uneasy, and not about to be agreeable. "You might as well sit down," he said to the two of them.

The warden leaned back in his chair. "You get a letter from your lawyer, boy?" he asked.

"Yes, sir."

The warden ignored Ruggles for the time. "Well," he went on, "I mean to tell you, boy, I've gone to some lengths for you. Now I think it's about time you do something for me in return. Here I am sitting in this place with somebody who killed a draft dodger, and you and Mr. Ruggles here are just acting as if no word about this is out on the floor, in the air. Nobody knows nothing. And yet—let me remind you, I have done these little favors for both of you."

He turned quickly to Ruggles. "Isn't that so, Mr. Ruggles? You with the cushy job in the library. You who can get a son of a bitch like Red Pennington to hold an audience with you. And yet you don't seem to feel like sharing anything with me, the man who is responsible for that *cushy* library job." He swung back to Cal, "And for letters recommending that your case be given careful, I said *careful* scrutiny." He took a deep breath.

Cal was spellbound. It was like listening to a singer, or a famous speechmaker. The ups and downs in tone, the sweetness and the threat.

"You start, Ruggles," the warden said. "Once again, you tell me what you know or what you think."

Ruggles looked considerate. He looked contemplative. He

shook his head sorrowfully. "No one's bragging about this one, boss."

Now Cal knew why the warden did things for Ruggles. It was to keep up these symphonic interchanges.

"Goddammit," the warden shouted, "is that all you can say? I've had to take every kid in this place who even looks like he might have known a draft dodger and put them in solitary. I'm not going to have a rash of killing in this goddamned place, not on my record, no sir, and you're telling me, you, the great prick of this whole place, you haven't heard a fucking whisper?"

"That," Ruggles said, leaning forward in his chair, "is *exactly* what I'm telling you." Now he was the authority. Serious. "I don't get no feel that this is a conspiracy, no bunch of bongos getting together and raising the flag. No feel at all. I can't even get wind that the kid was popped for that reason. Might have had a drug line."

"Shit," the warden said, "the killer carved the word *coward* on his back."

"How the hell am I supposed to know that?" Ruggles said, clearly unhappy that he did not.

The warden sneered at him and turned to Cal. "You hear anything about that? Anybody accuse you of being a sympathizer?"

Cal shook his head. "Nobody talks to me." It made him sick to think about someone slicing a word onto the flesh of another.

"You're telling me that noise isn't around the floor?"

"Hasn't come by me," Ruggles said.

"Well, either you're losing your touch, or this is a goddamned well-kept secret. Hard to believe."

"I think you're looking for one man," Ruggles said. "And hell, it could be anybody."

"Maybe," the warden said, rubbing his chin. "Maybe."

Cal looked at Ruggles just as the warden spoke again.

"I want, in twenty-four words or less, to know what the hell the two of you are up to with all the questions about some man from the past."

"It's got nothing to do with the killing," Ruggles said. "So if we might be *ex*-cused..."

Cal expected the warden to hit the roof, but the man just leaned back and laughed.

"I gave you the word before, Ruggles, so quite stalling and cough it up. I can deal with two problems at once."

"It's my fault," Cal said quickly, and even Ruggles looked startled, as if he wasn't ready. Cal's carefully outlined strategy vanished.

"Let's hear it."

"I asked Ruggles to help me find out who my father is."

Ruggles groaned.

The warden's smile faded. He leaned forward, and Cal stared at him, determined not to be thrown by his own unexpected beginning.

"You what?" the warden said. Whatever he had expected from the two men, this was clearly not it. "Your father?"

"Christ," Ruggles said. "Jes-sus Christ."

"Shut up, Ruggles," the warden said. He turned back to Cal. "You better explain the hows and whys of that, boy, and I haven't got all day."

Cal took a deep breath, and began with his mother and the photograph of the man in the World War II uniform. He told the story as quickly and clearly as he could manage. Every once in a while, the warden would stop him with a "Whoa, boy, run that by again," or would not and say, "Hmmm." Ruggles just fidgeted impatiently, and Cal expected him to break in any moment with a much shorter version. Finally, Cal got to the letter from Mary Beth, and the fact that all of the things from his past were gone. It seemed like a good closing note.

The warden leaned back in his chair. "I knew it, Ruggles. I suspicioned something like that. You think you're so damned smart."

"I like to do a fellow a good turn when I can," Ruggles said.

"Sure you do," the warden said. "You must have heard some right tall tales. You can spin them out for me someday when I'm real bored."

"That doesn't matter," Ruggles said. "We got something."

The warden turned to Cal. "You did?"

"*I* did," Ruggles said.

"From Pennington?" the warden asked.

"From Pennington," Ruggles answered, as if to make clear that he was the spokesman now.

"Suppose you just tell me what that big redheaded bastard

had to say and let me judge whether you've got something or not?"

Ruggles could tell a right bare-bones version. There was nothing mentioned about Red's wife and child. No mention of a deal.

"So we got an approximate date and place. Now the problem is to find out who the son of a bitch is."

The warden sat, twirling a pencil between his thumb and forefinger.

"You're telling me Pennington just spilled this all out to you because you asked? Because he likes you?"

Ruggles grinned. "Sure, he did. You know me. Mr. Nice Guy."

"You don't," the warden said leaning forward and staring hard at Ruggles, "perchance have something on Pennington? Some little nugget of information you're neglecting to impart? Some little tie-in to this killing?"

"I don't need anything like that, and you know it," Ruggles said. He seemed perfectly at ease to Cal. This all seemed to make no never-mind to him.

"Hmm," the warden said, using the pencil to make a note. "Hmm. Wade County jail, July sometime, sixty-one or so."

"That's right," Cal said.

"Red might be bullshitting you. He's got a strange streak in him."

"It can be checked," Ruggles said.

The warden laughed. Cal was uneasy again. He was starting to get giddy. Was this a huge joke on him? Planted information, more games for bored men?

"And just how do you propose to check, Sherlock?" The warden literally threw the question.

It was Ruggles' turn to laugh. "Well, that's where you come in, see? You can check."

Cal couldn't believe it. Ruggles didn't ask the warden. He told him.

The warden tensed. "Well, Mr. Ruggles and Mr. Newkirk, I want to thank you very much for cutting me in on your little scheme. It'll give me something to do in my spare time."

Then the fist hit the desk, and the face changed.

"Who the fuck do you think you are, telling me what to do?" he shouted at Ruggles. He turned to Cal. "And you, you damned fool. Here you got a chance—a *chance*—of getting out of here, and you're already planning ways to get back in."

"It's not revenge," Cal said, his voice higher than he intended, the words again unexpected. Revenge? "I mean, I'm not looking to do anything to him."

"Oh, I see," the warden said. "I see. You just want to find this weasely bastard so you can run up to him and throw your arms around him and say 'Hi, Dad.'"

That did it. Cal felt as if his chest might explode. "Listen," he said, leaning toward the warden. "He's probably dead. I don't know. But I'm going to have to go on the witness stand, and what if they ask me...I mean ask about my father, and what he has done in life. What if they ask me that? And I say, I don't know, don't know anything because he just..."

"Simmer down, boy," the warden said. "I get your drift."

Cal took a breath. "I *do* think he's dead," Cal tried again.

"You think he's dead based on what?" the warden asked, and Cal could tell Ruggles leaned forward with interest.

"It's just a feeling. Like, wouldn't you know if your father or your son was dead even if you didn't know where they were?"

Cal didn't realize how dangerous the statement might have been until he saw something strange flicker in the warden's eyes. A candle of interest.

"Go on," the warden ordered.

"See, I've been thinking about all these stories, and I've been thinking I don't really know which one or ones of them are true. I mean, anybody could have lied to me at any time, right? I figure that if I find out for sure, I can stop having dreams I don't understand, and just get on with it, like a normal person, you know what I mean."

Cal was speaking faster than he could ever remember doing before, and the warden just blinked. Cal hoped he would not ask him to repeat what he had just said. It had to do with this belief business. Did he believe the truth or believe the lie? Were the sins of his father visited upon him? Did he molest a child and rape a woman?

"See," Cal went on desperately, "I feel like he's dead, but then I have to remember that my mother told me he was dead, and the truth is, I don't know who's dead and who's not." Cal took a breath. "See, I thought if we could find Pennington's man, and I went to Four Corners to see if my mother..."

"Whoa," the warden said, clearly unable to follow the line. He turned to Ruggles as if he were an island of reason.

"And you," he said, "what made you decide to help with this good deed?"

Ruggles, the sweet southern slide. "You know me. Got to keep the mind active, the brain working, the juices flowing. Like reading a good book, picking out the best sections."

"You're a sarcastic son of a bitch," the warden said, trying his own brand of truth.

Cal was astonished that the warden had not asked him to explain more. Fathers and sons. Connections.

Would he kill him if he found him? Maybe.

"So," the warden said to Cal, "you just want to know if he's alive or dead, and if possible, the circumstances of what he did to your mother, right?"

"Right."

"And you don't intend to contact him."

"No, sir."

"You're lying."

"I don't intend to."

"But you might, later."

"If he turned out to be a reformed man, I might."

"God, boy, you are dumb."

Even Ruggles muttered something snide under his breath.

"If you don't want to check," Cal said, the red in his face making patience impossible, "just say so. I'll find out myself when I get out."

"Oh, that's even better," the warden said. "You can get out of prison and then spend your time nosing around jails and carnivals and places where the finest members of society hang out. Good idea, boy, good way to get hurt or killed or thrown back in. Haven't you learned one pissin' thing in this place?"

Ruggles took over. "Well, we thought maybe it would be real simple for a man in your position to just find out about this man, save Cal here from having to find out the hard way."

Ruggles' timing was off. Just as the warden's face turned bright red and both fists were headed for the desk, a light of inspiration passed his anger. His hands were literally suspended in midair, paused, then one came down on the intercom buzzer.

"Send a guard for Ruggles and Newkirk," he said, "and get me every goddamned file on anyone in this place who might have a kid in Viet Nam."

It was as if he had forgotten about them. Cal and Ruggles stood and the guard entered.

"I don't want one word out on what you just heard, you hear me?" the warden said. "And I'll think some on your proposition."

With that they were dismissed.

"I didn't think you had it in you, kid," Ruggles said once they were back in the library. "I've never heard such a crock of shit in my life. A goddamned genius couldn't have sorted that out."

As the warden got closer to the man he was looking for, Cal waited numbly for the days to pass before his appeal. Sometimes, in his dreams, he saw time passing the way it did in old movies, one numbered, day-of-the-week card at a time. Occasionally another man came to Ruggles with *another* story about some man he had run across in *another* place, *another* decade, but the tales got weaker, less interesting.

"Shit," Ruggles said at the table one night, "I've had enough of this bullshit. Case closed."

And that was that. There was still the air of the unsolved crime, and the convicts' capacity to exaggerate, to speculate, turned back to the dead kid in the shower.

Cal tried to make plans, but would then be overcome with the feeling of "counting chickens." Bad luck. God knows, he'd had enough of that. The cell, the library, all continued to decrease in size, and Cal woke almost every morning gasping for breath.

"Keep your pants on," Ruggles warned.

And my shirt, too, Cal thought.

And then it broke. The warden found the killer, and the prison hummed in amazement at the result. A man no one had suspected. A reason that made perfect sense.

The warden sent for Cal.

"I've been thinking about you, boy, and what you should do about your past. I got some contacts in Four Corners, friends who owe me favors." He paused. "From the past."

"Four Corners?"

"This is assuming, of course, that your lawyer's got as good as he talks, and that you can get out on appeal."

"I understand that," Cal said.

"See," the warden went on, "I decided it's not a bad thing for you to find out about your mother, and if you've got other kin there, or whatever. I always knew about my folks, but I can understand how it might be unsettling if you didn't."

Cal was positive he could see some almost envious glint in the warden's eyes.

"Thank you, sir," was all Cal could think to say.

"And," the warden went on, "I've given some thought to searching out the man Pennington talked about. I've decided to take you at your word and give it a try if you will promise not to meddle in this yourself."

"What do you mean, 'meddle'?" Cal asked.

"I mean, don't go consorting with criminals or snooping around and making people suspicious. You're going to need all the help you can get. Most people still subscribe to the 'where there's smoke' theory, and I'm not going to all this trouble to get you a clean start in a nice little town to have you fuck it up."

Clean start. Cal wondered if there was such a thing. But then, there was nothing left of the past, nothing left in Yellow Fork. A box of clothes and photographs, moldering in the stink of a vacant garage. Gone.

"Now," the warden said, "it'll take some time, so don't get impatient. You just think about getting back to normal the best you can, boy." He leaned back in his chair. He smiled and folded his arms.

Counting chickens. Knock on wood.

"Something about old Cheever, wasn't it? Never would have thought he had it in him." The warden looked satisfied.

Howard, with his ill-fitting teeth and mild manner. Cal's first cellmate. Watkins had told Ruggles and Henry Whitehorse all about it, and from there the word had spread like crazy. It seemed Howard Alonzo Cheever's grandson had been killed in Viet Nam, and when the draft dodger came in, something snapped. A sight to see, Watkins had said, the old man crying. He'd had to stop and take his teeth completely out.

"'Course he'll be a damned hero when he gets back on the floor. Even the newspapers around here making him out to be a patriot." The warden laughed, then was suddenly serious. "Self-righteous bunch in here, don't you think, for a gang of thugs."

Cal didn't know what he thought. He'd never been able to shake the feeling that the dead kid in the shower could have been him. Without Ruggles. Without the warden.

And then he was dismissed, and Watkins took him back to the library.

When Cal told Ruggles what had happened, Ruggles sneered. "That lousy bastard," he said. "Least he could've done was tell me first." He opened the book on his desk without looking at Cal. "I'll remember that."

On the eve of the appeal, Cal could not sleep. A strange mix of hope and despair kept him awake, taunted him with visions of walking along a street, greeting people, buying a hamburger from an Arctic Circle, mixed with finding himself confined in an upright box, a cell that was so small he could not sit down. A coffin on end.

The only town he knew was Yellow Fork, and he couldn't go there.

He wondered as he waited if he'd felt the same way the night before he married Mary Beth, and he tried to remember. It seemed so long ago. An event in the life of someone else. All his small-minded hopes and small-staked dreams. A woman to love and take care of, and a home where he had always lived. He'd been a stupid asshole to think such a thing could exist. And even when he'd known, known that the stories his mother told him were just her dreams, her wishes in the matter, he'd gone right on thinking the way she did.

Ruggles began to snore.

Prison, and the sounds and smells, the sweat and the secrets, had changed all that.

Ruggles turned over and the snoring ceased.

Then Cal was dreaming, and this time he was the man in the penny-toss booth, only this time it was made of steel bars. He was surrounded by glass, and he could feel the evil look in his eyes. He watched the women lean over the bars, and toss coins at the bowls, the glittering prizes that belonged to him. He watched their breasts, straining at the summer dresses. He saw their eyes bright with hope. Mary Beth tossed a coin, and he caught it in midair between two fingers, then he put it in his mouth and swallowed it. Then with his stick, and a loud maniacal laugh he could not identify, he sent the bowls, the glasses, the figurines shattering to the floor of his carnival cell.

Someone screamed and woke him up.

Ruggles was staring at him from his bunk.

"Well, kid," he said. "This is it."

The call came at ten minutes after four. He stood in the warden's office and listened to his lawyer tell him that as of that moment he was a free man. Released without bail, justice at work for a change. The trial hadn't been set, but he hoped it would be within four or five months, outside. Cal could not leave the state, but other than that, he was on his own.

"Can I go to Four Corners?" he asked.

"It would be better if you were closer," the lawyer said, "but if you've got folks there where you can wait, we can work it out."

Cal thanked him. Free. He couldn't grasp it. The screams and the sound of breaking glass still rested there, making it difficult for him to hear anything else.

"Are you all right?" the lawyer asked.

"I'm fine," Cal said. "I mean it. And I appreciate all you've done..."

"We got them," was all the lawyer said.

Them.

The warden shook his hand, and before Cal knew what was happening, he was back in his cell with Watkins, gathering together the few things that belonged to him. Ruggles handed him a list and the first item on it was Jane Russell. For a minute, Cal was afraid that the tears in his eyes would show, but then he folded the paper, and reached out to shake Ruggles' hand.

"You remember, boy. I've got my fine reputation to uphold," he whispered. "You get on the trail of that Pennington woman soon."

Cal glanced nervously at Watkins, but the guard merely seemed bored with it all.

"I will," Cal said, releasing Ruggles' hand. "You can count on it." He tried to laugh, but something caught in his throat. "Thanks for..." He tried, but he couldn't go on.

"You be smart, boy. That's not always a cinch for you."

That old familiar look in Ruggles' eyes. Half dare, half something Cal could not name. He could only nod and turn away.

"Let's go," Watkins said.

"Right," Cal agreed. He couldn't turn back to Ruggles now. He muttered his good-bye, and he wondered, as he went down the corridor with the guard, if Ruggles had heard him at all.

There was no time for good-bye to anyone else, which was fine, Cal thought as the warden drove him to his home. Ruggles was the only one who mattered. And before he could catch his breath, he found himself sitting at the dining-room table listening to the warden and his wife tell about the founding of the prison library, and about other prisoners who had been released.

Cal could not get used to the quiet, leisurely pace of the meal. No clanking of metal trays, no low growl of complaints.

"Jimmy Settle has his own garage now, and a pretty wife and two children. He was one of the warden's boys." She wiped the corner of her mouth with her napkin. "They sent us a picture last Christmas. And do you know," she added, leaning forward and looking directly at Cal, "Marty Loomis is almost a dentist. Only one more year to go."

After dinner, the warden sat down with Cal and went over the names and addresses of his contacts in Four Corners. A rooming house, a temporary job. A warning. "You remember how much you don't want to go back inside, boy," the warden said. "You think about that every single day."

Later, when the warden's wife showed Cal to the extra room, she took his elbow and whispered to him, "You keep in touch with him, won't you? It's important to him." She hesitated as if she were about to say something else, then merely patted him on the shoulder and wished him good luck.

In the darkness of the room, Cal could not sleep. The silence was strange and gentle. A curtain moved at the window, and it seemed large enough and alive enough to be the sail of a ship. He tried closing his eyes, but then the faces of many fathers passed before him. They revolved—some strangers, some familiar. The man in the photograph, Ruggles, the warden. Henry Whitehorse, and Howard Cheever. Turning slowly while he, Callant Newkirk, aimed a rifle at the moving target.

The image left him breathless, and he opened his eyes. It

was better to stare at the distant ceiling scarcely visible then to be struck by the long cool steel of the rifle barrel, the cross-hair symbol of the sight.

Sons with fathers, fathers without sons. The missing-in-action were everywhere.

He was numb with it all by morning when he heard the warden rap on the door. "It's time," he said.

Cal bought a ticket at the drugstore that also served as a bus stop, using a portion of the prison release money. He had Mary Beth's money order in his pocket.

He stood with the warden in the early morning darkness, and waited for the Greyhound bus that would take him to Four Corners. When the bus arrived and the doors opened, he turned to the warden and shook his hand.

"Thank you," he said, picking up the small bag that contained everything he owned. "I appreciate your help."

The warden only nodded.

As the bus pulled away, Cal turned back to see the warden standing beside his car. He watched him until the bus turned a corner, and he was gone.

Callant Newkirk could not tell whether the sick feeling in his stomach was merely hunger, or if it was fear.

He thought with some comfort of the two lists in his pocket. Ruggles' requests. Jane Russell from *The Outlaw*. The address of Lucy Pennington. The small comforts from the outside he wanted sent to him.

The warden's note of confidence. A job at Hardy's Hardware Store. A place to live at 312 Elm. A spoken promise to look for the man Pennington had described.

Callant was Ruggles' agent in the field.

He was one of the warden's boys.

A new life. Counting chickens on the farm.

Part Three

Cal sat on the bus and tried to watch the passing countryside, tried to let the rise and gentle sway of the vehicle calm him. Most of the other passengers were sleeping, but every time he closed his eyes a feeling resembling fear made a bright red line in the darkness.

It's my eyes, he thought. That's it. He wasn't used to looking into the distance. Short-range sight. He had to learn to shift. There were not any gray walls to prevent him from seeing now.

The sun was coming up, and was caught occasionally by some object—a fencepost painted white, a window of a farmhouse in the distance—so that the soft greens and blue were sprinkled with irrational lights. When it made him dizzy, he had to look away.

It was silent on the bus except for the sound of the engine and a sporadic burbling noise from the elderly woman across the aisle from where he sat. She wore a black straw hat perched on her tight curls, and her chin drifted to her chest, then pulled back, at which point she made the slight sound. Even though two empty seats and the aisle separated them, Cal could smell the light powdery scent of perfume, and that too struck him as strange. Too strong, too soon. He focused on her hands and the short white gloves she wore, on the purse she clutched in her lap.

But then she opened her eyes, caught him staring, and he was forced back outside to the fields. Cattle were slowly rising to their feet, and Cal thought he heard the distant tinkle of a bell, but knew it was only his imagination.

It had all happened so quickly. And the warden had made it sound so easy. Even his own lawyer. Erase these past months. You keep in touch, boy, the warden had said, his voice lower than usual as they shook hands in the predawn darkness at the bus terminal.

No one had explained this seeing difficulty.

His hand went to his pocket. A list of things Ruggles wanted. The name and address of Red's wife. A money order. A woman's name, a business phone number. Words that spelled out the details of what was to be his new life for the next few months.

Did they know he was going to be afraid? They shouldn't have kept that secret.

The woman had moved her purse to her side, out of his sight. It made him feel guilty.

They passed granaries, and pastures, and he could see the early morning workers of the land, a lone rancher on a horse, a flock of sheep, a small town where the bus did not stop, and then they began an ascent into low mountains.

He checked his watch. An eight-hour ride. Time to adjust his sight.

They stopped for breakfast at a diner fashioned of logs, and Cal ate alone at the counter. His words sounded strange to him as he ordered pancakes and coffee, and he was afraid to look at the waitress as he spoke.

"I couldn't hear what you said," she told him, and he thought, Christ, I can't talk either. When he repeated the words, he was not at all certain he wasn't shouting. As she put his plate in front of him, he noticed that she had painted some of her fingernails, but not all of them, and he wondered what that meant.

The bus took on several more passengers at the diner, and he noticed to his relief that no one had taken the seat next to him. The travelers were awake now, talking, laughing, making plans. A young girl sat next to the elderly woman, and he looked sideways at her, avoiding turning his head in her direction. She wore a bright yellow-flowered dress, and she was talking to the woman, but he could not hear exactly what she was saying. A visit, an aunt, something. Her skirt was short, mid-thigh, and he could see a pale brown birthmark the size of a nickel. It was dotted with freckles. He'd never seen one like it.

He looked out the window again. The winding road led up into a canyon, aimed at the summit. Tall pines lined the road, but they went by too fast for him to catch them. Dark green blurs, with occasional tips of new lighter green growth. Some dead ones, gray, barren, victims of lightning or some fatal scourge.

"It's my grandson's birthday," he heard the woman say. "He's ten years old today."

"I bet you'll have a nice party," the girl replied.

Her skirt slipped up higher on her thigh as she shifted in her seat looking for a comfortable position. Cal went back to trying to catch the trees. One would be enough. He tried thinking of the lists again, but they were still just words on paper.

"I think I'll try to take a nap," the girl said. "I stayed up all night talking to my boyfriend. I won't see him for two whole weeks."

Two whole weeks are nothing, Cal thought. Nothing at all.

He should try to sleep, too. A kind of heaviness sat about his shoulders, crept up into the back of his head. He took off his jacket and made it into a pillow of sorts, and fitted it into the space between the seat and the window. He stretched his legs out into the area in front of the vacant seat next to him. Through half-closed eyes he could see that the girl had reclined her seat slightly, turned on her side, her back to him. He could still see the birthmark. He checked the old woman and could tell from the incline of her black straw hat that she was looking out the window.

He watched the girl squirm slightly seeking the right position, moving her shoulders, slipping down lower into the seat. He thought her knees must be crowding the woman next to her, maybe even touching her. The skirt slipped higher, and while he began to fear a startling exposure, he could not get his eyes to move. His own eyelashes made ghostly little lines across her body, as if he peered through a slatted blind.

It's all right, he told himself as he watched her. It's because I've been in prison. It's all right, all right. He took his coat pillow and placed it over his lap. No, it wasn't all right. Close your eyes, close them. Sleep. Please.

He closed his eyes tightly and concentrated. He kept his hand clenched over his coat. He imagined the muted trees passing by, and thought he had that mixed up. He was passing by; they stood as they always had, in one single spot. He tried to blur his hearing as one does sight so that the words the passengers spoke to each other became a drone. A steady tone that inspired sleep. Though he thought he felt the bus stop, thought he felt a shifting of weight as people moved around him, he refused to open his eyes. He felt something touch his leg and he withdrew into his own space. He would not look. He would not.

He could hear someone breathing. Someone close. He thought his seat slipped backward, not suddenly, softly, someone working a lever, and not against his will, not *against* it, he was reclining, sleeping on his side. He moved his hand and drew it down the side of the girl next to him. He knew without looking that he touched the yellow-flowered fabric of her dress, then the flesh of her thigh, and he placed his finger on the spot he knew to be the mark. She turned toward him, or he turned her. He didn't know which. Now both of his hands touched flesh, and he moved those hands, or she did, up under that fabric, up under that yellow-flowered dress. He moved them up until they touched a silken fabric, until they reached a ridge, and he looped his fingers through the fabric, and pulled down. It was easy, too easy. She was helping him, he could feel her fingers. Without opening his eyes, he could see her hands. Some of the nails were painted, some of them were not, and he knew he only imagined that. Those hands belonged to someone else. He knew he wasn't actually looking.

And then there was nothing between them except the breathing and the feel of soft skin. Someone's hand took one of his and moved it away from the birthmark, closer to the center of the body. He let it go, sliding along the smoothness, reaching for the texture and the warmest recess of all.

He found the place. His fingers touched that place and sent a singular shock of horror to his brain. There was no hair, just the same smooth soft skin, and the recess. He opened his eyes in terror. By his side lay the little girl, her eyes wide with amazement. Those eyes were not six inches from his own, and they just stared into his, pale and clear like the cat's.

Someone screamed, and he looked up into the face of the old woman. She stood above them, her face distorted with disgust, with rage, but all the sound from her open mouth ceased, and he saw her raise her purse, saw her throw back her head with such force that her black straw hat sailed out the window of the bus. Other faces appeared, and he thought he saw one he recognized, and he waited for the blow, the blow that was coming from the woman who no longer held a purse, but a cane or an umbrella, something long and hard and lethal, and he closed his eyes and prepared to shriek in pain.

He sat up quickly, hitting his elbow against the metal side of the bus, awakened by an explosion in his mind.

The girl was still sleeping across the aisle. The old woman's black hat was still perched securely on her head. There was no one next to him.

He clutched his tingling elbow, and a small voice in front of him drew his eyes upward.

"You bumped your crazy bone, didn't you?" a little boy said with a smile. "I saw you do it."

"Sit down, Billy. Right now," he heard a woman say, and the little boy disappeared.

"I didn't do anything," he whispered. I didn't do anything, he thought.

He repeated that phrase in his mind all the way to Four Corners. He let the passing scenery turn into a colored veil, let it numb him into semiconsciousness.

And occasionally he prayed. Please, he asked someone, don't let her get off in Four Corners. Don't let that girl in the yellow-flowered dress stop there.

By the time the bus pulled into Four Corners a little after two, Cal had managed to calm down. It was just the shock of being outside, he told himself. That was all. As long as he just concentrated on details. The job, the new place to live. If he just kept calm, everything would be all right. He tried to read the names on stores as the bus passed through the main portion of town. An ice cream parlor, the Twilight Lounge, A and D's market. Hardy's Hardware Store, where the warden had arranged for him to work.

Four Corners was remarkably like his home town. Almost, he thought, a mirror image with just enough distortions to fool him.

He stood and took his small suitcase from the overhead rack. He noticed with relief that the girl in the yellow dress was making no move to disembark. It was all over. He was fine now, fine.

He walked up the aisle toward the front.

"Four Corners," the bus driver said as the bus pulled up in front of a combination filling station and diner. "Thanks," Cal said.

The driver opened the door, and Cal started down the steps. In front of the diner, a young woman wearing dark glasses stood waiting. Her hair was bright blond, hanging to her shoulders. She waved boldly and came toward him. Mary Beth. He stopped short. *Crazy bone.* It couldn't be Mary Beth. She passed around him, and he turned to see her hugging a tall young man in uniform. He must have come in on the same bus. Cal shook his head. He couldn't remember Mary Beth's face. He had lost his ability to recognize.

He heard the bus pull away, and the sound of the young woman's laughter. He reached in his pocket and pulled out the warden's slip of paper that contained the address. 312 Elm Street. Though he'd memorized the numbers, he had the feeling it was possible for things to change. Letters, combinations.

He waited until the operator of the gasoline station finished counting out change to the driver of a truck before he asked.

"Could you tell me where Elm Street is?" he asked. In the open air, his voice didn't sound quite so strange.

The man looked at him pleasantly enough. "Visiting someone?" he asked.

"I've come here to live," Cal said. "I'm looking for 312 Elm." Direct, simple sentences.

The man laughed, and Cal thought the man's teeth were uncommonly bright for such an old person. They were perfectly even and polished.

"Mrs. Pincher's place," the man said.

"Right." Cal held up the paper so the man could see it. A kind of proof.

"She'll love to get her hands on you," the man said, the bright teeth gleaming with the broad grin.

Something in Cal's confused expression made the smile fade from the man's face. "Hell, I don't mean that way. Mrs. Pincher runs what we old navy men call a tight ship, but she's got the best damned cook in town. Lived there a while myself after my first wife died."

Cal had the sudden image of a huge rawboned woman with an apron and a cane, and then realized that he had conjured up a vision of Ruggles dressed like a woman.

"Go two blocks that way," the man said, pointing to his left, "one block north, and it's about three—exactly three houses down. Big yellow job."

Cal nodded, replacing the paper in his pocket.

"Welcome to Four Corners," the man said. "You just home from the war, boy?"

An irritated honking of a car at the service station pump saved Cal from answering. Close, he thought as he bid good-bye to the man, but no cigar. Different battlefield.

He walked down the sidewalk that was broken in several places, tufts of resilient dandelions already appearing through the cracks. It was as if, even in the bright sunlight, he should keep his eye about two feet ahead. Something about balance. But as he walked, he gradually expanded his field. Carefully, the way he was going to do everything else. He passed a house that contained a backyard filled with the rusting bodies of old cars. Another house where the lawn had been replaced with concrete painted green, where plaster of Paris ducks stood around a blue painted pond. An old man sat on the porch reading a newspaper. As Cal passed, the man put the paper to his lap and watched. Cal could not get over the feeling that the man had somehow recognized him.

"A tight ship." He wondered if the man at the gas pump had ever been in prison.

He could see now, as he turned the corner and discovered that the town was probably only three streets deep off the main street, that it was a good deal smaller than Yellow Fork. He could see the fields stretching out into the farms that bordered the town. Yes, he thought, thinking of what he had to do, and what he needed to find out, this was most certainly a town where everyone knew everyone else. He much did they already know about him?

Patience, the warden said. Get a good start. And Cal remembered the broad daylight nightmare on the bus and was worried.

Before he was ready, the yellow house loomed up in front of him. It stood taller and broader than any other one on the street. A large three-story frame house with a porch that went around three sides. And to say that it was yellow was an understatement. A lemon would look pale beside it, and the trim was so white it seemed almost electric. A "bright" ship, he thought, hoping to be clever.

There was a small hanging sign over the front door. Priscilla Pincher's Boarding House, it said in bright blue script. Priscilla Pincher. A Dickens-type old maid. Miss Priss.

He took a breath and rang the bell. Since the day was so warm, the door was open, protected by the screen, and he could hear the sound of footsteps approaching. He straightened his back, and tugged at his collar to make certain it was not crumpled under his suit. He tried to brush a wrinkle from the jacket.

"Yes?"

He could see the woman faintly behind the screen. He saw curls piled high on her head, and a slim body in some kind of light dress. That feeling of familiarity again, of recognizing and yet knowing he was wrong, irritated him.

"Miss Pincher, please," he said. "I'm a new boarder."

The woman unlatched the door, and opened it for him. "You must be Mr. Newkirk," she said as he stepped into the entry-way.

"Cal," he said, and the smile wouldn't come. He would have to settle for control. "I think she's expecting me."

"She is, *Mr.* Newkirk," the woman said, extending her hand. From her wrist dangled a charm bracelet with more little figures than Cal dared to count. He focused on the hourglass as the bracelet jingled in front of him. "I am *Mrs.* Pincher."

He couldn't explain his mistake. And he had to raise his eyes to meet hers. Slowly, up the center of her body, pausing for a moment on the full breasts, the line of cleavage, the way the fabric pinched together, up in the direction that line pointed, to lips painted bright red, to cool green eyes that stared at him as if they understood completely what he thought, exactly where he had stopped in that gradual ascent to her face, and it was all right with her, as if she thought it had been a little like a caress.

She was as old as his mother and she wore false eyelashes. She brought the unbraceleted hand to her lips. She was smoking a cigarette, and he had not even noticed.

"I'm pleased to meet you," he said. He thought there was something as cool in his voice as that ice of green in her eyes.

"Let's go in there for a minute," she said, gesturing toward the open double doors that led to a parlor. "I'll explain the rules to you, then show you to your room."

He followed her into the large room that contained old highly polished furniture grouped around an impressive mantel. He had never, in his life, been in such a place.

"This," the woman said with a sweep and a jangle of her hand, "is the parlor."

Red-painted fingernails. All of them. Long and sharp.

"Smoking is allowed here, and on the porch, and nowhere else."

While the words were firm instructions, from the tone of her voice, she might have been flirting or teasing him. He tried moving his eyes from object to object. A pale green vase with a rose painted on the front. A brass bent reading lamp. A tassel hanging from the handle of a side-table drawer. The hem of her skirt. Her ankles and the thin strap of the black high-heeled shoes.

"Most of these things have been in my husband's family for many years," she said as his eyes stopped on the clock on the mantel. "Louis the Fourteenth." He turned to stare at her. "The clock. Louis the Fourteenth," she repeated. "Why don't you sit down now. Over there." She pointed to a high-backed chair upholstered in brown velvet. She sat across from him on a small divan. She extinguished her cigarette in a clean crystal dish.

"To begin with," she said, leaning toward him, "you're the first prisoner I've had, of any kind. *You*," she put the emphasis there, "are an exception to one of my many rules." She put a finger to a curl on top of her head.

"I appreciate that," Cal said. "Ma'am."

"Mrs. Pincher," she corrected.

"Mrs. Pincher," he repeated.

"I have eight other boarders," she said, adjusting her brace-let. "All of whom will respect your privacy and will expect you to do the same."

Cal was dazzled by the incongruity of the words and the voice that spoke them. Privacy. He wondered how many of them had already been told he was a former "prisoner."

As if she could read his mind, she said, "They know you are joining them, and that you come from another part of the state. That's all they know, all they are entitled to know, and I do not recommend that you confess your tenure of the last few months or so because it will merely confuse them."

"I understand," Cal said, moving slightly in the stiff chair.

"Good. Breakfast is at seven sharp, and dinner is at six-thirty. If you require lunch to take to work, the cook will provide you with a sandwich, a piece of fruit, and some sort of pastry for an additional fifty cents a day, payable with your monthly rent."

"That sounds fine," Cal said.

"The rent," she continued as she reached into her dress pocket for her cigarettes, "is due at dinnertime on the first day of the month. It is to be put into an envelope, sealed, and given to me at that time."

Cal reached into his pocket, hoping in vain for a packet of matches with which to light her cigarette even though he knew he didn't have any. Get some, he thought. Be ready.

She pulled a heavy silver lighter from the pocket and lit her own, nodding to him in a gesture of appreciation at his attempt.

"This way," she said, standing. Once again, he followed. As they crossed the entry hall, he noticed the slight sway of her hips, slender beneath the fragile fabric. When it came to him that if one did not look to the hair or the face, she might have been his mother, he felt a little dizzy. Perhaps he didn't remember her that well. Maybe it was just the age. Maybe it was the dress.

She led him into the dining room and pointed to a chair to the left of the head of the table. "You'll sit here," she said. In the center of the table was a bowl of flowers, and Cal thought at first they were real and wondered why there was no scent. Then he saw they were made of silk, and he was uncomfort-able with that error, too.

The dining room table was polished to such a sheen that the artificial flowers were reflected there, and Cal had a quickening desire to put one finger to the surface, to make a mark there, but he did not. Not then.

"We have one glass of wine with dinner, with the exception of Mrs. Mortensen, who cannot abide alcohol, and if you wish a cocktail before dinner, you must take it in the parlor. You may purchase your own bottle, and store it in the cabinet there, suitably marked with your name. I do not allow drinking in the rooms," she said, and once again her braceleted hand moved up to smooth a curl, "nor do I allow guests. All socializing is done in the parlor."

The words came at him like a train on a fast track. He wanted to tell her to slow down so he could get it all. He wanted to tell her that the men he knew spoke in three-word sentences; they didn't fire a volley of polite rules and regulations, and he clenched his fists at his side, noticed the tension, released the clench, and rested his anger in his eyes, in that darkening line of cleavage, the soft revealed fullness. She wasn't going to scare him.

"Do you understand?" she asked.

"I understand," he said quietly.

"Fine. I'll show you your room."

As he followed her up the two flights of stairs, something else occurred to him. Somewhere else he might have seen her. She looked exactly like the women in the old movies his mother had taken him to see. Cigarette-smoking, narrow-waisted, broad-shouldered, high-haired women in soft dresses. Mrs. Pincher was right out of the early forties. The house itself might have been a movie set. He put his hand on the banister. It was as if time had gone backward here. He wanted to point that out to her so she would know he understood something. But instead, he stared at the seams of her stockings.

Mrs. Pincher opened a door with a skeleton key, and walked directly to the window of the room and raised the blind. She turned to face Cal as he stood in the doorway, and crossed her arms in front of her. He noticed she no longer had the cigarette but could not recall when she might have put it out. "Your room will be cleaned and your linen changed on Wednesdays," she said as he stepped timidly inside the door.

"As you can see, we have a schedule here. Something I suspect will cause you no difficulty."

His face reddened at the reference until he noticed again that she was smiling slightly. Still, he wondered if she was one of those woman who might have driven a man mad enough to commit a crime.

"This is very nice," he said, walking to the bed, feeling again more acutely the inadequacy of his own words. He ran his hand over the ivory chenille spread, and up onto one of the four polished posters of the bedstead. He put his suitcase on the floor.

"No shoes on the bedspread," she said, walking toward him.

The room was light and pleasant, and uncluttered. There was a bureau next to the door, a desk with a chair against the wall across from the bed, and a brown striped easy chair with a reading lamp by the window. The walls were pale yellow, and the floor was covered with a worn but originally elegant rug of pale green, brown, and yellow leaves and flowers. There were two watercolors of autumn scenes above the desk, and another over the head of the bed.

"I paint as a hobby," she said, moving to straighten one of the pictures. "The bathroom is down the hall to the left, and the bathing schedules and the rules are posted on the back of the door." She opened the door to the closet and pointed to a chrome rack. "You keep your towels here," she said, pointing to the white ones already in place.

Cal did not know what to say. It was as if the room moved in around him, frightening at first, then embracing. Like a dream. A negative of the one on the bus.

"This is very nice," he said desperately. He walked to the desk, and touched the dustless surface with his index finger, leaving just the trace of a print.

"I'm glad you like it," she said, walking to the door. "You'll be comfortable here," she said without a trace of uncertainty, as if she herself could will it. "I'll call Mr. Hardy at the hardware store," she added, "and tell him you've arrived."

"Thanks," Cal said.

She started to laugh and he felt a flash of anger. He hadn't said anything funny, unless his confusion was amusing.

"Hardy's Hardware Store," she said. "Rather sounds like a laugh in itself, doesn't it?"

Cal looked at her blankly, and then she was gone.

Hardy's Hardware Store. Then it came to him. Hardy, har, har. At least he'd solved one damned puzzle.

He hoped his meeting with the hardware store owner was going to be easier, less filled with words and suggestions he did not understand. He sat down on the edge of the bed.

He'd traveled a universe on that bus, he thought, in less than a day. He shuddered at the thought of the girl in the yellow dress.

He wondered what had happened to Mr. Pincher. He imagined an emaciated old man in a wheelchair in the attic, and he didn't know why. Maybe it was all the old furniture.

Another mystery.

His meeting with Mr. Hardy was brief and to the point. After a crisp two-pump handshake, the thin sixtyish man with sparse gray hair led him through the store. "Paint section, tools, screws and nails, electrical." Again, Cal had to struggle to keep up with the clipped breathless words. Mr. Hardy was a man who did not look another directly in the eye, and it made Cal remember the warden's words. *Don't go out there looking guilty, boy. Got to look at people straight on.* He wondered if Mr. Hardy had a secret, too. What his connection was with the warden.

Mr. Hardy led Cal to his small cluttered office at the back, but did not suggest that he sit down.

"You need a short-sleeved white shirt and black trousers," he said. "Get them at Wellman's mercantile in the next block. If you don't have the money right now, he'll let you charge them, and we furnish the vests," he said, pointing to the bright red one he wore.

They were all, Cal thought as he listened, making damned sure he wouldn't make a mistake. Mrs. Pincher with her rules, Mr. Hardy with his complete instructions. He wanted to protest, but did not.

"Jimmy Lee Lucus," Mr. Hardy went on, "he's the young fellow out there in front now, he'll be the one showing you the most. He's got two weeks before he has to report, and when we get busy you'll have to learn real fast. People are impatient these days."

"Yes, sir," Cal nodded. Black pants, white shirt. Next block.

"Open at eight-fifteen, close at five-thirty, and all day Sunday. I expect you'll be prompt." He rubbed the point of his vest between two fingers, and looked around his own office as if taking inventory.

"Yes, sir," Cal said quickly, trying to keep up.

"See you tomorrow." Mr. Hardy shuffled impatiently.

"Yes, sir, at eight-fifteen." Drilling with the National Guard. About face, turn. Cal bumped into a chair as he did so.

"Mr. Newkirk?" the man said in a softer tone, and Cal turned back to him.

"Cal," he said, trying to sound casual.

"Cal." Mr. Hardy cleared his throat. "Rupert Hansen," he said, and it was the first time Cal knew the warden's name was Rupert, "is one of the finest men I've ever met."

"Yes, sir," Cal agreed, wondering at the slight catch in the man's voice. "He is that."

"Eight-fifteen."

"Thank you."

Cal walked through the crowded aisles of the store and wondered if he would ever be able to sort everything out. He nodded to the young man who stood behind the counter, careful to look him in the eye, and the boy nodded back, flipping his long blond hair away with a twist of his head. He looked barely sixteen, Cal thought as he stepped onto the sidewalk. Not old enough to know much of anything, and he was off to the war. Jimmy Lee Lucus reminded him of the dead draft dodger, an uneasy omen.

Cal put his hands in his pockets as he walked toward the vertical sign that said Wellman's. Before he knew it, he was humming a song to which he could not remember the words or the title, and he shivered in the sunlight of ghostly implication. He hoped it was from a long-ago movie, a song he might eventually remember on his own.

After purchasing his new uniform, he walked back to Mrs. Pincher's, passing by the feed store and nursery. On the sidewalk was a bench of potted geraniums in brilliant shades of orange and red for sale. Red Pennington. His scarlet wife.

He wanted one of those plants with the blazing clusters of blossoms. He wanted one even though his mother had hated them. And like the prisoner or child that he still was, he would have to ask permission. Mrs. Pincher and her rules. He'd put it on his sill and tend it until it filled the window with red.

It would help kill the memory of the girl in the yellow-flowered dress, and give him something to watch grow as he waited for the new trial.

At six-twenty, Cal stood in the entry hall, just outside the still closed dining-room doors. He wore his suit, and rocked back and forth on his feet, listening to the sound of quiet conversation from the parlor. Were they speculating about him? He was afraid to stop the conversation by entering the room. He'd had enough of that. He thought he heard Mrs. Pincher laugh, and it made him angry. He looked at his face in the mirror and practiced blurring his vision, an ability he'd found useful both in court and in prison. He merely had to appear to look at people directly. He didn't have to actually do it. Thus far, he had had only one encounter in the house. An elderly man who had nodded to him in the hall upstairs.

He looked at the tall clock that stood next to the dining room doors. Almost six-thirty. Yesterday, he was in a cell in a prison, now he stood in the foyer of an elegant house. The ticking of the clock seemed to grow louder, and he turned to watch the heavy pendulum swing. Edgar Allan Poe. A detail Ruggles would appreciate.

Right on the stroke of the half-hour, Mrs. Pincher emerged from the parlor and walked to the doors.

"Good evening, Mr. Newkirk," she said pleasantly.

"Good evening," he replied, "Mrs. Pincher."

She smiled at him as she opened both doors. She was wearing a different dress, a soft green clinging one in much the same style as the one she had worn earlier. Around her neck was a black velvet ribbon with small pearls attached. It reminded him of something vaguely evil.

"Come in," Mrs. Pincher said, holding her hand out to him, the same bracelet of the afternoon jingling on her wrist.

He stared at the offered hand. "Come on," she said, almost teasing him, and he cautiously extended his own. Her grasp was cool, dry, *powdered in death* he thought before he could stop himself.

"You are to sit here," she said, placing him behind the chair he already knew was his. Perhaps she said it more for the others. She smiled, releasing his hand. "We wait until the women are seated," she warned, and he wanted to tell her that he knew something about manners, that his mother had taught him *that,* at least.

The other boarders entered, carrying the remnants of conversation with them. Cal skewed his vision, just in case, as they took their appointed places. He noticed the man across from him bend to pull out the chair for the old woman he assumed must be Mrs. Mortensen. He glanced to his left and felt more than actually saw the middle-aged man who stood next to him. No clatter or trays, no hiss of profanity.

Almost everyone was seated before he noticed that Mrs. Pincher was still standing expectantly, and he moved quickly, pulled out her chair, and stared at her soft shoulder as she settled into her place.

"Why thank you, Mr. Newkirk," she said, the same trace of benign amusement in her voice.

He then sat down in his own place, nervously bumping his knee on the table leg as he did so.

"Tonight," she said as if calling the meeting to order, "as is our custom when we have a new guest, we'll have an aperitif to get us through the introductions." She reached with one slender hand for the cut-glass goblet that contained a peach-colored liquid.

Again Cal had the sense of living in a dream. Everything moved so slowly. He could feel the hands reaching for the glasses. He could not reach for his own; he knew his hand would shake.

"This is Mr. Newkirk. He will be living here and working at Mr. Hardy's store. I'm sure we will all do our best to make him feel at home."

Cal heard the murmur of acquiescence and felt annoyed.

"On my right," Mrs. Pincher said, indicating the gentleman Cal had encountered in the hall, "is Mr. Henderson. He is retired from the railroad, a conductor. He can tell you many amusing stories of his travels."

Mr. Henderson nodded to Cal, putting a finger to his bushy mustache as he did so.

"How do you do," he said.

"Sir," Cal replied.

"Next to him," she continued, "is Mrs. Mortensen."

The elderly woman touched the glasses that hung around her neck and rested on her bosom, and she smiled generously at Cal.

"Mrs. Mortensen was the town librarian until her retirement this past year. Now she volunteers there twice a week." Mrs. Pincher smiled at Cal. "She is our resident literary authority."

"And a vicious gin player," Mr. Henderson added, causing the woman to lower her eyes flirtatiously.

Cal almost said, I worked in the library, too, then realized he might have to explain where.

"You'd do well not to engage her for money," Mr. Henderson said, and the other laughed.

"How do you do," Cal said.

"Mr. Simmons," Mrs. Pincher continued around the table, referring to the tall thin man sitting next to Mrs. Mortensen, "is the farm loan officer at the bank."

The man raised one hand in a greeting and he had almost the longest fingers Cal had ever seen. Cal felt his own hand raise involuntarily and he placed it back in his lap. He nodded instead. He looked at the woman next to Mr. Simmons. She was a soft plump woman of perhaps forty with fluffy blond hair. She held her glass in one hand and looked at Cal with more curiosity than the others had. As if she knew something.

"Mrs. Lewis writes for the local newspaper," Mrs. Pincher said, and Cal thought he detected a colder tone in her voice. "Food, dress, social calendar, and gossip. We have to be careful what we say to Mrs. Lewis."

There was another murmur of amused agreement.

"Nice to make your acquaintance, Mr. Newkirk," Mrs. Lewis said properly, raising her head slightly, as if to say, I'm not quite the gossipmonger Mrs. Pincher implied, but one should be cautious anyway.

"Thank you," Cal whispered.

He looked to the man who sat at the end of the table, across the vast expanse of china and crystal from Mrs. Pincher. He was not like the others. He leaned back in the armchair casually, almost defiantly, a smile or a leer, Cal was not sure which, on the lip beneath a carefully trimmed line of mustache. Cal's concentration sharpened. The man might have been imitating Clark Gable, and was doing it with some success. The dapperness, the devil-may-care. The man did not look at him, but stared directly at Mrs. Pincher. Electricity, no doubt about it.

Mrs. Pincher took a sip of her aperitif.

"Mr. Tonelli," she said, "is from Italy. He has spent the last three years with us providing a touch of the cosmopolitan."

The man narrowed his eyes in condescending acknowledgment of his position.

Cal wondered what else he did. All the others had been introduced by profession. Was Mrs. Pincher keeping him?

"How do you do?" Cal said, uneasy with the formal words.

"Very well, thank you, sir," Mr. Tonelli replied. The trace of accent was educated and sophisticated. He did not sound like a gangster.

Cal had to lean forward to see the next resident. He was, Cal decided, the closest in age to himself. The man had blond wispy hair, slightly thinning on top, and wore horn-rimmed glasses. College, Cal thought. He wore a tweed coat that looked too warm for the evening.

And again, Mrs. Pincher with what now seemed an uncanny way of reading Cal's mind, said, "Mr. Dennis looks exactly like what he is," she said, and there was the hum of light laughter again. "He teaches history on the high school level, and would like to specialize in the sixteenth century, but they won't allow it."

"That's not true," Mr. Dennis said, looking over his glasses at Cal. "I gave a lecture on Karl Marx to my students and had to appear before the school board and defend it. They prefer to believe he never existed." He sighed. "'Talk about George Washington,' they said."

"Oh, William," said the young woman sitting next to him. "I mean, *Mr.* Dennis."

"That brings us to Miss Mayfield," Mrs. Pincher said, her

voice once again warm with something that seemed to promise affection. "Miss Mayfield has been charged with the formation of young minds. Second- and third-graders, to be exact."

The young woman was thin and pretty in a wholesome way, and she too leaned forward to smile at Cal. "We hope you'll enjoy living here," she said.

She looked a little like Mary Beth. Be careful, he wanted to tell her. You too can change into someone else.

"Four Corners is really a most nice community and I just know you'll find us to be friendly and..."

Mrs. Pincher tapped lightly on the edge of her plate with a spoon, and Cal turned quickly at the sound.

"Now, Miss Mayfield, there will be plenty of time for you to give Mr. Newkirk the bright side of life in Four Corners."

"Yes, Mrs. Pincher," Miss Mayfield said, reduced to an obedient student herself. She could not, however, resist just the slightest flutter of one of her hands, and Cal remembered the cool powdery feel of Mrs. Pincher. He rubbed two of his own fingers together to see if any trace remained.

"Finally," Mrs. Pincher said, and Cal found he had to pull backward and turn to the side to see the man next to him, "we have Mr. Johnson, court clerk and superb chessplayer."

The man with the round open face turned to Cal, and extended his hand. As Cal responded, he noticed the blond hairs and freckles on the back of the man's hand. He was the only one, Cal thought frantically, that he could imagine in prison gray, and he realized it was simply a matter of the man's size. Large-boned, a paunch of a stomach.

"How do," the man said. "How *do* you do?" he corrected. "Do you play?"

Play what? Cal's hand began to shake, and he pulled it away quickly. Chess. Of course.

"No. I mean, a little." He remembered trying to teach Mary Beth the moves. Where does the horse go? But I don't want to move it that way. Why can't we just move all the things the same way and it will be easier?

"Mr. Johnson will be glad to instruct you," Mrs. Pincher said. "You watch him take on Judge Harter on Wednesday nights, and you'll wonder how he still has his job."

"I worry about the judge's blood pressure," Mrs. Mortensen volunteered, still toying with her eyeglasses.

"I worry about the judge's sanity," Mr. Tonelli added, "but perhaps it is merely his belief in American justice."

Mrs. Pincher rang the small silver bell by the side of her plate, giving Mr. Tonelli, with his slight Italian accent, the final word.

By the time the dinner—fresh vegetables mixed and perfectly cooked, a pleasure Cal had forgotten existed, a fluffy yellow rice, and half a broiled chicken with Waldorf salad on the side—was over, Cal knew the library hours, the day the newspaper came out, that interest rates were rising at an alarming rate, and that the current case in court involved the murder of a cow.

He watched the others carefully, studied the utensils they chose to use, practiced nodding at appropriate times.

Mr. Henderson, perhaps forgetting the house rules, perhaps merely hoping to run one by, broached the subject of Cal's past, and was quickly admonished by Mrs. Pincher

"Now Mr. Henderson, you know we need to learn not to dwell on the past but to look to the future."

Her statement did, however, give Cal the perfect opening. There was something odd about this assemblage of people; it was as if they had been handpicked to be his consultants in his search.

"I am," he ventured as the spring-faced girl servant cleared the dishes away, "really interested in history, especially local history since I'm new here."

Mrs. Mortensen fairly tingled with excitement. "Tuesday evenings," she said triumphantly. "I work at the library then, and I will take you there personally and show you the old newspaper file." She paused, looked down the table to Mrs. Lewis. "We have every copy of the *Four Corners Clarion* ever printed, many of them before our own Mrs. Lewis's time." She smiled at Mrs. Lewis, who apparently could not decide whether to be flattered at the favorable age reference, or offended at the notion that perhaps she didn't know everything after all.

"At the newspaper," she chimed in, "we have extensive files, Mr. Newkirk, should you find an event that you want *additional* information on. We can't print everything, you know." She tossed the ball back into the middle of the table.

This was too remarkable, Cal thought. One day in a prison

when nobody wanted to tell you anything of importance, the next sitting around a polite dinner table with diners bursting with the need to tell him something, anything. He saw himself briefly as a rather sedate Ruggles of this table. The toughest one there. It made him want to laugh with the irony of it all.

Almost everyone went on to volunteer something. Mr. Dennis promised a sociological overview of small-town structure in the America of the sixties, and Miss Mayfield offered to let him visit her class as if the secret were contained there.

Mrs. Pincher promised nothing, and Mr. Tonelli seemed bored.

After the dinner was over and the guests had either adjourned to the parlor or to their own rooms, or in the case of Mr. Dennis and Miss Mayfield to what they had promised was only to be a short "after-dinner" walk, Cal found himself desperate for the solitude of his new room. At the same time, he did not want to appear rude, standoffish. Not when these people had the wealth of information he both wanted and needed. Careful, be careful.

He stood in front of one of Mrs. Pincher's bookcases, pretending to scan the titles.

Mr. Johnson tapped him on the shoulder. "I should have mentioned to you," he said quietly, "that the courthouse has its own history, too. Oldest adobe-block building in the town."

Cal nodded in appreciation. It was all too perfect. He smiled as he pulled a book from the shelf, and then he knew what it was like. A game of Clue. Summer evening, his mother and Dave, tired of Monopoly. Colonel Mustard had been his favorite character, and he always took the yellow piece. The library, the parlor, the dining room. A wrench, a candlestick, a gun. The weapons. A perfect setting for a murder. Mrs. Pincher's Boarding House. Who would be the victim? Mr. Tonelli. Otherwise, everyone would think he was the killer. Yes, Mrs. Lewis had done it in the bedroom with the candlestick. He was going to have to go upstairs, get away before he began to laugh uncontrollably. The pressure of it all.

"Excuse me," he said suddenly, causing both Mrs. Lewis and Mrs. Mortensen to look up from their respective chairs with startled looks. Then he realized it had sounded as if he were going to make an announcement. The red rose in his face again. "It was very nice to have met all of you." He cleared his throat. "Tomorrow's my first day at work, and all, and…"

"Why we understand perfectly," Mrs. Mortensen chirped. "You've had a long trip—probably—and you should go to bed."

Mrs. Pincher, leaning against the back of Mr. Tonelli's chair, merely said, "Good night, Mr. Newkirk. It's a pleasure to have you with us." The slight smile, the odd tone.

Cal, nodding and bowing and backing out of the parlor door. Cal, fairly running up the stairs to his new room.

Once inside the door, he found himself leaning back against it, the knob in his back. He felt his knees weaken, and he began to laugh quietly as he slid down the door until he was sitting on the floor hugging his knees.

So that was how it was going to be. That clear moment of insight. It was going to be easy to get them all on his side. Yes. That awkward moment of confusion. Boyish innocence born out of desperation. Turning the tables, Mary Beth. He had learned something from her after all.

He stood and moved to the bed where he dutifully took off his shoes before putting his feet on the bedspread. As if anyone could see, he thought. As if anyone knew.

No one had recognized his name. Four Corners seemed to have forgotten his mother.

Secrets. Tricks. Sell tickets and play the part.

He was suddenly exhausted. He stumbled through the preparations for bed, and soon was alone in the darkness with only the moonlight casting shadows on the wall.

And as he watched, the shadows took the form of girls dancing in a ring. He heard Mary Beth laugh, saw the little girl stumble slightly, his mother in her blue organza dress, Mrs. Pincher poised for the tango. And then the window was filled with red blossoms that burned brilliant in the night, and the dancers were gone.

Days in the hardware store were madness. "Spring," Mr.
Hardy had said philosophically, "that eternal season for the
fixing up of things." Mr. Hardy, Cal decided, would have been
happier about it if he were a greedy man. Instead, he seemed
merely more perplexed that people had not had the foresight
to buy well in advance. In the meantime, Cal ran the maze
of shelves and supplies with about the same desperation he
imagined the laboratory rat assumed. Everyone was painting,
pruning, repairing something. Exterior paint, interior paint.
Wiring, tools, new screen doors and windows, brushes, and
ten-penny nails. It gave life in the prison library the quality
of a film shot in slow motion.

It's good, Cal would think when he could catch his breath.
Can't think, can't worry. He focused on learning the business,
and the callused hands of carpenters and amateurs alike. He
went home each night to Mrs. Pincher's in a state of request-
filled exhaustion. He dreamed about socket wrenches and
hacksaws that only occasionally took the form of the shadow-
dancing figures of his past. Jimmy Lee Lucus, preoccupied
perhaps with possible death on the upcoming battlefield, was
little help, and Cal tried not to bother him. He prided himself
on a pose of cooperativeness.

He found the gentle concern of the other boarders only
slightly less disquieting than the mayhem at work, and he
found himself ready for sleep by nine. He heard them whisper
about adjusting to a new place, followed then by their own

stories of such times in their lives.

He had slipped out after dinner three times under the guise of an after-dinner walk and getting to know the town, and had found himself on Cedar Street in front of Lucy Pennington's house, but he had yet to catch a glimpse of the woman or her child. He had noticed with some amusement coupled with an uncomfortable superstition that Lucy Pennington had a row of geraniums on her porch, and that they were just like the ones he now had on his windowsill in his own room.

With Mrs. Pincher's permission, of course.

"Geraniums? If you can stand the smell, I don't see why not. They should have saucers under them so you do not spot the sill." She had shaken her head. "They make me sneeze, I must tell you."

"Be careful not to overwater them," Mrs. Mortensen had advised. "The leaves turn yellow." Later, he'd heard Mrs. Mortensen remark on what a nice boy he was, and he thought geraniums could mean more than one thing.

An impatient letter arrived from Ruggles, so he made a Sunday run at Lucy's house. He had to be careful not to appear to be loitering. Mrs. McNee's words. *I think he followed some girls one night.* So he walked slowly, approaching the house where the lawn needed cutting and the fence needed paint. Just as he was passing, a young boy came running onto the porch and down the walk. "You come back here, you naughty boy," a voice called from the house, and a middle-aged woman appeared, wiping her hands on a dish towel. The boy was climbing the gate, laughing, and the woman called to Cal, "Don't let that rascal get away."

The woman certainly was not Red's wife. Maybe her mother. Cal felt himself begin to sweat. The giggling child was almost over the gate, and Cal had to reach out and grab him around the waist and hold him kicking and waving his arms in midair as the heavy woman came down the steps.

"You naughty, naughty boy," the woman said, taking the child from Cal and whapping him soundly on his bottom. The boy struggled away and ran for the house.

The woman sighed. "Thank you," she said to Cal without really looking at him. "That boy could have been to Kentucky by now." With that she ambled up onto the porch and back into the house. Cal had no choice but to move on. The boy looks fine, he would write to Ruggles. He waited briefly at the corner to see if anyone else would appear, but finally went on. By the time he arrived at Mrs. Pincher's he had a plan.

The moment presented itself at dinner through the courtesy of one of Mr. Henderson's stories about his grandson. "A hellion, if there ever was one," he said. "Just like I was."

Cal began. "I was walking along today," he said quietly as the girl cleared the dinner plates, "and this little boy came running out..." He told the story, the street, precise detail.

"Sounds like Lucy Barnett's little boy," Mrs. Lewis said. "That's a sad story. She married this horrible man who..."

"We don't gossip at dinner," Mrs. Pincher interrupted.

"Well, it sounds like Lucy's mother was watching the boy," Mrs. Lewis said primly, and then, as if she were determined not to be completely overrun by Mrs. Pincher, she added, "You will never guess who I saw today." She dabbed at her lips with her napkin.

The serving girl came into the dining room carrying a tray of pieces of strawberry pie, and began to place them on the table.

No one asked Mrs. Lewis *who*.

"I think I will have some coffee this afternoon, Virginia," Mrs. Mortensen said to the girl as she placed a plate in front of her.

Cal saw a faint smile on Mrs. Lewis's lips.

"There she was," she went on, "walking down the street just as if all was right with the world, at least with her world."

Mr. Tonelli waved away the pie, and Virginia shrugged.

"Mr. Tonelli," Mrs. Pincher said, "would you prefer an apple, or an orange?"

"Nothing, thank you," the man said, leaning back in his chair. He alone seemed interested in what Mrs. Lewis had to say. "Now who might that have been, Mrs. Lewis?" he asked. "A celebrity in Four Corners?"

"Virginia, bring a little extra whipped cream for Mr. Simmons."

"Yes, ma'am."

"Well," Mrs. Lewis continued. "I saw *her*. Miss Maria Borelli." She looked at Mr. Tonelli as she spoke, but then turned to Cal. "She used to live here. In your room."

Mrs. Pincher put her fork on her plate with a little clink. "Mrs. Lewis," she said, the warning tone in her voice demanding attention from everyone. "Kindly keep your gossip confined to your column."

"I simply thought," Mrs. Lewis said, staring at Mrs. Pincher, "that you all would be interested to know that she is still in town. After all..."

"That is enough," Mrs. Pincher said. "Quite enough."

Dessert and coffee were consumed then in virtual silence as Cal tried to look back and forth between Tonelli and Mrs. Pincher, searching for some clue. Tonelli. Borelli. A hint of relation; that was silly. You weren't cousins because your names sounded alike. Maria Borelli. Why had she left? Another mystery in this living game of Clue.

He thought about pursuing it with Mrs. Lewis later, but decided he'd better save his questions for matters truly important. Miss Borelli was not top priority on his list of mysteries. It was interesting to note, however, the existence of another forbidden game. He was more the watcher than any of them dreamed.

Later, he passed Mrs. Lewis on the upstairs landing, and he could see that she had been crying.

"Is there anything I can do for you?" he asked her. "Are you sick?"

Mrs. Lewis shook her head. "This really is a lovely place to live, Mr. Newkirk," she said. "We should all try to remember that."

A tight ship indeed. But that wasn't always so useful. Did Mrs. Pincher suspect he knew Lucy's husband? He'd have to be extra careful now. Maybe Mrs. Pincher, curious for once, would ask him about it, and then he'd get plenty of information.

The watcher waiting. He wrote Ruggles a note promising more, and describing his new life. The pit and the pendulum. A woman from an old movie Ruggles might have seen.

The next day was Jimmy Lee's last. He shook hands with Cal and Mr. Hardy at closing time, and he and Cal left the store at the same time.

"Listen," he said to Cal as they stood on the sidewalk, "some buddies of mine are having a good-bye blast at the Circle R tomorrow night. Come over, if you want." He smiled at Cal, the sad smile of the doomed. "We're going to get good and drunk."

"Sure," Cal said. "I'll try to make it."

The Circle R. Hawley's Bar. Mary Beth and Kenny Larkin, and too much bourbon and prison. It would be dangerous, but Cal was feeling brave now and couldn't refuse.

"And good luck," Cal called as Jimmy Lee headed off down the street.

"Shit, I'll need more than luck," Jimmy Lee said, kicking at the concrete with the toe of his tennis shoe. "All those crazy gooks."

"Going out, Mr. Newkirk?" Mrs. Pincher called from the doorway to the parlor. Mr. Tonelli appeared at her side, one of his thin brown cigarettes held in his teeth like a cigar.

Cal stopped in the entryway and turned to face her. A resentment at being confronted rose, and he tried to shake it away. This isn't prison, Mrs. Pincher, he wanted to remind her. And you are not my warden. You are not my mother. Mother.

"Jimmy Lee Lucus is going to war," he said before he could temper the dramatics of the situation. "He invited me to a going-away party."

"Jimmy Lee Lucus," Mrs. Pincher said, with evident disdain. "You be careful of the crowd he runs with."

"Now, Mrs. Pincher," Mr. Tonelli said, chiding her, "they are merely a group of *young* people, not a band of thieves."

Mrs. Pincher's false eyelashes flickered and Cal wondered what choice words she would have later for Mr. Tonelli.

"I will merely remind you," she said to Cal, the familiar tone of bemusement in her voice, "that you are not allowed to have guests in your room."

"Mrs. Pincher," Mr. Tonelli added with an affectionate look at her, "is an incurable romantic."

Cal swallowed, nodded, and took his leave.

He walked along the sidewalk, headed directly for the Circle R. The jeans he wore were new and stiff, with that chemical smell, and slight scraping noise as his thighs rubbed together. He had put on some weight at Mrs. Pincher's, but he looked better, not worse. Healthy, he thought. The jeans and casual knit shirt were the newest additions to his wardrobe, purchased during his lunch hour. Everything was going just fine, fine indeed. Looking good, better, best. Becoming, actually, part of the pose.

It was dark, and he should have brought a jacket. He walked faster to keep warm. Sometimes, when he looked around at the faces at the dining-room table and tried to remember how Henry Whitehorse looked in comparison, how Ruggles had controlled everything, he had the same peculiar sensation of living his life in someone else's movie. That was all that was wrong. Somebody somewhere knew all the characters, knew who they were and what made them work. Knew about Maria Borelli, and what had happened to Mr. Pincher. They knew about his mother and his father, and who Mr. Tonelli was. Somebody decided where he would be, and knew who he was, too. Was his father a man who now looked like Mr. Tonelli? Age about right. Mustache. He'd remember that when he wrote to the warden. I'm tired, he would plead, of looking at every man who's in his forties who has dark hair and a mustache and wondering if the man is my father. Made him sound like a crybaby. Baby. Well, he had to face it. He was the youngest person at Mrs. Pincher's. He had been the youngest at Ruggles' table. He hadn't done much to prove himself more capable. He could start on that right tonight. Get in there with Jimmy Lee and his beer-drinking buddies and be one of them, only older, wiser. And he'd take another run by Red's wife's place, make another check to keep up his part of that bargain.

As he turned the corner of Cedar Street, the sun slipped abruptly, as if a hand had given it a giant push, and Cal fell comfortably into the cover of dusk. There was a large elm near the corner, and he stood beside it. If anyone should see him and ask, he would say he was supposed to meet someone. He could see lights in the house, but a yellow blind was drawn over both front windows. He thought he saw a shadow, but couldn't catch it. He reached down near the base of the tree where a stringer of climbing rose stretched on the ground. He plucked a small red flower and held it to his nose as he watched Lucy's house.

A horrible man. Red Pennington, the jealous husband. Cal shivered. He should have worn a coat. He looked at his watch. He heard a small child cry in another house, and two teenage girls came out of the house directly across from Lucy's. He crushed the rose in his hands. He would have to move along. The girls carried school books, and he wanted to call to them, Walk the other way, don't come by me, please, then thought how crazy that would sound. Scare them. Leper. The girls didn't seem to see him. One handed the books she carried to the other.

"Are you sure you don't want me to walk halfway with you?"

"It's hardly dark at all."

Cal started to perspire. Would they see him run away and wonder?

He moved quietly away from the tree. He had to get around that corner, behind the hedge, out of sight, and then run like hell for the lights of the Circle R. He brushed the side of the hedge as he moved around the corner.

"Did you hear something?" he heard one of the girls ask.

"Don't try to scare me, Judy."

"Be scared," he thought. "Be scared, honey." His mother running down the street. Who knew what kind of person hid at the other end of the street? He walked quickly away, his hands in his pockets, his head down.

"Well, hello Cal," a voice said, and he nearly fainted.

He looked into the face of Mr. Hardy.

"Taking my after-dinner walk," the man said. "Going to see Jimmy Lee away, are you?"

"Yes," Cal said, shivering still. "Cooler than I thought it would be."

"Bill-ee," a woman called, her hands cupped around her mouth as she stood on her front porch. "Time to come in."

"Isn't Jimmy's party at the Circle R?" Mr. Hardy asked.

"Yes," Cal said.

"Shoot, boy, you're walking the wrong direction."

Cal felt slightly dizzy. He couldn't think. "I was just walking," he mumbled.

"Come on," Mr. Hardy said, "I'll walk partway with you."

Walk partway. Don't go alone. "You know, Cal," Mr. Hardy said, pulling Cal in the right direction. "You don't need to be nervous. People in Four Corners are right understanding, as a rule."

Cal nodded, *saved again.*

He was thoroughly chilled by the time he arrived at the Circle R. He pushed open the rough-hewn door, and was assaulted by the sound of loud music. He was astonished at the noise and color and smoke of it all, as if he had never before experienced anything like it. He had to shake away the notion that he was a man from another time and place. The beat was steady, strong, and people were dancing. Johnny Cash and the strong steady rhythm of the bass.

He looked through the bar filled with people who were about his age, trying to locate Jimmy Lee. Young men with longish hair. Cal felt ancient beside them, a new sensation, and one that, at least for the moment, he cherished. He thought of the young men in cowboy hats who had probably come in from the outlying farms and ranches as boys, and the young women with bright shiny hair, blond, brunette, auburn, that picked up the light in their eyes and the glasses they held and tossed it playfully across the room, as girls. They smiled at their friends, and sipped the top of the foam on the beer, and laughed as if there was nothing to worry about, as if Jimmy Lee were invincible.

Cal still searched for Jimmy Lee, stretching to see over the heads of two pretty young girls who stood near the door whispering some romantic secret or dream. One of the girls twisted her ring while the other leaned close to her ear, and the ring twister smiled and said just loud enough for Cal to hear, "Did he really say that? Honestly? When?"

At the end of the bar, Cal saw Jimmy Lee. He was sitting, or almost sitting, on a bar stool, and he looked as if he could barely hold his head up. In front of him was a row of beer mugs, some empty, some still full. Cal pushed through the people. He better speak to Jimmy Lee quickly from the looks of things.

He tapped him on the shoulder and said again, "Good luck, kid."

Jimmy Lee looked up at him, his hair falling down over his eyes, and said, "They're going to cut my damned hair, did you know that?"

"I know that much," Cal said, and patted Jimmy's shoulder. The boy nodded ever closer to the bar, and finally just put his head down on one of his forearms.

"Rest a minute," he said.

"Too much party," said the young man who had walked up behind them.

"Right," Cal said, and tried to move away. He didn't like people coming up behind him. People who weren't expected. Mr. Hardy on the street. Had those girls seen him?

"You work with Jim, don't you?" the young man said. "Live at Pincher's place?"

Cal could see that Jimmy Lee's friend was not in much better shape; he had to steady himself against the bar stool.

"Right," Cal said, turning away from the man.

"Name's Bud," the man said anyway.

Cal waved at the bartender, who brought him a beer. "Four bits," the bartender said, and Cal put a dollar on the bar.

Bud picked up one of Jimmy Lee's untouched beers and drank. Foam streamed down from both corners of his mouth, and Cal wanted to get away from him, but didn't want to make him angry.

Tightrope, he thought.

Then Bud was pulling his arm. "Come on," he said, "I got someone for you to meet." He was insistent, drunk, eyes determinedly ahead. Cal had to concentrate to keep from spilling his beer. Bud kept pushing him toward a room in the back. Cal could see a pool table, other booths. It was lighter in there and the smoke hung low over the table.

"There's Maria," Bud said, drawing Cal through.

Maria Borelli? The woman whose name had stopped after-dinner conversation cold?

Suddenly they were before a table and Bud was leaning over as if he had to be within six inches of someone's face in order to recognize him, and two other men sat at the table, and one other woman with long red curly hair was laughing, not with him, but at him. When he stood aside to pull Cal into the circle, Cal's mouth opened in surprise, and he felt the perspiration begin as he looked into the gray-green eyes of a woman who looked enough like a picture of his mother taken twenty-five years before to have been her sister. Sister. His mother's? His?

"This here's the guy who lives at Pincher's now," Bud said, hitting Cal in the chest with his gesturing arm.

The woman looked mad enough to start a fire.

"So why should I care, Bud? So why you drag him over here?"

Trace of an accent. Cal could not take his eyes off the woman's face. The same long dark black curly hair. The gold loop earrings, bright red lipstick, a spot of color on each cheek. She brought a cigarette to her lips, and that took the feeling away from him for a minute—that and the accent—and she inhaled, expelled the smoke, and looked at Cal as if it was his fault.

"Good luck," she said to Cal coldly. She turned her attention to Bud. "Take your friend away, eh?" she said. "We got our own party here. No visitors."

"Nice to meet you," Cal said, grabbing the wavering Bud, and the calm way he said it made her blink.

As soon as he could find a vacant place he parked Bud there, moved to the end of the bar, and ordered another beer. Whatever had happened between Mrs. Pincher and Maria Borelli must have been something, he thought. He moved down the bar until he could find a stool, and saw, when he sat down, that he could see Maria Borelli and her group framed in the mirror. They laughed and talked, and she seemed preoccupied with her fingernails.

What had she done? It certainly seemed as if everyone knew what but him. He shivered again, looking around. The Circle R was far too much like Hawley's for comfort. All he would need now was the woman who looked like Mary Beth to come strolling in, and he would be convinced that he'd never really left Yellow Fork after all. His mother was young and alive. And he was in that place like on the "Twilight Zone." When all of this was over, he was going to head for New York City.

"Cal?" He turned to face a pretty blond girl and he nearly laughed with fright.

"Hi. Remember me?"

He was too stunned to reply. His vision blurred and he could not make out her face. He was going crazy.

"I'm Jimmy Lee's sister. I met you at the store."

Cal just stared at her.

She laughed. "You were pretty busy. I guess you don't remember."

"I remember," he lied. He had to stop shaking. It wasn't Mary Beth. She didn't even look like her.

"Poor Jimmy Lee," she said nervously. She nodded in the

direction of the booth where Jimmy Lee had been taken. He was asleep, his head on the table.

"Quite a party," Cal said. He couldn't think of anything else. She just stood there, looking down at her hands. Her hair, now that he could focus his eyes and see it, was straight and shoulder length, and he could count ten or twelve freckles on her cheeks. She seemed remarkably out of place in the bar, and it made the stale smoke and the smell of beer unbearable.

"It's real close in here," he said. He had to get away. "Think I'll get some air." He stood up from the stool. He couldn't worry about rudeness, not when he was cracking apart.

"I know," she said. "It's depressing. Could I go out with you for a minute?" She glanced around anxiously. "I mean if you're not leaving altogether."

He had no way out of that. "Sure," he said.

Outside, the night seemed to have warmed some, a change in wind direction, something. They turned off the main street at the first opportunity.

"I forgot my coat," the girl said.

"So did I."

The girl walked with her arms folded in front of her. "Were you in Viet Nam before you came here?" she asked.

"Why?" Was it his imagination, or did the breeze shift, bringing a cold whisper with it?

"You must have been somewhere. I don't know. It's funny. The people who come back don't want to talk about it."

"No. I lived in another part of the state," he said. "Worked at a smelter."

They passed the dark public swimming pool, and Cal could see the light of the moon reflected on the still water.

"They just filled it for the summer," she said as if she could read his mind.

Cal remembered the days that seemed centuries ago now. The feel of the water as he cut through it, the cheers of the high school crowd as they urged the swim team on. Pull, pull, the girl in the bathing suit at the end of the lane, the man with the stopwatch. The click of a thumb as he stopped the second hand, the pat, pat, pat of the girl's feet as she ran the time to the desk.

"I was on the swimming team in high school," he said.

"Maybe we could go together sometime." She added, "Oh, in case you forgot, my name's Kayleen."

"Hello, Kayleen." He smiled, though it was a struggle.

They started off down the sidewalk again in silence. The air was helping, he thought. Clearing away those smoky terrors. A light breeze rose and fell, rattling the new leaves in a spring tree. A dog barked three times, then howled in the backyard of a house they passed, and she shivered.

"You lived here all your life?" he asked.

"Every day of it," she said. "I'd like to move away, but I don't know how."

"This seems like a nice enough place."

"If you knew Four Corners as well as I do..."

"I'd like to know more," he said.

They crossed the last paved street of the town, and paused on the corner. "It's getting warmer," she said. "Isn't that odd?"

It was true. The wind was southerly and slight, whispering away the chill.

"That means it will probably rain tomorrow," she said. "Which way do you want to go?"

Cal looked down the sidewalk that fronted the row of houses that formed the line of demarcation between town and field. He looked out across the flatness of new grasses blowing lightly.

"There," he said, pointing toward the horizon and the moon. "Is there a path?" He wondered if the houses had been there in his mother's time. Perhaps this was the very street she had run down frantically trying to escape the man. He could make out the hulking black forms of barns dotting the fields. The low-lying sheds. Right there in front of him.

They passed lilacs in bloom and when they turned into the alley, he heard the sound of the irrigation ditch, full with the spring runoff. He remembered the kitten, and the blue liquid eyes, and he had the painful desire to confess to the slight girl who walked beside him, forcing him to take another deep breath of resolve.

"Jimmy Lee used to catch horned toads in those fields and put them in my bed," she said as they walked. "I used to scream and scream while he laughed."

Jimmy Lee, fighting in a jungle while helicopters whipped

the sky into a frenzy, rising clouds of smoke and fire and the rhythm of artillery.

Boys and their games. Make the girls scream, scream. As men they had even greater tricks. Henry Whitehorse and Howard Cheever.

They turned down a dirt road that seemed to stretch out into nowhere. A few crickets promised the summer that was soon to arrive, and some strange night-flying bird rose up from the field and flapped away across the sky.

"Want me to tell you a ghost story?" he asked maliciously, wanting to generate the shiver that had twice now made her seem so delicate.

"I'm too old for ghost stories," she said, shaking her head.

He looked at her pretty face, her young face. You're never too old, he thought. But if she had any ghosts, she hid them well. "I'm only teasing," he said.

They had walked another hundred yards or so when she suddenly stopped. "Let's go back," she said. "I'm cold."

He knew suddenly and absolutely that she wanted him to kiss her. How would he ever explain to her? This girl he had just met, who, because it was a little chilly, wanted him—him—to kiss her. In an instant, Mary Beth pinned to the living room floor, the little girl stretched out beside him, a girl with a birthmark on her leg, a dark-haired woman kept prisoner in a barn by his blood.

"I'll take you back," he said, and he looked away into the darkness. Would his terror ever end?

"Would you just walk me home instead?" she asked. "It's not very far."

He thought it sounded like an apology. Together, they turned back toward the few lights of the town and away from the black floating fields that hid the horned toads and musty abandoned barns of the past.

She insisted he stay for a glass of lemonade. She went to get sweaters, a pink one for her, a gray wool cardigan for him. They sat on the front porch of her house.

"So," he said, trying to relax, "what is there to do in Four Corners?"

She shook her head. "Not much, I can tell you that. What did you like to do when you were growing up?"

"The usual," he said. He didn't want to go back to Yellow Fork, even for a minute. "Track team, swimming team."

"It's funny about being a kid," Kayleen said. "I mean, I took dancing lessons from Mrs. Rudd, and piano lessons from Mr. Clancy, as if I would ever be able to use those things." She turned to him. "I mean now, I can pick out a tune here and there, but I can hardly put on a pink net costume and dance around a stage. It feels somehow like I was fooled." She paused. "I look at my mother. You should see her pictures when she was young," she said. "She was beautiful. Now she's old."

Cal thought of his own mother, lovely even on her deathbed, and tried to calculate the difference.

Her mother had grown up in Four Corners, too. As had her father. "Two silent people," she said, shaking her head. "It's like a prison here."

Cal almost laughed a cruelly knowing laugh.

"How old is your mother, anyway?"

She looked at him, startled by the question, clearly. "I don't know," she said, glancing away. "I don't even know. Forty something, I guess."

Perfect. She would have known his mother, probably.

"When I was a junior," she said, jiggling the glass and watching the ice, "I was queen of the prom."

"You're a very pretty girl," Cal said.

"And I'm still in Four Corners."

"Other places aren't much different," he said.

"I just don't believe that," she said, lifting the glass to her lips. "I won't believe that."

He saw to his dismay that tears were forming in her eyes.

"And now, Jimmy Lee is going away. I know he might have to go to Viet Nam, but he might not, too. He might go to Europe, or somewhere nice."

Cal put his arm around her shoulders. "He might."

She shook her head. "Really, actually, I'm afraid he's going to die."

A truck pulled up in front of the house, bringing the sounds of drunken laughter, the slamming of doors, shouted curses, the clatter of a beer can as it hit the sidewalk. The porch light came on, and a man in striped pajamas came out just as three boys clumsily struggling with the starchless body of Jimmy Lee came through the gate.

Cal turned to see a woman behind the screen door in a bathrobe and a hairnet. She held her hands tightly in front of her in an angry formation of prayer.

Cal stood to help with the incoherent Jimmy Lee. The girl and her parents stood silently as they passed by and took Jimmy Lee into the house and dropped him onto the living room couch. Once everyone had gathered to stare down at the boy who was off to war, the boy who sang disconnected strains of "When Johnny comes marching home again," in his sleep, Cal could see that the mother's eyes were red from weeping, and that Kayleen was pale with the terror of it all.

"We'll get him to bed," the man said. "You all be on your way."

"I'll help," Cal said, bending over to get Jimmy Lee to his feet. "I work with Jimmy at Hardy's."

Kayleen's father nodded. "Seen you there."

While Kayleen ushered the other celebrants out the door, Cal and Jimmy Lee's father marched the soldier down the hall to his room.

Cal found Kayleen standing on the porch. She pulled her sweater around her again, and another shiver descended.

She looked at Cal, speechless, her eyes filled with terrible questions. He murmured "Good night," aware of the sound of a woman crying quietly in the background.

As he walked home, he recounted his own mysteries. He decided, as he turned the corner and went up the steps of Mrs. Pincher's boarding house, that it all came down to the same thing. Life and death and the constant battle to understand the difference.

It was three o'clock in the morning and Mrs. Pincher was sitting alone in the parlor in her dressing gown. In the dim light from one corner lamp, Cal could see that she held a glass of wine in one hand, and a cigarette in the other. He wondered if this was a nightly custom, if she, in fact, ever slept.

"So how was 'good-bye to Jimmy Lee'?" she asked.

Cal hated the edge of the question. He turned without answering and mounted the stairs to his room. He thought he heard the soft sound of laughter from the parlor, and he imagined the slight creaking of the stairs as he walked. Perhaps his weight made faint cracking lines in the plaster as the house aged overnight. Underneath all of this, behind the carefully curtained windows and the latched screen doors, were the answers to his questions.

It was an odd sound, perhaps someone calling his name, but a sound that passed or at the same instant made him sit up in bed. He was perspiring in the darkness. Silence. A light tapping, fingernails on glass or a restless limb of a tree. Another sound, perhaps a small pebble thrown up from the yard to signal him. Come on down here, whispered, come on, Cal, come on. Another pellet, two, three. He was standing at the window. There she was, looking up at him, her long, almost white-blond hair a graceful arc in the darkness. *It's me*, rising up through the night, an arm raised, a hand beckoning, *it's me*, singing up through the new leaves of the tree.

He was out on the high wooden landing looking down at the whitewashed boards that crisscrossed the house, that formed a ghostly fire escape, and he started toward the ground. His feet were heavy on the wood. He was afraid of sound. *It's me, Cal*, drifting in melody, the white half moon of a promising face. He put his fingers to his lips to hush his own heart. He reached the second level, the parallel catwalk, and he passed two dark windows, and he thought he heard the sound of breathing, but perhaps it was his own.

He stopped. The third window. The curtains were parted slightly, and an elongated diamond of light crossed his path, blocked his path like a deadly transparent wall. He heard a groan.

The girl waited, still, as motionless as a statue in the middle of the lawn. He had to get by.

He moved close to the window, prepared to dip below the sill and crawl past the barrier. A short shrill scream that was quickly quelled made him look inside the room. Two tall red candles burned beside the bed, and he could see the man and the woman. Their naked bodies were not white, but rather an electric orange, as if the red candles cast red light. The woman's hands were above her head and she seemed to struggle beneath the man, the man with black hair, the man who buried his face in her belly, moved down between her thighs, holding her legs apart with his great hands that were stained with hair, the man who with a rough twist of his head was profiled in the window, locked between her legs, and she still hid her face from it all.

Through the slightly parted curtains Cal saw the white bared teeth, the black mustache, the vicious mouth open and attacking. The woman seemed to be twisting into the bed, burrowing away from the man who was more beast than human.

Cal could not move his legs.

The man straightened and crawled up over her like a snake. He wrapped her legs that now seemed disconnected, as if in the blink of an eye he had dismembered her, around his waist, then grabbed her long black hair in both his hands.

He's killing her. Cal felt the words rise in his throat. He had to stop it. The man was bending her and breaking her, and he was going to pull her hair from her head and wear it around his neck like a scarf. Cal was strangling in his own fear. His mouth opened in a rage at it all, and no sound came forth. He could not breathe.

With a final violent thrust at his victim, the man yanked the woman's face into the candlelight, forcing her out into the night where her blind eyes saw nothing.

There, contorted in absolute ecstasy, was the face of Maria Borelli.

A loud single crash. A gunshot. A slamming door. A car, too close, backfiring.

Cal forced his eyes open. Darkness, silence. A slight scrape of a branch against the window of his room. He lay there, not moving, until everything had vanished except the face. The open red lips, the long-lashed fire-lit eyes. The black hair on the pillow and the protracted moan.

He wanted Maria Borelli in the middle of the night.

As it goes when one has a dream that is frighteningly realistic, Cal had a difficult time in the presence of any of the principal players. He dared not even look in the direction of Mr. Tonelli. To compound his problem, Mrs. Pincher seemed annoyed with him, a fact made evident by her either cool or barbed remarks at the dinner table. When he entered the room, she seemed to stop talking and stare at him. The yellow house on Elm no longer seemed so safe.

At the store, he worried about encountering Kayleen. The memory of a girl in a white dress beckoning.

He received a rather cryptic note from Ruggles suggesting forthcoming information quickly. He was afraid to approach Lucy's house again after his awkward meeting with Mr. Hardy. He had to cross the street one evening on his way home to avoid a face-to-face with Maria Borelli.

He awoke one night, soaked with perspiration, the words "Leave me alone, all of you" caught in his throat like a scream. Mrs. Pincher, in particular, watched him too much.

"Our Callant is branching out," she said one night at dinner. "Getting into the swing of things."

The other boarders ate silently, as if afraid to hear what might follow. "Ah to be young and foolish again," she said, cutting off the corner of her lemon meringue pie and placing it gracefully in her mouth.

"Now, Mrs. Pincher," Mr. Tonelli said, leaning back in his

chair as he always did when he was about to bait her. "You do yourself a disservice."

Cal squirmed. The only thing worse than enduring Mrs. Pincher's sarcasm was somehow feeling that Mr. Tonelli was defending him. He did not want the man as an ally.

He spent hours in his room trying to reconstruct a plan, trying to get some calm, some order back into his mission.

He wrote to Ruggles explaining that he needed more time. He also reminded him that the warden, thus far, had not fulfilled his part of the bargain. Perhaps Red had made the whole story up.

But it was Mrs. Pincher who gave him the most difficulty. What did she want from him? Was she angry because he had not stopped that night after Jimmy Lee's party? Did she want a report the way a mother did? Or did she want company of another sort?

He didn't like either possibility, but he had to do something to appease her.

Saturday, on his way home from work, he stopped in front of two children, a boy and girl, who were selling branches of lilacs from a bucket of water on the corner. They must have been six or seven years old, and looked like twins.

The private enterprise of the young. He and Dave selling tomatoes from his mother's garden. They'd filled his wagon with the red ripe fruit, and wheeled it optimistically down to the main street and set up business to make the fortune that would buy them double-decker ice cream cones for the rest of their lives. Odd. Mrs. McNee had been their first customer, and they had pocketed her money and laughed behind her back and called her "fat" as she walked down the street. Dave, never the shy one, was the barker. "Best tomatoes in the world," was his modest cry.

All this came back to him as he examined the branches of lilacs, a peace offering for Mrs. Pincher. The little boy eyed him suspiciously, and to his dismay, the little girl lifted up her dress to scratch a large mosquito bite on her thigh. A red welt. A mark. He had to look away.

A wagonload of tomatoes, and the big boys coming down the street.

"I think I'll sample this one," Georgie Weller had said,

picking a tomato from the wagon. He had mashed it ingloriously into his mouth, the seeds and juice streamed down his chin.

Cal selected three good-sized branches of flowers, and held the dripping stems in his hand. "How much?" he asked the little boy as he shook the water from his hands.

"Three dimes," the little girl said.

The big boys and the tomatoes. Dave, it must have been Dave. He was the one who loved to throw things. The air suddenly filled with ripe tomato missiles. Georgie Weller took one right in the side of the neck, where it splattered and ran down inside his shirt.

Cal searched in his pocket for the money. His hands shook as he placed the three dimes in the outstretched hand of the little girl.

He and Dave had returned to Cal's mother's house covered with the seeds and the juice of their first business venture.

He imagined the bucket of lilacs overturned, the little girl screaming and crying as a big boy whipped her with the falling lavender blossoms.

He blinked away the image and remembered his mother squirting him and Dave with the garden hose to wash away the bloody seeds.

He wanted to run. "Thank you," he muttered to the silent children. "Good luck," he added, thinking everything was a near miss these days.

As he turned down the street he heard the little boy. "Give me the money," the boy said. "I keep the money."

He looked back in time to see the boy snatch the dimes from the little girl's hand, and all he could think was that someone should tell her to keep her dress down, to keep herself covered.

He walked two blocks before he noticed he held the flowers so tightly his hand was imprinted with hard lines. He looked at the delicate blossoms, inspecting them for signs of impending death, but they were as firm and resilient as ever. He had done no damage so far.

With cold determination, he walked up the steps of the yellow house.

Mrs. Pincher was coming down the stairs, and Cal would remember, later that night, the way her face softened back into grace as he held the flowers out to her. Both little boy and suitor, he trembled.

"I thought they were real pretty," he said simply.

"Why, thank you, Mr. Newkirk," Mrs. Pincher replied, putting the flowers to her face. "They have such a lovely distinctive scent."

He nodded, unable to recall.

"Go on up and change for dinner, then come have a nice cool drink with me in the parlor," she said.

It was as if he had just returned from a trip.

Twenty minutes later they were alone in the parlor. The others had adjourned to the porch due to the heat.

"So tell me how you're really doing, readjusting and all," she said, putting a bourbon and seven-up into his hand.

Was that his failure? The lack of progress reports?

"Fine, I think," he said. "Hard to meet so many new people."

"Yes," she said, gesturing for him to sit down. "I can imagine." She exhaled a stream of smoke. "There are all kinds in Four Corners."

The slight burn of the bourbon gave him courage. "I was in prison with a man from here," he said. He watched her carefully for any sign of disapproval that might force a quick retreat.

"I wondered if you'd run into Red Pennington."

"I didn't know him very well."

"That's good for you."

"Doesn't his wife live here?"

"You don't want to get to know Lucy Pennington, although compared to him I suppose she's not a bad sort."

Cal sipped his drink, and Mr. Tonelli appeared in the door.

"This is certainly a cozy gathering," he said, gesturing with his arm at the emptiness of the rest of the room.

"Why don't you join the others on the porch?" Mrs. Pincher said firmly.

Cal saw what he thought was a quick flash of anger in Mr. Tonelli's eyes, but then the customary arrogant smile appeared.

"I actually intend to enjoy the solitude of the garden before dinner," he said. "I trust we'll be dining on time." He turned without waiting for any response and was gone.

Was he jealous, Cal wondered? That would be good.

"I didn't know," he went on with the subject of Red, "why he was in prison. Sometimes those things aren't discussed."

"He's a vicious bully when he drinks, which is most of the time. He beat the man he worked for senseless over some misunderstanding, a man who had taken him in and given him a good job."

Cal glanced at the clock in the hall. Not much time.

"But he has a little boy, doesn't he?"

Mrs. Pincher looked at Cal and laughed. "*She* has a little boy. Whether he has one or not is a matter of debate." She sipped her drink.

That, Cal thought angrily, was the very kind of speculation that had gotten him convicted of a crime he didn't commit.

"I'm sorry," Mrs. Pincher said, as if in response to some look from Cal. "Perhaps that was too cruelly put."

"Pennington talked a lot about his wife and kid," Cal said. "Seemed like he really loved them both. He didn't seem like such a bad guy."

Mrs. Pincher placed her cigarette in the ashtray, leaned forward, and took Cal's free hand. Her clasp was cool and warm at the same time, powdery and caring.

"Listen to me, Callant. Prison was a very different thing. Prison is exactly what it is defined to be. A place where people are not free. Not free to be good, not free to be bad. Lucy was what we call in this town a 'wild' girl. No one knows why. Nice enough family. She was just always in some kind of trouble. I suspect she's not terribly bright. Anyway, Red was just another form of that trouble. With any luck, he won't come back for her."

There was nothing remarkable about her words, or even the way she said them, but something about the way she held his hand and the concern in her eyes made it all a serious warning.

She let go of his hand and stood up from the couch.

As he stood to join her, Cal said, "Sometimes I think I just don't understand people very well." Like you and Mr. Tonelli, he thought.

"You just talk to me about anything that confuses you," she said, and Cal looked past her to the lilacs that stood in the vase on the hall table.

"Thanks," he whispered. "I'd appreciate that." He smiled inside. She'd given him a perfect excuse for the future.

"You can't trust everyone," she added, standing back from him. Suddenly, he could smell the lilacs.

"I met Jimmy Lee's sister," he ventured.

"Kayleen? She's a nice girl, a sweet girl. I never liked Jimmy Lee much, though."

"I could tell that," Cal smiled. A nice girl, a sweet girl. A girl who might tell him a lot if he could manage to be calm about it.

"Well," Mr. Tonelli said from the entry hall, "that little walk has certainly sharpened my appetite." Mrs. Lewis was at his side.

"Is it time?" she asked.

Mrs. Pincher did not answer. She led them into the dining room without a further word.

It was as if the lilacs in the entry hall had somehow absorbed the past tension. Dinner was once again filled with good-natured conversation, earnest speculation about summer. One by one the boarders gave Cal their recommendations as to how to spend the warm night. After dinner, he played a game of chess with Mr. Johnson, and was beaten quickly and badly although Mr. Johnson said he was much improved.

He went for a walk once the sun was down, and found himself, quite unexpectedly he thought, in front of Kayleen's house. Fate, he decided, and renewed courage. The memories of the mangled tomatoes and the little girl were gone, as if both had been a mere daydream of long ago.

A sweet girl, a nice girl. Trust.

The doors and windows of Kayleen's house were open and he could hear the sound of a television set, and voices that seemed to be calling from room to room.

After all, she had seemed to like him, he thought as he walked up to the door and knocked. He could hear the sound of tires screeching and sirens screaming from the television, and then Kayleen's father was there.

"Is Kayleen here?" he asked, even though the man had not inquired as to his business.

The man opened the door, and Cal stepped inside. He could hear a small child crying somewhere else in the house.

"Mother?" the man called, and Kayleen's mother appeared

in the kitchen door drying her hands on her apron. "He wants Kayleen."

The man did not seem to recognize him, and before Cal had a chance to refresh his memory, the man had returned to the chair in front of the television set, joining two young boys.

Mrs. Lucus came forward.

Cal extended his hand. "I don't know if you remember me. I worked with Jimmy Lee." She made no move to take his hand, so he placed it awkwardly in back of him.

She smiled. "I remember you. Jimmy Lee got to his training camp all right," she added.

"That's good. Is Kayleen here?"

"I suppose so," the woman said wearily. "You wait here."

He watched her walk up the stairs. She seemed much older than Mrs. Pincher, much older than his mother, although he knew that was not true.

As he waited nervously, he knew they must think him a suitor. Kayleen would think that, too. A nice girl. Remember that. Normal, act normal. A shy young man, but one with nothing to hide.

Soon Kayleen and her mother appeared at the top of the stairs, and Kayleen peered down at him.

"Hi," she said. "I'll be down in a minute."

It seemed like a good deal more than a minute to Cal as he stood there. More cars collided on the television show, complete with the sound of breaking glass and more sirens. At last she came down the stairs.

"I wondered if you'd want to get a milkshake or a beer, or something," he said.

"Sure," she said, smiling. "I've been wondering if you'd call."

Her expectation sent a wave of dizziness through him, so he concentrated on her face. Freshly scrubbed. He could smell the soap. She took a sweater from a coat rack by the door. "Just in case," she said.

Later he would think that things could not have worked out more perfectly if he had written a script, and he would wonder what fateful hand designed it so.

He set the course himself, once they decided on a milkshake. He led so they would have to pass Lucy's house, and he set the stage by asking polite questions as they walked. Who lived in the green house? What was the woman who sat on her porch with five black cats at her feet like? They passed the high school principal's house, and the place where Kayleen's very first boyfriend had lived before his family moved to Wisconsin. They passed an old house where a candle burned in the window.

"I used to be terrified of that woman. We all thought she was a witch. She used to scream and wave a broom at us when we passed, and threaten us if we came into her yard. Of course, at night some kids would run through just to antagonize her." She laughed. "I was never brave enough."

Mary Beth, Cal thought wryly, would have led the pack.

"Now I feel sorry for her," Kayleen went on. "But I'm still afraid. She stops people on the streets and tells them the future whether they want to know or not."

Cal had the peculiar sensation of knowing the woman, but could not think why. The future. He shuddered to think what she might have to say to him.

As they approached Lucy Pennington's house, Cal could see a young woman sitting on the porch. She sat with her arms around her knees and stared out at a lone water sprinkler that sprayed the hopeless lot of untamed grass. Just as his lips were forming the question, the woman called out.

"Hey, Kayleen."

"Hi, Lucy."

They stopped, and the young woman got to her feet and came toward them. She wore tight white shorts and a blue halter top, and had long curly red hair that hung well past her shoulders. She was the woman who had been sitting with Maria Borelli the night of Jimmy Lee's party, and Cal could see immediately why Red was so worried.

Lucy leaned against the closed gate, and Cal heard the steady sound of the water sprinkler and saw the bright drops of water that pinged on the overturned tricycle she had not bothered to move out of the way.

"You hear from Jimmy Lee?" Lucy asked, looking at Cal with some curiosity.

"He got to camp all right," Kayleen said. "This is my friend, Cal Newkirk. Lucy Pennington."

"Nice to meet you," Cal murmured. She showed no sign of recognition of his name. Red had been lucky enough not to mention him at least.

"I don't suppose you've got any cigarettes," Lucy asked. "I tell you, sometimes I think that kid will never go to sleep, and I can't go for even a minute until he does."

"Sorry," Kayleen and Cal said in unison, prompting a nervous laugh.

"We could get you some and drop them off after we get a shake," Cal volunteered, and he felt Kayleen tense beside him.

"Oh, gee, would you?" Lucy brightened immediately. "Wait right here."

Cal watched her run up the walk to the house, watched as she bounced up the steps, the shorts barely concealing her body.

"Her husband's in *prison*," Kayleen whispered as if to point out that he had made a mistake. He wanted to laugh at her innocence.

Lucy reappeared with three dollar bills clutched in her hand. "Would you mind getting a six-pack, too, and Marlboros?" she asked, directing her question to Cal with what he could only describe as a note of flirtation. "Any kind of beer's okay."

Cal took the money from her outstretched hand. "Now, there's no hurry," Lucy emphasized, but Cal could see that was not true.

He knew the woman stayed leaning against the gate as they walked away. A kind of prisoner herself.

"It's not that Lucy's so bad," Kayleen said. "I guess she's just lonely. That can happen real easily in Four Corners."

"Won't hurt to do her a favor," he said, feeling the softness of the bills in his hand, remembering the tone of her voice. What if he were to make a play for Lucy Pennington? Take her up on some unstated invitation. That would make some letter to Ruggles. Still, she hadn't gone off and left her little boy. His own mother, always there, always faithful to her son. Mrs. Pincher, waiting.

In the ice cream parlor, much to Cal's dismay, they ran right into Mr. Dennis and Miss Mayfield, who acted as if they had just been caught in the woodshed. Miss Mayfield giggled nearly uncontrollably—something she was not allowed to do at Mrs. Pincher's—while Mr. Dennis stood to invite them to sit down and join them.

"Now don't you tell Mrs. Pincher," Miss Mayfield said.

"I won't," Cal agreed. This was going to slow things up considerably. He wanted to get back to Lucy Pennington.

Kayleen was explaining that Miss Mayfield and Mr. Dennis taught at the very schools she had attended, that in fact, she had been in one of Mr. Dennis's classes.

"A good student, too," Mr. Dennis said without a smile.

A young girl came and took their orders, and after much indecision, Miss Mayfield settled on a raspberry milkshake, reminding Cal of Mrs. McNee and seeds in her teeth, while he and Kayleen ordered chocolate.

"We were just talking," Mr. Dennis said as they waited, "about why there isn't more reaction against the war in Four Corners. How we just ignore the fact that the city streets are filled with protesters." He pursed his lips in disapproval.

"Kayleen's brother was just drafted," Cal said quickly, hoping to cut the conversation right there.

"He didn't want to go," Kayleen said softly.

"No one wants to go to war," Mr. Dennis continued. "Particularly a war that is immoral and illegal."

The waitress served the milkshakes, giving Mr. Dennis a contemptuous look as she did so. "My father was proud to defend his country in World War Two," she said angrily as she put Mr. Dennis's vanilla shake in front of him abruptly. She walked quickly back to the counter and said something to an older woman who was eating a sundae. The woman turned to stare at them.

"That's exactly what I mean," Mr. Dennis said, stirring his shake with his straw. "People here are a bunch of blind sheep, following a dishonest government."

"William," Miss Mayfield pleaded. "Let's not go into this now."

Cal could see Kayleen's face reddening, and he felt helpless to change the tide.

"Well, I wouldn't go," Mr. Dennis said.

"You're not going to be invited, isn't that so?" Cal could

not resist. He hated the confusion he felt.

"That isn't the point," Mr. Dennis went on. "No one should go. I would take jail first."

Cal laughed. He couldn't help it, and Kayleen said nervously, "I really should be getting home."

"I don't see what's so funny," Mr. Dennis said.

"Nothing," Cal said. He had to be careful. For the first time, he wanted to tell someone where he had been and what it was like, about the dead kid in the shower, and Howard Cheever, the unlikely murderer. "I think you don't understand as much as you think."

He would leave it at that, no matter what.

"I think it is terrible that we send poor kids like Kayleen's brother off to kill innocent women and children in some country where nobody wants us to begin with," Mr. Dennis said quickly. "They don't even understand the issue."

"My brother went to fight for freedom," Kayleen said, and Cal could hear the tears in her voice.

"Now you've hurt her feelings," Miss Mayfield said. "Say you're sorry." A teacher addressing her first-grade class.

"Let's go," Cal said to Kayleen, and she looked at him gratefully.

Mr. Dennis's face was almost purple. He took a deep breath. "Kayleen, I'm sorry," he obeyed. "It was tactless of me."

Kayleen nodded slightly, and Cal glared at him.

"Well, have a nice evening," Miss Mayfield said brightly, as if nothing had happened. "We'll see you at home, Mr. Newkirk."

Cal shook his head in amazement all the way out the door.

They walked in silence to the corner market where they purchased the cigarettes and beer. Once off the main street and into the comparative darkness of the side street, Cal stopped Kayleen. "Listen," he said. "I'm sorry about all of that. Don't be worried. Jimmy Lee will be fine."

Kayleen nodded sorrowfully at his words. "He's really confused about it all. I know that much."

Jimmy Lee and the rest of the world, Cal thought. He had to recognize his own ignorance. He was so involved in his own battles, the wars, past and present, seemed to belong to others, not to him. He found the words "My father was a war hero" playing in his mind. Saw his mother's lips forming the syllables. But his father wasn't a war hero. He was a rapist, dead or alive; he didn't even know which. Kayleen took his free hand, either to give or to get comfort, he didn't know which, and he struggled to relax.

There were four cars and a pickup in front of Lucy's house, and they could hear the music as soon as they turned the corner. Patches of light from the windows lay in squares on the porch and the still-turning water sprinkler had created an overflow stream onto the front sidewalk that forced Cal and Kayleen to walk carefully around it.

"Oh no," Kayleen said. "I don't feel like a party."

"I know," Cal said. He squeezed her hand reassuringly. "We'll just drop this off." He could see through the screen door seven or eight people clustered in the living room, and since it seemed unlikely a knock would be heard, he opened the door and stood aside for Kayleen to enter. Once again, she crossed her arms in front of her. Cal looked around. It was like the Circle R and Hawley's. It could have been one of Tina's parties. He halfway expected to see Dave or Kenny Larkin. Mary Beth.

"There you are," Lucy said, swooping down on them and taking the bag from Cal's arm. "Such good delivery people. Come have a beer."

"Just one," Cal said before Kayleen could object. The music was so loud, he had to shout. The Beatles.

"This isn't going to mix very well with a milkshake," Kayleen said as Lucy handed her a beer.

"Just one," Cal repeated. He had to lean close to her ear so she could hear. "It'll cheer you up. Think of it as showing me life in Four Corners."

Kayleen smiled weakly. "There's not much to see."

The minute the music was over, Kayleen was surrounded by people asking about Jimmy Lee. He was amazed at how politely she replied given what had just happened, after the upset. He recognized one of the young men from Jimmy's party, and a house painter who was a regular customer at Hardy's.

"How you doing," the man asked, nudging by them into the kitchen. He didn't wait for a response, and Cal began to tap his foot to the new song on the record player. Then he saw her. Alone, in the corner, was Maria Borelli.

"Come dance with me once," a young man with stringy blond hair said to Kayleen, "for old time's sake."

Kayleen held Cal's hand tightly, then looked up at him as if both asking and fearing permission. Cal shrugged, and she released his hand and walked into the center of the room with the young man. Cal leaned against the door of the kitchen and pretended to watch Kayleen while actually keeping his eye on Maria. The dark-haired woman returned his gaze once, and looked quickly away. She seemed to be having trouble lighting her cigarette, as if her eyes wouldn't focus, and Cal saw a book of matches on the table, reached for them, and walked over to her. He was only half aware of Kayleen's blond hair curtaining her face as she danced.

Bending over to Maria, he struck the match and held it to the shaking cigarette. He wanted to say, You'll never guess where I saw you last.

"My hero," said Maria.

"You're welcome," said Cal, and he sat down on the arm of the sofa. Look a ghost in the face and it will go away, he thought.

Someone stumbled and sent the needle screeching across the record into silence.

"Dammit," Lucy called, "be careful of my records." The high-pitched wail of a child punctuated her sentence. "Hell," she said, extinguishing her cigarette and heading for the bedroom.

Kayleen appeared at Cal's side and placed her hand on his shoulder. Cal heard a door slam, and someone changed the record. Now it was Johnny Cash, and "Folsom Prison."

"That's Lucy's favorite song," Maria Borelli said, "isn't that a kick in the head."

Cal could see that she was almost too drunk to move.

"We should go soon," Kayleen said. "I have to get home."

Cal nodded. He heard the child cry again.

"You're the one," Maria said, tugging on his arm, "took my place at witch Pincher's house, aren't you." She laughed.

"I guess so," Cal said, and he slipped his arm around Kayleen's waist. It seemed the perfect time.

"You be careful," Maria said, waving her cigarette at him. "She'll cut your balls off and serve them up for dinner."

"Cal," Kayleen pleaded, pulling at him.

"I don't think she'll do that," he said, and then there was that flash of recognition. Maria who looked like his mother and talked like a whore and had taken off her clothes for another man in his dream and made him watch.

"No? Take a good look at Tonelli. See if you think he's still got his." She dropped her cigarette on the floor, and Kayleen bent to retrieve and extinguish it. Maria merely let her head fall back against the couch, and tried to manage a laugh.

"She was in love with that Italian man," Kayleen whispered to Cal. "Maria was."

"Kayleen, could you come here a minute?" Lucy called from the hallway by the bedroom. With a sigh, Kayleen went to join her.

Cal stared down at the drunken woman. The beautiful face twisted into anguish, into violence. He wanted to slap her for the betrayal. Instead, he leaned over to her.

"Tonelli seems to me to be a man who has everything he wants."

Maria raised her head and stared at him. "Get away from me, you bastard."

Cal smiled at the accuracy of her statement, and left her. He walked down the hall in search of Kayleen. Maria Borelli didn't know what she was talking about.

He stood by the bedroom door and peeked inside. Kayleen was sitting on Lucy's bed, rocking the child in her arms, crooning to him, while the child choked and sobbed. Lucy stood over them, her hands on her hips. Kayleen's hair looked silver in the light from the bedside lamp, and he was hypnotized by the sight of her. He could almost feel her arms circling him, rocking him, but the hair next to his face was long and black like Maria Borelli's when he closed his eyes. It made him angry to be tricked.

"What do you think's the matter?" he heard Lucy ask softly. "Doesn't he feel hot?"

Kayleen nodded, and Cal stepped into the room.

"What's the matter?" he asked, and Lucy turned to him. Gone was all the flirtatiousness, all the garish smiles.

"He's sick," she said.

"He's got a fever," Kayleen added. "He feels like he's burning up."

"I don't know what to do," Lucy wailed.

Cal went to the side of the bed and placed his hand on the child's forehead. The little boy whimpered and turned his face into Kayleen's breast, but not before Cal could see the look of Red Pennington about the boy's eyes.

"You'll have to call Dr. Ray," Kayleen said, "and ask him to come over."

"But what about them?" Lucy asked, gesturing with one hand in the direction of the living room.

"I'll tell them he's sick and ask them to leave," Cal said. "Or I'll try."

"Call the doctor," Kayleen repeated, and Lucy moved to the telephone by the bed.

"Would you?" She turned to Cal.

He nodded, and went back into the living room. He walked to the record player and turned it off.

"Hey," the young man who had danced with Kayleen protested.

"Lucy's baby is sick," Cal said. "Everyone will have to leave. She's calling the doctor"

There was an awkward silence, and then the guests, as if stunned, began to pick up the pieces of the evening.

"Someone will have to carry Maria," the house painter said, "she's out like a light."

Cal began to gather up the empty beer cans as the others began to gather up themselves and their belongings. There were curt nods of good night, and then the welcome sound of car engines starting, and the rise then fall of noise as they drove away.

The house was silent except for the whimpers from the bedroom.

By the time the doctor arrived, there was little evidence of the party except for the slight haze of blue smoke that hung in the air.

Cal showed the disgruntled, disheveled old man to the bedroom door, and as Kayleen joined him, they heard the doctor say, "So what have we this time, or is your worry-wart mother just acting up, hey boy?"

They walked back to Kayleen's house in silence.

At the front door of her house, he looked down at her and found her face wet with tears.

"Hey," he whispered. "You were great with that little boy. Don't be upset."

She pushed past him, flung the screen door open, and he could hear her crying as she ran up the stairs to her own room.

As he walked home, he tried to figure out what had happened. Was it Mr. Dennis? Lucy and her baby? Did she misunderstand his talking to Maria Borelli?

"Don't you come in my yard," a voice shrieked in the night, and he stopped in fear. There, framed by the light from inside her house, stood the old woman who told the future.

"I know you," she shrieked. "You stay away."

He hurried on, chilled by the sound of her voice, the black shapeless silhouette in the door. A crazy woman who screamed at everyone.

Why had she pretended to recognize him?

She would explain it to him later in a dream. An old crone who didn't know the future, but somehow divined the past.

Cal sat at the desk in his room writing a letter to Ruggles. The window was open and a Sunday morning breeze blew the curtains, and he could feel cool air on the back of his neck. It was very simple, he told him in the code they had arranged, the woman Ruggles knew in Four Corners was a good mother and a faithful wife. He would let him know if there was any change in that. Unfortunately, he had been unable to locate Jane Russell, but Ruggles should not give up hope. Had Ruggles gotten the box of stuff he had sent?

It was more difficult to think of things to tell Ruggles in a letter than Cal had imagined it would be. I'm making progress, he wrote, thinking that sounded much too vague. Getting ready for the new trial, I mean.

That seemed like a lie, but he couldn't explain. I haven't heard from the warden, he added, then signed the letter with an angry scrawl.

He wondered how Kayleen was feeling. He still had no idea what had made her cry. Maybe she had just been worried about Lucy's child. She was such a tender-hearted girl.

Mary Beth. Selling everything without so much as a twinge. $265.00.

He took a deep breath. It shouldn't be that hard to simply go to the telephone and call Kayleen and ask her. Ask her what? Why were you crying last night? It sounded like a song. He considered going for a walk in the sunshine to see if it would purify his mood, and then stopping by the Lucus house. It seemed too revealing somehow. He didn't want to scare her.

He would call.

There was a telephone on the table in the hall outside his room, and a small local phone book in the drawer. It was odd, he thought as he peeked out of the door to make certain the telephone was free, that he had never had any reason to use the telephone here.

The hall was empty. He pulled out the small chair and sat down. *Lucus.* He was surprised to find five more families in the area with that name. Lucus on Green Street.

Then it occurred to him. *Newkirk.* Maybe there were other members of his mother's family she had neglected to mention along with the number of other things she hadn't told him. Maybe Four Corners was fairly teeming with cousins or aunts and uncles. N. Newkirk. There were no Newkirks in the area at all. In town or in the outlying farm communities. He turned back to Lucus.

Of course. If his name had been familiar, someone would have mentioned it. He heard those conversations all the time in Hardy's.

"Your name Watson? You related to Billy Watson who lives over by Sugar Creek? Brother, huh, uncle, huh, cousin, huh?"

Of course, Mr. Hardy knew everyone in the county.

Cal leaned back in the chair. But it was odd, too, with what had happened to his mother, that no one had said, "There used to be a Newkirk woman lived here twenty odd years ago." People in Four Corners were proud of their good memories, especially for names and dates and gossip. Maybe they were embarrassed to bring it up.

"Are you going to use the telephone, Mr. Newkirk?" Mrs. Mortensen called from her partially open door.

"Oh," he turned to her. "Sorry. Yes. I'll only be a minute."

"There's no hurry, dear," she said.

Cal smiled as he noted the Lucuses' number again. Mrs. Mortensen had taken to calling him *dear* when Mrs. Pincher was not present. There was something about the way she said it that he liked.

He dialed the number. Mrs. Lucus answered on the fourth

ring, and Cal imagined the house full of people who could have answered, and heard Mr. Lucus say, "Mother, phone's ringing."

She called Kayleen to the phone.

"I wondered if you'd heard how Lucy's boy is," he asked.

"I called this morning. He has an ear infection so the doctor gave him a shot and some medicine. He'll be fine."

"He had that high fever from an ear infection?"

"That's common," Kayleen said. "My little brother gets them all the time."

"You sure know a lot about kids," Cal said.

"More than I care to," she answered.

Cal cleared his throat.

"Listen, would you like to go to the movie tonight?"

"I don't think so. I'm not feeling very well."

He said he was sorry to hear that. He asked if there was anything he could do, bring her something, and to each question she replied with the fewest words possible. He started to feel panicky, and thought, don't be silly. She doesn't feel well. That's all. The flu, something. She doesn't know anything about you. You didn't *do* anything to her. He could feel his heart begin to pound. Sitting in a sunny upstairs hall on a Sunday morning with his heart threatening to break through his chest, with his speech almost breathless.

"Maybe I could call you later in the week?"

"Maybe," she said. "I have to go."

He replaced the receiver. He could not imagine what had gone wrong.

"Finished now, dear?" Mrs. Mortensen's tiny voice. "My, do you have a pain in your chest?" She crept out of her door and started for him as if she had a cure.

"Indigestion," he lied as the beating subsided.

"You better whisper that, young man," the old lady said. "If Mrs. Pincher heard..." She shook her head to indicate that certain disaster would follow.

Cal smiled and stood. He helped Mrs. Mortensen into the telephone chair.

"My, how sweet of you," she said, fluttering her spare lashes at him. "Now, let me see, where is that number?"

No Newkirks.

"Listen, Mrs. Mortensen," Cal began. "I've been meaning

to go to the library, to look at some of the history of Four Corners—you know, the things I've talked about—and I wondered if you might..."

"Dear, any time you want to go, just let me know. I even have a key." She smiled, holding a scrap of paper close to her eyes. "In fact, Thursday night would be perfect for me."

"Great," he said, wishing she had made it sooner. Patience, the warden whispered in his ear. He backed into his room, smiling, bowing as he went, watching the lady dial carefully, deliberately. As he closed his door, he hoped to hear her say something like, "I want a sawbuck on Crazy Irma in the fourth," but heard instead, "Mrs. Carlisle? This is Elvira Mortensen from the library drive."

He sat back down to his letter. He wrote a postscript about the boy, and the fact that there were no other Newkirks around.

That afternoon, Cal and Mr. Johnson played their regular Sunday game of chess on the front porch instead of in the parlor. It looked as if summer had arrived for sure, and Mr. Johnson said so three times.

Cal studied the board. He'd tried reading the book on chess Mr. Johnson had lent him, and while it helped some, Cal didn't think he was going to live long enough to win a game from this man. It was, however, taking him longer to lose.

Mr. Johnson didn't seem to care how well or how badly he played as long as he did. He helped Cal, explained strategy, and talked about the weather. He took one of Cal's knights, giving up only a pawn in the process.

On the other side of the porch, Cal could hear Mr. Henderson telling Mr. Simmons about the time the train was caught for five days in the snow over Cutter Creek pass, and Cal wondered how many times Mr. Simmons had nodded to that same story. It would have been something to see Maria Borelli in this household. Something indeed.

"Mr. Newkirk, it's your move. I just took your king's rook."

Cal sighed and turned his concentration back to what was about to be another defeat.

It didn't take long. Mr. Johnson leaned back in his chair and lit his pipe. "You're improving. Don't get discouraged," he said. "Patience, that's what it takes."

Cal nodded. He was feeling better. So Kayleen didn't seem to want to see him. It was probably for the best. It was a beautiful day. He wanted to stretch out on the lawn with the grass prickling at his back, put his hands behind his head, and watch the big fluffy white clouds roll by. With any luck, the backyard would be empty.

He excused himself, and walked around the veranda to the steps that led to the back lawn. There was a wooden picnic table, and he wondered if in summer they would occasionally eat outside. Something told him it was unlikely. There was an apricot tree with the hard green fuzzy balls that would be soft orange in a couple of months, and an apple tree with faint spots of red already.

Perfect, he thought, heading for the apple tree. No one around. He stretched out and took a deep breath. Relax. Calm down. Patience advocated by everyone. He hadn't seen Miss Mayfield and Mr. Dennis yet. They had not been to breakfast. He wondered if they had spent last night in one bed or another arguing about the war, or at least about Mr. Dennis and his tactlessness. Sneaking around like children to argue politics. He wondered if Miss Mayfield giggled when Mr. Dennis made love to her.

Lying on his back, he tried to make the cloud formations into giant bumble bees or Indians, and came up with soft breasts and intertwined bodies. All on a summer's day, a summer's day.

A bee flew close to Cal's face, and he held perfectly still as he had been trained to do from childhood, and the bee, soon bored with him, moved on to the honeysuckle to join the others.

Summer's day. The queen of hearts, she made some tarts, all on a summer's day. The knave of hearts, he stole those tarts, and took them clean away.

He wished the sound, the tone of Kayleen's voice on the telephone didn't still bother him. He wished he'd been able to tell her about the old woman screaming at him so perhaps she could have talked the fear he felt away. He closed his eyes. Patience. Lucy was done with. Wild Lucy, Mrs. Pincher had called her. Wild wild Lucy in the tight white shorts. Not-too-smart Lucy.

Maybe she only made one mistake. Caught in the woodshed or behind the barn with some boy with his pants down around his knees. Poor Lucy. Ruined. He felt uneasy with desire, and the little girl in Yellow Fork surfaced. A girl raped by her father's words, he decided. They should both hate that man for his interruption. Five minutes later, he thought, perspiring, and everything would have been all right. Now it was going to take a second trial.

"Would you like a lawn blanket?" Mrs. Pincher asked, casting a shadow across his body. He had not heard her coming.

He raised up on his elbows, shading his eyes from the sun in order to see her. She stood close, so close he could see above her knees beneath the skirt. She stood there, as if she knew he could see, daring him to look. A little girl with a kitten.

"No. I'm fine, thanks."

Her head seemed small from the foreshortened angle, and he could see a slight trail of cigarette smoke although her hand was hidden. Against the sun, she looked black.

"I never liked the way grass tickled. Made me feel as if something alive were crawling on my skin." There was something odd in the way she said the words. He'd noticed the tone a lot lately. Several times he had seen the light from her bedroom window casting its rectangular glow onto the lawn in the middle of the night when he, too, still adjusting to freedom and a view, had stood at the window of his own room.

"Do you want me to get a blanket for you?" he asked.

"No. Thank you. I only came out to check the roses. For aphids."

He lay back down, and covered his eyes with his hand.

She paused, and he wondered why she didn't walk away. He could feel her presence like the breeze. He cleared his throat. "Mrs. Pincher?" he asked, keeping his eyes shut.

"Yes."

"I met Maria Borelli last night, at least I met her for the second time, actually."

"Well. What did you think?"

"She was drunk. Crude. I didn't like her at all."

"There are many things that can be said about Miss Borelli," Mrs. Pincher said. "You've mentioned only a few."

He felt her turn, felt it almost as distinctly as if the hem of her skirt had swirled across his face.

When next he looked at her, she was kneeling down in the roses, but he was certain she only pretended to look for aphids. She sat too long without moving.

That night he failed to keep Maria Borelli from his dream. The old woman on the porch shrieked at him again, only this time she insisted he come closer and be identified. In the dim candlelight, her face changed in waves between a very old withered woman he didn't know and a twisted Maria. She had five black cats at her feet, and he remembered in the morning that the cats belonged to someone else. I know you, she said. I knew your mother and I knew your father. Then she stopped. She started over, erasing her previous words with a hand trailing mist. I know you. You're the man that raped that pretty girl with the dark hair. I was a crow that sat on a sill and watched. I know you, yes I do. Remember that crow? Ah, too busy, evil one, too busy to see me. Then her face was dark and a cat crawled up her skirt like a spider.

What about the future? Cal had asked, watching the cat climb toward her face, seeing white claws rising, step by step.

She started to laugh, and the strength of that woke him up. Strangely enough, it was the image of the cat that seemed to gradually turn into an enormous spider that kept him awake. It was not her words, the very threats he made in his soul to himself. It was the changing of things. Her face, the time, the cat, the obscuring mist that took away belief, or the value of words once said.

It was the shifting that made him feel that all was hopeless. So many stories told, so few facts known.

Don't give up now, Ruggles said suddenly. You fool. Don't let an old witch beat you with a stick.

It made him angry to think about the dreams. Parts of them always lingering into his day, the aftertaste of some sour substance taken inadvertently. He thought it was like fighting some damned war where the enemy kept changing shape, and attacked only in darkness, making him whirl endlessly in search of the hidden position, unable to determine the line of fire. He supposed he should be grateful that the spirits did not loom up in front of him in the hardware store, sending him screaming into the street for everyone to see and wonder. The discomfort of memory was not such a high price to pay for keeping them in that dark slumbering place. For all of the threats, suspicion, they had only been able to ruin him once, and that was long ago. He saw the little girl and the kitten as part of a dream let loose before he knew what was happening, and he had been imprisoned because of it. Now, as he took care of business, he thought he knew something about being a jailer. Every concrete block he could construct on fact from his past went into the making of that protective wall, and when all of the pieces were in place, he would be a free man. He would tell his own truth.

And Mrs. Mortensen, in her soft blue-gray way, was going to help him. She was his date, his current lady love. He couldn't think about Kayleen now, or Maria Borelli, or even Mrs. Pincher. Mrs. Mortensen was going to introduce him to his mother and wouldn't even know it.

Thursday night, as promised, Cal and Mrs. Mortensen set

off for the library. Because her foot was ailing, they walked
slowly, her arm through his, and it occurred to him that she
was old enough to be his grandmother. She talked lovingly
of the past, of her youth. He liked the sound of her voice, the
feel of her arm, and the faint odor of her perfume mixed with
the summer night air.

"Even after we had been married five or even ten years,"
she said, "Mr. Mortensen would walk me to work and come
for me at the end of the evening hours."

Cal wondered if, when he grew old, his own past would
melt into romantic memory the way hers had. Or perhaps she,
too, fought the nightmares with daydreams.

Once at the library, Mrs. Mortensen introduced him to the
narrow-faced woman who sat behind the desk with a distinct
air of possession.

"This is Mr. Newkirk from Mrs. Pincher's," she said. "I'm
going to show him a little of Four Corners' history."

The woman, without smiling, said, "Well, Elvira, you're
certainly the person to help him with that."

The library was housed in an ancient red brick building
with high ceilings and tall windows with raised venetian
blinds. The windows were open and the sounds and smells
of summer nights floated refreshingly in and around the cu-
bicles defined by shelves of books. Honeysuckle, jasmine.

"We really are the county library," Mrs. Mortensen said.
"The largest branch."

Cal looked at the children's section. It might have been the
very one his mother had taken him to in Yellow Fork. A round
low table and small chairs. A stack of children's magazines in
the center. He had picked his books from there, and his mother
had carried home the large ones, the novels with plastic protective covers. She read them in bed at night. Before she went
to sleep. Alone. He wondered if the stories she told to him
had been written by someone else. Lines from a romantic
novel.

"Now, dear, where do you think you would like to start?"
Mrs. Mortensen said.

"The newspapers, I guess. Isn't that what you suggested?"

"Well, that would be a good idea."

"I thought I would start back about twenty-three years. That's
about how old I am."

"Let's see," she said calculating. "that would be 1944." She smiled at him as if she understood perfectly. She patted his arm, and looked up at him.

"1944. That was the year Mr. Mortensen died."

"I'm sorry," Cal said quickly. "I didn't mean…"

"No need to fret. He was a wonderful man, and I have my memories."

How many times had he heard those words. Amazing coincidence.

The periodicals were kept in the deepest left-hand alcove in the larger room. There was an oak table and two chairs. A perfect place to study, he thought. Mrs. Mortensen moved to a cabinet with large flat drawers.

"They're stored by year," she said. "You know the *Four Corners Clarion* is only a weekly, so there won't be much national news."

"I'm interested in what happened here," he said.

She looked at him quizzically, but turned to the cabinet, scanning the plates that identified the time. She pulled open the sixth drawer down.

"Can you lift this out, dear?" she asked, pointing to a large flat glue-bound volume of papers. "1944." She shook her head. "It seems like yesterday."

He lifted the volume out of the drawer and placed it on the table. Was she going to sit there beside him and prevent him from really getting at what he wanted? It wasn't good that the year had a special interest for her. He wanted to go directly to July.

"I'll just leaf through it, if that's all right," he said, pulling out one of the chairs. When he looked at her face, he could see the faint trace of tears in her eyes.

"You know," she said, "we got three new catalogs this week. I think I'll just sit in the reference section and go over them. You come and get me if you have any questions."

"Thank you," he whispered. He made a vow then. As a kind of payment, he would sit with her some evening and ask her every question he could think of about her life. It would be like an interview. He thought her shoulders seemed a little stooped as she walked away.

He opened the volume. While the papers were yellow, they were in remarkably good condition. He decided the people of Four Corners did not spend inordinate amounts of time perusing a past they probably preferred to recall from what was not, rather than what was, printed there. All he needed was a brief mention of the incident. A name. A description of the event. He took a small notebook and a pen from his shirt pocket. His hands were shaking as he opened the book to the middle. May 16, 1944. The headline announced that the city council had decided that this year's Memorial Day observance would be particularly dedicated to those who had lost their lives in the ongoing war. There was a picture of a group of people clustered around a table as a man signed something. A bright-faced boy, a new Eagle Scout, was identified. A new zoning law discussed. He turned the pages to July 1. There was a picture of the groundbreaking for the new public swimming pool, the very one he and Kayleen had paused by the night they met. A man with a shovel in his hand. The mayor. There was a schedule of events for the coming Fourth of July celebration.

Perfect, he thought.

The occasion was to be at once solemn, and joyful. They were to celebrate the freedom, the independence, the American way, and at the same time remember the fight that went on to preserve that freedom.

A parade at 9:30 in the morning. A picnic sponsored by the Veterans of Foreign Wars in the park at noon. A reading of the Declaration of Independence on the bandstand at two. A band concert at four. A dance in the Eagles' Hall at eight, featuring Al Winslow's orchestra.

A carnival would open at one in the afternoon and run until midnight in the vacant lot at the corner of Green and Second.

Cal felt his heart begin to pound. The carnival. There it was, in print. He put his hand on the page, covering the information, and took a deep breath. Maybe he didn't want to know after all. Perhaps he needed more time. Courage. He remembered the swimming pool in his home town as he stared at the groundbreaking ceremony that took place in Four Corners almost twenty-three years ago. Cal and his fifth-grade friends, kicking and splashing, dunking each other, running until the lifeguard shouted at them to stop. The slapping sound of bare feet, the devil-may-care jumping into the middle of the giggling girls, causing waves of water to get into their eyes and their noses. Giggles and shrieks and choking on top of it all. Cal diving backward into the pool to the cheers of his friends, and the dull pain as his head hit the bottom or the side, he never knew which, and the screams as his head began to bleed, and the lifeguard pulled him from the pool. Blood streamed over his shoulders, and someone carried him into the dressing room while his friends stood around him shivering in their wet suits, quaking with fear.

The pale face of his mother, summoned from home, and the way she held his hand as the doctor at the clinic put in the stitches and took the X-rays.

"It doesn't really hurt," he kept saying. He couldn't wait to see the picture of his head.

But when the time came, when the doctor came back through the door and attached the film over a lighted screen, Cal didn't want to see. He didn't want to know what was underneath his skin and his flesh; what would remain if everything else were horribly peeled away.

That was how he felt then, and how he felt now as he looked at the newspaper before him.

Then he had summoned his courage and forced himself to look at the X-ray. He never could see the crack in his head, although the doctor pointed it out to him. He had survived the experience by pretending it was someone else's head.

That wasn't going to work this time.

A carnival on the edge of town. Would the next issue have a headline about his mother? Would her face stare out at him, smiling girl in a cap and gown, a picture resurrected from the newspaper morgue? That's what they did with victims of automobile accidents. What would they call it? In 1944? Before he could stop himself he imagined the headline MURDERED above her photo. A terrible error.

He turned the pages. The newsprint felt dusty in his fingers. He passed by the want ads, the obituaries, the calendar of coming events. The supermarket ad with prices so low they seemed to be mistakes. An ad for the local Chevrolet dealer with a smiling man pointing to a new car, with a bubble that came out of his mouth saying, Now's the time to buy.

The picture in the center of the July 8 edition was one of the first-prize-winning float in the Fourth of July parade. A young woman dressed as the Statue of Liberty held the torch high, and the headline read, LION'S CLUB TAKES IT AGAIN.

Cal scanned the page. A boy and a girl stood proudly in front of bicycles waving American flags. The mayor had proclaimed the celebration an enormous success. Ernest Wilkerson had died at the age of ninety-two. A chicken-killing dog was on the loose.

Nothing. Cal turned the page. A gossip column talked about families who were reunited for the holiday. Mr. and Mrs. Tommy Littlejohn were the proud parents of Melinda Sue, born on the Fourth of July. Mrs. Lawanda Baker was hospitalized with an emergency appendectomy. The 4-H was planning its annual campout.

Two more pages of ads. The police news. Cal felt almost faint. Jim Medina had been jailed for drunken driving. Lorenzo Hogue and Herbert Olsen for illegal sale of fireworks. Elmer Lucus had reported the theft of twenty chickens and local juveniles were suspected.

Nothing. The back page contained an ad for the Buick dealership as if in response to the Chevrolet man from the week before.

Of course. Maybe his mother had been kept captive for the three days or so. The paper might have gone to press before she was rescued. Calm down. Think clearly. Patience.

July 15, 1944. Local man killed in tractor accident. A dim picture of one George Morgan. The chicken-killing dog was now thought to be only one of a pack. The board of the irrigation company expressed fears over a shortage of runoff water. The new PTA president and her officers posed for the camera and expressed concern over new textbooks. John Miller had enlisted and gone off to join his two older brothers who were already serving abroad.

Cal was now shaking from the soles of his feet to the top of his head. He turned the rest of the pages. The local newspaper had not even seen fit to acknowledge what had happened to his mother. The police report was just another series of traffic violations and one reported stolen car, later found abandoned outside of town. Juveniles suspected again.

He put his head in his hands. He'd been so positive it would all be there. The whole ugly story. The publicity that had made it impossible for his mother to remain in the town in which she had grown up. The humiliation of it all. He looked to the hospital news. Mrs. Baker had been released; Harvey Elder had been admitted. Not even a mention of an unidentified woman recuperating from an assault.

Had the story simply been too sordid to print?

No. Something else wrong. What if, after all this, he was in the wrong town? What if Dave had somehow misheard? Cal had been so positive of that one detail, and yet—he had to go on.

July 22. Funeral services for George Morgan. Three dogs caught and disposed of. The school board president resigned. A group of citizens had petitioned the city council to prevent another carnival from being allowed to use the lot at the corner of Green and Second. They cited noise and dirt and unsavory characters.

The carnival was gone.

"Well, how are we coming along?" Mrs. Mortensen said, leaning over the table. "I knew George Morgan," she said wistfully, seeing the funeral notice. "He was a hardworking man."

"It's very interesting," Cal said, hoping the tremor in his voice did not show. Where would the records be? The court? The city hall? The library suddenly seemed too warm and he thought he wasn't going to be able to stand it much longer. He wanted to get out on the street and run away from the disappointment.

"Let's see," Mrs. Mortensen said. "You're on July." She began to turn the pages. She stopped on September 9. "There's my Harry," she said, pointing to the picture of a robust-looking man in an American Legion hat. HARRY MORTENSEN DIES, it said simply, and an article followed.

Harry Mortensen, 47, died at his home on Tuesday after a lingering illness.

"Of course the picture was taken before he got sick," Mrs. Mortensen said. She continued reading the article, moving her finger down the page. Mr. Mortensen was the principal of the high school prior to his early retirement in the spring of the preceding year. Active in the American Legion, the Kiwanis, and had been treasurer of that organization. He was originally from Iowa, and had married the former Elvira Smith, who survived him. Their only son, William, had been killed on November 16, 1942, while serving with the Allied Forces in Europe. Services were scheduled.

The information wound around in Cal's head, a qauzy protective bandage. Killed in the war. "He looks like a nice man," he heard himself say, thinking how strange it was she had never mentioned the lost son. Suddenly, he felt entombed, as if he had been the one killed, the son never mentioned. His mother did not exist in the pages; it was as if she never existed and he had to latch on to someone, belong somewhere. He could feel the anger surfacing again, threatening the summer night.

"Everyone loved him," Mrs. Mortensen said, and for a minute Cal could not remember who she was talking about. He needed to save them both from 1944.

"Let's go get a sundae," he said, closing the book quickly. Something cold to wake him up.

"I can't think of anything I'd like better," she said as she reached for the handkerchief she kept tucked in the bosom of her dress. "I think I'll have a strawberry one."

As they walked along the street, Cal felt his throat constrict, his arm begin to shake. He wanted to stop her, shake her, and shout, *There was nothing there for me.* She lived in that town. She was there. Surely she must know what had happened to his mother. He imagined her terrified eyes behind the glasses, a quivering mouth. He hated the impulse; he had to stop it. There were other ways. Other records. This damned town, he thought, glorified the war and disregarded a local atrocity. He didn't understand.

That night he dreamed a driverless tractor was headed straight for him while a dog barked in the distance.

The next day, he went to the city hall on his lunch hour. The young girl behind the desk was eager to oblige once he told her he was trying to write a story about small-town crimes of the past.

"For the newspaper?" she asked.

"For a magazine," he said, hoping she would be even more impressed.

"No kidding. One sort of made up? I never knew anyone who wrote stories before. Don't you work at Hardy's?"

He nodded, and she presented him with the files from 1944.

"We haven't really had much happen around here," she

added. "It's really a pretty safe place to live. Not like those cities."

July. He tried to read, although the words tended to dance in front of his eyes. She leaned over the counter, a dreamy look on her face. "I write poems," she said. "For birthdays and things like that. Everyone seems to like them."

"That's nice," Cal said, turning a page. So far, it was a terse version of the newspaper. How could they ignore it here?

"The biggest thing I ever heard of was the murder," the girl said. "They still talk about that."

"Murder?" Cal stopped and looked up at her. Red's case?

"A Mr. Wiggins killed his wife and his horse. No one's ever been able to figure out why he killed the horse."

Accidents. Maybe they had listed it under accidents. He reread the information about George Morgan and the tractor. A little boy had been struck by a car but escaped with only a badly scraped leg. He closed the file.

"Well, thanks," he said to the girl. "I guess I'll have to think of something else." What the hell was wrong here?

"The man went to prison," she said.

Man? Which man? The driver of the car?

"Prison?" he asked, the familiar embarrassment starting up the sides of his neck.

"The man who killed his wife and his horse."

If Cal had not been so confused, he might have laughed out loud at the statement. He wondered if the headline in the *Clarion* had read, MAN KILLS HORSE. What was wrong with these people, with this town, he asked himself as he left the courthouse. For the first time, a conspiracy presented itself as a possibility. Had someone known he was coming and removed all the evidence of the crime against his mother? Perhaps the rapist was not a carny worker after all, but the mayor or some prominent citizen who had paid to have the whole mess kept quiet. There had to be something, somewhere. His mother was fading, losing substance. Soon she would be no more real than those shape-changing faces in his dreams.

A man passed him on the street, nodding, saying, "How do," walking on, and Cal thought he did not know the man, then remembered he was a customer. But who else was he? Was it possible that they all, everyone in this damned town knew who he was, and were keeping the damned secret behind "how do's," and fallacious smiles? His stone wall was dissolving into a row of blood-red dying flowers. The night people were edging into the daylight, and he had to stop them.

The rest of the day at the hardware store was terrible. He thought he detected flickers of recognition in the eyes of the carpenters and house painters. He heard Mr. Hardy tell someone to go back to the root of the problem and he imagined a coffin in the ground entangled with those roots, and then Mr. Hardy said something about "rot" and Cal could smell musty earth, and the stench remained in his nostrils for the rest of the day.

It took all his self-control at dinner to listen to Mrs. Mortensen proudly describe their outing, to keep from shouting at the boarders, *There was nothing there.*

He paced in his room. It was too warm, too closed. He considered running away from everything. Packing his bag and stealing away while all of the secret-keepers slept.

Go back to the root of the problem. The root. He stared out the window as the moon rose over the fields in the distance. The root.

He heard someone laugh. Someone walking along the street, invisible in the darkness. A girl, a woman. Was it Kayleen pointing at his window, explaining his strangeness to some confidante? Someone like Tina, or Mary Beth? Lucy? That's where Cal...He stopped. Cal who? There were no Newkirks in Four Corners. Was that what *they* all knew? That Newkirk was not his name?

So that was it. How could he have been so stupid? He'd been so preoccupied with finding the identity of his father, it had never occurred to him that *Newkirk* was not his mother's real name. She had confessed to making up *Callant*. She had been proud of that creation. A romantic name to match the stories that she told. Stage names to suit her purposes, and the roles they had both played all those years.

"Try to be smart," Ruggles had said. Smart.

Still, Dave's mother's cousin had recognized *Carlotta*. Cal had just assumed she had recognized *Newkirk*, too. If only he'd had the courage to press Dave then, perhaps even to confront the cousin. Too late now.

Callant Newkirk. A complete work of fiction. A name without substance. Was this how it was going to be? The more information he gathered, the less he would know?

They were escaping, all of them. Come back, go back. Where did one look for a woman, long gone, without a name? He didn't even have a picture of her.

Picture. Someone who looked like Maria Borelli. Younger. Younger than Kayleen.

He had one more place to check before he would have to reveal what he knew of his past, before he would have to ask the direct questions.

One more opportunity. Tomorrow, he would take it.

He took a late lunch. As he walked, he thought if this worked he would still owe it to Mrs. Mortensen. The school where her husband had been principal. Two blocks away. He could only hope that even though it was summer vacation, there would be someone there. As he approached the building, he was struck with the horror that it was a new building, that it would not contain anything or anyone old enough to remember, then he thought that was absurd. Records traveled; they were packed up in boxes and moved. There was a man in a gray uniform mowing the lawn, and Cal nodded to him. He looked like a prisoner.

The front door was open, and he walked into the empty hall. The floors were polished and locker doors were all neatly closed and newly painted. Cal stopped. Every hallway in every school must bring back the same feelings. The echoes of friends hurrying between classes, the laughing, the pushing, the flirting and the planning and the wishing for miracles that seemed possible. Easy days. And then the halls were empty again.

To his left was the office, and he could hear the lonely sound of a single typewriter.

The woman at the desk jumped when he said, "Pardon me."

She was pretty in her bright pink sundress, and she smiled at him once she took a breath.

"I'm sorry," she said. "The principal is out."

"I really only wanted to look at some old yearbooks," Cal said, putting his hands on the counter that separated him from the rest of the office. It occurred to him that he was becoming an accomplished liar.

"Recent ones?" she asked.

"Not really. 1938 to 1942."

"Well, we have them," she said, then hesitated, and Cal thought he saw that flicker of recognition he feared. "Is this some kind of research project?"

Cal folded his hands to keep them from shaking. "One of my teachers," he said, "went to school here, and I just thought I'd look up and see..." See what? He looked down at his hands. "Well, just see what she was like."

The woman smiled. "Oh, I see. What was her name?"

You don't see, he thought, but think anything you want. "Well, that's it...her name was Mrs. Kelly when I had her for sophomore English." He was amazed at how easily boyish he could sound. "I really don't know her maiden name, but I'm sure I'd recognize her picture." He knew he should force himself to look at the secretary, and so he raised his eyes to her.

She looked at him sympathetically now, fooled. She got up from her desk. "You just wait here."

He began to perspire again. He heard the sound of the lawnmower as it passed by the window. A loud bell rang, and he jumped, then froze. *I've been caught* was the first thing that came into his mind. An alarm for a prisoner escaping. A siren on a street.

"Sorry," the woman said as she placed four slim volumes in front of him. "The bells ring whether there are students here or not. They just can't seem to tell the difference."

He ran his hand over the plastic-encased book that was on top, almost as if he could divine a presence.

"You can sit over there." the secretary said, gesturing to a row of four chairs along one wall. "I really can't let them out of the office. They're the principal's collection."

He nodded his thanks. He took the chair in the corner, and started with 1938, which was on top. The freshman class.

For once, something was easy. There she was, on the third page of faces he scanned. Carlotta McKeller. Here I am, she smiled out at him. That wasn't so difficult, now was it? Clear-eyed, long lashes. Smiling because she didn't know what was to come. It took his breath away.

The telephone rang, and the secretary whispered, and Cal wondered if she was telling someone about him. It didn't matter; at least she wasn't watching him as he ran his finger over his mother's young face. She was mentioned only once in the index in 1938 so he moved on to 1939. This time there were three page numbers by her name, and he searched for the first. In passing, he came upon the full-page photograph of Harry Mortensen, who smiled forth with authority. "He treats all who enter through these doors with fairness and concern," written beneath his name.

Sophomore class. The same young girl with longer, fuller hair. She smiled, showing her teeth this time. Page 48. Carlotta McKeller, secretary of the sewing club, modeling a dress she had made. Page 56, member of the drama club in her role as Juliet. She wore a long white dress and held her palms up in a position of pleading.

She had never told him about her acting. She'd given that experience to a friend he now suspected lived in her imagination the way the mythical father had. Perhaps she was afraid to tell him that truth. Perhaps she had feared he might suspect the rest.

Juliet, he thought in a moment of craziness, wherefore art thou, Romeo, and he had to shake the giddiness by closing the book.

1940. He moved slowly now, mechanically, as if the pictures could be frightened from the pages and she would, once again, vanish. Carlotta McKeller, Junior. Five numbers this time, and he was anxious, now, as if he were approaching the last pages of a mystery. Vice-president of the sewing club. Hero in *Much Ado About Nothing,* wearing what appeared to be a bridal dress. A bride she had never been. He should have known something when she wore blue. Periwinkle blue? Hero. What an odd name for her. His father, war hero. He did not know the play. Carlotta McKeller and her princesses. A full page of glory at the Junior Prom. Her escort was not named, and he imagined a man with a mustache lurking outside the range of the camera, watching.

She wore gold earrings now, new in her junior year, and she was beautiful. The other girls paled beside her, and he was filled with love again at her presence.

"Did you find her?" the secretary asked.

He moved his hand from the picture. "No. Not yet. At least I'm not sure."

"Well, take your time."

He could tell she knew he was lying.

The last picture showed her receiving a drama award, a certificate clasped in her hand, smiling at Harry Mortensen, who was not yet ill.

1941. A senior. A young woman so radiant that her picture seemed taken by someone other than the regular photographer, and the image was so real it brought her voice back to him along with the scent of her perfume. She called to him, then threw back her head and laughed when he pretended to hide. The earrings flashing, and the brightly painted nails, shocking red as she put her hands to her face in mock surprise when she found him.

Time was running out on the noisy clock on the wall. Each minute marked with a click of the unsubtle hand. Cal turned the pages quickly, saw his mother in another hand-sewn dress, this time president of the sewing club. Lady Macbeth examining her hand, chairman of advertising for the yearbook, chairman of the Senior Hop. Carlotta McKeller, outstanding senior girl. Interests: drama, sewing. Best-dressed girl, well-liked by all. "I hope to travel all over the world," was her ambition.

She'd never told him any of that. She had been utterly convincing as the happy, proud mother who wanted Park Place and Boardwalk in Monopoly. Two pieces of cardboard with green houses and red hotels. He shook his head. She had never given him one single reason to feel sorry for her, not one. And until Dave told his story, Cal had assumed she was the happiest mother of all.

He stopped. He'd missed a picture. He looked at the clock and searched for the number. He passed it in his rush, and for a moment thought someone had cut out the page. But there she was again. I found you, she seemed to say. Once again, I found you.

She was queen of the Harvest Ball, and she stood with her three attendants in front of a bale of hay. She was laughing and wearing what must have been a gold cardboard crown, and she held the hand of the girl who stood next to her. As he scanned the other faces, one caught him. Wait. She looked familiar and for a minute he thought, this is the movie star, there was someone after all. She didn't make it up. The girl was blond, and very pretty. He tried to put a name to her from films or magazines. Just the trace. Then he knew. It was the eyes more than anything else. He read: Millie June Beckman. The pretty blond girl holding his mother's hand was Kayleen's mother.

Another bell rang, and he jumped. He was late, too late. Carlotta McKeller, outstanding senior girl and yet a couple of years later they would not even acknowledge her assault with an anonymous note in the paper. Why? How could everyone have simply ignored her tragedy?

Kayleen's mother would know.

"You found her, didn't you?" the secretary's voice was soft, romantic. Understanding. "I can tell from the look on your face."

"No. Well, yes, sort of. I think it's her."

"Which one?" the secretary asked. "Maybe I could help."

"I have to go," he said, closing the book. "I'll be late for work. Thanks."

He had to run most of the way to the hardware store. He didn't want to have to answer any questions. He'd found her. At damned long last, he had found her. She wasn't made of mist. She wasn't an illusion. She was back where she belonged, and he wasn't going to doubt her again.

He was breathless as he put his vest back on.

Now if the warden could find the man Pennington described, and if he could get Kayleen's mother to tell him what she knew, he would have parents again.

A father and a mother. For better or worse.

When he got home, there was a letter from his lawyer on the table in the hall. The trial date was set. August 28. He expected Cal to return at least a week in advance so they would have plenty of time to prepare his testimony. Things looked good, but he wanted to be certain everything went their way. He hoped Cal was well.

It didn't leave much time for Cal in Four Corners. He wished he had someone to share the good news with, but it was impossible.

Cal wondered how much of his life was going to be spent either keeping secrets or unraveling them. As he sat at Mrs. Pincher's dinner table, the face of his mother, shining out from the long-ago pages, made a kind of scrim through which he saw, or didn't see, what was going on at the moment. He wanted to stop the everyday conversation, stop it dead cold in the middle of the main course, and say, listen all of you— today I saw my mother, today I found the pages that defined her for four years, four years before she vanished from this community. Don't any of you wonder whatever happened to Carlotta McKeller?

Mrs. Pincher commented upon his lack of appetite, and he brushed her aside with "late lunch," but didn't miss a certain irritation in her expression. As the dinner dishes were cleared, and dessert served, he felt a pressure to startle them all, and knew it was not the time. Not yet.

"Well, Mr. Newkirk?" Mrs. Mortensen was staring at him.

"Do you mind? Oh, you don't mind if I tell."

He didn't know what she was talking about. Wait, he wanted to shout. Tell what?

"Mr. Newkirk had the most interesting idea," she said. "He went to the newspapers in the library to find out what was happening twenty-three years ago, and it prompted me to think." She stopped and placed her hand over her coffee cup so Virginia would not pour her any more. "I thought it might be nice if we were all to tell how we spent some Fourth of July in our lives. Nice and patriotic and all, and it would give us all a little history lesson."

Virginia placed a bowl of raspberries and cream in front of Cal, and history, history rang in his head. Carlotta McKeller was raped on the Fourth of July, and you didn't even mention it in the paper. What about that Mrs. Lewis? What about the court records? Where were all of you? I was conceived in one of those dilapidated barns while fireworks made children ooh and ah. *August 28.* Would they mention his trial if they knew?

"You Americans are so sentimental about your holidays," Mr Tonelli said.

"You've lived in this country over twenty years, Mr. Tonelli," Mrs. Pincher said. "I find it amusing you do not yet consider yourself one of us."

Over twenty years. Where did he come from? Mr. Henderson said something about the train, but Cal was concentrating on Mr. Tonelli, who stared at Mrs. Pincher with one eyebrow raised.

Miss Mayfield giggled, and it made Cal shake his head. History. She was a majorette, of course she was. Short skirt, baton, leading parades.

Mrs. Mortensen wanted something more factual, not just little personal reminscences. Carlotta McKeller. That was a fact.

"Well," Mr. Johnson said, "there's one here who doesn't think this country is up to much, Elvira. Seems like he might be happier in Russia, or China." Mr. Johnson looked at his hands.

Cal knew what was going to happen even before Mr. Dennis slammed his spoon onto the table, and he wanted to raise his hand and say stop it, stop it all, but it was too late. Mr. Dennis was shouting. "Don't you people read the newspapers? I don't mean the *Clarion,* I mean the national news. Don't you know what is going on, what this country is involved in?"

"Mr. Dennis," Mrs. Pincher began, leaning forward in warning.

"No. You listen. This country may well be involved in what is a totally illegal war. Not maybe. *Is.* This war in Viet Nam is illegal. Immoral."

Cal wanted to explain to Mr. Dennis that the *Clarion* did not report immoral acts. And that Dennis should have kept his opinions to himself.

"Why talk about the past?" he went on. "We need to pay attention to now. We are *killing,* killing innocent people, and we're sending innocent young men to do that."

"We've got to stop communism," Mr. Henderson said.

"Our government is lying to us," Mr. Dennis pleaded. His face was bright red now, and his glasses were slipping down his nose. "Doesn't that matter to you?"

"People are lied to all the time," Cal said. "There's nothing new about that." His words sounded so distant he wasn't certain he actually spoke them.

"Does that make it right?" Mr. Dennis went on. "Like sheep..."

"You're talking to veterans here," Mr. Johnson said, a tremor of anger in his voice. "We fought to protect our country."

Somebody didn't protect Carlotta McKeller. Not Mr. Johnson, or Mr. Henderson. Mr. Tonelli. Cal looked at the faces at the table. It was as if it all stopped to give him the time. He could hear Mr. Dennis shouting, Mrs. Pincher pounding on her glass with a spoon, the steady beat, her words admonishing Mr. Dennis, and he looked at each face and measured it. Mrs. Mortensen and her dead unmentioned son and her eyes filling with tears. A somber Mr. Tonelli. Mr. Henderson trying to get to his feet, to defend his country once again. Miss Mayfield, her baton gone, her face white with terror.

"You can all wave the glorious flag and talk about history," Mr. Dennis shouted. "I'm sick of it." He pushed back his chair, and stood. For some reason, he fixed his gaze on Cal, and Cal pushed back his own chair, ready to go at him, not because he was wrong, but because he was so stupid, because he was hurting everyone, and then Mrs. Pincher's cool fingers were around his wrist like a single handcuff, and Mr. Dennis was gone.

"Callant," she said softly, "please sit down. Please."

Miss Mayfield ran sobbing from the room.

He sat down. Something gone from him. He clenched his fist. He didn't even know why he was so angry at Mr. Dennis. He suspected much of what he said was true. But it was so goddamned ugly. He had the sickening feeling there weren't going to be any more war heroes. It made his mother's story more useless than ever.

Mrs. Pincher was apologizing, and he couldn't stand it anymore. "Excuse me, please," he said quietly, and she nodded.

It was not until he was in his room that he remembered that she had called him Callant instead of Mr. Newkirk, and he wondered if he had imagined it. No. He could hear the breath in the way she said it.

He had to get out of the house. An island. Everything was confusing. Something about seeing the pictures, something about refusing to accept Mr. Dennis and *his* time. He had the feeling his mother lived in a small house somewhere in town, and that he could walk over and see her, ask her a question or two, and listen to her laugh. Watch her make a pitcher of iced tea, hear the ice cubes swirl, see the steam rise as the ice was dropped into the hot tea. Smell it, feel the glass in his hand, and his mother would be so glad to see him again, so alive and well and doing fine.

He wanted to cry because it wasn't true. He had never missed her so much. There wasn't even anyone to talk to about her. No one. The longing was so intense, it began to take a physical shape in his mind, and he closed his eyes and saw Kayleen.

He couldn't tell her everything, but he wouldn't have to. He could talk to her. A nice girl, a sweet girl, a tender understanding girl. He'd seen that. She didn't have to understand, she just had to listen. And he could study Mrs. Lucus, look into her eyes. If he was going to have to ask her for the story, he wanted to be ready. He didn't want her to refuse him.

And he decided that dropping in would be best, as if he hadn't planned it at all.

When Mrs. Lucus answered the door, he had an overwhelming desire to say, I know who you are, and he continued to think that even as he asked for Kayleen, even as Mrs. Lucus turned her face away from him as if she were afraid to be recognized, even as he listened to the perpetual sound of the television set, as he was invited in.

And when Kayleen appeared, looking skeptical, he said quickly, "I'm sorry I haven't called before. I was just walking and it's such a nice night, I thought maybe we could go out for a while."

A young boy called, "Ma, can we have popcorn?"

"It's getting dark," she said.

"We won't stay long, I promise." He forced himself to reach for her hand. Promise. He wanted to tell her that if she wouldn't be afraid, neither would he.

Her hand was soft in his as they walked.

"Things have been so busy at the store," he said. "Sometimes I think I hardly have time to think."

"That's okay," she said. "I mean, it wasn't that I expected you to call or..."

He hoped she couldn't detect the slight trembling he felt inside. "But I wanted to call," he lied. No. It wasn't a lie exactly. "I've had some things I had to take care of."

They passed three little boys who were carrying pails and flashlights. Worm hunters, out for bait.

It reminded Cal of yet another business venture. The boys could have been himself and Dave all those years ago before. The scheme had come to an end when his mother had opened the can he had stored in the refrigerator. It was full of nightcrawlers, and she screamed and dumped the whole squirming mass upside down on the floor.

"I thought they'd like it better where it was cool," he had explained as she stood with her hands on her hips surveying the damage. He'd picked them up from the floor one by one. For weeks afterwards, whenever they had spaghetti, he'd said, "Ah, worms," and made his mother wince.

"Ever go fishing?" he asked Kayleen.

"I've been, and I hate it. It's boring."

He had to admit he agreed.

They passed by the park and the empty bandstands that would soon be draped with the red, white, and blue bunting of the coming holiday.

"Let's sit over there for a minute," he said to the girl who walked beside him. "Up there, on the stage." He wanted to tell her about Lady Macbeth and Juliet. One black, one white, and red the color in which they joined. He shivered.

The wooden stairs creaked as they climbed them, and when they reached the platform, Kayleen sat down on the edge, dangling her legs over the side. The white of her sandals looked strangely fluorescent in the fading light, her skin dark. Some of the light from the street lamp reflected in her hair. He sat next to her.

"Mr. Dennis blew up at the dinner table tonight," he said. "About the war."

She brushed a strand of hair away from her face.

"Sorry," he said. "Didn't mean to bring that up again. I know you were really upset when I took you home."

"That wasn't it," she said. "It was seeing Lucy and her sick baby, and thinking about my mother and how someone always seems to be crying."

"You were really good with that little boy."

Kayleen turned to him. Her eyes were strange, distant in the near darkness.

"I want to leave Four Corners soon," she said. "Get away from here. Go to college, maybe. Or to a city and get a job."

Suddenly he wanted to hold her. Keep her there with him. He wanted to explain to her that it was dangerous to think that way. His mother, wanting to travel the world. Look what had happened.

"Four Corners seems like a nice place to me," he said, although he knew he would be leaving, and it made him feel dishonest.

"That's because you've already been somewhere else," she sighed. "I've never even been out of this state."

Because he wanted desperately to protect her, he put his arm around her shoulders. His own trouble would have to wait. He felt her stiffen slightly, and he hoped she wasn't afraid of him. No need then. Not then.

"You see," she went on, "my mother must have had plans too, plans to get away. Everyone does here. But then she met my father and fell in love with him, and look what happened."

"But if she loves him, is it all so bad?" If she just knew, he thought. About "out there."

"Is it so wrong for me to want to do better?" She looked at him. "There's nothing to become here. Nothing to be except a wife and a mother. Why did I have to learn things in school that I'm never going to use? I studied, studied hard. For what?"

"I guess I see what you mean," He said, but he knew he didn't, not exactly. He'd always assumed Mary Beth wanted to be a wife and mother. Always assumed his own mother was happy. Perhaps neither of those things was true, either. "I just never thought of it."

"Did you go to college?" she asked.

"No." He wasn't prepared for questions. "I worked at a smelter."

She paused, searching his eyes for what was clearly missing. "Why did you come here?"

He could feel his heart pick up the pace. Sort out the primaries, leave the ugliness out. "I had a good recommendation for the job."

"But is that all you want to do? Work in a hardware store forever?"

It occurred to him that there was no *forever* in his life. That he was living it in pieces of information about the past, and in getting from one court-appointed date to another. He was never going to be able to explain some of it without telling all. What did he want to do? When all of this was over and done with, what in the hell was he going to do?

Guilty. Would he hear that word again? Would September bring a return to prison? He tried to scare that possibility away.

"When I save enough money, I'm moving to a city. Maybe New York. See the world," he added, trying to laugh a little.

Her arms went around his neck, and she held him. He could feel the delicate bones in her back, and the fear of the future in her breath against his face.

"Would you take me with you?" she asked.

His mind filled with maps of untraveled roads, directions never taken. Buildings so tall one couldn't see the sky, let alone the fields and abandoned barns.

"Sure, I'll take you," he whispered, hoping she believed him. In the distance, shrouded in mist, was the gray prison wall.

A few minutes later, Cal and Kayleen left the bandstand and the oddest sensation came over him. It was as if he stood across the park, across the dark expanse of lawn with someone else and watched them. A different field of vision altogether. There they were. A girl and a boy. She in a white skirt, he with a matching shirt. And as he watched, he was older, and a woman was with him. They were out for an evening walk, away from their house, which was silent because the children were gone. Maybe they had forgotten how to walk hand in hand, how to lean toward each other in whispered moonlight conversations. They paused briefly and watched without speaking, taken back in time to the summer evenings of their youth and their courtship. He reached for the woman's hand, and she leaned her head on his shoulder, and they watched the young couple disappear. Remember when you gave me the gardenia, the woman said to him, and he kissed her on the top of her head. They walked away from the couple that had crossed their path, back toward the memories that formed the glue of their lives. Photographs pasted in a scrapbook, or mounted into black corners. A man in a uniform and a woman in a blue dress, leaving for their honeymoon.

His ghosts had risen again, and he had become a myth. If Dave had kept a secret, it might have been the truth.

"I feel better," Kayleen said.

The siren in the firehouse rose with the single note and fell again, announcing ten o'clock.

"Come sit with us and have some popcorn and lemonade," Mrs. Lucus said from the shadows of the porch as Kayleen and Cal entered the yard. In the dark, Cal could see that Mr. and Mrs. Lucus sat together on two lawn chairs, a small table between them.

"You don't have to," Kayleen whispered to Cal, "if you'd rather not."

"I'd like to, just for a little while," he said loud enough for the Lucuses to hear. Mr. Lucus rose without a word, and reappeared with two more lawn chairs. Kayleen went into the house for glasses, and Cal settled into the chair next to Mrs. Lucus.

"This is the nicest night we've had yet," the woman said. "Summer's here for sure."

"Yes," Cal agreed, trying to see the woman's face in the darkness, searching for the girl who held his mother's hand in the Harvest Ball photograph. Did Mrs. Lucus still have that yearbook, or had it been thrown away? Did she take it out on lonely nights when her family was asleep and look back to those pages with longing? Did she wonder what had ever happened to her friend?

A broad flat flash of light lit up the sky in the distance.

"Sheet lightning," Mrs. Lucus said, rubbing her arms as if chilled. "I love to watch it even though it gives me the willies. Odd to see lightning and not hear the sound of thunder."

Cal could hear the ice rattling in Mr. Lucus's glass.

"First time I saw it, I thought I'd gone deaf," Mrs. Lucus added. "I kept counting, like you do to find out how far away it is, and nothing happened."

Crickets began to sing in the grass, and Kayleen brought the glasses and lemonade, poured him one, and sat down next to her father. Cal could barely see her, and he wondered what she was thinking about. Was she already starting to dream on his promise? Mrs. Lucus passed the bowl of popcorn to him, and he took a handful. He tried squinting, to see if he could make the lights of the town and the stars blur into illuminated windows of skyscrapers far away.

You've found enough, a voice said to him. Forget the past now. Go on and be happy with summer nights such as these.

No one spoke. They sat on the porch, two couples lost in thought, and watched the occasional flashes of light on the horizon. They sat mesmerized as if enchanted by the flickering of a quiet fantasy on a movie screen, eating popcorn and drinking lemonade.

Suddenly, there was the scent of approaching rain in the air, and a distant roll of thunder.

"Best be getting in," Mr. Lucus said.

Cal reached Mrs. Pincher's just as the storm began. He lay in his bed and watched the lightning flash, and he counted the way Mrs. Lucus had done when she was a child to see how far he was from the strike. The crash of thunder, a cloudburst in the night, the rain hard against the windowpane.

Carlotta McKeller. August 28. What then?

The days passed quickly now. Cal spent his days at the hardware store, and his evenings with Kayleen. At first, they spoke in general terms of what it would be like to move someplace else, what it would be like to leave a place where one had family, friends, history. Cal looked forward to the time with Kayleen, and found the word *love* entering his thoughts, and he wondered if it could possibly be true, or was this the "summer romance" he heard others speak of in romantic tales of the past.

One evening, after dinner, Kayleen appeared at Mrs. Pincher's, a map of the United States and an almanac under her arm.

"Come on," she said. "Let's sit on the side porch and I'll show you what I've found."

The other boarders smiled at each other. Young love, they whispered. The future before their eyes.

They sat down at the wooden table, and Kayleen spread out the map. She had drawn a large red circle around four cities. Denver, San Francisco, Chicago, and New York.

Cal, back in the warden's office, tracing the lines between states, waiting for good news or bad. It made him shiver, even though the night was warm. Will you take me with you, Kayleen had asked, and he had agreed. He might not be able to keep that promise, and he couldn't even explain that to her. Counting chickens again, Ruggles warned.

Kayleen opened the almanac, and her face was hidden by the curtain of blond hair. "Now the thing about Denver is this," she said. "It's not as big, and it might be easier to get work there. It might be less scary to start out there."

Cal nodded. What could he do in Denver, or anywhere for that matter? Smelters were in small towns, not the cities Kayleen had marked.

"I guess they have a lot of snow there," Cal said. A courtroom with snow falling outside. Watching it through the windows. There would not be snow on August 28.

"Maybe we could learn to ski," Kayleen said, turning toward him. Such hope in her eyes, he thought, such anticipation.

"Maybe," Cal said. A *maybe* was not so much of a lie.

"But listen to this," Kayleen said, reading from the almanac. "Chicago has ninety-five institutions of higher learning." She shook her head. "Imagine that. We could each work part-time, and go to school the other part."

I may have to get my college in a prison library, Cal wanted to tell her, but he couldn't, not yet. His business in Four Corners wasn't finished. New York, San Francisco.

"What kind of jobs do you think we could get?" he asked. He was feeling more and more anxious.

"I think girls can always get jobs as waitresses," Kayleen said. "I wouldn't mind doing that. Maybe you could work in a store. You have experience and all."

Experience. The pins on the warden's map. Signifying what? He began to perspire.

Kayleen closed the book and looked at him. "Are you all right?" she asked, and he had to turn away from her concerned face.

"I don't know," he whispered. "I feel like I'm getting the flu or something." He wiped his brow with his hand.

"You're really perspiring," Kayleen said. "We can go over this tomorrow when you feel better."

He nodded, and watched as she refolded the map. "Sorry," he said, wishing she knew exactly how sorry he really was. He was just like his mother, spinning fairy tales to someone else. And just as he had done, Kayleen believed.

He walked her to the front gate, thinking he needed a drink of water, quiet, darkness. She stretched up to him, and kissed him on the cheek. "Mama and Daddy want you to come to our Fourth of July picnic," she said.

"Fine," he said. "I mean, I'd really like to do that."

He watched her walk to the corner, where she turned and waved at him again. He thought she seemed disappointed, that she didn't have the same energy in her walk, in her face, and he knew it was his fault. He felt like a thief.

And as if that were not difficult enough, that continual feeling of betrayal, the third of July brought more trouble. First of all, due to a late customer at the store, Cal was almost late to dinner. He was the last one to enter the dining room before the doors closed. Mr. Tonelli's chair was empty as was Mr. Dennis's, and Miss Mayfield had clearly been crying.

He had forgotten. Mrs. Mortensen was going to give her tribute to the holiday. Unkind of the two men not to be there. Mrs. Pincher was cold, and he didn't envy the men once she had a chance to tell them what she thought of this behavior. In a shaking voice, one he assumed was replete with rage, Mrs. Pincher ordered an extra aperitif for everyone and while the boarders, rather grimly, in his opinion, sipped glasses of dry sherry, Mrs. Mortensen read her solemn tribute.

He looked around the table at the assortment of kindly faces and thought, this is like a family. Concerned, caring, gentle. As if it were Thanksgiving instead of a summer's eve, he silently counted his blessings.

Mrs. Mortensen's voice trembled slightly as she read. It was, she stated, a time to think about heroes. Those brave men who fought in the Revolutionary War, the defenders of justice and equality in the Civil War, those who had traveled to far shores in the World Wars to save humanity, and last but not least to think of those now in Southeast Asia who believed, in spite of all, that the cause was one of justice and democracy.

Cal decided it was just as well that Tonelli and Dennis were not there. Tonelli with his sneering; Dennis with his hysteria.

"I know there are some," Mrs. Mortensen went on, "who question our place in the world today, but it's important to remember that we live in the world's greatest, most generous country, and if, if we are approaching this wrongly, certainly our remarkable system of government will see the light."

Cal hoped that would be true on August 28. The American system of justice and the light.

Mrs. Mortensen sighed. "In closing," she said, "I would like to take this minute to remember my—our—son who died in World War Two, and to hope that all wars, within and without our country, will end soon."

With tears in her eyes, she sat back down at the table to the quiet applause of her closest friends.

"To Mrs. Mortensen," Mrs. Pincher said, raising her glass, and Cal was close enough to see the tears in her eyes, too, "for her lovely and quite appropriate tribute."

"And to the end of all wars," Mr. Henderson added.

It all seemed so large to Cal. The end of all wars, within and without. Each of them must have struggled, and who was to say but what their questions might have been as encompassing as his own. *Now* was what was important. The person he was now. Not the past, but the future.

And as he listened to the pleasant dinner conversation that followed, he could not help worrying at Mrs. Pincher's strange silence. She made no explanation of the absent members, and she merely rearranged the food on her plate. Once, Cal felt her staring at him, and when he raised his eyes to meet hers, he caught an expression of glassy emptiness that made him look away.

When dinner was over and the others adjourned to the front porch for more speculation on the state of things, Mrs. Pincher touched his arm.

"I have something for you," she said, and the tone of her voice made him afraid. He had a sudden vision of Mrs. Mortensen opening a telegram.

Before he could shake that notion, she handed him an envelope.

"I didn't want the others to see this," she said.

He looked down to see the warden's return address. Now, of all the times, a letter. It didn't seem right, not this evening when all he wanted to do was call Kayleen at the home where she was babysitting and tell her that everything, *everything* was going to be all right.

He could not even murmur a thank you. She touched his arm gently, as if she understood, and left the room.

Upstairs, he sat at his desk simply staring at his name on the front of the envelope. Throw it away, his mother whispered. It doesn't matter anymore.

But Mrs. Mortensen had opened the telegram about her son. Jimmy Lee Lucus had opened the envelope he must have known contained a summons to war. Perhaps Ruggles had hesitated over the letter about Lucy Pennington, afraid of what he would have to tell Red.

He'd closed his eyes too many times already. He'd run away from Dave; he'd lied to his mother, the sin of omission. He'd run quick and hard and breathless from the thought of what another ten minutes with the little girl in the long soft grass might have meant to them both. On the eve of a national celebration of heroism, he sat trembling in his room with a simple letter.

And to his further dismay, a singsong chorus of little-girl voices echoed, "Sticks and stones may break my bones," and he completed them as he began to laugh, "but words will never hurt me."

Sticks and stones and guerrilla warfare in Southeast Asia. A live grenade in a foxhole. The bombs bursting in air. The rockets' red glare. He was losing his mind to music.

He opened the envelope. He started slowly, carefully. The house was absolutely quiet, as if it, too, waited.

> Dear Callant,
>
> I know it's been some time since your release and that you expected information before now. Well, the fact is, I've had some grave misgivings about our bargain and almost decided not to tell you what I found out. Then I figured, hell, you'd probably just drive yourself and a lot of other people crazy while you played amateur detective.
>
> Did manage to track down the man Pennington talked about, or at least it's the jailer's best guess from his records. Now listen, Cal, this is an ugly story, and I just don't see what good is going to come out of you knowing it. You should also remember that unless this Herman Beloit (AKA a dozen other names) would somehow be willing to

confess to the situation with your mother, you
can't be certain who he is anyway. He might not
tell you anything. Worse, he might lie just for the
fun of it.

I advise against contacting him. Who knows what
inner itch drives a man like Beloit to his actions. I
recommend you put all this behind you, and go
on with your life. I stress that this is all just
someone's best guesswork.

Cal paused at the bottom of the page. Herman Beloit. What
kind of a name was that? French? Beloit. He wondered if
there were other Beloits in the area. Sinful relatives.

Again, I hesitate to tell you all this, but it is
important that you let this rest, so I'm going to
just tell you everything available on this man.
Here it is, for better or for worse.

First of all, he was dishonorably discharged from
the army in 1942. Reasons unclear. From that
point on, he was arrested with fair regularity in
every place from Utah to Texas to Washington. He
was quite a drifter, maybe followed the rodeo
circuit, might, and I stress the word *might*, have
traveled with a carnival. Five rape charges prior
to 1949, none of them stuck. Five assault arrests,
and two six-month terms in county jails. A slew of
drunk and disorderlies. From 1949 to about 1958
he seems to have been out of the country.
Merchant Marines probably. Committed his
crimes elsewhere. Hard to tell. Surfaced again in
1959 with a series of charges that didn't stick.
1961 was when he ran into Pennington. Rape
charges again and the woman refused to testify.

Dishonorable discharge. Ironic. The picture of the man in
the uniform. His mother's war hero husband. A man to look
up to indeed.

Had she known any of this? To his relief, he knew she could
not have.

And this man, this rapist had remained almost totally free all those years, and he, the son, convicted for something he had not done. Wasn't life a series of interesting turns. He could feel the cold descending.

> In 1962 they finally got him. He was tried and convicted of murder in Texas. Now listen, Cal, this is gruesome business, and I don't really have many details. Seems he went into a cafe one night late, drunk probably, and ended up abducting two sisters who worked there as waitresses. A Carmen Hernandez, 32, and an Alicia Rodriguez, 30. Apparently drove them out of town to a deserted shack, raped them, then carved them up with a Bowie knife. They caught him a week later in New Mexico.

Cal felt sick to his stomach. He put his hand over the letter. Two women, probably with long dark hair and gold earrings. Hidden away and tortured. He tried taking deep breaths. It didn't help. He ran from his room for the bathroom.

Then it was over. There was nothing left. He stood at the sink running cold water into his hands, bringing it to his face. Baptism. Immersion. It would not wash away. He saw a raven sitting on a fencepost.

He could not absorb it all. His own room was suddenly strange, a place he had never truly been. The gentle room, the gentle people in the house.

He sat back down at the desk, too numb to do anything else. Maybe he was imagining this all. Another dream, a branch against the windowpane. But the letter was there. The pages filled with awkward type. An *O* that was always gray. A blurred capital *R*.

He tried to finish the letter, hoping for a clue that would make it all a mistake. Herman Beloit was on death row in the Texas State Penitentiary. Might be executed, but capital punishment was on the decline. On to more cheerful news, of a sort. Ruggles' assistant after Cal had not worked out. Managed to get hold of some drugs and went crazy, nearly destroying Ruggles' meticulous system. He'd been replaced by an embezzler with an eye for detail and organization.

And the night before, someone had stabbed Red Pennington, and he wasn't going to make it. His wife had been notified. Cal stared at the warden's signature. So Lucy Pennington was about to be a widow. Perhaps she already was. Would she take her son onto her lap and say, "You father was a wonderful man, kind and gentle?" He tried to imagine that, to hear her voice.

He had to get away. He went by way of the crisscrossing structures on the side of the house, the scaffolding of his dream.

He walked steadily, deliberately along the streets of Four Corners, passing but not seeing the houses he had come to know. He walked away from the center of things out into the yellow fields of summer. He stood finally, a trespasser in someone's field, and looked to where the sun was falling into the sea of grain.

He longed for the sea he had never seen.

He did not know how long he stood in the field, thinking and yet not thinking, about Herman Beloit. He didn't cry; he didn't scream. When the last light of day was gone, he merely turned on his heel and retraced his steps back to Mrs. Pincher's. He considered his choices. He could refuse to believe what the warden had told him.

But the words were there on the paper. Burning the letter wouldn't erase them from his memory. He considered raising his fist to the sky and cursing the heavens. Goddammit, why do you give and take away? Why is that always part of things? A fatal trickster. Another black secret to keep along with all the others. A simple-minded repository for countless sins.

Confession. The sins of the father are visited on the son. Someone else's religion. He had nothing. He wanted to kill Herman Beloit, and he wasn't even going to be able to do that. American justice was going to rob him of that.

He wanted to tell just one person so someone would understand. He wanted to be recognized as a haunted man.

And then he would be gone. He shivered with the knowledge of that. And then, he would be gone.

He would slip out of the clothes of this past and give his history to someone else. He would run to the mountains or to the shore, and never again speak to another living human. He would end the line of Herman Beloit forever. No child, no feeling.

The trial. He'd have to wait for the damned trial.

There was a light on in the parlor at Mrs. Pincher's, but there was no one about. He started up the stairs to his room, then stopped. He saw a faint strip of light from under Mrs. Pincher's door. She must still be awake.

He would give this all to her, the best keeper of secrets he had ever known. And he thought it remarkable as he turned and descended the stair, he was the calmest he had ever been. Perhaps as cold as Herman Beloit had been when he killed.

He knocked lightly at her door.

"Yes?" Her voice sounded odd, strained, as if she had been waiting for him.

"It's Cal," he said. "I wondered if I could talk to you."

There was silence, and he waited. He heard her hand on the doorknob.

"Cal?" she repeated his name as if it might be a deadly trick. "Just a minute."

It occurred to him as he waited that his mother's door had never been closed against him. It seemed odd now, in view of the other secrets she kept so well.

After a moment, Mrs. Pincher opened the door and, with her face turned away from him, gestured for him to enter.

He had never seen her room before, and stood dazzled by what he saw. It was elegantly, lavishly furnished. Dark rich fabrics and carpets. The walls contained not her own spare landscapes, but ancient paintings in dark tones and heavy gold frames. She stood, her back to him, in front of an ornately carved round table at which were placed two velvet upholstered chairs. He could hear her placing ice in glasses, and saw a bottle of whiskey on a silver tray in the middle of the table.

"Sit down," she said, pointing to a chair. As he pulled the chair out from the table, she turned and handed him a drink in a heavy crystal glass. With her own glass, she clinked them together.

"A toast," she said, "to God knows what."

She stood in front of him, a long silk robe knotted lightly at the waist, her breasts loose underneath, the line of her cleavage evident. From the light of the lamp behind her, he could see the clear outline of her body. He moved his eyes up her body to her face. He blinked. Her eyes were red from crying, slightly swollen. The false eyelashes were gone, and her eyes flickered naked in the lamplight.

"Try to pretend," she said, "that I don't look wretched." She pulled her robe more closely about her, and sat down in the chair opposite him. With shaking hands she lit a cigarette, and exhaled a stream of smoke toward the ceiling.

You have good reason to be afraid, he thought suddenly, but when he leaned forward, he could see that it was not fear, but drunkenness that made her eyes waver so.

"What's wrong?" he asked, waiting to hear something dangerous.

"You were the one who wanted to talk," she said, with a wave of her hand. The end of the cigarette made a little red arc. A premature firework. "Welcome to my sanctuary."

Don't feel safe, he wanted to tell her. Not now, not tonight.

"I came to talk about the letter."

"Letter? Oh, yes. A voice from the past." She tapped her cigarette angrily in the ashtray. "You ought to forget the past," she said. "Otherwise, someone might make you live it."

He had the maddening feeling she had opened the letter, opened it behind the doors of her "sanctuary" and read every cursed word, and he wanted to make her confess.

"You don't know what was in it," he said.

"It's not my business," she said.

"But it is," he said. "Don't you think you should know who sleeps in one of your rooms upstairs?"

She stood from the table and began to pace. "Don't you think I know you?" she asked.

The old woman, flapping in black, recognizing him before anyone else.

"No," he said simply, turning in his chair to follow her with his eyes.

She paused by the bed and stroked the carved post. She touched the heavy brocade spread reverently. He watched the hand that held the cigarette, afraid of a spark, a fire that would consume them both.

"I always check references," she said. "One cannot have too many references. You need to know everything possible about someone. They can fool you, you know. They can trick you. They can lie. They will say they are telling the truth, and that is the greatest lie of all."

She turned, sat down on the bed, crossing her legs and

causing the robe to part, revealing the flesh of one thigh. She no longer looked devastated, and he could not take his eyes off her.

"I never lied to you," he said, standing up from the chair, leaving his glass on the table. There was something terribly wrong here. He began to feel the heat in the room, a summer furnace.

"How do you know?" she asked. "How do we know without a real test?"

She leaned forward slightly, almost revealing a breast.

"You see, my dear, what happens is this." She put her glass to her lips and drank, never taking her eyes off his face. "You build a little safe world and you build it carefully. You make a life that is tolerable, not just tolerable, *preferable* to all those around you. An elegant room like this. A room in a mansion of some other time. No dirt, no sordidness. You build an oasis against the barbarism one is continually surrounded by." She smiled at him. "Mr. Pincher understood that theory. He made his place, then found someone—me—to fit into it perfectly. When he was gone, I altered it to my own taste." An ash fell from her cigarette, and she brushed at it with her foot.

"And then one day, by mistake, you let a barbarian in disguise into your room. Into your sanctuary."

She did know. She sat there on her damned satin bed, swinging her bare leg just enough to make him look, and she kept him there anyway.

She reached over to a night table by her bed, and put out her cigarette in a china tray.

"Come here," she said, smoothing the place on the spread next to her.

She wants to die, he thought desperately, watching her hand made the smooth circles on the bed. That's what this is all about. She sat there patiently, swirling the ice in her glass, and daring him.

Condemned, he moved to her side, and she reached for his hand, and he was lost in the grasp of her fingers. He thought the lights went out, but he had only closed his eyes and she sighed gently in the darkness.

He was going to have to stop her now, or tangle her in the violent sheets of her own bed, quieting her words forever.

"You shouldn't have let me in," he said, opening his eyes

and facing her. The softness in her eyes turned first to confusion, then to an alert fear.

"Oh, my dear," she said, and he wrenched his hand from hers, and stood up from the bed. He wanted desperately to leave, but could not. He clenched his fists at his side, his back to her.

"You've misunderstood," she said quietly, and her words became those of many separate voices. Misunderstood.

She was standing behind him, now, and she touched his arm. "I wasn't talking about you, Callant," she said. All the traces of drunkenness were gone. "Not you."

"My father," he said, and his words rose like a growl in his throat, "was—is—a murderer."

"That was what the letter said?" she asked, as if that did not necessarily make it so.

"Yes."

She walked past him to the table. He could only watch as she poured some whiskey into her glass, and then some into his.

"You'd better sit down," she said, facing him.

She was different now, as if all that had gone before was another one of his horrible dreams. She was the lady of the house, the mother confessor. She was once again the woman he had come to see, to confide in. He thought he must certainly—this time—be losing his mind.

They sat at the table while he told her everything. When he finished, she had tears in her eyes and she reached across the table for his hand.

"But it's over now," she said. "Can't you see that? It doesn't matter about your father. You write the story of your own life now."

He had not been able to explain that that was impossible, not with all the memories plaguing him.

Then it struck him. It hit him suddenly from behind, a dark-haired man with a stick.

"Mrs. Pincher," he said softly, "where is Mr. Tonelli?"

She seemed to draw herself up in her chair. A brave woman, facing the words.

"He has run off," she said, "if a snake can run, with that Borelli woman."

Another battlefield casualty.

"I'm sorry," he said.

"I'm not. Not about that precisely. About other things, those terrible 'might-have-beens' that haunt women my age."

"I think I have to go away," Cal said. "Someplace where I don't know anyone."

Mrs. Pincher stood from the table.

"It's too late to talk about it now." She paused. "And too soon at the same time. Let it sit awhile." She laughed and took his hand. As she led him to the door, she held his hand tightly, and he was a little boy again, and he wondered what it would take to lead them both to safety.

"You help me," she said as she opened the door, "and I'll help you." She reached up and kissed him lightly on the cheek.

"This hasn't been a great day for either of us," she whispered.

In his room, he undressed for bed and set his alarm. It was only five hours before he was to meet Kayleen at the parade. He lay awake as the gray dawn crept in under the shade. He finally slept with the peculiar sensation that his mother was sleeping peacefully in her room with the door open down the hall.

But in a dream he would not remember but only sense the next day, he walked the long corridor of the prison toward a chamber. He walked with a priest who called him Herman Beloit, and rattled rosary beads in his hand in time with the step.

Something tickled his nose, brushed by his face, vanished. A floating web perhaps, a long-legged spider. Something burned at his forehead, then slipped into a pounding as he contemplated opening his eyes.

And he knew if he opened his eyes, he would look into the blue eyes of the gray kitten. Then the little girl would appear. He had to get away first. He could taste the alcohol from the night before, sour in his mouth. His head pounded. He had to run, leave before it all began again. God, he couldn't get his legs to move, couldn't get his arms to support his weight to raise him from the ground. What was wrong? What if the girl came and lay down beside him, and he reached for her? What if the father didn't stop it but watched with some insane lust of his own? He had to open his eyes and run away.

He stared at the ceiling of one of Mrs. Pincher's bedrooms. His room. He turned to the clock. Five minutes before the alarm was to go off. In five minutes, he could have taken that little girl. He reached to stop the clock, and vowed never to take another drink, and then remembered that it was the Fourth of July, and that sun that cracked around the drawn blinds was going to come at him mercilessly when he went outside.

Mrs. Pincher wanted him to take his time, wanted him to think things over before leaving. He didn't think that was going to help. He was going to have to tell Kayleen, if not today, tomorrow. It made him feel like a coward to contemplate it. A coward and a breaker of promises. But in view of what he might become, he thought as he swung his feet to the floor and rested his head in his hands for a moment, she should count herself lucky. If she only knew.

"Happy Fourth of July," he said to his reflection in the mirror. "You're a dead man." And the thought of him walking through the celebration knowing a secret that no one would suspect made him smile. One of those hollow men from another planet. He took two, then made it three, aspirin.

By the time Cal joined the Lucus family at the agreed-upon place, he could already hear the sound of the band, and the Lucus children, who were perched on the hood of the family car, strained to see.

"You look like a movie star in those dark glasses," Kayleen said, smiling and taking his arm.

"I'm in disguise," he whispered. "A handsome stranger."

She laughed. "You sound different, sophisticated."

"It's all an act," he said, "just to please you."

She leaned her head against his shoulder. An American Legionnaire passed by, and Cal bought little American flags on sticks for everyone in the family. Mr. Lucus put his in the band of his gray felt hat. There, for the rest of the day, the flag was to flutter in the breeze.

"I can hear the band," Benny Lucus called. "It's almost here."

It was true. The sound of the drums, the *rat-a-tat-tat*. The solid pulse of the big bass drum that Cal felt was doing a fair imitation of his heart. He twirled the flag on the stick between his fingers thinking he had been here before, heard it and seen it all, and maybe through some trick, he could be fourteen again, and start all over. Dave wouldn't tell his story, and his mother wouldn't die, and he would let Mary Beth be someone else's wife. The little girl would have been visiting her grandmother in another city that day.

There was the rising wail of the fire truck siren, the truck that led them all, led the majorettes who carried the banner that said Four Corners High School, the banner of purple edged in gold fringe, and as he watched, the letters scrambled and flew and came down reading Yellow Fork, and he clapped and cheered along with all the rest.

"I'm going to be a fireman," the middle Lucus boy said. "Like my uncle George."

The band stopped in front of them. The tuba, bending, dipping, a boy twirling drumsticks, batons flying into the air, a glimpse of satin shorts and epauleted uniforms of white. "The Stars and Stripes Forever," or "Be kind to your web-footed friends, for a duck may be somebody's mother."

The Four Corners Veterans of Foreign Wars, some marching, one man, his hat slightly askew and a hand paralyzed and limp in his lap, was wheeled in a chair. There was the smell of popcorn and peanuts and balloons and gunpowder in the air. Of summer heat and small firecrackers. Bombs bursting in air over Viet Nam and Berlin.

"That's one of my best friends," Kayleen said pointing to the girl who was dressed as the Statue of Liberty. "Isn't she pretty?"

The girl was smiling, staring straight ahead, concentrating on keeping her balance. She was dressed in a silver robe, and she stood in a light blue sea of paper napkins tucked into chicken wire. Underneath the sea, the ocean white with sprayed on foam, a nearly sightless driver attempted to move the float smoothly down the street without running over the veterans or into the back of the band. It made for a jerky journey and the Statue of Liberty had reason to be nervous.

And behind her a solitary man wearing a Lone Ranger mask sported a sandwich board and a large yellow peace symbol. Printed underneath, in clumsy black letters, was "The Footprint of the American Chicken." It was hard to tell whether the applause was for him, or for the Statue herself.

The American Chicken. The American Eagle, and the float from his past entered the parade of the present. It squeezed in behind the chicken, and blocked Cal's view of what followed. A ten-foot-high eagle with wings spread. Perched ready for flight on clawed legs designed by Dave's father for the scout troop float. Dave and Cal and the rest of the troop had walked proudly beside it, thrilling to the applause as they passed, each boy in uniform with merit badges carefully sewn on by his mother. Under the wing of the American Eagle. The designer himself was underneath it all, the giant bird and the fruited plain, peeking out, praying.

Then it had happened. Jimmy Billings in his clown suit, riding the bike with the crooked wheels, cut in front of them, and Dave's father threw on the brakes and the American Eagle wobbled once or twice, then pitched forward, plunging its beak into the plain, and thrusting its butt into the air.

It could not be righted, and there was no escape. Cal and Dave and the rest of their troop walked along, trying not to laugh, covering their mouths with their hands, and endured. At the end of the parade, Dave's father, in full view of his entire troop, got out from under it all, placed his hands on his hips, and looked at the eagle. "God damn fucking hell," he said. Women paled, men cleared their throats, and Cal and his friends looked at Mr. Langley with wide-eyed admiration.

Oh, to laugh again. And he knew he smiled. Before he told her good-bye, he would tell Kayleen that story.

The local National Guard unit marched, boots heavy on the streets, and Cal could feel the familiar cadence, and he was back in his own unit, marching in his own parade. He would have to find a new unit if the trial went his way.

The sound of applause rippling along the line of people made Cal stretch to see. A young man in an army uniform sat up on the back of a convertible. A hand-painted sign on the car door said simply, LANNY JAMES, VIET NAM WAR HERO, in alternating red and blue letters. Lanny waved to the crowd, unsmiling, eyes blank.

"He lost his leg," Kayleen said. "Just above the knee."

And the last float, the one sponsored by the Lion's Club, followed. Three pretty young girls in white dresses held hands underneath a sign that said UNITY. Cal glanced at Mrs. Lucus. Do you know where your friend Carlotta McKeller is? he thought as he watched her smile and wave at the girls. Do you care?

The horses were last. The Bit and Spur Riding Club on palominos that tossed white manes against tawny bodies and crisscrossed, riding in limited formation, depositing bright green heaps to be cleaned up later.

"It was the best parade ever," Kayleen said.

Cal wanted to tell her he didn't know. There were things too complicated to define. Parades. The American Eagle and the American Chicken. A raven on a post, a hawk circling in the sky.

Instead, he smiled. It was easy to do today, and he didn't
know why. "I'll bet," he said taking her hand, "that you say
that every single year."

The Lucus family picnic was such mass confusion on so
many levels that it was possible for Cal to stumble through it
almost unnoticed. Kayleen commented that he seemed a little
quiet, and he said he thought he might be getting a summer
cold. Mrs. Lucus offered to make him some hot tea, but he
declined that. Mr. Lucus seemed perfectly content to have
another man who didn't feel like talking around. He played
ball with Mr. Lucus and the two middle boys. He tossed the
littlest girl in the air until she giggled so hard she begged him
to stop. And all the time, he felt his vision narrowing. The
mosquito bite on one boy's cheek. An angular scar on Mr.
Lucus's forearm that Cal noticed as the man flipped the hamburgers on the grill.

Once he thought of announcing his departure at an appropriate moment, and then realized that one would not arise,
not on a holiday like this. He could ruin everything, and he
didn't have the stomach for it.

Mrs. Lucus called for helpers to carry things from the kitchen,
and Cal volunteered. He passed Kayleen carrying plates of
pickles and onions, and she smiled at him sympathetically,
wishing away a cold that was a lie.

"Did you ever think," he asked Mrs. Lucus as she handed
him the potato salad, "about living somewhere else, away from
Four Corners, I mean?"

She looked puzzled, and it occurred to him that the ante-
cedent to the question was in his mind, that it really had no
connection to her. But then she smiled and shook her head.
"Kayleen's been telling you about her plans, hasn't she. The
girl's got the wanderlust."

"But when you were younger, you and your friends must
have thought about the city, or something, too," he said as she
dished pickled beets one by one into a blue glass bowl.

"Mother, these hamburgers are ready," Mr. Lucus called
from the yard. He sounded impatient.

"I guess we did," she said, screwing the lid back on the
beet jar. "But then Mr. Lucus asked me to marry him, and
well..." she smiled. "You can see the results of that."

She doesn't, Cal thought, look the slightest bit unhappy now. He felt misty-eyed with envy. Where was he ever going to find that kind of peace? How could he ever have a child and have to tell him about his grandfather? He tried to imagine what it would be like to tell Kayleen about his past, and it made him feel ill.

"You take those things out, dear," she said to Cal. "I can manage the rest."

The meal was mayhem. The baseball players refused to wash their hands and had to be sent from the table twice. The baby pounded her cup on the tray of her highchair. Cindy, one of the sisters, wanted to get her ears pierced.

"Margie Duncan got hers done," she whined.

"Not now," Mr. Lucus warned.

"I mean, really, you never want to talk about it."

Cal was having trouble with the food. The drink from the night before seemed determined to rise above. Cindy was listing names and ages of girls with pierced ears, and Kayleen was starting to squirm.

"Nice girls," Mr. Lucus said, determined to make this the final word on the subject, "do not have pierced ears."

Cal stopped, his fork in midair. Carlotta McKeller with the gold loops in her ears, holding onto the hand of the girl Mr. Lucus had married.

"Times are different now, Daddy," Kayleen said.

"Not in Four Corners," her father replied.

"That's right," Kayleen said, and Cal could hear the tears in her throat. "Not in Four Corners."

"We'll have no more of this talk," Mrs. Lucus interrupted another protest from Cindy.

"I'm going on the hammer this year," Ben said.

"Oh no you're not," Mrs. Lucus said. "That thing is dangerous."

If Cal could have forgotten the statement about the earrings, he would have been amused at the series of arguments over other challenges.

Nice girls. Did that mean, he thought slowly, that the people in this town thought Carlotta McKeller got what she deserved? Was that why there was no mention, no record anywhere? Because it didn't matter what happened to woman with pierced ears? The thought was so insane, he thought it might break his head open the way Mr. Lucus was cutting open a water-melon with the swift stroke of a huge knife.

And after the boys had spit the seeds as far as they could, after the contest had been declared a draw, after the baby was put to bed and Mrs. Lucus won two straight games of hearts with a flair for shooting the moon, Mr. Lucus ordered beers for the four of them, and Cal thought it was the first thing all day that had made his stomach feel better.

And as they sat in the pleasant Lucus backyard, it was as if Cal could feel himself gradually drawing away, as if he some-how rose above everything and floated with the rather numb-ing objectivity he attached to willing ghosts.

The past was in the air, too, and Mr. Lucus caught it, and began to talk about World War II.

"Of course, I couldn't go," he said somewhat sadly. "At that time if you worked in farming or mining, some defense-related industry, you served your country by staying home. It was hard not to be a bigger part of it." He sighed. "My dad and I had the biggest victory garden in these parts."

"Well," Mrs. Lucus said smiling, "except of course for the Weylands'."

"Hmm," Mr. Lucus said, neither agreeing or disagreeing. "And old Mr. Gristina only grew tomatoes. Italians are like that."

"You always mix up Mr. Gristina and Johnny's father, Mr. Paci. He was the one who grew tomatoes."

"Point's the same," Mr. Lucus said. "Everyone did some-thing."

And as the stories shifted and changed before his eyes, Cal saw rows of burgeoning tomato plants, red, ripe, full, and the patches of red spread and splattered, and became the ravaged bodies of men in trenches, and when he tried to shake that away, he saw the white-naked body of a woman smeared with blood, a soldier with a bayonet standing over her, and then there were two bodies, and a man in prison gray, faceless, unknown, and a cell that reminded him of his own.

He wanted more than anything, before he said good-bye, to whisper, "My father was killed in the war."

"It wasn't George Murray who got all those medals; it was his brother Calvin," Mr. Lucus said. "Hell, I ought to know, I've listened to his stories often enough."

Stories. Always the stories. And where was the truth? In a hateful letter in the top drawer of his desk.

The sun was slipping and the first few sounds of early evening fireworks began. Yards somewhere in town were filled with children in nightclothes who had to be in bed by eight even on a holiday. Cal felt a significant chill. It was almost over. Tomorrow he would vanish without a trace and become a part of one of those stories remembered without regard to accuracy.

He would say farewell to it all in the damned dingy dust of the carnival while the others about him wandered in the innocence of ignorance.

In wars, one knew the enemy by the way he spoke and the uniform he wore. The flag that flew, the lines drawn.

He thought he was like the battlefield, littered with corpses where the sun was hot and bright in the day, and the stars burned cleanly at night. He was no longer a participant.

"Are you sure you're okay?" Kayleen asked as they approached the carnival. "You're so quiet."

He put his arm around her, thinking he should spare her when he could. "I'm fine. Just a little out of it, I guess."

"My family's pretty overwhelming when you get them all together like that. Did you notice with all the war talk, they didn't mention Jimmy once? They're really scared of what will happen to him."

People have a way of ignoring the unpleasant, he wanted to say, of forgetting things they don't wish to recall.

"I didn't want to bring it up either," he said. "Sometimes it isn't necessary to actually say the words. They probably thought about him all the same."

He could feel Kayleen's puzzled look, but couldn't face her. They turned the corner and the carnival materialized out of the summer dust, a gaudy bawdy lady waving her arms and singing a tawdry song. They stepped inside the well-worn ropes, and Cal felt as if he were entering a room where someone had died.

The lights burned yellow and white and blue and red through the mist of the fine textured dust that rose from the footsteps of the patrons. The rinkytink music from the carousel, the murmur of voices, of cheers, the clatter of lead-bottomed bottles falling to a soft ball and a perfect throw, the calls of the barkers competing for the quarters and the dollars and the eager hands that took folding money from worn bill-folds in back pockets.

They passed a young couple, the boy's tattooed arm firm around the girl's bare summer shoulders.

"Whew," Kayleen said, "I think I'm going to sneeze."

He looked down into her eyes that seemed to glitter with some unspoken belief in the excitement of it all, and he thought, be afraid, Kayleen, be afraid for all that can happen here. The ends of his fingers tingled as if they were going to sleep.

The dust made it difficult to breathe. The hammer twisted and turned and flashed light, the occupants screaming, up and down. The Ferris wheel, slow and languorous, turned almost silently in the night, giving up shining faces to darkness at the top of the arc. A brazen woman with bright red hair and scarlet lips sold them orange tickets for the rides, turned and walked away from them, two large holes in her mesh stockings. A faded beauty, a slight limp. Painted by it all, looking used.

Kayleen greeted friends, introducing Cal if they had not met before. Mr. Hardy, looking disgruntled at the noise and dust, said, "Happy July Fourth," as his two grandchildren pulled at him in opposite directions and begged. Cal said good-bye to him with his eyes.

They got in line for the Ferris wheel, and when Kayleen shivered slightly, Cal hugged her again. Just a little longer, he thought.

High above the carnival, in the cool above the trees, he held her hand and looked down. The seat swayed and he wondered if anyone, ever, had stood up there, climbed over the edge of the rail, and plummeted down through the workings to oblivion. Crucified on the wheel, sacrificed on a meaningless altar, while a horrified crowd watched and asked why.

They were spending too much time at the top, as if he were being dared to act. Swaying, back and forth. Was it broken? "Rockabye baby...cradle will fall." Looking down, he saw Mrs. Mortensen and Mr. Henderson. They seemed to be picking their way through the refuse of a bombed-out building. Tentative, fearful.

Then the wheel began; it began the slow spinning circle

with every seat taken. Kayleen, skirt fluttering on the descent, her hair blowing back on the rise. Cal could hear the clicking of the gears. Mr. and Mrs. Lucus shouted to them and waved, and he ached for the kind of good-bye he and Kayleen might have had had things been different. Setting off for California, goody-bye and good luck. And then it was over, and the operator released the bar and held the seat steady while they stepped away.

On the ground, they passed the penny toss that was now the dime toss, and the glass was not cobalt blue and lime green, not pale orange and yellow. Now things were black and white and shaped like animals—bears, tigers, a leopard with green glass eyes with an ashtray on its elegant back. The concessionaire was a small man who looked like a monkey and waved his stick in a harmless stupid way at the passers by. An impotent conductor. The penalty had been castration. The sins of the fathers...

Cal picked out the prettiest thing he could find, a white bowl with a rose in the bottom, and pitched two dollars' worth of dimes before he won it. As he handed it to the smiling Kayleen, he wondered if she, too, would weave stories around such a dish, a bowl filled with fruit in the middle of a kitchen table, with her children sitting there, eyes wide. A husband in the backyard mowing the grass.

He was my first love, and he was killed in the war.

A gift was a gift, and Kayleen kissed him on the cheek.

He bought her a plastic kewpie doll on a stick, and she laughed in embarrassment at the nakedness beneath the blue and cerise feathers. The doll reminded him of Mary Beth, and he thought he should take the present back, plunge the stick into the ground, and burn Mary Beth at the stake. There were different ways of saying good-bye.

Two of Kayleen's brothers ran by with three others boys, lost in the love of misdirection, of too many possibilities.

"Can't I have a quarter," Ben begged Kayleen. "Please." And Kayleen reached into the pocket of her skirt and produced one for each of the brothers, who ran again into the dust.

"Hit and run," she said. "They're experts at that."

Mr. and Mrs. Lucus found them, the baby crying inconsolably on Mrs. Lucus's shoulder, and Cal wanted to ask her if she was the one, the one who all those years ago had taken yet another crying baby home, a baby who took her to safety, leaving his mother unprotected.

"We're taking the little ones home," Mr. Lucus said. "The boys can take care of themselves."

"Have fun," Mrs. Lucus said, and they were gone.

In a small town, even the artificially beautiful die young. Families gathered at pickup trucks to go back to their farms. Teenage couples started for cars and secluded country roads. Young men with cans of beer headed whooping into the distance looking for what they had not found at the carnival. The Ferris wheel stopped, and the concessionaires closed up their makeshift shops, and covered the treasures with tarps. The lights went out, one by one. They would spring to life another day, Cal thought. Tomorrow, and he would be gone.

As Cal and Kayleen walked away, the noise ceased as abruptly as if one had closed the lid of a coffin for the last time.

Kayleen danced along beside him, holding the bowl to her chest. "I loved it," she said. "No one ever won anything nice for me. Do you know how many places those people who work in that carnival have been? Just imagine, all over the country. I mean it's dirty and all, but just think of the places they've seen."

The street was dark. Only a solitary light here and there. A small bathroom square, a low orange burning of a lamp in a living room that waited for someone not yet there. He could hear the sound of Kayleen's shoes on the concrete as she did a little tap-dance step. She did a slight soft shoe in front of him, turning flirtatiously. "Remember how they always danced along the street in those old movies? Like this?" She whirled around and her skirt flew up. She held the bowl over her head, and he imagined it flying up into the sky, then falling faster than a comet, falling to the sidewalk and smashing into a million pieces of meaningless glass.

"Let me carry that for you?" he called to her. He didn't want her to break what was left of him, that bowl that was to sit on her table and remind her of him.

"No, no, you don't," she called, laughing back at him, "Indian giver, Indian giver," and she began to run. "It's mine." She looked back at him, her hair swirling about her face, her eyes catching a piece of moonlight, and he stopped as her hair turned black, as it fell longer and thicker, and hid her face.

"Wait," he called desperately, but she ran on, and he started to tremble. The white of her dress was blue in the moonlight now, and one pale arm arched at her side, the mooncircle of the bowl that became her face, and the unmistakable glint of gold rings in her ears.

He stepped behind a tree, out of her line of sight. In his hand, he held a stick. A stick that was a magic wand, and he pointed to the bright glass trinkets that surrounded him. While he called, he watched the young woman with the long dark hair, the shy way she stood away from the crowd. He beckoned to her with the stick. "Come on, pitch a penny and win a dish." He wanted her there with him, wanted her closer so he could reach out and touch one of those earrings, so he could tell her that nice girls don't have pierced ears, and that he would wait for her until the lights of the carnival died. He tried to tell her that with his eyes, but she wouldn't obey, and he thought she should be taught, should be shown.

The lights were gone and he was behind her, hiding in the darkness. She glanced backward as if she were frightened, and he thought, you should be, you should be. I'll catch up with you; I always do, and he knew he could run silently, he knew how to slink along innocent streets like this one, streets where some were wise enough to hide from him and the false world of glitter he promised. He laughed. She didn't even know he was there, and he would be on her before she knew what had happened.

A dog barked in the distance. A white cat crossed the street in front of him, home from the field with a mouse in its mouth. Slinking under a gate, down the path beside a house, and the man with the stick followed the cat, soundlessly as if he were its black twin. Through someone else's backyard, into the alley, and he ran along the road, the weapon in his hand, knowing that the girl with the long dark hair would have to cross his path and that he could see her because she wore white, the same way he had seen the white cat.

And he thought he heard her call for help, and he knew he was near, knew without knowing exactly why, that he would meet her at the end of the alley, but that he would be there first because he was fast and sure, and then she would be sorry, so sorry that she had teased him the way the other girls in other summer dresses had tormented him. He could hear the sound of water running in the ditch, and he knew it hid the sound of his steps. As he neared the sidewalk, he stepped into the willows that edged the small stream. He parted the rushes and saw her coming. She called a name he did not recognize, and he thought she was laughing, but he turned it into crying, and he thought if you are crying now, you will be screaming soon, and all the time she came closer. Soon he would be able to reach out with the arm that held the stick and grab her. He would twist her into the willows, tie her with the long strands, and carry her away to a hidden place. There was no turning, no stopping, and now she came quietly, and she looked back over her shoulder.

With a silent leap, he was on the sidewalk, his arm around her, the stick held like a knife against her throat. The sound of the water, torrential in the ditch, and a slight helpless scream. The colossal sound of breaking glass, the ringing of a single shot, and something in his chest broke.

He released her. He stood in dumb horror and stared at the shattered bowl at his feet. Kayleen stood before him now, trembling, tears streaming down her cheeks. In his hand, he held the kewpie doll on a stick.

"Oh, my God," he said. "I'm sorry." He could feel the eternal sob rising in him, and he threw the stick doll into the water and covered his face with his hands. He could not stop shaking. He said he was sorry, over and over again, his own religious litany.

She touched his arm. "It doesn't matter," she whispered. "It was my stupid game."

He sank to his knees as if to pray, and she put her arms around him, holding him, rocking him as if she understood. They knelt, the sacrificial bowl shattered between them, until his eyes were dry.

It took every ounce of strength he had ever had to walk her home. He heard himself promise her another bowl, and he knew he would do at least that much before he left.

He would give her that, with love.

And as he walked, he thought his mother's soul had surfaced to save him again. The goodness had conquered what must be a blood-running tendency. But what about the next time? Who would he frighten to death on some dark street when that monster surfaced inside him again?

He hadn't known what he was doing. He had become something evil, and only the sound of the breaking bowl had brought him out of it.

His mind had played one sophisticated trick too many.

Damn you, Herman Beloit. Burn in hell for us both.

He did not sleep at all that night. He lay with his eyes open, tired of pretending that which escaped him. He tried remembering the pleasant times of his childhood, but always the feeling, and it was only that, not an image but a feeling blocked him.

He tried to decide where he would go, as if even this darkness time could not be wasted, and he came up with nothing. Where would he wait?

At eight o'clock in the morning, he called Mr. Hardy and told him he was ill.

"Probably something you ate at that carnival," Mr. Hardy said both sympathetically and contemptuously. "Nobody buys anything the day after the Fourth anyway."

Mrs. Pincher knocked on his door and asked him if he was all right, and he said he just needed to sleep. He tried sitting at his desk, a piece of paper and a pen in front of him, feeling he should write to the warden, and not a single word of explanation came to him.

Finally, he crossed out the warden's name, and printed, in determined block letters, I NEVER HURT ANYONE. Underneath, in small tentative script he explained, *I only frightened them.*

Shortly after noon, he went out the back way. Down the wooden landings that might have been a fire escape. He thought he should buy something to eat, but the thought of putting food into his mouth made him wince. And he thought it was nice that the day was cloudy, overcast. The threat of a storm making the air heavy. He could smell approaching rain. There seemed to be nothing to do except walk. He passed the five and dime, remembered he promised to replace the bowl, and went inside.

He stared at the shelves. There were wooden bowls and plastic bowls, cheap cut-glass punch sets, plain white ones with hairline cracks in the glaze, all of them ugly. He didn't know how long he stood in the aisle before a woman finally said, "Can I help you find something?" and he almost laughed. Without a word, he turned and left the store.

Just before closing time, he went to the bank and withdrew all of the money he had saved. He thought, as he pocketed the bills, that he did not owe one cent to anyone. He could buy a bus ticket to anywhere, if he could just get a destination. He would go to the bus stop and ask for a schedule.

As he turned the corner, he saw a house he had never noticed before. Climbing roses and vines almost hid the small structure from view. A worn wooden sign hung above the front porch. Mrs. Goodson's Treasure Shop. The gate was ajar, as if permanently captured by age and the concrete walk.

The porch was covered with tables that held old bottles, sun-tinted milk bottles, ancient battered soda pop containers, and a collection of perfume vials. There were medicine bottles, and three dented milkcans.

RING said a small yellowed sign by a bell pull. The sound it made reminded him of Christmas.

"Yes," a small old woman asked from behind the screen.

"I'm looking for a present for someone," he said. "A glass bowl."

As if he had given some magic password, she opened the door and let him in.

"I have beautiful bowls," she said. "All of them are old. Real antiques."

She had pure white hair in little circle curls, and she smiled a plump invitation to him. She looked like every picture of Mrs. Claus he had ever seen.

Her living room was crammed with glassware, figurines, a rack of old chiffon dresses and satin gowns. A mannequin stood in the corner wearing a black beaded dress and a feather boa. The paint was coming off her face, and Cal could not look at her again.

"There is a method to my madness," Mrs. Goodson laughed, pointing to an archway that led into a dining room. On a large oblong table was an assortment of china and crystal that would have put any carnival patron into a trance. There were goblets that changed color as he moved around the table. Cut-crystal pedestal dishes, lacy edged plates with fading flowers in the center. There were large bowls and small bowls, all of them shiny with care.

It was a dazzling sight, and he felt clumsy and slightly dangerous in the room with so many delicate objects.

"Did you have something specific in mind? A special kind of bowl?"

"A kind of fruit bowl," he whispered. "One that might sit in the middle of a table and..."

And what? He could not say remind someone of me.

"I know exactly what you mean," Mrs. Goodson said, pointing to a cut-crystal bowl near the center. "Now that's a lovely one. French. A real treasure."

It was too fancy, too elegant. He would be afraid to touch it, let alone carry it along the street to Kayleen's house. The crystal facets looked sharp enough to cut one's hand.

"I don't suppose you have anything blue?" he asked. The thought make him feel giddy, light-headed. A blue glass bowl.

"Cobalt glass? My, you're young to be interested in that." She smiled at him with an unnerving steadiness.

"Is that dark blue?" he asked.

"Come with me," she said, and she led him away from the crowded table to a large glass china cabinet in the corner. She took a tiny gold key from her pocket and opened the case. The entire second shelf was filled with dark blue glass. Plates, cups and saucers, goblets, cordial glasses, and one perfectly round simple bowl on a stack of dinner plates.

If it had been identical, he thought, he would have lost his mind instantly and run screaming into the street, but it was not. The bowl his mother had on the table had a slightly scalloped edge. The shape was just different enough.

"How much is that?" he asked.

"Oh, dear," Mrs. Goodson said, folding her hands in front of her. "I really didn't mean to sell the cobalt."

"But it's just exactly what I wanted," he said quietly. Now he was beginning to see. That was why she had so many things. He looked at her knowing he should feel angry and tricked, but he felt only compassion. She didn't want to sell anything.

"Who did you want to give it to?" she asked.

"My mother," he said. "She used to have one just like it, but it was broken. I've looked a long time for a way to replace it."

Mrs. Goodson was wringing her hands now. "I've had that bowl for forty, maybe even fifty years. I think it was my grandmother's." She looked confused, concerned. He wondered if she suspected she lied, or if she even knew for certain that she did, and could not admit it.

"I would pay whatever you wanted," he said, putting his hand to the wallet in his back pocket. "You have lots of beautiful things here, but that is exactly the bowl I need for her."

Mrs. Goodson sighed. She reached to the top shelf and took down a tiny sterling silver cup lined in gold. "Look at this," she said, pointing to the engraving. "Wesley Andrew Garret, 1932. I never knew this person." She turned the cup gently in her hand. "Such a nice thing for a little baby to have, don't you think?"

"Please sell me the bowl," Cal said.

She put the baby cup back in its place on the shelf, and turned to him. "We could wrap it in some real pretty paper. I could probably find a box for it."

He thought she was going to cry, but he was determined to stand there in spite of everything.

"I would always be grateful," he said, that stranger that sometimes put odd words into his mouth surfacing again.

"I don't even know how much it should cost," she said, and he knew it was difficult for her to admit.

"I could give you fifty dollars."

"Your mother is a lucky woman to have such a nice son," she said, reaching for the bowl. "Let's say thirty-five."

He sat at her kitchen table with a glass of iced tea in front of him as she wrapped the bowl. She folded layers of white tissue around it, and wrapped the box with a paper covered with lilacs, and white crinkly ribbon that she curled with her scissors.

As they walked to the door, she said softly, "I think I'll close up for the day. Feel a little tired with this weather and all. It hangs so heavy this time of year."

He thanked her, and as he went down the walk, she called to him from the porch. "Come back again, young man. Come back for a visit."

He could not escape the feeling, as he agreed to return, that he would never find this house again. He supposed he believed it did not really exist.

It took a flash of light, a rising roll of thunder, and a flat drop of rain to his forehead to bring him back to life. He did not know how long he had walked the streets of Four Corners, the package held tightly under his arm. It was almost dark, and the rolling blue-black clouds promised a cloudburst.

He turned and began to run down the street in the direction of the Lucuses. The rain fell faster, mud splashed onto his pants, and raindrops fell in his eyes. He thought he might be struck by lightning, and the bowl would shatter, and he would have betrayed the woman who had sold it to him because she trusted him. Lightning doesn't strike twice, Hail Mary, full of grace, the sound of his footsteps on the rain-washed streets.

Suddenly he was on the Lucuses' front porch, banging on the screen door, the question stuck in his throat. *Why did you let my mother go? Why didn't you help her?* There was a blinding flash and a great crash of immediate thunder just as Kayleen opened the door.

She pulled him into the house. She threw her arms around him saying, Where have you been, where have you been, and he wanted to say Around the world, but had already told his lie for the day.

"It's Cal," she cried as he tried to catch his breath, "and he's soaked from the rain." The Lucus family appeared in the living room, took one look at him, and ran for help. Mrs. Lucus returned with towels, and Kayleen went for some dry clothes, and before he knew what happened, Cal found himself in the bathroom with a pair of jeans and a shirt that belonged to Jimmy Lee. He changed into the clothes, the jeans tight in the thighs, but what did it matter, and he tried to dry his face and his hair with the towel. He didn't know if he was crying or not, and when he looked at his reflection in the mirror, he wondered what had happened to the present. Where was the carefully wrapped blue glass bowl?

"We have some tea for you," Kayleen said through the bathroom door. "When you're ready."

There had to be a way to make them explain, he thought as he stared at his ragged face in the mirror. There had to be a way. He took a breath, swallowed the tightness in his throat, and went to join the family.

They were in the kitchen. The large table was heaped with boxes of pictures and scrapbooks. Kayleen pulled him into the empty chair next to her and pointed to the clutter on the table.

"We're working on the scrapbooks," she said.

Where was the gift? He looked frantically around the kitchen, but there was no sign of it. Had he dreamed the entire thing?

"I went to the store and Mr. Hardy said you were sick, so I called Mrs. Pincher's but she couldn't find you."

"Are you still cold?" Ben asked.

"I went for a walk," Cal said, reaching for the tea. Too many questions. His hands were shaking. "I lost track of time, something." Where was the box?

"These storms come on real suddenly in these parts," Mr. Lucus said.

"I try to get these kids to keep their books up," Mrs. Lucus said, "and it's a struggle. I keep telling them they'll be glad when they got old like we are that they have these pictures to remind them."

"I want to watch television," Cindy said.

"Not during an electrical storm," Mrs. Lucus said. "It's a good time to catch up on this." She put a stack of photographs in front of Cindy, who shrugged and picked them up listlessly and began going through them.

"I look ugly here," she said, turning the picture face down on the table.

Where was the box?

"This is mine," Kayleen said, opening the white book in front of her. "Wait till you see what a fat baby I was."

A tiny silver baby cup. He couldn't ask the question, demand his answer with the children there.

A door started banging somewhere, and Mr. Lucus rose to see to it. The smell of the summer rain came in through the screened windows. Cal could hear the sound of the drops on the roof.

Kayleen pushed her book in front of him, and a bright round-faced baby looked boldly from the first page.

He and his mother had never owned a camera. He recalled now that he had asked for one and gotten a clock radio instead. The only photographs they had owned were his school pictures and the one of the man in the uniform. And the one Dave had taken.

"We had more pictures when Granddad was alive," Mrs. Lucus said. "He was a real camera bug. Always thought the camera was a real miracle."

"This is me when I was three and took dancing lessons," Kayleen said, pointing to a picture of a little girl in a chick's costume. She had her hands on her hips.

He had to get into the living room and see if the box was there.

"And this is my first day of school."

A girl in a plaid dress. A girl on the stand testifying against him. This—is—the—man. He blinked. Then his mother, smiling in her cap and gown.

"I wonder what happened to my yearbooks?" he asked. "We didn't have a camera."

"How could you have lost those?" Kayleen asked. "I have all of mine in my room. I'll show them to you sometime."

"I used to look at my mother's," Cal said, glad it wasn't exactly a lie.

"Where was she from?" Kayleen asked, turning the pages of her own book.

He wasn't ready. Not yet. "Is this Jimmy Lee?" he asked desperately, pointing to a little boy in a baseball uniform.

"I guess mine are in the attic somewhere," Mrs. Lucus said with a sigh. "Though I don't suppose I have them all. Money was so dear then."

"That was my first boyfriend," Kayleen explained. "He moved away."

Mr. Lucus returned. "Baby stirred a little, but didn't wake up. Can sleep through thunder but wakes up if a pin drops in the next county." He shook his head. "Show Cal the victory garden pictures, the ones we told him about on the Fourth."

In the attic. Pictures of his mother, covered with dust, but safe. His own, mildewed, rotted in a garage in Yellow Fork, then thrown away.

"Cal probably doesn't want to look at a bunch of photos of us when he can see Kayleen as queen of the Junior Prom," Mrs. Lucus said. She smiled, and her prettiness came through and Cal wanted to say, You go into the attic, you get your pictures now, and I'll search for that box wrapped in lilacs and curly ribbon. He felt feverish.

"We've seen them a million times," Ben said. "A *million*."

"You go get ready for bed then," Mrs. Lucus said, "and the rest of you, too. But tomorrow, you're going to finish this year's sections, you hear me?"

Cindy and boys left the room as if they were freed prisoners.

Mr. Lucus laughed. "Hard to instill a sense of history in those rascals. Pass the book over here."

Mrs. Lucus handed him the dark brown book, and Kayleen leaned against Cal's shoulder. Mr. Lucus skipped by pages quickly, by Christmas trees in black and white, a woman leaning against a tree, solemn-looking people facing the camera, until he came to the garden.

"That's Millie and her mother standing by that low rock wall. Look at that corn, will you?" A woman that looked almost like Kayleen's mother stood with a girl that could have been Kayleen. Family. Family traits. A cold-blooded murderer in a prison in Texas. Front-facing photograph. Side view. Did Cal have his eyes, his cheekbones? The picture blurred.

Mrs. Lucus, her hand on her husband's shoulder, leaned over the book. "Show him our wedding pictures," she said, and Mr. Lucus turned the pages too quickly. Cal wanted to stop him. Go back, go back, not forward. Why was he always so helpless?

There was a sudden bright flash of lightning, and an immediate crash, and the room was dark.

"Oh, my," Mrs. Lucus said, "the first power failure of the summer." Cal heard her move to the kitchen cupboard. The darkness didn't surprise him at all. Another instance of perfect timing. Now he couldn't see pictures; now he couldn't look for the lost present. He could feel the pages of the scrapbook underneath his hand.

"Utility pole, most likely. That was a close one. I'll be right back." Mr. Lucus was a shadow that moved from the room.

Mrs. Lucus struck a kitchen match and lit three candles in holders and placed them on the table. "I wonder about those kids upstairs," she said, and Cal could see dark lines of worry on her face in the candlelight.

"They would be screaming bloody murder if they were awake," Kayleen laughed. "They went to bed just in time."

"Or they're telling ghost stories." Mrs. Lucus frowned. "And then they'll scare themselves to death."

Murder and ghost stories. Did they make them up, or were they true?

"I need to find more candles," Mrs. Lucus said. "If I just kept a better organized kitchen."

"I'll go to the foot of the stairs and see if I can hear anything from the kids," Cal said. It would at least be a chance to find the gift. He could give it to Kayleen, grab Mrs. Lucus's scrapbook, and run away with it. No, that was wrong, he thought as he took one candle and went into the living room. Kayleen and her mother were discussing the hidden candles. He held the candle in front of him, and turned slowly in the room. He thought he heard a slight gasp from upstairs, then realized it was a muffled giggle. The living-room furniture cast large and looming shadows in the flickering light, a tall highboy seemed to move. The numbness was still there, in his mind, in his heart, and it was getting worse. He couldn't think where the box might be. He walked around the end of the couch toward the television set, the silent screen catching the flame, suggesting another person in the room, and he jumped at first, another huge crash of thunder with a simultaneous flash of light, and there on the end of the couch was the box.

He felt the blood begin to flow back into his cold hands. It was all right. He hadn't imagined it. The box was there, wrapped with lilac paper and white ribbon. He picked the box up, put it lightly to his ear, and shook it. It felt like the bowl. It didn't seem to be a trick. This was not a horror show where strange boxes contained amputated hands, an eye for an eye. Why did he think of that? He would give Kayleen the bowl and leave. Like he planned. Under cover of thunder and darkness.

He could not stand any more.

"Cal?" Kayleen stood in the doorway.

"I'm coming," he said, turning to face her. The candlelight from the kitchen flickered behind her.

"I almost forgot to give you this," he said, handing her the box.

"That is for me?"

He felt the smile, more than saw it.

"I'll bet I know just what it is," she said as he led the way back to the kitchen. "I'll bet you went back to the carnival today."

"No," he said. "I didn't go there." No, he wouldn't be tempted to do that again. He was through tempting ghosts.

"This is for me," Kayleen said to her mother. Mrs. Lucus was bent over her scrapbook. "Can I open it now?" Kayleen asked, and Mrs. Lucus looked to Cal to answer.

"Sure. I mean, please," he said. Mrs. Lucus's hand covered a photograph, and he strained to see. His breathing increased. Something familiar about the girl who was visible. He heard the sound of tearing paper. "I'm so excited," Kayleen said. Cal wanted to take Mrs. Lucus's hand and lift it away. He knew, he was certain, that under that palm, under Mrs. Lucus's eyes, the eyes that watched Kayleen open her gift, was his mother.

"Oh look," Kayleen said, lifting the bowl from the bed of tissue. "Move the candle closer; look how lovely."

Cal stared at Mrs. Lucus's hand. He watched as she lifted it slowly from the page, watched as she reached for the candle, moving it so everyone could see the bowl, and the light passed over the photograph, and Kayleen held the bowl to the light, and through the blue reflection, through the soft haloed light, he saw the picture. The very one. Shiny, cracked some with age. Pasted in a book.

"I've never seen a more beautiful bowl," Mrs. Lucus said softly. "Really, Cal. Where on earth did you ever find it?"

Kayleen's eyes were full in the light, and Cal looked at her face, then to Mrs. Lucus.

"Who," he said, pointing to the picture of Carlotta McKeller, "is that girl?"

"Pardon me?" Mrs. Lucus asked, and Kayleen stopped turning the bowl.

"I asked who that woman is. The one with the long black hair."

"Oh, you couldn't possibly know her, dear," Mrs. Lucus said. "She's gone."

"Gone where?" Kayleen asked, putting the bowl down in the middle of the table. "Oh, it's perfect. Thank you."

"I've seen her," Cal said. "Somewhere." He could feel it all coming back. The anger. The unanswered questions. Why didn't anyone help her? Millie June Beckman held her hand in friendship and all she could say now was that she was gone.

"Well, the truth is," Mrs. Lucus said, "I suppose you might have seen her somewhere else. She left here over twenty years ago. I don't know where she went. It was a sad story."

"The one who's holding your hand? The beautiful one?" Kayleen asked. "What happened to her?"

Cal felt the heat from the candle flame on his face. He was light-headed again, and he reached out with one finger to touch the bowl, to test its existence. He was going to hear another version. Point of view Millie June.

"I told you about her, Kayleen. Sometimes you don't listen. She was my friend who was so anxious to get away from here. Wanted to go to Hollywood, be an actress. It wasn't that she was a bad girl, either. Not cheap or flighty. Good student, friendly. Like you. But she had all these big dreams."

"Don't lecture me, Mama," Kayleen said. "Not in front of Cal."

"It's not a lecture, honey."

"So did she go to Hollywood?" Cal asked. "Have I seen her in the movies?" He could hear the accusation in his own voice.

"Well, no, at least I don't think so." Mrs. Lucus looked at him. Even in the dim light, he could see that she was puzzled.

"I don't remember you mentioning her," Kayleen said, and Cal wanted to tell her to shut up and let her mother go on. Let her mother tell her how she abandoned her friend when something awful happened to her.

"It's not something you tell in front of young children," Mrs. Lucus said, and she brushed a stray blond curl from her face.

The room was suddenly terribly sultry, and Cal thought he would burst with the pressure. Burst, break, grab her around the throat and shake the words out of her. The confession. Kayleen was talking about the bowl again, jabbering, and Cal had to ask.

"Well, what actually happened? I'm curious now." Come on, his tone of voice coaxed. Step into my web. Tell me your crime. Confess.

He saw the distance in Mrs. Lucus's eyes. Saw her float into the past. She described his mother again. Lovely, beautiful girl. A seamstress, and his mother's face, her smile, she turned before the mirror, slowly now.

"She had no mother and father to guide her, but oh, how the young men flocked to her."

No, Cal wanted to say. They didn't after *that*. She kept them all away.

"I guess we were all a little jealous." Mrs. Lucus sighed. "To have so many suitors and not want any of them. Oh, she'd go on dates with them, dances, the like, but she always said that as soon as she saved enough money, it was off to California for her."

Jealousy. Kayleen shifted impatiently next to him, and he reached onto the table and gripped her hand.

"This is eerie," Mrs. Lucus said. "I think it must have happened right around this time of year. Carnival was in town. It always comes on the Fourth."

The lights, the music, the man with the stick. She really was going to tell him.

"We all went to the carnival. It was a real event in those days. Not much happened around here, and the war was such a worry."

"It still *is* an event for Four Corners," Kayleen said.

Her mother frowned at her. "Well, there was a young man from Evanson. Nice young man, quiet, sensitive. Handsome, from a good family. We were all a little silly for him."

The pressure in his head again. He knew he held Kayleen's hand too tightly, knew because she looked at him questioningly, and he could not let go.

"Well, Carlotta had gone out with him a few times. More than that, I suppose, and he was completely smitten with her. She just kept telling him about California and Hollywood. He took to following her everywhere. Persistent. Everyone excused it because he was in love, and he was such a nice boy, a handsome boy."

I don't care about him, Cal wanted to shout. I care about *her*.

"Well," she went on, "he followed her around the carnival, I guess. No one really knows for sure."

The man, the murdering man with the stick, the man with

a broken blue glass bowl and a piece of rope. But the bowl wasn't broken, it was sitting on the table in front of him. Not that bowl, another bowl. Not the blue one, ever.

"Maybe she decided to let him walk her home, and maybe he was just so desperate with love he didn't know what to do."

"Mother," Kayleen said, "what happened?"

"He took her to someplace outside of town, a cabin, a deserted barn or house. I can't remember. I guess he thought if he could just keep her long enough, he would convince her."

"To marry him?" Kayleen asked.

Wait a minute, Cal wanted to say. Who took her away? A man from the carnival. Who was this other boy?

"That's what he said later," Mrs. Lucus said.

"Later?" Kayleen asked.

There was something wrong. Terribly wrong. This wasn't the same story.

Mrs. Lucus was suddenly uneasy. "Well, the fact of the matter is, I guess he had his way with her, and I can tell you she wasn't that kind. Must have been pretty frightening for them both. And then little Boyd Masters was out there looking for cats, the kind that are wild and live in deserted barns, and he came across them. Robert Kirkwood took off running, and little Boyd was left there with poor Carlotta crying, so he got his father, and they took her home. Of course the whole town found out about it. Small towns can't keep secrets like that."

She paused, shaking her head. Her eyes went lovingly to her daughter.

Too many images, too many words. Robert Kirkwood. Herman Beloit.

"What happened to him? Did he go to jail?" Cal knew his words were too loud. He just didn't care.

He could no longer see anything.

"Jail?" Mrs. Lucus said. "Oh my, no. It wasn't that he really wanted to hurt her. Even Carlotta understood that, because she told me so herself. But some people made it into an ugly story. All that jealousy. An evil impulse in some. Most of us knew the truth, though. He was just hopelessly in love."

"What happened to them?" Kayleen asked.

"That's the saddest part," Mrs. Lucus said. "And you know, she was a good friend of mine, and I never got to tell her good-bye. About a month later, even though she'd seemed fine, she was just up and gone. I never found out where she went."

"Yellow Fork," Cal whispered.

"What did you say?" Mrs. Lucus asked.

Cal shook his head. "What happened to him?"

Mrs. Lucus shivered, putting her crossed arms on the table. "And here I talk about the children telling ghost stories. It must be the storm, and the candles."

"Where is he?" Cal repeated.

"He ran off to the war. His poor parents. Nice people. He ran off, and then a few months later, he was killed. France, I think. He was their only child."

Mrs. Lucus's eyes suddenly filled with tears.

"Oh my, Jimmy Lee," she said.

Kayleen rose and went to her mother. She put her arms around her neck, and whispered, "He'll be all right. You know he will."

The room turned in on itself. The flickering candles blurred into hazy moons, then became a string of lights that surrounded a terrace and the strains of "Stardust" rose in his head. A couple danced, a woman in a blue dress and a man in a uniform. Perhaps she had loved him anyway, and found out too late. Everything she told him was true because it might have been.

"Do you know for sure that story is true?" Cal asked.

Mrs. Lucus blinked. "Well, pretty much of it," she said. "Carlotta told me some of it, and Mr. Lucus's brother was a good friend of Robert Kirkwood's. There's no reason not to believe it." She sounded wounded by his mistrust.

Mr. Lucus was suddenly standing in the kitchen.

"Pretty new bowl," he said pointing with one long finger. "Power isn't likely to be on soon."

"I have to go," Cal said. "It's late."

"Cal gave me the bowl," Kayleen said.

"You can bring the clothes back anytime," Mrs. Lucus said.

"Tomorrow," Kayleen added, and she kissed him on the cheek.

The storm had washed all traces of summer dust from the sky. As Cal made his way back to Mrs. Pincher's, the power was restored and the houses were lit all at once. Because it was so late, the lights were promptly put out again, one here, another there. Water rushed by in the ditch, and there was a refreshing coolness in the air. The stars sparkled brighter than ever against the black; they reflected in puddles of water in the street, and the moon, although hesitant, made its way through.

It was quiet except for the sound of his footsteps as he walked, and the occasional dripping of rain from the fences and burdened plants. Cal thought as he walked about the man in the uniform, the photograph his mother had showed him all of his life. He wondered if it could possibly have been Robert Kirkwood.

When he reached home, he sat at his desk and tore the letter from the warden into small pieces. Herman Beloit would have to be someone else's father.

What was the saying? The third time's the charm. He was going to take this story and live with it as truth.

He put his face down on his arms, and quietly cried with relief.

Early the next day, he took the bus to Evanson. He had pleaded another day of lingering illness to Mr. Hardy, and been excused. If he could verify Mrs. Lucus's story, there would be many to whom he would owe an explanation. The warden, Ruggles, Mrs. Pincher. Dave. It was up to him to clear up the decades of misunderstanding.

In the Evanson library, equipped with Mrs. Mortensen's research skills, he found the announcement of his father's death in the *Bulletin*. February 19, 1945. He wondered if his father had lived if he would have felt a mysterious moment at the birth of his unknown son. Would the sounds of shelling have been silent for an instant, giving the soldier a vestige of peace?

Cal stared solemnly at the photograph, blurred by poor ink and time. He was amazed at the resemblance. A man in a uniform who looked nothing like the framed picture of the man his mother had, but a man who could have been Cal himself.

He wondered, as he sat in the library, if his father, at the moment of his death when his life supposedly passed before his eyes, thought of his mother with love or with rage. She remembered you, he whispered to the soldier. You were the man she danced with in her deathbed dream. He was certain of that.

It took him awhile, wandering through the Evanson cemetery, to find the plot. It was a small rectangle, surrounded by a low wrought-iron fence. How different from the un-marked place where they had taken holly in winter, flowers in summer.

A large granite marker contained the names of three people. Robert Kirkwood, 1923–1945. Ethel Frances Marson Kirk-wood, 1902—. Charles Orville Kirkwood, 1900—. Two bloom-ing rose bushes on each side of the marker, a flat plaque in the earth to identify Robert's grave. A bronze American flag, embossed beside the name. Two yet-unused places. Living grandparents.

The plot was carefully tended, and Cal thought sadly how neglected his mother's grave must be by comparison, and that he would have to return to Yellow Fork and see to it. Two rose bushes in bloom. One red, the other the yellow with pink edges Peace rose that had been his mother's favorite. Such irony, coincidence. He would reunite them through the flow-ers.

He stood patiently, waiting to divine some essence from a spiritual presence. He stood with his hands in his pockets, a slight curve to his spine, a breeze ruffling his hair. He saw them dancing again, alone in the moonlight, the stringed lights, the orchestra in black and white, and he heard the music. The man in the uniform, the woman in the blue dress. The sound of the water lapping against the pier. He tried to penetrate the earth with that vision.

The man had gone off to war and never come home. A sad, though not unusual, story.

He knelt down by his father's grave. He ran his fingers over the bronze plaque.

"Let me tell you," he whispered, "about what a wonderful person my mother was, how she loved me and cared for me. How she told me every heroic thing about you. How she kept you alive long after the fact."

Finally, he stood from the grave. As he left the cemetery, a pesky black crow flew from tree to tree along his path, chat-tering. You mistook me for someone else, he scolded the bird and the old woman who had frightened him. A simple case of mistaken identity The fact that he himself had made the most profound mistake would take time to reconcile. The mis-guided things he had done would take time to rectify. But on the witness stand, he would say, *"My father was killed in*

World War Two. A hero's death in France."

Would it be possible, if he came back to Four Corners after the trial, to explain everything to Kayleen and her family? He would have to try, or he would be running forever.

Once he found the address in the phone book in the drugstore, it didn't take him long to find the house. Evanson was smaller than Four Corners. He stood across the street from the pleasant two-story house, white frame with a full porch across the front painted green. There was a circle of pink and purple petunias in the middle of the large front lawn, and the iron and wood pillared fence had been freshly painted. It brought to mind the plot, his father's home now. Someone took plenty of time with the garden. It would be something to tell them about, a common topic. He could describe his mother's garden, the tomatoes, lettuce, the carrots, the berries picked and bottled, the apples cored and cooked and kept in the cellar. The flowers that changed from spring to fall.

Perhaps they would cry impostor and send him away.

A mailman came whistling down the street, the springy step of a man who loves to carry news. He sang through the gate and up onto the porch of the Kirkwoods' house as if there were nothing sacred about it at all. He called through the screen door to people Cal could not see in words loud enough to be heard from where Cal stood.

"Isn't this a honey of a day?"

The lid of the mailbox falling with a light metallic clang, the steps taken two at a time by the whistling man with the mail on his back, the gate latch clicking into place behind him.

A little girl on a bicycle passed by him and said "Hello" as if he were a friend. He nodded back at her as she passed, watched as the bicycle wobbled a little. She was a beginner.

When he turned back to the house, an elderly woman with carefully curled gray hair was lifting the lid of the mailbox. She removed a letter, adjusted her glasses slightly, and stared at the face of the envelope.

And then, as if she could feel Cal watching her, she glanced across the street at the tree. But as if he were nothing to be concerned about, she turned and went back into the house.

He could send them a letter.

He could leave them alone.

He closed his eyes, and tried to remember his mother as she sat at the table on the porch playing Monopoly with him and Dave. "This is as good a time as any," she said as she purchased a hotel for Park Place.

He had to try. For all of the grace his mother had given him, for all of the love, he had to try to explain.

He moved away from the tree, hesitating only slightly before he crossed the street.

He pushed the doorbell and heard the chimes ring inside the house. The woman appeared almost immediately, and then a tall thin man behind her.

"Yes?" the woman asked, behind the screen.

Cal took a deep breath. "My name," he said, "is Callant, and I'm Carlotta McKeller's son."

The woman put her hand to her breast. The man stepped up to the door, adjusted his eyeglasses, and peered through the screen at Cal in silence.

I look exactly like *him,* Cal thought, facing the man and woman. Exactly.

The man slipped one arm around the woman's frail shoulders. With the other, he pushed open the screen door.

In a voice trembling with memories, he said, "Come in. Please."